# OHIO *Weddings*

LOVE COMES TO THE LAKESHORE
IN THREE ROMANCE NOVELS

BETH LOUGHNER

ISBN 978-1-59789-987-1



All scripture quotations are taken from the King James Version of the Bible.

This book is a work of fiction. Names, characters, places, and incidents are either products of the author's imagination or used fictitiously. Any similarity to actual people, organizations, and/or events is purely coincidental.

Cover image: Altrendo Nature/Getty

Published by Barbour Publishing, Inc., P.O. Box 719, Uhrichsville, Ohio 44683, www.barbourbooks.com

*Our mission is to publish and distribute inspirational products offering exceptional value and biblical encouragement to the masses.*

ecpa Member of the Evangelical Christian Publishers Association

Printed in the United States of America.

Dear Readers,

Thank you so much for joining with me on a journey to Bay Island. This wonderful island is full of people like you and me who have many of the same day-to-day struggles we encounter. Our churches, like the one on Bay Island, are full of wonderfully redeemed believers who come with many different quirks and personalities that God expects to become as one unit. Throughout the Bible, God used the most unlikely and mismatched followers to complete His incredible work. It's the same today.

If you're like Jason and Lauren, may you find it in your heart to forgive and be forgiven. Larry and Becky learned how to make a dreamer and a realist function together as a godly team. . .and so can we. If you're caught up in life's goals, worries, or deceptions, take it to God. Like in Nathan's and Judi's case, there isn't a hole deep enough that we can dig ourselves into that He can't fix. God has the power to heal all wounds.

God is amazing! He can take a group of all ages, economic statuses, educational levels, and personalities and make them work as one body. Marvel in His perfect plan.

So kick your feet back and enjoy your time on the island.

Beth

www.bethloughner.com

# Bay Island

# *Dedication*

Thanks to all who helped make *Bay Island* come to life. Without my family, it would have been impossible to make this dream come true. A special thanks goes to John Pierce who spent hours editing the manuscript for typos and grammatical errors. He might have given me up as a lost cause but he didn't.

Where would this author be without the help of her editors? A big hug goes to Tracie Peterson and Rebecca Germany for believing in me and *Bay Island*. Their expertise helped make Bay Island the place it is today.

# Chapter 1

Lauren Wright leaned heavily against the white painted rail, her hands tightly gripping its cool surface. Great belches of diesel fuel fumes reached to the upper deck of the ferry, giving her stomach an uneasy roll. Her eyes remained fixed ahead.

Bay Island loomed in the distance, drawing closer and closer as the boat plowed its way across Lake Erie. The once familiar trip now seemed out of place, distorted—suffocating. Five years' absence hadn't been enough.

A light breeze wafted across the warm waters, lifting the ends of her hair from her shoulders. Lauren gave a long, drawn-out sigh. A lifetime wouldn't be enough. A sense of dread overtook her again. She should never have come back. Tom Thurman had been wrong in asking her to come, wrong to think the past could be remedied.

The Bay-Line Ferry slowed, the steady noise of the throttle dropping to a hum as the boat edged toward the dock. Ferry workers scurried about, throwing thickly twined ropes to the waiting dockworkers in blue shirts. Reluctantly, Lauren followed the other passengers down the steep, narrow steps to the lower deck where her car was triple-parked in the gridlock of vehicles.

Skirting around the cars, she stopped suddenly, her eyes darting nervously toward the crowd waiting at the dock. What if. . . ? The thought hadn't occurred to her before. What if she were to meet Jason at the dock or on the road to Piney Point? What would she do? *No, no, that couldn't happen! He'd never recognize me—I've lost weight, I've changed, I'm more sophisticated now.* Still her heart pounded with agitation.

Lauren slipped quietly behind the wheel of her small sports car. Soon the line of cars ahead began crossing over the ramp, slapping the metal plate as it bobbed with the boat—*clang, bam, clank, bam.* Her car followed suit, and Lauren's hands were sweating as she steered the car down the main road.

Nothing much had changed at first glance. Beckette's Souvenir Shop had a bright new awning over the storefront, and the bike rental shop now had an enclosed building, but the simple store styles were still there. As she rounded the last corner, though, Lauren's eyes widened in surprise. The once familiar run-down Dairy Barn and Suzi's Boutique were gone. In their place was a newly designed shopping area. Levitte's Landing!

Lauren drew the car slowly to the curb as she gaped. Levitte's Landing! Jason

Levitte's design. Jason's dream. He'd spoken for years about building the shops, designing a wharf-style area that would attract tourists. Slowly she counted the stores—eighteen, nineteen, twenty. It seemed so enormous—so crowded. People milled about the area, many watching as a small cruiser boat anchored itself alongside several other boats at the dock. Minutes ticked by as she continued to stare.

"You're parked illegally, ma'am. I'm going to have to ask you to move."

Startled, Lauren took a calming breath before turning toward the voice. The tall, imposing figure of a police officer now stood by her door. "Oh, I'm sorry, I didn't—"

The officer leaned his tall frame down, alert blue eyes searching the back seat before returning his gaze to hers. A flicker of recognition crossed his face. "Lauren?" The sandy-haired officer moved closer, his tone less imposing now. "Is that you?"

Lauren shielded her eyes from the sun with one hand. "Yes," she answered hesitantly.

"You don't recognize me?" He laughed, his lopsided grin pulling to the right. "Larry—Larry Newkirk." He extended his hand through the open window.

"Larry—?" Lauren grasped his warm hand, her mind reaching back in time, dissolving into nothing. "I'm sorry—"

"I'll have to admit I'm a whole lot taller and more handsome now," the man said, his smile widening. "You might best remember me as the high school senior who helped you with the Christmas play at church a few years back."

Lauren looked him full in the face, finally brightening with relief. "Of course, I remember you. And you're right; you are a whole lot taller."

"And more handsome, let's not forget," Larry added with a pleasant, low-rumbling laugh.

She offered him a small smile. "And more handsome."

"What brings you back to these parts?" he asked congenially. A split second was all it took before an uncomfortable look crossed his face. "I'm sorry! I didn't mean—"

"It's okay, Larry," Lauren assured, pressing a smile to her lips with effort. "I'm just here for a short vacation."

"At Piney Point?"

Lauren nodded, suddenly wishing she could end the conversation. "Well, I really—"

His brows drew together suddenly. "Does Jason know you're here?"

The question caught her off guard, tearing at her heart, the same heart she'd been convinced was healed. "No," she replied slowly. "And I'd really rather keep it that way—for right now."

"I understand," he answered, his voice taking on an odd quality. "If you need anything—"

"Thank you, but I'm sure I'll be fine." Lauren gave him a dismissing nod of her head, rolling up the window in one quick move. It took all she had to keep her foot off the accelerator until he'd moved. When he finally did, she maneuvered quickly into traffic.

It was too crazy, her coming back. Tom Thurman had convinced her to come back, convinced her there was no future for the two of them if she didn't. Oh, how she'd tried to tell him two weeks earlier that coming back to Bay Island would result in no good.

"I think you should go," Tom had said, sitting on the edge of her desk in the accounting department that day, munching an apple while she worked.

Lauren looked up from the billing statement she held and eyed him in disbelief. "You can't be serious." She glanced about the room to ensure it was empty.

"They've all gone to lunch," Tom said intuitively, glancing at his watch. "Exactly where we should be right now."

"I'll be done in a minute."

"So?"

"So, what?"

Tom lowered the apple from his lips. "You know exactly what. I'll be through with seminary in less than three months and getting ready for missions training by Christmas. Where does that leave us?"

Lauren gently laid the billing statement aside and looked up at his strong profile. His coal-black hair shone in the florescent light above, and she gave him a whimsical look. Tom had been her rock for the past three years—loving, kind, gentle—real husband material. Yet, there was something. . .something that held her back. Not that she could put her finger on it exactly. Maybe it was a lack of romantic oomph that was causing her to hesitate.

"I don't know what God wants for us," Lauren finally said. "I don't even know what He wants for me."

"I know! That's exactly what I'm trying to tell you," Tom answered, his hand coming down over hers. "God has called me to missions, that much is clear. You haven't felt a call for anything in nearly five years."

"That's not fair, Tom," Lauren interrupted, her face reddening.

Tom lifted his hand, leaving coolness in its place. He swiped his hand over his face in a show of impatience. "It's very fair. You can't deny we have something very special together, and I've told you how much I love you, but you've got to know God's calling takes precedence over all that."

"I know."

"But if God has called me to missions and not you. . ."

Lauren gave him an apprehensive smile. "It'll all work out, Tom. A lot can happen in six months before your missions training." *Maybe God will change that direction. Being a pastor in the States would be nice. I could be a pastor's wife—but please, not a missionary. I don't want to go to Africa or Brazil.* She squashed those thoughts. "Maybe God will give me a desire to go into missions by then."

Tom shook his head. "Don't you get it? God's not going to call you anywhere, not until you've resolved the issue you left behind on Bay Island."

Lauren balked. "Bay Island has nothing to do with it."

"Doesn't it?" Tom asked, his voice giving rise to an unusual fervor. "You've never forgiven God for what happened on Bay Island, and you ran away from the problem before—"

Stunned, Lauren stood to her feet. "You weren't there! I didn't run away! I was pushed away. You didn't feel all the gawking eyes at church or hear all the whispering tongues." Unwanted tears welled in her eyes. Giving them an angry swipe, she continued. "I'd done nothing wrong, absolutely nothing."

Tom immediately pulled her into his arms. "I know. I know," he whispered gently into her hair. Slowly he pulled her back. "You and I both know you never sold those drawings. Most importantly, God knows."

Lauren shook her head miserably. "But he—they never believed me."

"You mean Jason, don't you? Why, you can't even say his name! You were once in love with Jason Levitte," Tom stated matter-of-factly.

"But—"

He laid a gentle finger on her lips. "Wait until I finish." A deep breath escaped. "No matter what you feel toward Jason right now, you were in love with him five years ago. You told me you'd forgiven him for falsely accusing you, even though you knew he still believed you'd sold him out."

"That's true!"

"That's nonsense!"

"How can you say that?"

"Because you're still angry with him, and you're still angry with God." Tom pulled her close again, his face pleading. "Haven't you ever wondered why you never get too deeply involved in any church ministries? You don't trust God anymore. He didn't make things right when you thought He should."

"I'm just cautious, that's all," Lauren answered, pulling herself away. "You're psychoanalyzing this whole thing too much. I've put Bay Island behind me. Please don't go dredging it up all over again. Bay Island has nothing to do with you and me."

"I wish it were so." Tom gave a sigh. "I want you to tell me, truthfully, if you really believe you've forgiven Jason, that you harbor no anger toward him whatsoever. Tell me if Jason were to walk in here today, he'd be welcomed like any other brother in Christ."

"Tom, this is crazy," Lauren pleaded.

"No, it's not!" he retorted. "Let's get this out in the open." He leaned forward.

"Tell me! Would you welcome Jason in here today?"

Lauren frowned. "Just because he's forgiven doesn't mean I ever want to see his face again."

"See! You're still angry with him," he said gently. "Just admit it!"

An answer didn't come to her right away. "He should have known better," Lauren finally said. "He should have known I'd never cheat him. Tara set him up—set me up—and he couldn't see it. Men can be so stupid!" She hadn't meant for the words to escape her mouth, and she immediately tried to snatch them back. "I didn't mean that."

"Yes, you did, Lauren."

Lauren hated it. She had meant it, every word of it. Yes, she was angry. Yes, God should have cleared the matter up by now. She'd given Him five years—five whole years.

"Lauren, I've prayed about this for months," he openly admitted. "And I really feel you need to talk this thing out with Jason. Then maybe we'll have a better sense of what God wants in your life."

"It's not fair, Tom. Going back to Bay Island could very well blow things up in my face. Nothing good could come of it." Lauren picked up the billing statement again, staring aimlessly at the figures. "Somehow, I know I'd—I'd lose you."

"The only way you can lose me is if you choose to do so." Tom's loving tone almost undid her. "And there's only one way to find out."

"There has to be another way," she reasoned, wrinkling the yellow paper with her grip.

"There's only one way. Go to Bay Island." Tom slowly took the paper from her grasp and ironed it out on his leg. "If not for yourself, then do it for me. I just know the answer's there."

"I can't just pick up and go," Lauren argued.

"Take a week's vacation," Tom suggested. "You have plenty of time coming, and your parents' cabin stands ready and waiting."

"I don't want to go."

"I know, but promise me you'll think about it."

"I'll think about it." *But I won't like it.*

# Chapter 2

Soft pine needles blanketed the tree-lined road leading to Piney Point. Lauren purposely slowed the car to a crawl, breathing in the long-forgotten smells of pine and dewy foliage. An unexpected lump formed in her throat. Until now, she'd not realized how much she missed the place—the place she'd once considered a sanctuary.

The four-room cabin came into view as her car rounded the last turn, and Lauren immediately focused her attention on the large front deck. The screen door was propped wide open, its wood frame wedged tightly into place by a tipped lawn chair. A large box fan was busily sucking air from inside the door opening.

Lauren saw no one as she parked the car beside the cabin, the tires settling into old, shallow ruts cast perfectly to her wheelbase. Funny, after all these years. It was as if time had stood still—waiting.

Lauren stepped from the car, slowly taking in her surroundings. A strange ache settled over her. How could Piney Point feel so welcoming, yet uninviting, all within the same moment? Her thoughts were quickly interrupted by the loud echo of footsteps coming across the wooden deck.

"Come on over here, and let me get a good look at you," greeted a loud, familiar voice. The ample-sized woman strode down the deck steps toward her, a wide, toothy grin plastered on her face as she wiped her dusty hands on the blue apron tied around her thick waist. "Girl, it's so good to see you."

Lauren gave the woman a full grin, relief flowing through her as she happily let herself be enveloped in the woman's bear hug. "Tilly, it's good to see you, too."

"I should say so, girl," Tilly exclaimed, giving Lauren several welcoming swats between the shoulder blades with her big hand. Lauren nearly choked. Finally the woman forced Lauren back, eyeing her critically. "The years have been good to you, Lauren Wright; I'll have to give you that. And look at your hair. What have you done?"

"Had it cut and styled. It's been this way for quite some time," Lauren answered, fingering the curled ends. "Do you like it?"

"It looks mighty fine, it does," Tilly said, smoothing the ends brushing Lauren's shoulders. "Just never thought you'd ever let a pair of scissors near it."

"Yeah, well. . ." Lauren never finished the sentence. She knew what Tilly was thinking. Lauren's long hair had been the first thing to catch Jason Levitte's attention, and he'd never hidden the fact that he'd loved her flowing tresses. The hip-length hair had been the first thing to go after she left five years ago.

"And that outfit is really cute, too."

"Thanks," Lauren murmured self-consciously, taking a look down at her denim jumper and white sneakers. The outfit was more casual than she usually allowed, but she'd determined to spend part of her vacation doing just that—vacationing.

"Your mom said you'd be coming today," Tilly went right on talking. "The cabin's clean and waiting for you. It's a mite stuffy, though. Don't know why your parents don't rent it out anymore, being high-peak season and all. But I guess that's none of my business." Tilly stopped for a moment's breather. "There's no sense standin' out here jawin', is there? Come in and look around."

Tilly led the way up the deck steps, and Lauren followed quietly behind. The swishing rhythm of Tilly's full skirt stopped when she paused long enough to set the fan aside from the doorway. They stepped inside.

"The phone should be hooked up sometime today, and the groceries your mom asked me to order are all put away. Even fixed that old finicky paddle fan," Tilly said, snapping the switch on the wall up and down to prove it.

"Tilly, I don't know what to say. The place looks great. I had no idea you'd be here getting the place ready. Mom never said anything."

"You know your mother," the older woman clucked, giving a heavy shrug of her shoulders. Lauren walked to the kitchen, one hand skipping lightly over the laminate surface. "How have you been, Tilly?"

"Finer than honey," Tilly answered, her eyes twinkling. "I couldn't be any finer now that you're back home."

Home! The word struck an odd chord in Lauren. Piney Point had always been a home away from home. For nearly a year, it had served as her only home. But her home was in Cincinnati now. Her job was there. Tom was there.

Tilly Storm was the nearest neighbor to her parents' cabin, her own cabin only an eighth of a mile farther along Piney Point. Lauren's earliest recollection of Tilly was on her tenth birthday, the year her parents had bought the cabin. Tilly had fixed a big picnic lunch for her family, and Lauren thought the welcome basket was for her, for her birthday. No one had ever told her otherwise.

Over the years, Tilly became a permanent vacation fixture to Lauren, and she'd often dreamed of living on the island year-round as Tilly did. For one year that dream had come true—the year she'd met Jason.

"I'm assuming Jason still lives on the island," Lauren asked casually enough, belying the way her heart raced as she spoke his name aloud.

Tilly's smile dimmed. "Well, yes, he still lives on the island." There was caution in her voice. "He's moved to the north side, though. Built him a fine home at the inlet."

Lauren briefly turned her face from Tilly as she pretended to peruse the pantry cabinets. "At Muriel's Inlet?"

"Yep, that's the one. Built there about two years ago."

The blood nearly drained from Lauren's face. Muriel's Inlet! Surely Jason wouldn't have built the house he'd designed especially for her. Muriel's Inlet had been the intended location of their future home. True, they were never officially engaged, but they'd talked and dreamed of living at Muriel's Inlet in that house. What could he have been thinking? What if Jason had married? Could he have been so foolish as to marry Tara? She'd never bothered to let that horrible thought enter her head before.

"Has he married?" Lauren risked asking.

Tilly's dark eyes grew keen. "No, girl, he hasn't." Her lips thinned out into a frown. "Don't reckon he ever will."

Lauren busied herself opening drawers, avoiding a reply. What could she say?

Tilly gave her a penetrating look. "I suppose you're here to get things settled between the two of you?" Silence. "I'd say it's about high time. It was bad business the way things were left. I'm glad you're going to work things out. I see now that neither one of you have been right since."

Lauren closed the last drawer more firmly than intended. "Don't go getting your hopes up, Tilly. I have someone else waiting back home." *My lifeline from this place—from Jason.*

This news drew a concerned wrinkle across Tilly's brow. "Your mom said—"

"I know what Mom said," Lauren interrupted with a sigh, remembering her mother's hopeful insights from an earlier conversation. "I'm not here to renew any relationships, just to set things straight. Then I plan to enjoy a few days of my vacation before going back home."

Tilly studied her. "I hope you can work things out, girl. It's been a mighty shame the way things turned out."

Lauren smiled. Girl. Tilly had called her that ever since she could remember. The familiar sound of it had a comforting appeal. Then a frown slipped over her mouth. There was nothing really happy left on Bay Island, not anymore.

"Is Tara still hanging around?" Lauren finally asked. Tara! The name itself burned like fire under her skin. It was hard not to hate her. She'd been the one to deliberately deceive Jason, the one who single-handedly destroyed Lauren's reputation, effectively running her off the island.

Tilly seemed taken aback by the question, and a look of disapproval crossed her face. "I know how she did you wrong, Lauren, but don't you think that's a bit—cruel?"

"In what way?" Lauren asked, astonished.

Tilly paused to study Lauren a moment. "You don't know?"

"Know what?"

Tilly seemed confused. "When's the last time you and Jason spoke?"

"The day I left here, five years ago," Lauren replied. "Why?"

"Then you didn't know Tara died last year?"

Lauren numbly shook her head, taking in the words. "Tara's dead?"

"You haven't talked with anyone from the island since you left?" Tilly asked again, as if the concept was too incredible to believe. "You never heard?"

Lauren pulled out one of the heavy maple chairs from the kitchen table and sat down. There was more unpleasant news ahead, she was sure of it. "I've pretty much avoided any Bay Island news over the years, Tilly, but evidently something bigger than my own fall from grace has happened here since I left." The words sounded flippant and unfeeling, but Lauren truly didn't care.

"I'd just supposed Tara had called you."

"Called me?" Lauren asked in disbelief. "I should hardly think Tara would call me."

"She'd said she called you," Tilly answered, clearly disturbed by this new revelation.

"I promise you. I've not spoken to Tara or to Jason since the day I left here." Lauren's voice held an edge of sharpness. "No offense to the dead, but since when did Tara's word carry any scrap of truth?"

Tilly shook her head vehemently. "Oh, Lauren, don't say such a thing."

"Tilly, I didn't come here to fight with Tara or Jason or anyone else. I've come to set things straight." Lauren's voice sobered. "I'm here to clear my name."

"But that's just it. Tara cleared your name two years ago."

The statement came like a bolt of lightning. Lauren swallowed quickly. "What are you talking about?"

Tilly blew out a lungful of air. "I'm gonna have to have coffee for this one," she announced, turning to the cupboard doors. Silence reigned as Tilly pulled out the filters, then the coffee canister, then the sugar bowl.

"Tilly," Lauren blurted out in exasperation. The wait was too much to endure. "You can talk while you fix the coffee. What did you mean about Tara clearing my name?"

"It'll be only a moment," Tilly answered, ignoring Lauren's mounting frustration. "Want some?" Tilly extended an empty coffee cup toward Lauren.

Lauren only shook her head, rubbing her temples impatiently. Why couldn't Tilly just get on with it?

"There," Tilly finally said, bringing over a brimming mug of coffee that threatened to spill over. Slowly she sank into the chair. "It's a rather long story. Where should I begin?"

"At the beginning," Lauren answered. "What's this business about Tara?"

Tilly seemed to have difficulty knowing where to start. "Well, after you left, the town was pretty much in an uproar over the drawings that were stolen and sold to that firm on the mainland. Of course, few of us knew the real truth about Tara then."

That was an understatement, Lauren thought spitefully. Even the church people had mentally convicted her without a trial. In all fairness, though, looking back, Lauren could see how they were used. Tara had orchestrated the deception with such methodical precision that the circumstantial evidence was hard to ignore.

"Things did settle down eventually," Tilly went on. "But then Tara was diagnosed with brain cancer about two years after you left. Guess the guilt was tearin' at her more than any of us knew. She even told her doctor that the cancer was a judgment from God for something she'd done in the past."

Lauren listened solemnly.

Tilly took a nervous sip of coffee. "Jason was by her side through all the radiation treatments and doctor visits. By then they'd only given her three months—four tops. That's when she told Jason the truth about what happened, how she'd left the forged note on your desk, and how you'd delivered the plans to Williams and Tolbert. Tara even told him about all the little things she'd done to discredit you." She gave a weary shake of her head. "Jason was devastated—of course." Another shake of the head. "Oh, it was truly pathetic."

Lauren ignored the sympathetic inference. "You mean to tell me Jason's known for over two years of my innocence?" Lauren nearly exploded. Of all the nerve! Never once did he attempt to call and apologize for his brutish behavior. Not once! Lauren stood angrily to her feet.

"Sit down, Lauren," Tilly demanded sternly. "You have to listen to it all." When Lauren dropped back in the chair, sulking, Tilly continued. "Jason didn't make it easy on her, if that's what you're thinking. Tara wanted God's forgiveness, to become a Christian, but Jason knew from all the years of trying to reach her with the gospel, she'd have to come to God on His terms, not hers. I think Tara thought God would cure her of the cancer if she made things right."

Tilly folded her hands. "Jason just told her the truth. She was going to die no matter what she chose to do. There wasn't going to be any last-minute reprieves whether she got things right or not. She had to know it was her eternal soul at stake, not her physical life. Tara made a choice that day to follow Jesus."

Lauren didn't like what she was hearing. Anger simmered hot inside her soul as unholy thoughts revolved. Wasn't it just like Tara to squeak into heaven after all she'd done, after living the kind of life she had for twenty-five years?

"Tara went before the church that next Sunday and confessed, telling the whole nine yards of it," Tilly continued. "Jason told Tara she'd accused you falsely in public and that she'd have to exonerate you publicly. After she told the church, he demanded she talk with you."

"She never called," Lauren told her dryly.

Tilly looked thoughtful for a moment. "I thought for sure she had, but maybe she died before she could do it."

Lauren nearly snorted but thought better of it. "Things certainly aren't turning out as I'd expected," was all she would say.

"You need to talk with Jason," Tilly advised.

"Oh, we'll talk, all right," Lauren promised. "And I can't think of any better time to do it than today."

Tilly looked worried. "Better give him a chance to explain, girl," she admonished. "Don't go at him with both barrels shooting."

Lauren paused a moment to calm her thoughts. Tilly was right! The golden opportunity was at hand, and she didn't want to muff it. Maybe this thing could be wrapped up nice and tidy, much earlier than expected. Somehow that didn't seem quite possible. Besides, Jason had a lot of explaining to do.

# Chapter 3

A stiff wind blew through the open six-seater golf cart as it sped along the paved road skirting the shoreline. Lauren pressed her foot hard against the accelerator, running the electric engine for all its worth—all twenty-five miles per hour of it.

Jason! What could have possessed the man to go to such great lengths to finally clear her name, yet leave her to lie in its poison for no cause? What good could he have hoped to accomplish? And the house! How would she react if Jason had actually built her dream house—possibly for another woman? It wouldn't be long until she'd find out. Muriel's Inlet was less than a mile away, and she'd have plenty of time to catch a peek at the house before finding her way to Jason's office. He'd be at his office, of that she was sure. His Saturday hours hadn't changed, according to Tilly. He'd been a workaholic then and was most assuredly one now.

That Tilly had thoughtfully recharged the battery of her parents' cart was so appreciated. Lauren had always loved puttering about the island in the thing, especially when the weather was as glorious as it was that day. If only her mission were as pleasant.

Lauren drew in a deep breath. An earthy moisture was coming across the lake, mixing itself with the abundance of island honeysuckle. There was a rainstorm coming. Lauren could smell it. Rhythmic waves lapped loudly at the huge rocks as she passed an open stretch of shore. Several other carts passed by in the opposite direction, each driver giving an easy wave of greeting. Lauren smiled and waved back absentmindedly, her thoughts still churning.

Jason! She'd rehearsed their meeting so many times in her head it was quickly becoming a blur. No introductory statement seemed right. *Hello, Jason, remember me?* Or maybe the direct approach. *Jason, we need to talk. What were you thinking? How could you have kept silent?*

Would Jason even have an explanation for his behavior? He'd been so sure of her guilt five years before. That fact alone hurt more than anything. The memory of that ugly day was forever etched in her mind, a memory that now circled like a hungry vulture.

"Jason," Lauren had called to him when he'd entered the office that afternoon. "We need to go over the Ross account. Do you have time now or—"

Jason had stopped at his open office door, a manila envelope tucked under his arm. Icy gray eyes fixed on hers, and she instinctively stopped midsentence.

He was quiet for several long seconds. "I want to see you in my office right now. You won't need the Ross report," he said, his voice low and menacing.

Lauren became uncomfortably aware of the sudden tension in the room. Only two other workers, Tara and a receptionist, were within easy earshot, and they seemed to be holding their breath in wait. Never before had Jason used that tone with her.

Lauren felt her cheeks go warm, but she confidently rose from her chair and walked the length of the hallway to his office before pausing at his door.

"Close it behind you!"

Still Lauren said nothing, then quietly closed the door. He faced her from behind the desk, his large frame hovering, waiting. His features, too finely chiseled to be truly handsome, now seemed carved out of stone. His square, determined jaw was clenched. Jason was furious. That much she could tell. But at what—or whom? Jason was never one to rant or rave, or to raise his voice, yet she felt his anger, radiating as it was now.

"Sit down!"

"I'd rather stand, thank you," Lauren replied, her defenses rallying. She bravely neared his desk. There was no doubt now. She was the target of his anger, although she could conceive of no reason why she should be. Something serious was at stake. "What's wrong, Jason?"

His eyes narrowed dangerously. "You tell me," his harsh voice demanded as he suddenly withdrew the contents of the manila envelope. Several eight-by-ten glossies slid haphazardly across his desk as he tossed them toward her.

Lauren let her eyes wander to the black-and-white prints. Gingerly, she picked one up and then another. "What are these?" she asked, studying the office building which was focused into view on the prints. A small gold sports car in the right-hand corner caught her eye. Her car!

Jason didn't answer but extended yet another photo toward her. Lauren silently took it. Her own image peered back into the camera's zoomed lens, apparently as she was leaving the office building.

"I don't understand, Jason," Lauren spoke, desperately keeping her voice calm. "Why do you have these pictures?" She fingered through several others. It was obvious the photos had been taken the previous afternoon while she was on an errand delivering a tube of drawings to the mainland.

"I had you followed."

"Followed?" Lauren eyed him indignantly. "Jason, have you gone stark-raving mad? Why would you have me followed?"

His smile wasn't a pleasant one. His shoulders straightened beneath his checked shirt and blue tie. "I'd hoped it wasn't true, Lauren, but these pictures don't lie." He ran his hand impatiently through his blond hair. "Why would you do this to me?"

"Do what to you?" Lauren was reaching the point of exasperation. "I delivered the drawings as you asked. Was there a problem with the drawings?"

"I asked you to?" He spoke brusquely, disregarding her question. "That's a lie."

Lauren flinched at his venomous tone, then forced her shoulders back in a show of courage. "Yes, you! You left the message on my desk asking me to deliver the tube of drawings."

"You stole those drawings, Lauren," Jason accused. "You stole those drawings and sold them to Phil Tolbert."

"Stole your drawings!" A hollow laugh erupted. "You can't be serious, Jason."

"You're about to see how serious I can be," Jason threatened.

Lauren stared in disbelief. Was this the same man she'd fallen in love with over the past year, the reasonable man with whom she'd dreamed over their perfect house, the man who'd actually sketched the designs lovingly into form?

"I have the proof, Lauren, if you'd care to look at it."

"Proof?"

Jason silently opened the top drawer of his desk and handed her a business-size envelope. Lauren withdrew the contents.

"These are my bank records," she breathed incredulously, looking up at Jason. "What are you doing with these? And how did you get them?" Her eyes fell back to the copied statements in her hand, settling on the account balance highlighted in yellow. Twenty thousand! Never in her life had she accumulated that much money.

"Was it worth the money?" His taunting words shot through her.

"Jason, I swear, I have no idea—"

"I do," Jason interrupted, stabbing his finger at another photo of her and Phil Tolbert. "What I don't understand is why. Did you need the money? You know I'd have given you the shirt off my back if you'd just asked. Did you think I'd never figure out what you'd done until everything was drained, including my business?"

Suddenly Lauren knew. A tiny light began to glow. Insignificant events that meant nothing before meant everything now. There was the day her purse was missing from work. Frantically she'd searched, only to have the purse show up a half hour later in the same spot where she'd left it. And what about the mysterious blips from the computer indicating her password commands were malfunctioning, or the funny feeling she'd had when Jason left the message for her, not Tara, to deliver plans to Phil Tolbert?

Tara! It had to be her. Lauren had known there would be trouble from the first day she'd laid eyes on her. Tara had her hopes set on Jason, and although she was only twenty, ten years his junior, she wanted no one encroaching on her territory. Jason was blind to the facts, that much was obvious. Lauren's attempt at pointing out that certainty to him had met with an adamant denial.

"She's only a kid in need of the Lord," he'd said.

Tara had worked as Jason's assistant for nearly a year before he'd met Lauren on the island during her vacation. Jason and Lauren had built a long-distance, occasional-visit relationship over that year, finally resulting in her taking permanent residence on the island, working as his accountant. Tara hadn't liked the intrusion but appeared satisfied with the current attention Jason had given her in his many attempts to reach her with the gospel. But Lauren saw through Tara's facade easily. Tara had no real interest in spiritual matters, but she was more than willing to string along a willing Jason—just long enough to keep his attention and time focused her way.

But would Tara stoop to such depths to remove Lauren? An uneasy suspicion settled the question. Yes! Yes, she would!

"There has to be an explanation, Jason," Lauren pleaded.

"And what would that be?"

Lauren took a deep breath, suddenly afraid. He'd never believe Tara was capable of setting her up. He was much too blind concerning the young girl. But Lauren had no choice except to attempt reasoning with the man. "It's obvious that I've been framed—there's no other explanation. I would never hurt you, Jason, you know that. How could you even think me capable of doing something like that?"

Slowly he walked around the desk until he stood before her. "How, indeed?" He gave her an odd, level look. "And just who then, Miss Nancy Drew, do you think is capable of doing such a thing?"

His arrogant tone wound the tension one level higher. There would be no reasoning with Jason, not at that moment, and his cavalier acceptance of her guilt irked her. "If you were so clever," she was stung to retort, "you'd know."

He gave her a smoldering look but said nothing for several seconds. Instead, he gathered the glossy photos and stuffed them back into the folder. "If I'd been so clever, I'd never have let myself in for this mess, Lauren."

The utter contempt in his voice shook her. It was coming to her very quickly that she was engaged in a battle that might never be won.

"I want you to clear out your desk," he demanded.

Lauren knew in that moment the final irrevocable act would take place. He was letting her go, detaching her from his work and most of all, his heart. She stared stonily at him.

"It's best to keep this little affair quiet, don't you think?" he went on. "I have no desire to press charges, but I do want the money back."

"The money?" Lauren blinked. "But, Jason, I have no idea where that money came from or who it belongs to."

"I know who it belongs to. It's mine, and I want the money back!"

Lauren glared defiantly up at him. "You're impossible." She leaned close to his face, anger surging through her veins. "I told you once a long time ago we should have never been paired, that dating someone who's obsessed with moving up the financial ladder of success was a bad idea. People with money think about only one thing: protecting themselves and their assets. Didn't I tell you that? You're so suspicious of everyone's motives, you can't even think straight enough to see the obvious." Lauren had to fight to keep her voice even. "I'll leave your precious little office, Mr. Big Shot, but if you want the money, you'll have to take it the same way it got there—without my help or my knowledge."

Lauren didn't wait for a response but turned on her heel and quietly left his office. Ignoring the subtle stares of the office staff as they returned from lunch, Lauren efficiently emptied her desk of every personal possession. Tara was conspicuously absent, which boiled her blood another ten degrees higher. With her chin held high, Lauren gave a final glance back at her desk before exiting the front doors.

It wasn't until two months later that Jason spoke again with Lauren—the day she'd left the island for good.

"You're leaving?" Jason asked coolly, leaning on the hood of his black sedan as he watched Lauren pack the trunk of her car.

"It would seem so," Lauren answered with a hard edge to her voice. "Is there something you wanted, or did you just come by to gloat?" Why had he shown up? She didn't need any more grief. The faster she packed and left Bay Island, the better.

He didn't answer right away. "No, I just thought you might have something to say to me before you left."

Her gaze raked over his face. All her pent-up frustration of the past weeks, all the resentment she felt toward Jason and her fellow church members threatened to blow. The news about her alleged wrongdoing had spread fast across the island and through their church, thanks to Tara. It hadn't surprised Lauren. But she was surprised and dismayed at her church family, who seemed even less forgiving than the rest.

Lauren swallowed hard, fighting back the sting of tears as she thought about the dwindling number of students in her junior Sunday school class. Parents had pulled their children from her class when they'd heard. The glances, the whispering—it was too much. It was time to leave the island, her church—and Jason. It was the only way. She'd tried to brave it out, hoping against hope her name would be cleared. But it hadn't. Why was God allowing this miscarriage of justice?

"Let me help you," Jason said, stepping forward to take the heavy suitcase she was about to heave into the trunk.

Lauren quickly tugged it out of his reach. "No, thank you. I can get everything myself, if you don't mind."

Jason clenched his teeth, and she saw his jaw muscles twitch. "I'm trying to be as understanding as possible."

"It's a bit too late for that," Lauren retorted. The heavy bag landed with a thud in the trunk. She stopped and looked at him. "But I do have something for you."

He looked puzzled as Lauren opened the car door and scooped her purse out from the front seat. Quietly she searched through the contents.

"Here!" Lauren handed him a dark blue checkbook. "I've taken out what's mine. Do what you want with the rest of it." Why he'd never claimed the money before now was beyond her.

Jason accepted the book. "I've figured out where the twenty grand came from," he told her, then paused. Lauren ignored the bait and piled in another bag. "The money was taken from the supply fund in the form of a check made payable to cash," he went on. Still, Lauren packed. "Aren't you at all curious how I've tracked it?"

"Not at all," Lauren answered, slamming the trunk lid shut. "Matter of fact, I don't much care what you've found or haven't found. The bottom line is you think I ripped you off, and that's all that matters in the long run, isn't it?" She swung around to face him. "But I will tell you one thing. The truth has a way of coming out. Oh, it may take another week or a month or maybe even a year, but the truth will eventually come out, Jason. When it does, don't bother calling to apologize. It'll be too late for anything to be done about it by then."

"I think we both know the truth." His tone was disconcerting, as was the expression in his eyes. "I'd have forgiven you if you'd just admitted what you'd done."

Lauren laughed. "On the contrary, I have already forgiven you for the false accusation. I can only ask that God will do the same." *That should heap some self-righteous coals on your head.*

Jason slowly shook his head, an action Lauren interpreted as pity. "Where will you go?"

"Why should it matter?"

"I still care about what happens to you."

Lauren opened the door of her car, tossing her long French braid to one side as she slipped inside. "That's mighty neighborly of you," she retorted, starting the car. "But you lost that privilege the day you accused me of the unthinkable."

With that, Lauren propelled the car forward, never looking back, never seeing Jason's expression.

# Chapter 4

As soon as Lauren rounded the bend at Muriel's Inlet, she saw it. The beautiful house stood regal and tall, a commanding sight at the top of the sloped acreage. Lauren let the cart coast to a stop on the graveled shoulder. Looking up, she merely shook her head in disbelief. *Jason, how could you?* The coloring, the windows, the decorative trim—everything was exactly as she'd dreamed, right down to the white Adirondack chairs gracing the wide wraparound porch.

Lauren alighted from the cart to get a better look. Every door and window was shut tight, an emptiness seeming to surround the house. The driveway was vacant. No one was there to keep Lauren from openly gazing at the structure.

The tall Cinderella-type tower immediately caught her attention. It jutted off the second floor with a large stained glass window on one side and a small balcony facing the lake on the other. Puzzled, she drew her brows together. The tower had never been part of the original plans. Yet she couldn't deny the beauty it gave the home, the fairy-tale wonder it evoked.

Her gaze wandered across the perfectly landscaped lawn, which extended well out of view. It was hard to believe Jason had actually forged ahead with the building plans. And for what? The large house was much too big for him alone. Another thought stirred. Maybe he wasn't alone. Tilly said he hadn't married, but that didn't mean there wasn't someone special in his life, a future Mrs. Levitte. Could he be so callous as to build Lauren's dream house for another woman?

She looked beyond the gazebo in the side yard, the white cast-iron tea table set inside giving it picturesque perfection. Everything looked perfectly in place. It was as if life on the island had never changed or paused for a moment because of her departure. Didn't those on the island realize the sacrifice she'd been unjustly asked to pay. . .how those events shaped her life, nearly unraveling her faith in God?

Several minutes lapsed before Lauren settled herself back into the cart, her melancholy mood causing a long, deep sigh as she slowly turned the cart around. She wasn't ready to face Jason, not just yet. Things were happening too fast. There were too many things defying logic or understanding. Thoughtfully she drove one block down to the public access path which led to the rocky shore. The familiar rock structures were the same, a welcoming sight she'd enjoyed years ago. Slowly she stretched her frame from the cart and walked to the shore. Lauren was pleased she could still climb the steep, pitted rocks surefootedly.

The wind tugged at the hem of her dress as she gingerly stepped from one stone to another. There was a definite smell of rain now, and the choppy waves indicated the storm would present itself in only a few hours. Lauren eyed the point, a large rock fifty feet into the deep water. Cautiously she made her way across, jumping rock to rock, careful to keep her white shoes dry.

The view was spectacular as always. From the point, one could clearly see Muriel's Lighthouse at the tip of the shoreline. How many times had she sat on that rock, looking, taking in the sounds of the water and screeching seagulls?

Lauren turned around and looked past the short cliff where Jason lived. The house was hidden from view, everything except for the tower, which also enjoyed an unobstructed view of the lighthouse. She turned back to the water, mesmerized. Minutes ticked by. The wind picked up, throwing water higher, an occasional gust causing the water to kiss at her feet. Eyes closed, she drank in the smells and sounds.

"Lady!" A man's urgent voice interrupted the tranquility.

Lauren turned slowly to face the distraction, her heart sinking straight to her sneakers when she caught sight of Jason making his way down the rocky cliff. His unmistakable figure stopped halfway down when he noticed her undivided attention.

"It's not safe out there," he yelled against the wind. "You'd better get back to shore." He waved for her to come in.

It was apparent he hadn't recognized her. Lauren didn't move but continued to stare at him, and he began his descent again. His blond head bobbed several times from the rough terrain. His footing slipped on the loose stones, but he quickly righted himself.

Jason finally made it to the shoreline, and Lauren wondered if he'd recognize her now with the distance closing between them.

"You need to come back," Jason yelled again, concern still vibrating in his voice. "Are you stuck out there?" Lauren's relative calm must have given him cause to worry, for his forehead wrinkled in deliberation, his gaze fixed on hers for several seconds. Then he seemed to grow impatient with her silence. "Why won't you answer?"

Lauren watched as Jason suddenly began making his way across the same stones she herself had traveled. His long legs brought him farther into the waters, drawing him closer and closer. Unnervingly, his eyes never left her. Lauren scrutinized his expression, wondering if he'd yet made the connection. She couldn't tell. It wasn't until he'd safely reached the point, when he stood only five feet from her, that his realization became quite evident.

Their gazes locked for several moments. Finally, he broke the silence.

"So, you've come back." Although his tone was gentle, it was flat and oddly insulting. The wind ruffled his loose pullover shirt as he folded his arms across his chest, waiting.

"Yes!" Lauren finally tore her gaze from the gray eyes fixed on her. She let her eyes roam over the churning waves, desperately trying to collect her thoughts. They weren't supposed to meet like this, unprepared and by chance. She could barely catch her breath, let alone conjure up her earlier anger toward him, the anger he deserved. The sight of him completely unraveled her.

"Why didn't you answer? I thought you were some loon trying to commit suicide." His tone let her know he was annoyed.

Lauren let her gaze wander slowly back to his face, tipping her chin up high. "Guess I couldn't resist the temptation of climbing the point just one more time." She drew in a breath. "I didn't want to be disturbed."

"It's my business to disturb those who trespass on the point," Jason declared with authority. "This is private property now."

She caught the full meaning of his words. "I suppose that shouldn't surprise me. Everything at Bay Island has changed." Her voice was deceptively calm, and she applauded herself.

His gaze roved over her, settling on her hair as it whipped about her face in the wind. "You've changed quite a bit yourself. I see you've cut your hair."

There was no sense asking what he thought about the shortened version; Lauren already knew, and she suspected he knew why she'd had her beautiful mane cut. She also knew he'd noticed her new slender figure, but the "new her" gave Lauren no pleasure at the moment. "A lot of things have changed in the past five years." She tilted her head. "How have you been, Jason?"

His face remained expressionless. "I've managed. And you?"

Jason wasn't making their unexpected reunion any easier. And it was obvious he was nowhere near being the least bit repentant about his past actions against her. Instead, he seemed angry, as if expecting something from her.

Lauren shrugged. "I suppose I've done all right—all things considered."

His jaw muscles twitched. "You seem to have done exceptionally well, if you ask me." He shifted his six-foot frame. "And to what do we owe this unexpected visit, Lauren?"

This was Lauren's chance to let the years of rehearsed words spill out, to live the scenes she'd evoked in her mind, the ones in which she triumphed. Five years of the drill should have prepared her better. Instead, she felt empty, drained. Thoughts circled aimlessly, unable to take form.

A sudden gust of wind pushed against her, and Lauren scampered backward, nearly losing her footing. Jason's hand shot out, locking on her arm as water lapped across the tops of their shoes.

Lauren shrugged off his grasp. "I'm okay!"

Jason seemed irritated by the interruption. He pointed toward the incoming dark clouds. "The clouds are starting to build to the north," he said. "We'd better head back to the shore before we both get swept out to sea."

Jason threw her an expectant glance before hopping down to the next rock. Lauren grudgingly followed his lead. Twice he grasped her hand to help her across the more treacherous areas. Lauren's hands burned at his touch. Why did he still affect her to the point of craziness? Something was so disjointed about his behavior, and it bothered her terribly. It was as if nothing had changed, as if he was still angry with her. He hadn't wanted her to come back. What was wrong with the man? He owed her an explanation and at the very least, one or two sheepish looks of embarrassment. But he'd given her none of that, none at all.

Lauren stopped suddenly, and Jason threw her a quick glance.

"What's the matter?" he asked impatiently.

"What's the matter?" she echoed sarcastically. "For starters, your attitude. I'll never understand you, Jason Levitte!"

"Join the crowd," he remarked flippantly as water licked at his shoes again. "But do you think we could discuss this on dry land? We'll both be soaked if we wait here for the storm to push in any further."

Lauren moved reluctantly, caring less about getting wet than his attitude. He was as commanding as ever, even to the point of protectiveness, but she wasn't fooled into thinking he cared one iota about her. It was just his way, regardless of what he liked or disliked. Even in his contempt for her five years earlier, he'd tried his best to extend a way out for her, misguided as it might have been.

"We'll go to the house," Jason said as soon as they reached the shoreline. "We're way overdue for a long, hard talk, and I definitely have a few things to say."

Lauren eyed the visible tower. "I'd rather talk right here, if you don't mind." She had no desire to see the house which held her wasted dreams, to possibly see another woman's handiwork displayed.

Jason followed her gaze, and Lauren thought he'd paled for a moment, but he gave no indication when he spoke. "I don't plan on standing out here with the storm bearing down on us, nor do I have any intention of letting you go this time. At least not until we've properly hashed this thing out. It's been too many years coming. Now, are you coming to the house or not?"

"No," Lauren told him firmly. "I'm not going up to your house. Do you think I'm blind? Did you think I wouldn't recognize it? You built my house, Jason, the one I invented and dreamed of." She was angry and hurt by his offhanded manner. Didn't he know the house represented his ability to go on without her, the ability to disregard her memory as if she were nothing? "It's cruel, Jason. Did you do it for spite, hoping to see the day I'd view it as a memorial to what could have been?"

Jason said nothing for a moment. "No. That's not why I built it."

"Then why, Jason?" she demanded. "Did you take a leave of your senses? Why did you waste your time building this house when you should have been trying to find me? I deserved the courtesy of being told I'd been cleared." The hurt in her gut cut like a knife. "I couldn't have been that hard to find."

"No, you weren't hard to find at all," Jason said sharply. "Twenty-five thirty-six Brandon Parkway, Cincinnati, Ohio. How could I forget? It's blazed into my memory."

Lauren froze, her body, her mind, turning to stone. "You knew? You've known all this time where I lived, and you never thought to call me up and tell me? You couldn't have phoned and said, 'Hey, Lauren, the truth is out now. Guess I made a little mistake'?" Frustrated anger seared at her throat. "Didn't you think I deserved that, Jason Levitte? It was heartless and inhumane to let me go on thinking people still hated and despised me."

"They never hated or despised you," Jason snapped. "I know it was rough—"

"Rough!" she nearly spat. How dare he! "You want to hear what rough is?" But her words stopped cold. No, she wasn't about to let him gloat over her misfortunes, to let him know how she'd left her faith until Tom Thurman had nurtured her back to spiritual health again. Tom! Why had he ever insisted she come? Where was he now when she truly needed him?

"Let's speak about being heartless and inhumane," he demanded back, his voice brusque. "Let's talk about Tara and her feelings."

Lauren couldn't believe the man's audacity. "Tara and her feelings?" she asked incredulously. "What about mine? Or have you forgotten who the real victim of this charade is?"

"In the end, we were all victims, Lauren." His eyes challenged her to disagree.

"Oh, yes," Lauren said tartly, throwing all caution to the wind. "I've heard about Tara's so-called conversion. Pardon me if I'm a bit skeptical."

He watched her with narrowed eyes. "You've changed, Lauren," he finally said. "And I must say, cynicism doesn't become you. Tara did her best to explain things to you and ask your forgiveness. But you'd have none of it, would you?"

Lauren forced herself to meet his gaze. "Have none of what?"

"Tara's apology, of course." He eyed her suspiciously. "Don't play innocent."

This was the second time Lauren had heard of the mysterious conversation she'd supposedly had with Tara. "I've not spoken with Tara since I left here," she challenged.

"That's impossible. I was in the room when Tara called." His eyes narrowed. "I heard her half of the conversation, and it wasn't pretty, I can tell you."

There they were again! Back to square one—him accusing, her denying.

"I'm telling you, Tara never called me," Lauren protested angrily. "Choose what you want to believe, but at least let your memory serve you right. We went through a similar scene like this five years ago. I don't plan on going there again. Just remember who told you the truth then."

The fierce fire in his eyes dimmed as he rubbed his hand thoughtfully across his jaw. "You're right. I don't understand what's going on." He gave an exaggerated sigh. "And I don't plan to make the same mistake twice."

A loud bark erupted suddenly from atop the cliff. Jason jerked his attention to the offending noise. A black Labrador retriever peeked over the cliff's edge, resounding another bark before sniffing at the air toward them.

"Stay up there, Butch," Jason commanded the dog.

A woman immediately joined the dog at the cliff, glancing quizzically between Jason and Lauren. Her petite form struggled slightly with the wind, her long black hair fanning out behind her.

The woman called to Jason uncertainly. "You have a call from Levitte's Landing, and they say it's urgent." She looked back at Lauren, caution in her eyes. "Do you want me to take a message or can you come?"

Lauren watched the indecision in Jason's eyes. "Go ahead, Jason," she told him. It figured! Finally they'd reached a point in their conversation where it was beginning to go somewhere, and his work interfered—again. Why didn't that surprise her? How many times had their dates and plans been interrupted by business?

"Tell them to hold on. I'll be up in a minute," he answered the woman abruptly. His focus returned to Lauren as the woman and dog turned away. "I'm sorry, but I really do have to take the call." Still he didn't move.

"I understand." She didn't.

"No, you don't," he replied without rancor. "You never did understand the demands of my work." He looked back to the cliff. "It looks as if now is not the best time for us to go up to the house anyway." He thought a moment. "Are you at Piney Point?"

Lauren nodded.

He consulted his watch. "Give me two hours, and I'll be there. We'll get this whole mess straightened out." She felt him move closer to her. "Temporary truce?"

She was silent, thinking. "Temporary truce," she finally agreed. Very temporary.

He nodded his head grimly but said no more, hurrying up the steep path in the same way he'd come.

Lauren watched him disappear over the top. She wasn't going to hold her breath waiting for his visit. When it came to business, she knew exactly where she stood—dead last.

# Chapter 5

Lauren listened as hard rain pelted the galvanized roof of the cabin. The vengeful sound turned deafening at times, much like her own thoughts, loud and overwhelming. Lauren let the calico print curtain drop lazily back into place as she turned from the rain-blurred window. One wary glance at the clock let her know Jason's two hours had come and gone. Not that she really expected him to come on time.

Jason was perpetually late. Lauren was forever punctual. It was a subject they'd actively debated in years past and one she couldn't win. Of course, there was always a legitimate excuse for his lateness. How could she compete with success?

Five o'clock! If she were truly honest, there was a sense of relief mixed in with the anxiety she felt over the delay. The first two hours had given her time to better sort the complexity of the situation. In less than six hours Lauren had learned some cold truths—truths she never expected nor really wanted to believe.

Jason was a total mystery. He'd admitted knowing her whereabouts over the past years, going so far as to say her address was blazed into his memory, yet he never bothered to phone or see her. It simply didn't make sense. Could he have been so put out by Lauren's supposed rejection of Tara's apology that he'd written her off completely? If only he'd called himself.

But most intriguing was the house. Lauren hadn't missed the almost sad quality present in Jason's voice when she'd touched heavily on the subject. Yet he'd never given her an answer as to why. If he hadn't built it for spite, then for what? He certainly hadn't built the house for her. It was obvious he still held great contempt for her and had ill-judged her—again.

Another thought crossed Lauren's mind. Who was the black-haired beauty on the cliff? Had Lauren imagined the tension this woman created or how abruptly Jason tried to shoo her away? Something akin to jealousy sparked through her at the thought. Who was she and why was she at the house? Jason had all but given Lauren the bum's rush after the woman's arrival.

Lauren walked aimlessly back to the window, peering out with unseeing eyes. Why should she even care who the woman was? Jason and she weren't in love anymore. That fact was indisputable. She'd once heard it was impossible to fall out of love, just as it was to fall in love. Lauren supposed it to be true. But their love hadn't fallen from anywhere; it had been crushed into millions of tiny pieces before finally being ground into fine dust. There was nothing repairable about that!

Lauren had always believed God's will dictated there was one man for every woman, but her experience with Jason shot down that belief pretty quickly, too. She'd loved Jason with all her heart and yet, over time, she'd found another to love, hadn't she? She'd been so sure at the time Jason was the one, the one she'd be spending the rest of her living days with. God's blessing had been upon them, she'd felt sure of it. But it never happened, and Lauren had learned her first real lesson about trusting reality, not emotions. How could her feelings have been so misguided? Wasn't true love supposed to conquer everything, even scandals and desperate misunderstandings?

The shrill ring of the phone cut through her thoughts. Lauren looked at the clock again. There was little doubt in her mind who the caller would be, excuse in hand—of course.

But it wasn't Jason's voice she heard on the line.

"I see you've made it safe and sound!" Tom greeted her happily. "Did you have a nice trip over to the island?"

Lauren strained to hear as the rain seemed to increase in strength, pounding the roof without mercy. "Tom, I'm so glad you called," she finally responded, plugging one ear with her finger. She pressed the receiver even tighter to the other ear. "And yes, the boat trip was fine."

"What's all that racket?" he asked loudly. "Sounds like a freight train coming through."

"A storm's blowing in across the lake, and it's pouring buckets right now." Lauren stretched the cord as far as it would go to the kitchen table. "How are things in Cincinnati?" A pang of homesickness nettled at her heart.

There was laughter in his reply. "Worried the college can't get along without their best accountant?" he asked. "Everything seemed well under control when I went by there this afternoon for my exam."

"Oh, Tom," she immediately interrupted. "How did your first orals go?" She grimaced guiltily. She'd forgotten about his exams, neglected to pray for him. It was inexcusable.

"Pretty well," he answered. "It's just one of those things where you answer all the questions to the best of your ability and hope you gave them what they were looking for. At least day one is down, and I only have two more to go." The noisy rain died down, and his voice grew softer. "I appreciated your prayers. I could really feel them today."

Lauren bit her lip in self-reproach. The prayers he felt weren't hers at all. She'd been too engrossed with her own problems to even remember. It was as if she'd stepped from one life into another, the latter as disjointed and lost as the first. "I'm sure you did very well, Tom," she finally said. "You always do."

"Such faith in your man. I like that." Tom laughed amiably.

Lauren was glad Tom couldn't see the worried expression on her face. An uneasy feeling tapped at her gut, a feeling of uncertainty. She disliked it when he spoke possessively like that. His words, although innocent, seemed to ensnare her. By rights, any woman would be thrilled with the prospect of being possessed by a man like Tom. But she wasn't! And she feared their relationship was about to change. Would she be the same woman after a week on Bay Island?

Tom seemed to sense her troubled thoughts. "Have you talked with anyone on the island?"

"I met Tilly earlier," she answered hesitantly. "And I've seen Jason."

"Oh?" Lauren detected a bit of caution in his low voice. "How did it go?"

"Not very well, I'm afraid." Her fingers doodled imaginary circles on the maple kitchen table as she gave Tom a rough sketch of the events and information she'd learned that day. "As you can see, I'm not quite sure what to make of it. My name's already been cleared. Technically, my objective for coming here has been met." She paused thoughtfully. "Maybe I should come home."

There was an audible sigh. "No, you need to stay right where you are." His voice grew terribly serious and weighty. "It doesn't sound as if much of anything has been resolved. There's still more work to be done, a few more wrinkles to iron out." He paused. "Are you going to church tomorrow?"

Lauren let out a soft groan. "Yes, as much as I dread going." She could only picture the scene in her mind, how the church members would react. Would they greet her openly, offering their apologies, or would they ignore her, shying away in embarrassment? Either scenario made for an unpleasant morning.

"You can do it!" he encouraged. "I know it's been hard, but you'll be so much happier when this whole thing has been flushed out of your system." Tom's voice turned teasing. "Then we can get on with more important business, if you know what I mean. I was thinking a small grass-hut wedding in Africa or Bangladesh might be fun."

Lauren cringed. There he went again.

"I was only joking, Lauren," he quipped, obviously sensing her silent discomfort. "You know I'd never push you into missions or marrying me. I'm a patient man, and I'm confident God will show us just what He wants before December."

"I'm sure He will," Lauren agreed. Relief tickled her heart. Five months seemed like a long reprieve at the moment.

A sudden, loud bang erupted from the front door. Lauren's startled gaze darted nervously toward the noise.

"Can you hold a minute, Tom?" She put the receiver on the table without waiting for his reply.

Lauren stopped dead in her tracks as the door jolted open without warning and a tall, blue-slickered figure barged purposefully inside. Blatant fear tore through her until she recognized Jason's face emerging from under the rain-soaked hood. Large drops of water cascaded off the slicker and onto the floor, instantly forming puddles at his feet. Jason held a drenched cardboard pizza box in one wet hand.

"Take this, would you, please," he instructed, shoving the box toward her.

Lauren took the drooping box as her racing heart and senses began recovery. "Let me get you a towel." Quickly she deposited the pizza on the kitchen counter and disappeared down the short hallway to the bathroom. She emerged a moment later with a large brown towel.

Jason shrugged the dripping slicker off his shoulders.

"Let me take that," Lauren said, exchanging the wet slicker for the dry towel. "You're drenched."

He gave a wry chuckle. "Tell me something I don't already know."

Lauren hurried through the kitchen and into the utility room with the raincoat. "I didn't know it was supposed to rain like this," she called loudly as she reached for the coat hook. Returning, Lauren gazed across the large room which served as the living, dining, and kitchen area. She watched Jason towel-dry his blond hair.

"They didn't predict this much rain," he responded, now wiping the towel down his glistening arms. He glanced at the kitchen clock. "I tried waiting it out but finally gave it up. I didn't want to keep you waiting any longer." His comment held a double meaning which wasn't lost on her.

"You could have called," she told him. But then again, he was always good with excuses. There was no sense bringing it up. "It doesn't matter anyway. As long as you're here now."

Jason's gaze riveted to the kitchen table. "Did I interrupt something?"

Lauren let her eyes follow his line of vision. The phone! She'd forgotten Tom! Warmth crept up her neck. "I am on the phone. Just—just make yourself comfortable." She looked uncertainly at his wet clothes. "Dad still has a couple shirts and shorts in the back closet if you want those. They're probably a bit musty-smelling, but at least they're dry." She seriously doubted Jason would fit comfortably into her father's extra-large clothes.

"I'll be in the bathroom, changing," he announced, looking pointedly at the phone. "Don't keep him waiting."

Lauren cast Jason a quick, surprised look but didn't respond. She was sure she'd heard a soft chuckle before he vanished down the hall and into the walk-in closet.

Lauren kept a wary eye toward the hallway as she returned to the phone. "I'm sorry, Tom," Lauren rushed, her voice low. "I didn't mean to keep you waiting."

"Was that Jason I heard?"

Another wave of warmth crept upward. "Yes. He just came in." She felt awkward and uncomfortable. "He's changing out of his—his wet clothes." She stopped for one horrified second. "I don't mean in here! In the bathroom, of course." Immediately she rolled her eyes. *What is wrong with me?*

"It's okay," Tom responded with a reassuring laugh. "I'm not the jealous type."

Nervously, Lauren tucked a strand of hair behind her ear. "There's certainly no reason for you to be jealous."

"You almost sound hurt that I'm not," he teased. "I suppose I could show a little jealousy if that'd make you feel any better. Might be good for your ego, you know. Is that what you want?" he asked, giving a full laugh.

Lauren imagined his grinning face, dark and handsome, the large dimple on his cheek deepening. "No."

"You forget, my dear Lauren, I trust you implicitly, no matter what or how the circumstances appear." The amusement had left his voice, and Lauren caught his meaning full force. Before she could respond, he went on. "I knew going into this you'd have to meet with Jason—probably more than once, but it's a gamble I'm willing to take." His lighter tone returned. "Just make sure he's out of there by midnight, Cinderella. I may not be the jealous type, but I do have my limits." Another easy laugh came across the line. "There! Is that enough jealousy to keep your ego intact?"

Lauren smiled to herself. "More than enough." Movement caught her eye, drawing her gaze toward the figure coming down the hallway.

Jason walked into the open room, stopping to give her a full, modeling twirl. The oversized clothes swirled loosely with him, sagging terribly on his tall frame. His eyebrows inched upward quizzically for an opinion. Lauren gave him a warning glance but found it hard to keep the smile off her face.

"Lauren?" Tom's voice brought her back.

"Sorry."

"I'll call you Monday evening about the same time. Will you be around?"

"I'll be here," she answered distractedly.

Lauren watched as Jason traipsed into the kitchen and turned on the oven before rummaging loudly through the cookware cabinet. He finally produced a round pizza pan and quickly stripped the pizza from the soggy box and placed it on the pan before throwing it into the oven.

"I may have to visit the library Monday," Tom continued on, oblivious to her lack of attention. "If I do, it may be eight or later before I get home to make the call."

Jason walked silently to the back porch door, coming back a few seconds later, his arms full of kindling wood.

*What is he doing?* She wondered if he'd lost his mind.

"And, Lauren?"

"Hmm?" she answered absentmindedly.

Jason walked past her and deposited the kindling in the holder by the fireplace. His eyes danced mischievously, obviously fully aware of the distraction he was making.

"Remember to pray on Monday. I need to pass these orals."

Lauren snapped her attention back. "I'll be praying for you all day, I really will." Did Tom suspect she'd neglected him in prayer today? Struggling hard to keep her focus from Jason, who was lighting the dry twigs in the fireplace, she turned her back on him. But her mind refused to budge. Why was Jason lighting the fireplace in July? For the first time, she noticed the cold draft invading the room, most surely brought on by the northern storm.

"Take good care of yourself," Tom instructed, interrupting her thoughts once again.

"I will," Lauren responded. Her voice softened out of Jason's hearing range. "I really miss you, Tom. Take care until I come back."

Tom murmured something in response and hung up. She was still clinging to the phone when Jason passed her again with another load of firewood. The wood dropped noisily into the basket as she slowly replaced the receiver.

"I'm warming the pizza," Jason commented when she walked into the room. "Thought a small fire might chase away the cold."

"That's fine, Jason," she responded casually, relieved at the evenness in her voice. "I see you found the clothes all right."

"Don't see how these kids today function with loose britches," he said, adjusting the waistband as he hunkered down to tend the fire. "How do they keep these things on?"

Lauren only shrugged, wondering if Jason's bantering was for his benefit or hers. She'd do well to remember he still had a lot of explaining to do.

At Lauren's ambiguous shrug, Jason stood abruptly from his squatting position. "I suppose you're ready to get on with it," he taunted gently.

"Yes," she answered bluntly.

A grim expression overtook his face. "Well, I'm not!"

Lauren gave him a sharp glance. "What do you mean?"

"Not on an empty stomach, I'm not." Jason breezed past her to the kitchen, leaving a bemused Lauren behind. "I think better on a full stomach."

# Chapter 6

Have you got any pop?" Jason rummaged through the kitchen drawers, finally pulling out paper plates and napkins.

*Just make yourself at home, why don't you?* Lauren was tempted to say it aloud as she stared silently at the man's back. Since Jason's arrival, he'd buzzed about the cabin as if their five-year separation had never occurred. Something was wrong with this carefree, amicable behavior. Just that afternoon he'd been unflinchingly cool, and now he was forcing levity into the atmosphere.

Lauren walked carefully past him, maintaining a fair distance. "I'm sure there's some pop in the fridge, but it's probably not the kind you like." She opened the refrigerator door, staring at the contents. A frown crept over her lips. Figures! She pulled out a can of her favorite and one of his. "Guess you're in luck."

A satisfied grin spread over his face. "Doesn't sound like you were the one doing the shopping. It must have been my guardian angel who was so thoughtful."

"No, it was Tilly," she responded with some exasperation. Tilly's initiative to also buy some of Jason's brand of soda, one she herself detested, bothered her greatly. There had to be an unhealthy, preconceived idea somewhere in Tilly's mind about her and Jason. It could only mean trouble.

His mouth quirked. "Sometimes angels come in different forms."

Lauren ignored his attempt at humor by searching through the hutch for a trivet. A moment later she heard the oven door creak open.

"I don't know about you," he called out to her, "but I don't plan to stand around in the kitchen exchanging pleasantries all day. I'm hungry and I mean to eat."

She placed a large silver trivet in the middle of the dining room table and glanced into the kitchen. "The pot holder's in the middle. . ." The words died away as she caught his intent stare.

"I know," he assured, his words a mere whisper.

*Of course he knows,* she thought with a sigh. He knew every nook and cranny of the kitchen, maybe even better than she did.

Jason slowly opened the middle drawer and pulled out a flowery pot holder. Lauren watched him drag the hot pizza pan from the oven and move quickly from the kitchen, right past her and the table, and into the living area. Hot steam trailed behind him.

"Where are you going?"

"In front of the fireplace. Where else?"

Lauren stepped back, her voice taunting. "Just like old times?"

Jason gave a slight start as he lowered the pizza onto the stone ledge of the fireplace. He turned slowly, his dark gaze penetrating. There was an awful silence. "No," he finally said. "We both know the good old days can't be brought back again. But if you'll remember, we did call for a temporary truce. I thought it'd be nice to sit by the fireplace. If you object—"

"No," Lauren said contritely. "It's all right." Without hesitation, Lauren brought over the two sodas and plopped herself down on the carpeted edge of the flagstone. Why did she have the feeling Jason was gaining the upper hand on the evening?

Jason fed the fire once more before securing the fire screen. "Still take your pizza with pepperoni, peppers, and double cheese?" he asked, scooping up several small squares. He handed her the plate.

Lauren looked thoughtfully at the pizza he gave her. "You still remember?"

She felt the odd look Jason gave her, but he said nothing as he filled his own plate. Slowly he lowered himself to the floor. "Of course I remember," he finally answered. "It's a little early in the ball game to have my memory going." The corner of his mouth lifted slightly. "We consumed more than our share of pizzas in the past. It would be hard to forget." There was something playful and tender in his tone.

Lauren's heart tugged at its warmth. "We did eat our fair share." She picked up a piece and examined it. "I've added Italian sausage to my repertoire. Didn't want anyone to think I was in a rut."

"I'll keep the new information on file." He watched as she took a bite.

Lauren held his gaze for a long second before finally breaking eye contact. She looked down at her plate again in silence. Not a companionable silence, but a stiff, prelude silence that waited for the inevitable. She couldn't help but wonder what he was thinking. Meeting him like this was harder than she'd imagined, and her emotional energies were ebbing fast—just when her defenses needed to be at their greatest.

"You're not eating." Jason's glance lighted on her.

"To be honest, Jason," Lauren admitted, setting the paper plate down, "my stomach's been in knots ever since this trip was planned."

"Then why did you come?" he asked much too casually.

Lauren had no intention of explaining Tom's request. She'd already said too much. She couldn't very well admit her fears to Jason. By all rights, he was still her adversary. She was right to be wary of him. Jason had been in a position to search out the truth five years ago, but instead, he'd cast her aside, treating her as a pathetic liar who was totally expendable. He deserved her animosity. Why, then, did loneliness rush in on her as she looked at Jason's waiting expression?

"You wouldn't understand," she finally said with resignation.

"Try me!"

Lauren sighed. How could she sum up the honest reasons as to why she'd come back? True, Tom had firmly nudged her into action, but if the truth were to be told, she'd come to face the ghosts of her former life. If she faced them, maybe, just maybe she could finally shut the door to their existence.

"What's happening in your life now?" Jason prodded again. "Something's made this trip necessary."

"Maybe."

Jason opened the fire screen and stirred the fire with the poker. "It only makes sense, Lauren. Five years is a long time to break total contact with the island and then," he paused, snapping his fingers for emphasis, "all of a sudden show up. Something's occurred in your well-ordered life to spur you into action."

"My well-ordered life?" she repeated blankly.

"Your life has always been ordered," Jason told her pointedly. "You like all your ducks in a neat, little row."

Lauren had to stop this maddening line of conversation. He was creating a diversion from her true mission, delaying the explanations due on his side.

"Although I'm sure my orderly life is of great interest," she began with a bit of sarcasm, "it's the issue of false accusations that brings me here." Lauren let her fingers glide nervously over the flagstone. "But in a sense you're right. I am at a point in my life where I'd like to move on without Bay Island hanging around my neck like an anchor."

"So you've come to set the record straight?"

"In a nutshell—yes."

"And you say you've never heard anything from anyone on Bay Island in five years?" Jason sat relaxed—too relaxed—his long legs stretched out lazily, crossed at the ankles. "Could it be that a special someone in your life has spurred you on after all these years?"

Lauren didn't like the way Jason was interrogating her once more. If there were to be any more cross-examinations, she'd be the one doing the questioning—not Jason. "I haven't come to discuss my life with you, Jason, but to find out why things happened as they did five years ago. I had no knowledge of Tara's death or her confession to you and the church."

But Jason was persistent. "You didn't receive a call from Tara?"

"I told you, Jason," she responded, exasperated, "Tara never called me. I never spoke to her."

He looked perplexed for a moment. "I don't understand it."

"Has the possibility ever crossed your mind, Tara may not have made the call?" Lauren pointed out logically. "We've both seen, firsthand, Tara's talents in the area of deception. Could it be possible she was still protecting what was dear to her?" Her voice dwindled to a soft sigh. "She was in love with you. You'll admit that now, won't you?"

Jason looked at her coolly. "Let's not go into that again."

"How can we avoid it?" Lauren sat up straight and leaned forward. "I was a threat to her, Jason, and as much as I tried to tell you, you couldn't see it. The whole scheme she'd pulled off was for one purpose, and one purpose only—to get rid of me. Without me, you were free again. Maybe she was still holding on to that. Maybe she feared I'd come running back to you once this mess was finally cleared."

"Ready to start all over again, is that it?" he finished for her, disbelief on his tone.

"Something like that."

There was a moment of silence as his gaze seem to pierce her very being. "Would you have come back?"

Lauren let her gaze drop pensively toward the bright flames of fire before shaking her head. "Five years is a long time," she whispered, her voice husky. "My life's changed—I've changed. You've changed." She slowly turned toward him. "And you hurt me, Jason, like no man ever has or ever will again. A hurt like that doesn't just go away—not even with time." Lauren stopped, aghast at what she'd just admitted.

Jason sat up from his relaxed position, letting his hands dangle thoughtfully between his knees. "I'll never be able to live down what I allowed to happen to you," he freely conceded, his face grim. "I may not be able to assume all the fault, Tara had her share, but it ultimately fell to me to determine how to handle the situation. I managed it badly. I protected my pride more than anything else." He raked his long fingers thoughtfully through his hair. "I can't tell you how many times I've asked God for His forgiveness."

Lauren glanced up sharply, leveling him with an accusing look. "And what about my forgiveness? Did you ever think to ask for my forgiveness?" There was an aching pause. "Why didn't you call me, Jason? Why didn't you tell me you were sorry?"

Jason slowly rubbed one hand over his bristly chin, the five-o'clock shadow making the defined angles that much more prominent. "I'd planned to."

"When?" Lauren scoffed. "Next week? Next year?"

"After Tara talked with you," he answered, his voice dropping a decibel lower, "I'd planned to call you."

"And?"

"And then Tara phoned you."

Her gaze swept over him. "You wrote me off after she'd told you of my horrible behavior. Is that it?" Lauren couldn't believe it. How could Jason be taken in not once, but twice? "You never questioned the validity of her story?"

Jason frowned at her. "You weren't there, Lauren. Tara did change after coming to Jesus." With a defeated sigh, he rubbed his chin again. "Would you have me believe she faked it all, and in the end, died without Christ?" It was clear the possibility not only appalled but frightened him. He shook his head. "I won't believe that."

"You'd rather believe Tara than me?"

"I didn't say that." He looked at her crossly, his tone turning icy. "You keep making it sound like a contest exists between you two. Lauren, the woman's dead."

*And she's still wreaking havoc in my life!* Jason could be so dense at times. "I didn't say that," Lauren retorted, taking the chance to steal his own line. "But maybe you're right. How can I compete for the truth when you never give my reasoning a chance? Why is it so hard for you to believe me?"

When he spoke, his tone thawed, but the taunting inflection remained. "I do believe you about the phone call, Lauren." He released an exaggerated sigh. "I don't understand it, and I'm not ready to brand Tara a fake, but I do believe you."

Lauren detected the catch in his voice. It gave her a small stab of satisfaction to know she'd rattled his cool exterior. "Thank you for saying so."

He looked at her thoughtfully. "What would you have said to Tara if you'd gotten the call?"

"I'm not sure," she answered honestly. "I'd like to say I would have forgiven her, given her a proper Christian response, but that little self-righteous pat on the back would be just that." Right now she didn't feel very Christ-like toward Tara, and she wondered if she'd ever allow God to help her in that area. As draining as the emotion of hate was, it seemed easier to handle and maintain than the alternative. Forgiving Tara would require more than she possessed. Wasn't she entitled to keep what little pride she had left?

"You couldn't, or should I say, wouldn't, have forgiven her?" The question seemed to be of great importance to him.

"I was never given the chance to find out what I would have done," she answered evasively.

Jason appeared to reflect upon her words. The crackling of the fire seemed to grow more intense in the silence. "I was with her when she died, you know."

Lauren said nothing but kept her eyes fixed on the fire. She hoped Jason wasn't going into any gruesome details meant to rip at her heartstrings.

"I think I was angrier with you as she lay dying than I was when I'd thought you'd sold my drawings." Sadness vibrated in his voice.

"Me!" Lauren gave a low cry, her tired heart reeling.

"She wasn't at peace, Lauren," Jason continued on. "She couldn't accept God's forgiveness without yours. I tried to tell her she'd done her best, that God would deal with the rest. She just couldn't see past it."

"Yet you never called me!" she stated incredulously.

"No," he answered, seeming to struggle for the right words. "That was the day I finally let you go. What little spark of hope existed died right there in that hospice room."

There was an awkward silence.

"And where are we supposed to go from here?" Lauren whispered.

"Forward, I hope," he answered pragmatically.

"I don't think it could go backward any further," she reasoned in all seriousness.

As if against his will, he smiled. "Don't tempt it."

Lauren gave him a nervous smile. Things could be worse. Or could they? "Do the people at church know about this phone call business with Tara?"

"No," he answered without hesitancy. "They just assumed things went all right, that everything was patched up between Tara and you. I'm sure some began to wonder, though, when you never came back."

"Well, I'm here now." She sighed wearily. "But little good it does at this point. The past can't be fixed."

"No, but we can alter the future." Jason stood, picking up the cold pizza pan. "Tomorrow I'm picking you up for church. That's the first obstacle to be dealt with. Secondly, I plan to find out what happened to the call you were supposed to receive from Tara."

Lauren stood and followed Jason into the kitchen. "How do you plan to do that?"

Jason ripped off a long sheet of aluminum foil. "I'm not sure yet, but I'll figure out something." Quickly he wrapped the uneaten portions. "And thirdly, I plan to enjoy the Skipper's Festival this week, regardless. I'll show you just how much I've improved my rock-skipping skills."

Lauren smiled. "You're still competing?"

"Yes. And I plan to win this year." He opened the refrigerator door.

"Jason?"

"Hmm?"

Lauren watched as he slid the leftovers on the top shelf before looking up expectantly. "Why did you build our—your house?"

His expression sobered. "That I don't plan to explain right now. I think we've got enough on our plates, so to speak, to deal with."

Lauren nodded silently, wondering, yet refusing to ask about the woman she'd seen at his home. Jason disappeared into the utility room, then reappeared with his blue slicker.

"Services start at ten," Jason said, opening the front door. "I'll be by at nine-thirty."

Lauren followed him out onto the wooden deck, their steps echoing softly in the darkness. "The rain seems to have stopped."

Jason nodded and took a deep breath as he looked up at the sky. "There's something so pure about the air after a good rain," he said softly. He leaned on the rail and looked out. "I've missed the view from Piney Point." Slowly he turned toward her, his dark eyes deepening. "And I've really missed you, Lauren."

She held her breath. "I'm glad you've come back."

An emotional lump was closing in on Lauren's tight throat. *Oh, please don't let me cry.* The threat subsided for a moment, allowing her to speak with a steady, clear voice. "I've missed you, too."

Jason moved closer. He reached out and rested his warm hands gently on her arms. "And I am truly sorry for the way I treated you and how this whole ugly mess turned out." He pulled her an inch closer. "Will you ever be able to forgive me?"

"I told you five years ago I'd already forgiven you," she replied in a near whisper. *Just please don't ask me to forgive Tara.*

He searched her face, his expression unreadable. "I don't believe you really have, and I'm not letting you leave this time until you do. I plan to make this up to you, Lauren."

"That won't be necess—"

"Yes, it is necessary," he said with conviction. Soft night sounds surrounded them, echoing as he slowly lowered his face to hers.

Lauren knew what was coming. Paralyzed, she let his lips brush lightly across hers, neither refusing nor responding.

"I will make this up to you, Lauren Wright. I promise!" With that, he bounded off the deck, down the wet steps, and to his car. "Nine-thirty! Be ready."

Lauren watched the road for several minutes after the sedan's taillights vanished into the darkness. Fear gripped at her heart. Jason's presence, his touch, his kiss—what was she to do? Her mind refused to believe, but her heart knew the awful truth. She was still in love with Jason Levitte!

# Chapter 7

"You look nice," Jason commented, swinging open the passenger door. "Blue has always been a good color for you."

Lauren murmured a polite response as she eased herself into the passenger seat. Instantly she felt the cool texture of the leather upholstery as it penetrated her lightweight skirt. The fresh morning air still held a damp chill.

Stress and fatigue—due to her maddeningly sleepless night—were taking their toll on Lauren's resolve. Thoughts of Tara had roved through her mind all night like a wolf on the prowl. Would it ever be possible to know the truth about the mysterious phone call? Was there any way to prove her own innocence? The taunting thoughts would not settle. It was like being accused all over again.

Jason had been with Tara when the call had supposedly been made. Lauren racked her brain for possible scenarios. The only person who could have possibly intercepted such a call would have been her sister, Cassie. But she'd only lived with Lauren for a brief, two-month period. A possible but not probable conclusion. And Cassie would have told Lauren if such a call had come. There was no explanation. Was Tara lying? Could she have fooled Jason with a dial tone pressed to her ear?

Jason slipped into the car, disrupting her thoughts. He paused to look at her. "Ready?"

"I suppose." Lauren rested her elbow on the door and rubbed her fingers along her temple. The headache plaguing her earlier seemed to step up a beat. An unnerving morning lay ahead, the next dreaded step she knew she must take.

"They're just sinners saved by grace," Jason said with a reassuring smile, seeming to perceive her thoughts. "Just like us." He grasped her hand and gave it a squeeze. "If it's any comfort, this is as hard for them as it is for you. They were really embarrassed and ashamed about how they treated you. Give them a chance to make it right."

Lauren was very aware of Jason's touch, his hand still firmly clutching hers. "I've tried hard to prepare myself for this, but I'm not looking forward to it." She took a deep breath, paused, and took three curious, successive sniffs. "Why does your car smell like fried chicken?"

"Probably because there's a pan of fried chicken in the trunk." He flashed her a knowing smile. "I've become a cook of sorts over the past few years."

Lauren waited for a further explanation, but it never came. "Maybe I'm better off not knowing," she mumbled softly to herself.

Jason released her hand, still smiling. Quickly he started the engine and maneuvered the sedan easily down the incline. "I don't always carry chicken around in my car," he baited.

"Oh?"

"Only for special events." He gave her a sidelong glance. "It's for the fellowship dinner after the morning service."

Lauren quickly turned toward him. "You never mentioned anything about a fellowship dinner," she groaned. Her temples began to throb harder. It was one thing to get through an hour-long service, and another to manage a fellowship meal.

He turned the car down Shore Lane. "You have to give the people a little time to get their nerve up, Lauren." His tone turned tender. "You'll do just fine—trust me. The fellowship time will give them an opportunity to talk with you, to be more relaxed. Then, by next Sunday, things will be much smoother." He laughed. "It may take Mr. Edwards at least that long to get his apology out."

Mr. Edwards! Lauren closed her eyes to block out the old man's image. The church elder had actually stood in front of the entire congregation and demanded her removal from the church roster. It was utterly devastating. The man had shown her no mercy.

"If Mr. Edwards needs more time, he'll be too late," Lauren said flatly, leaning back against the headrest. "I won't be here next week."

Jason snapped his head toward her. "What do you mean?"

"I'm only here for a week," Lauren explained matter-of-factly. "I thought you knew."

"A week!" he sputtered incredulously, frowning. "How did you ever figure to straighten out this mess in a week?"

Lauren gave him a level, logical look. "I didn't figure on anything." She could tell he was disturbed by her nonchalance. "I know a week isn't long—"

"Of course a week isn't long enough," he interrupted. He rapped his long fingers impatiently on the steering wheel. "We have a lot to work through." He paused and looked at her. "And what about the Skipper's Festival? You said you'd come."

"Oh, I'll be here for the festival." It was the old Jason talking now—concerned and commanding. And she had to admit, he looked unbearably handsome in his blue pin-striped suit. Combined with the thick halo of blond waves, the attraction was nearly too much. Lauren raised her eyebrows playfully. "I wouldn't miss your performance for anything. You might actually win the title this year."

Jason didn't smile but focused his smoky gray eyes on the road ahead. "Is there something—or someone—causing you to rush back so soon?"

Lauren knew the question was loaded. She certainly missed Tom, but not enough to rush home. And right now she didn't want to talk about Tom. The memory of Jason's kiss the night before was still too vivid to spoil—just yet.

"I'm on a week's vacation," she finally said. "There's a job to consider. I can't just take off when I want."

Jason wore an expression that told her he knew better. "A week just isn't going to be long enough." He seemed to pause and mull over the situation. "I'll take some time off this week. I don't want you leaving before I've had time to make things up to you."

Lauren smiled, inexplicably pleased. Then the smile slipped. How many times in the past had Jason expressed his wish to spend time with her, only to have his work suddenly intrude? And there was another woman to consider. Surely the woman wouldn't sit idly by as he divided his attention between the two. How did he plan to handle that?

Jason waited.

"I told you before. There's no need to make anything up," Lauren said slowly. "I know how important your work is to you." She looked distractedly out her window. The morning was alive with colorful summer flowers, all but unseen in her preoccupation.

"I'm not married to it," Jason responded, sounding a trifle annoyed. "The business is on its feet. It doesn't need the constant pampering it used to."

Lauren wasn't convinced. Just yesterday they'd been interrupted with company business, and they hadn't even been together for more than fifteen minutes. Still, if he could pull it off. . . The possibility of spending the week with Jason sent warmth through her veins. "You're liable to get a lot of tongues wagging if people see us together." A forced smile hid the weightiness of her next words. "Besides, you might have a special someone who wouldn't like it very much."

"Not exactly subtle, are you?" he deadpanned.

Lauren couldn't tell from his tone whether he was irritated or amused. "About as subtle as you, I believe."

There was a brief silence before Jason slowly shook his head. "Don't worry yourself. I can handle things on my end. It's rather complicated and much too hard to explain." He glanced at her. "And what about you? Is your special someone okay with this trip?"

"My special someone," she began hesitantly, "trusts me explicitly."

A pained expression crossed his face, and she immediately wished the words hadn't spilled out as they had. She hadn't meant to say it in such a way to hurt Jason. An appropriate retraction was forming when he interrupted.

"It's certainly a good thing he didn't see us kissing last night, then." Jason kept his eyes on the road, but Lauren could see their impish twinkle. He was actually enjoying her discomfort.

"Or her, either," Lauren retorted.

Jason faked a sigh of relief. "Or her, either!"

The atmosphere suddenly lightened, and they both smiled.

"Tell you what," Jason suggested. "Our own problems are complicated enough. Why don't we abandon the rest of our outside dilemmas for this week? It will be just you and me."

As he spoke, Lauren watched the church whiz by. She stretched her neck and thumbed back toward it. "You just passed the church."

Jason hit the brakes and looked in the rearview mirror. "See what you've done?" A slow grin crept over his face as he quickly wheeled the car back around. "Well? What do you say to my proposal?"

"Just you and me, huh?" Lauren met his teasing eyes with a smile. She liked the idea immensely. She knew it was emotional suicide at best, but how could her heart refuse? She wanted to be with Jason. Ramifications could be dealt with later. She stuck her hand out before him. "Deal!"

Jason looked quickly from her face to outstretched hand, a smile playing across his lips. He gave her hand a firm shake. "Deal!"

Lauren watched as the church whizzed by once more. "You just passed the church—again," she announced.

Their gazes locked and both broke out in laughter.

The church building was packed as Lauren scanned the crowd, seeing several new faces mixed with the old. Jason held his hand reassuringly on the small of her back as he guided her through the foyer. An unfamiliar woman took their food dish, and they proceeded into the sanctuary. For a moment their presence went unnoticed until Larry Newkirk intercepted them.

"It's good to see you again," Larry greeted, his warm smile aimed at Lauren. His gaze traced the length of Jason's arm, lingering at her waist. He nodded. "Jason."

Was it her imagination, or was there tension between the two men? Lauren shot a nervous glance at Jason. Jason, however, seemed perfectly at ease.

"How's the police job, Larry?" Jason asked in a light and friendly tone.

"Same as usual," Larry briefly responded before turning back to Lauren. "I forgot to mention yesterday when I saw you that I have something of yours you'll want back."

Puzzled, Lauren slowly shook her head. "Something of mine?"

"Your cross necklace," Larry explained. "You'd lost it during a drama rehearsal one night. Remember?"

Remember! Of course she remembered. It had been a graduation gift from her parents, which she'd worn daily for several years. Hopelessly she'd searched the church for weeks. When she'd left the island, she'd given it up for lost, as lost as her faith.

"That's wonderful, Larry," she gushed with anticipation. "Do you have it with you?"

"Sorry," he apologized. "I didn't think to bring it." He looked meaningfully at Jason before turning back to her. "I can swing by the cabin sometime this week with it if that'd be okay."

"Sure," Lauren answered hesitantly, feeling the increased pressure from Jason's hand on her back. "I'm here for the week." She glanced at Jason. He stood perfectly poised.

"I'll be sure to catch you before then."

They exchanged pleasantries for only a moment more before Larry wandered off to a beckoning friend and Jason ushered her further down the aisle toward the front.

"Better be careful with Larry," he whispered close to her ear.

Lauren drew her brows together in bewilderment.

He moved closer. "He's always had a thing for you."

"A thing?" It took everything within her to keep a skeptical chortle from erupting. "Jason, he was a drama student of mine, just a kid." Of all the ridiculous. . .

Jason kept propelling them down the aisle. "He's not a kid now!"

Lauren could feel several pairs of eyes trained on her back, and she said no more. Right now she had other, weightier things to deal with. She found her stomach muscles forming into knots. What was she doing here? The once familiar building seemed foreign, distanced by more than time. The people were strangers, pieces of a past life she no longer knew.

"Is this okay?" Jason asked, stopping at the third pew from the front. Before she could protest, he whispered, "Go ahead and sit down. I'll be right back."

Pride kept Lauren from detaining him, and he hadn't waited for a reply before disappearing. A tremor of distress flitted through her. Was she losing her mind? In less than twenty-four hours she'd done an about-face with Jason. She was once again the unassuming, starry-eyed woman she used to be.

"Looks like you've patched things up with Jason."

Lauren looked up and was barely able to move out of the way before Tilly plopped herself down in the pew beside her.

Tilly gave her a wide smile. "It's good to be back, isn't it, girl?"

Lauren nodded absently, knowing Tilly wasn't paying one bit of attention to her response. Instead, Tilly was looking over the congregation. Much to Lauren's horror, Tilly silently began summoning several from their seats. It wasn't long before numerous faces swam before her, greeting, talking, laughing—causing absolute chaos in Lauren's mind. Each seemed caught up in Tilly's exuberance.

"Oh, we're so glad you're back," Mrs. Phillips, the church librarian, cooed. "We were just asking about you last week, weren't we, Gertrude?" The older lady looked to the tall woman beside her who bobbed her head in agreement.

Lauren smiled. Both women had always reminded her of the two aunts in *Arsenic and Old Lace,* sweet and unassuming. "How have you both been?"

Neither got far into the conversation before the choir began filling the loft, dispersing the crowd.

Tilly squeezed Lauren's shoulder. "Told you everyone would welcome you back," she pronounced, slipping quickly out of the pew.

Lauren hazarded a look at her retreating back. Beyond, she caught a glimpse of the raven-haired woman in the back. Jason was at her side. Her heart sank. Lauren slowly faced forward. Once again, an immense wave of regret washed over her. She should never have come back. Up and down, back and forth. Soon she wouldn't know which way was anywhere.

The song leader was announcing the first hymn as Jason slipped quietly into the pew. Lauren kept her eyes fixed to the front. Still she couldn't hide the sight of him from her periphery. His presence, his control overwhelmed her. She felt him tap her arm.

"Sorry, I got tied up," he whispered when she turned toward him, his face a mock look of chagrin. He pulled out a blue hymnbook from its holder and held it before her.

Lauren wouldn't—couldn't—sing. The lump in her throat seemed to be growing by the second.

"Are you all right?" Jason was leaning close to her ear.

Lauren could feel his warm breath, smell the minty tang of a lozenge. She nodded, giving him a reassuring smile. He seemed convinced.

The service dragged, and Lauren forced herself not to look at her watch constantly. Her mind was too much in turmoil. Finally the closing prayer ended. But there was no escape.

Immediately, smiling faces accosted her as Jason kept the cordial introductions and updates coming. Lauren tried desperately to keep up each conversation but was hopelessly lost. No longer could Lauren discern the past actions of these people. With the exception of Mr. Edwards, most of the accusations were behind her back or silent in nature. Were these the same people who had shunned her so mercilessly five years ago?

"I'm starving," Jason finally announced to the group. "There's plenty of time to talk with Lauren over lunch."

The group disbanded happily, and Jason turned to her. "They may not come right out and apologize, but they're mending fences just the same by their welcome. You can see that, can't you?"

"It's hard to tell between mending fences and sweeping it under the carpet," she replied honestly.

Was accepting her back into the church circle, into their fold again, enough to exonerate the past? She didn't think so. But Jason's question had been a rhetorical one. Regardless, she was now a stranger. Like leaving the parental home to be on your own, things are never the same again upon return. Relationships change. Unwritten rules change.

Jason quickly threaded them through the food line, making sure Lauren tried his fried chicken. Everyone seemed carefree and happy, as if the clouds had parted leaving sunshine in their place. Somehow, she managed through the fellowship dinner. It seemed more of a performance on her part. Even Mr. Edwards received a polite and appropriate response from her repertoire. She wanted to forgive these people—and some she could. But for others, their hurtful words and actions of the past paraded across Lauren's memory as they spoke with her. Her mouth managed the right responses, only they never quite reached her heart. *Oh, God, what if I can never forgive? Am I destined to be out of Your will forever?*

"It time to go." Jason was gently nudging her elbow. Lauren tried unsuccessfully to hide her damp eyes. He gave her a crooked grin, laying his arm lazily around her shoulders. "It feels good to get everything settled, doesn't it?"

Lauren gave a lying nod.

"Now," he said teasingly. "I believe our week is just starting. Let's not waste one minute of it."

# Chapter 8

True to his word, Jason became an attentive fixture at Piney Point the next day. The squeaky screen door, the loose deck boards, the leaky faucet—each yielded to his skillful hands. For Lauren it was just plain déjà vu.

"What's next?" Jason asked, backing himself out from under the sink cabinet. He looked expectantly at Lauren while wiping a rag over the plumbing wrench. He tossed the wrench noisily into the toolbox.

Lauren flipped three grilled cheese sandwiches on the griddle. "I think you've just about fixed everything there is to fix," she told him with a smile. "Get washed up for lunch. The sandwiches are almost done."

"Yes, ma'am." He gave a mock salute and trotted off toward the bathroom.

Never in her wildest imagination had Lauren expected such a turnabout in Jason. Her heart was even more unprepared. She dreaded the fluttery feeling it gave every time he was near—a sure sign of impending disaster. And she was falling for his act. Where was her pride? Where was her sensibility? Jason was doing his best to make her stay on the island pleasant, but they couldn't just pick up where they left off. Yet what was she to do with the erupting feelings that mirrored her reawakening love—a love she thought had died? And what about Tom? The whole thing was getting much too complicated—just as she'd feared.

Jason reappeared in the kitchen as Lauren placed the coleslaw on the tray.

Jason picked up the tray. "I'll take that," he said with a charming smile. "Don't forget the napkins."

Lauren grabbed several paper napkins and followed him out to the front deck. The noon sun broke through the trees as swaying bits of puzzle-piece light danced over the picnic table. Jason set the tray down on the checkered tablecloth.

There was silence for several moments as they arranged the food. A warm, southerly breeze fluttered the paper plates until each one was properly laden with food.

Lauren looked up, venturing to speak first. "I saw Levitte's Landing when I came in on Saturday," she began. "It's really beautiful with all the walkways and dockside shops. When did you build it?"

"Finished it early last year," Jason answered, looking pleased at her interest. "I'm planning to expand the pier with two more restaurants and a couple of shops if the tourist numbers explode like last season." His enthusiasm seemed to ebb slightly, and he gave a careless shrug of his shoulder. "We'll see. I have a few other projects I might like to do first—maybe take some time off."

She nodded her understanding, noticing the change in his demeanor. Absent was the normal fervor he usually exhibited for his pet projects. Had Jason finally achieved a reasonable balance between work and his personal life or was something troubling him?

"I'd like to take you over there this afternoon," he continued on, a teasing glint in his eye. "I seem to remember how well you like shopping, and there are plenty of specialty stores to suit your fancy."

Lauren smiled. "I'd like that. I want to see the final design—all the details, you know. You certainly went through enough designing and redesigning. It should be perfect." She couldn't help but remember the many nights he'd worked and shared the drawings with her—cherishing each one as he would his own child. "I'm sure the final product's everything you wanted."

Jason raised an eyebrow but said nothing. His attention went back to his food.

Lauren shot him a nervous glance after a moment of silence settled in. "Are you ready to tell me about the house?" The house at Muriel's Inlet never left her mind. She'd looked for any opportunity to bring the subject up this morning, but Jason always seemed to head her off at the pass.

"No!" He took a sip of his drink, watching her over the rim of the glass.

She frowned as her gaze locked with his. Would he ever tell her? Jason shook his head at her as if to say he understood her questioning look. Lauren just stared back, contemplating her next move.

"Do you want to tell me about the woman—"

"No!"

Frustrated, Lauren leveled him with another stare. It was then she saw the spark of amusement crossing his face. The man was impossible.

"Is there anything we can talk about?" she asked with a smirk.

"No!" He smiled mischievously, and Lauren waited as he toyed mockingly with his coleslaw. "I take that back. We could talk about Cincinnati and the man—"

"No!" She jabbed her fork playfully in his direction.

"All right, then," he answered good-naturedly. "What's left?"

Lauren put her fork down and thought for a moment. Her mood suddenly grew serious. "Tell me about Tara. Tell me what happened."

Jason's brows creased over his half-hooded eyes, his reserve evident. "It will only start an argument, Lauren. I'm not sure we'll ever be able to agree to disagree. I do want to tell you about it—sometime. Now just doesn't seem like the right time."

"There will never be a right time," Lauren admitted with a sigh. "There are so many things I don't understand about what happened or about you, either. I need to know why."

Jason gave an elaborate sigh. Several emotions seemed to cross his tanned face as he sat contemplating.

"You're the one who said you wanted to make things up to me," she reminded gently. An insect buzzed near her ear, and she absently shooed it away. "We have to start somewhere."

She sensed resignation in his voice when he finally spoke. "What do you want to know?"

"Everything," Lauren pleaded softly. "Tell me everything that happened after I left the island. Tell me about the people at the church. . .about Tara's illness." She poked her index finger at her chest. "Help me to understand."

Jason nodded. "I'm not sure anything I have to say will make you understand."

"Try me!" Lauren desperately wanted to clear the cloud between them, impossible as it seemed.

Jason shoved his food aside with a deep sigh. Silence reigned for several seconds. "The day you left was especially hard," he began reflectively. "But I really thought your leaving would be the end of it, a time to forget, a time to go on with my life. The church seemed to settle down from the scandal, the work remained steady, Tara stayed on as my secretary, and I hired a new accountant."

Lauren leaned forward, concentrating on his every word.

Jason swung one leg lazily over the bench before continuing. "It was almost as if everything went back to normal until the day Tara was diagnosed with brain cancer. We didn't know at first it was cancer, but we knew it was serious. She said she smelled weird odors, and then the headaches came. The doctor ordered several tests and then a biopsy. By then it was too late."

"When did this all happen?" Lauren asked. The time frame was so important!

Jason squinted one eye in thought. "Almost three years after you left, I think. It all meshes together after awhile."

Lauren nodded. "Go on."

"Radiation shrank the tumor a little, and they tried to operate, but it was hopeless." He shook his head. "It was only a matter of time at that point. They gave her six months, maybe seven." He seemed to have difficulty forming his next thoughts. "Late one night after Tara realized death was inevitable, she called. She was so upset I couldn't make heads or tails of what she was saying. By the time I got there, she was hysterical. That's when the whole thing spilled out—how she hated you, what she'd done—how she'd set up the whole masterpiece."

Lauren picked up her glass of iced tea and took a sip. There were so many questions just begging to be asked. But she didn't dare interrupt.

"I don't think I need to go into detail about that." He took a sip of his own drink.

"Yes, you do," Lauren quickly corrected. "Tell me what she said."

Jason's jaw muscles tightened, and Lauren thought for a moment he wouldn't. Then something flickered in his eyes, and he began again. "I think you've already figured out how Tara borrowed your checkbook and rigged your account with the twenty thousand before setting up the last delivery. The rest wasn't too hard, and she'd kept herself pretty busy planting doubt in the minds of the other office staff as well. It was an elaborate scheme." There was an element of disbelief in his voice. "It's still so hard to fathom!"

"Did Tara ever tell you why?" Lauren asked softly.

He shook his head. "Not really. She mentioned something vague about trying to protect my interests, interests she thought you were somehow endangering." He shrugged one shoulder. "It really didn't make sense."

Lauren had to restrain the impulse to cry out. Instead she bit the inside of her lip purposely to slow her response. "She gave no details of her reasoning at all?" *There had to be signs, Jason!* "How did she act toward you after I left?" she prodded.

A brief look of annoyance crossed his face. "Lauren," he warned. "Let's not go there."

"Well," she encouraged cautiously, "just think for a moment." She met his brooding gaze. It was obvious Jason would have to be led by the hand on this one. "Did Tara stand by your side, pledging her loyal support after I left? Did she offer you solace at every turn? Was she magically at your side during every difficult moment?"

Jason looked at her and a laugh erupted. "Oh, come on, Lauren. You make it sound like I picked up with the first woman offering me a shoulder."

Lauren lifted a questioning brow his way. "That's not what I inferred. I'm only asking a question. Was Tara's shoulder always available?"

"Tara wasn't interested in me," Jason assured her. "She was just. . ." He seemed at a loss for words.

Lauren rolled her eyes heavenward. Men could be so dense! "She was just in love with you," she finished for him. Waving off the protest she saw brewing, she quickly pressed on. "It's all right, Jason. I accept the fact that you didn't recognize it. Her motive was ill-conceived, an oddball, sort of mixed-up mess. She probably didn't understand it herself."

She watched him lower his head for a moment before looking back up. "Psycho-speculation!"

"Maybe," Lauren offered gently. "Whatever the reason, it drove her to do what she did." She was amazed at her own relative calm. "But do you really think she was sorry?"

He hesitated. "I always thought so. But you've brought question to that, haven't you?" His brows drew together. "I still don't understand the missed phone call. I can't even begin to fathom what it means. But for right now, I have to believe she made a true decision for Christ." There was a terrible, tense silence before he continued. "You can't know what the thought does to me—"

"No, I can't," Lauren responded, touching his hand lightly. They were quiet for several seconds. "Do you remember what I said to you the day I left?"

He lifted his quizzical gaze, a smile tugging at the corners of his mouth. "Quite a few things, if I remember right."

She smiled back. "I told you the truth always has a way of coming out. It may take a day, a month, or years, but it always comes out." She tugged at his hand. "It was true then, it's true now. If there's one thing I've learned through this ordeal, it's that God does things in His own time and in His own way. We have to trust He knows what He's doing."

"You almost lost that truth because of me," he stated ruefully, shaking his head in self-reproach. "I'm glad you gained your faith back."

Lauren's head shot up. "What do you mean?" How could he know of the spiritual struggles, the struggles that nearly drowned her?

Jason seemed to take great care with his words. "I told you earlier, I've kept some track of you through the years."

Lauren couldn't decide if she should be elated or angry. The memory of the glossy photos came to mind; he'd spied on her before. "But why?"

"I never stopped caring about what happened to you," Jason answered casually.

Lauren had no problem reading between the lines. Caring about what happens to someone and caring for them were two different things entirely. She nodded and stood up. "Just like one of your lost lambs." Just like Tara! She began to slowly gather the plates but stopped. "If you've kept track of me, why didn't you contact me? Things might have turned out differently if you had."

"I'd planned to," he admitted, also standing. "But one thing led to another, and the thing with Tara's phone call wound my clock pretty good. I wasn't sure I even wanted to see you again." He paused. "And there were other things to consider."

Lauren dumped the forks and knives on the tray. "Such as?"

"Well," he hesitated, "there's Tom for one thing. You weren't exactly unattached—"

"Jason!" Lauren nearly cried. "You really have been spying on me!"

"I wasn't spying!" Jason refuted calmly.

"Of course you weren't." Lauren humphed at him and took up the tray. "You're really the limit, Jason Levitte."

Jason only smiled. "I told you this would start an argument!" He picked up the glasses and started for the door in front of her. "I've had enough serious conversation for one afternoon. We have better things to do. You said you wanted to go shopping. Why don't we get ready?"

Lauren stuck her tongue out at his retreating back. *The man has his nerve. He'd known about Tom all along. But how? He couldn't just drop a bomb like that and then change the subject.*

"Jason," she began in her no-nonsense tone.

Jason turned for a brief second. "I'm not discussing the matter any further at the moment, except to say, you don't have to worry that pretty little head of yours with visions of me staring in your windows or any other such wild thoughts. I think you know me better than that."

Lauren knew he'd say no more after meeting his determined stare. He was a stubborn man! Everything had to be in the right time and context for him. Yet, she had so many burning questions and so few answers.

They put the food away in silence. Lauren finally locked the front door and joined Jason on the deck.

"Ready?" Jason asked cheerfully.

"Lead on!" She'd play it slow. Some careful thought was needed on her part.

They started down the steps.

The shrill ring of the phone shot through the open windows. Lauren turned briefly but waved a hand toward the cabin instead. Whoever it was would call back.

"I had a wonderful time," Lauren said as she scrounged through her purse for the front door key. "I think I overspent, though." The afternoon had gone much too fast and not once did an opportunity come in which she could engage Jason in their previous discussion.

"Levitte's Landing will have to be expanded if you keep shopping there," Jason replied, shifting the heavy shopping bags from one hand to the other.

"I know they're in here somewhere," she groaned, still digging deep into the recesses of her handbag.

His own keys jingled as he leaned past her and easily opened the door.

Lauren breathed a sigh of relief as she stepped through the door and dropped her two packages on the end table. "Never could pass up a good sale," she said, grinning. Suddenly she spun toward him. "Wait a minute!"

"Yes?" Jason responded, letting the shopping bags from his own hand glide easily to the floor.

"You just opened the door." Her mouth gaped at the thought. "You have a key to the cabin!"

Jason only shrugged his shoulders, nonplussed. "I found it on the deck when you left here five years ago."

Lauren thought back for a moment. He was right. She'd left it on the table and meant to give it to Tilly, but Jason's appearance had rattled her.

"I'll give it back if it bothers you," Jason continued.

Lauren blinked once. "I don't suppose it matters," she finally said.

"It's up to you," he said in a carefree tone, fingering the key in question. "If it makes you uncomfortable, I can give it back."

"Let's not worry about it right now," she answered, waving him off. For some inexplicable reason, she didn't want the key back. There was an odd security in knowing he'd kept it on his key ring all these years.

"If you change your mind," he continued, "let me know." He looked at his watch. "I need to go now, but I'll be back in the morning—about nine—to nail down those loose shingles on the gable ends."

"You're leaving?"

Jason grinned. "For now. I have a few things of my own to tend to." He rubbed his chin. "Why? You don't want me to go?"

Lauren met his gaze. No, she didn't want him to go, but she wasn't about to let him know it. And he was being deliberately provocative. "No, that's fine. I have plenty of things to attend to myself."

He smiled knowingly. "All right, then." He leaned forward, giving her a quick peck on the cheek. "Until tomorrow." There was a slight pause.

Lauren braced herself for more, dreading and hoping, but it never came. Instead, Jason let the screen door thud softly behind him. The faint sound of whistling and echoing footsteps across the wooden boards followed him out. She stood stock-still until the musical strain drifted off into oblivion.

# Chapter 9

Lauren stared intently at the winding road long after Jason's car had disappeared from sight. Familiar forest sounds comforted then eluded her. Even the wing-clacking crescendo of the summer locust nearly went unnoticed in her absorption. What was she to do? Thoughts tumbled over each other until they drifted to the top like lottery balls, random and out of sequence. Jason had been right about her need for a well-ordered world. She'd denied it then, but in retrospect it made sense. Security and order allowed her to function. Flexible Jason would never understand that. Or maybe it was she who didn't understand Jason.

The sudden ring of the phone broke the spell, and Lauren jerked. An exasperated sigh escaped as she hurriedly entered the cabin and gave a nervous glance at the clock. She'd forgotten Tom—again! Hesitantly she reached for the receiver.

"About time you answered," greeted a booming female voice. Lauren exhaled a breath of relief as her sister, Cassie, continued on in her usual exuberant style. "I've been trying to reach you all day. Where have you been?"

Lauren smiled at her younger sister's bluntness. "I'm on vacation," she answered without remorse. "I was out shopping with Jason."

"Jason?" Her sister gasped, and Lauren could almost imagine her astonished look. "You can't be serious! You're on speaking terms with the man?"

Cassie was the brutally candid one, a trait Lauren both admired and hated. "Cassie," she slowly warned.

"Don't Cassie me!" she retorted. "Have you lost your mind? I don't understand how—"

"You don't have to understand," Lauren interrupted firmly.

Cassie ignored her. "Does Tom know about this?"

"Tom's the one who suggested it."

Silence from Cassie was rare, and Lauren capitalized on it.

"And I didn't call you earlier to talk about my shopping excursion with Jason," Lauren continued.

"The whole world's gone crazy," Cassie muttered.

Lauren couldn't suppress a smile. "I won't argue that fact."

"Well, the message you left on my answering machine sounded so cryptic. I knew something must be up," Cassie parried. "It has to be Jason! You should know being around him again is bound to bring trouble—"

"There's nothing wrong," interrupted Lauren again. Cassie had been Lauren's staunch defender when the trouble began on Bay Island, effectively building dislike for Jason in the process. It was evident Cassie's feelings hadn't diminished in the least. "I just called to ask you a question."

There was caution in Cassie's voice. "All right. What is it?"

"I found out a few days ago that Tara may have tried to call me, maybe about two years ago," Lauren began to explain. "She evidently spoke with someone—"

"That's right! She did!" Cassie broke in. "She spoke with me."

A queasy lump formed in Lauren's throat. "You spoke with Tara?"

Cassie went on undisturbed. "Yes, I spoke with her. I let her know in no uncertain terms her apology was a little too late and a little too phony."

"You didn't!" Lauren cried in disbelief. "Why didn't you tell me?"

There was a sigh on the other end of the line. "You'd been through enough, Lauren. It was time to move on. Things were finally beginning to look up for you and Tom. Tara and Jason would have only muddled things for you again. It just seemed best to not mention the call."

"But Tara was dying," breathed Lauren in a near whisper. She stretched the cord and sank into the kitchen chair.

"Dying?" There was a twinge of disbelief in Cassie's voice.

Hadn't Lauren herself expressed disbelief at the notion? Tara's craftiness made one wary, even of the impossible. "Tara had brain cancer and died over a year ago. Jason said she was trying to make her peace with God about what she'd done." Lauren suddenly felt sick at the thought.

Cassie was unconvinced. "She could have made her peace with God without dragging you through the ordeal with her." There was a stifling pause. "I'm sorry if I caused you any trouble. I really didn't think you'd speak with her, anyway." Her voice turned harsh. "You almost didn't survive Tara's interference the first time around."

Lauren gave a deep sigh. She couldn't fault Cassie for her protective instincts, misguided as they were, and regardless, there was nothing Lauren could do about it now. Her eyes focused on the packages sitting on the floor, the ones Jason had carried. Jason! He'd be overjoyed to hear the news—wouldn't he? Tara hadn't lied after all!

"Are you all right?" Cassie asked with concern after a lengthy silence.

Lauren managed a weak laugh. "I was just wondering how I manage to get into these predicaments without ever participating."

"Trouble does seem to follow you," Cassie agreed in all seriousness. "And that's exactly why you should stay away from Jason." She took a deep breath. "You're not trying to renew anything with him, are you? I mean, Tom's a great guy and with your luck—"

"Don't worry about me, Cassie," Lauren assured, thinking over her sister's words. Cassie had always fancied Tom. And if Lauren were to admit the truth, Cassie matched Tom much better than she. Cassie would fit in anywhere, including Africa or Brazil. Wasn't that an ironic twist?

Cassie gave what sounded like a snort.

"Everything will work out," Lauren went on. "And I do appreciate you telling me about the call—and for trying to protect me."

"Promise me you'll be careful. I don't want to see you hurt again."

Her concern nearly brought tears. "I will."

The two sisters spoke for only a few moments longer before Lauren slowly replaced the receiver.

Ugh! Lauren fingered her aching temples. Cassie would be calling back, she was sure of it. Her sister never gave up. Yet something loomed larger than Cassie's interference. There was no avoiding what had to be done now. Jason would have to be told! Oh, how she dreaded that! Bowing her head, she prayed for wisdom—a ton of it.

*God, how do messes like this get started in the first place? Did I do right when I left Bay Island five years ago? Did I follow Your will? I thought I did. I did what I thought best!* Her head slumped further. *I was innocent, Lord!*

Long meditative minutes passed. Lauren looked about the room as her thoughts drifted to Tom. What was she to do about him? She'd not given him the consideration he'd deserved—especially during his important exams. It was becoming quite evident something vital was missing in her heart for Tom. Love wasn't like that.

The truth was, she didn't love him—not the way a woman should love a man. The thought seared her heart. It wasn't fair to Tom. It wasn't fair to her.

Then there was Jason! She'd been living in a fantasy world the past two days with him. But what had she expected? Even if he still cared for her, he'd lived successfully without her for five years, never needing to see her face or hear her voice—not even once. She'd been easily replaced by Tara then and by a raven-haired beauty now—and there may have been more. It was hopeless to think anything positive was on the horizon. One futile tear trickled unchecked down her cheek.

Several minutes melted into the stillness, and the quiet numbed her whirling thoughts. But the silence began to break, gradually at first, then with increasing urgency. *Clomp—clomp—clomp.* Lauren drew her brows together in concern as the echoing footsteps grew closer and closer. She jumped at the loud knock.

"You in there, girl?" Tilly's boisterous voice carried through the screen door.

Lauren sniffed and swiped her hand clumsily across her face. It was dry. "Come on in," Lauren called, forcing brightness in her voice.

The door swished open, and Tilly lumbered her full figure inside. "Brought you some cookies." She plopped a plastic container of cookies on the table. "Snickerdoodles."

Snickerdoodles! Jason's favorite! Tilly was determined and persistent. The thought added more weight to her already heavy chest, and the wall of tears she'd successfully held off earlier threatened to break loose.

"Whatever is the matter, girl?" Tilly demanded when she saw Lauren's face. Swiftly she gathered Lauren to her, draping her arm heavily across her shoulder.

The tears could be held no longer. Unable to speak, Lauren could only shake her head despondently. Tilly led her to the couch, snatching several tissues from the box on the end table as they passed.

"Just cry it out," Tilly soothed, thumping Lauren's back encouragingly. "Cry it all out. Then you can tell me what's ailin' you."

Tilly let her have her cry, occasionally handing Lauren more tissues. Several minutes passed before Lauren gave a final wipe of the tissue and loudly cleared her nose.

"I'm sorry," Lauren squeaked out. "I didn't mean to unload like that."

Tilly waved her off. "Don't you worry yourself none about that." She cocked one eyebrow at Lauren. "Trouble between you and Jason?"

Lauren sniffed and nodded. "I talked with Cassie today, and she told me what I didn't want to hear." She went on to explain the entire miserable affair. "Oh, Tilly," she moaned, "I wish I'd never discovered the truth. At least my life was calm, even if a little boring, in Cincinnati." She swallowed. "Now I have to let go of Tom and lose Jason all over again."

"I understand about Tom," Tilly said. "If you don't love the man, you can't marry him. But what's this about Jason? Afraid he'll not understand about the call?"

Lauren shook her head. "It's more than that, Tilly," she answered sadly. "Jason and I—we can't just pick up where we left off. It's been too long—he doesn't love me."

"How can you say such a thing?" Tilly accused. "I've seen him here every day since you've arrived. What's that tell ya?"

Lauren lifted a weak smile. Tilly would never understand. "He's only trying to make up for how he hurt me," Lauren explained. "You know how he is." She hesitated. "And he has someone else, someone he's built the house for."

"What?" Tilly demanded with a laugh. "You mean Becky?"

"Becky?"

"Petite, black-haired woman?" Tilly described and Lauren nodded. "That's Becky Merrill. She's working for Jason over the summer while on pre-field ministry."

Lauren looked up at Tilly. "Missions?"

"The Congo," Tilly confirmed. "And I can't see Jason getting serious with Becky, especially not when she's leaving for Africa in a year." She chuckled. "And you of all people should know God has to call a person to the mission field. You can't just follow on the shirttail of someone who's heard the call."

The irony struck Lauren, and she gave a watery laugh. "Maybe Becky should meet Tom. Finally—a match made in heaven." A frown slipped over her lips. It wasn't really funny, not at all.

"What you and Jason need, Lauren Wright, is a good talking to," Tilly proclaimed. "I always told you Jason was the one for you. I still believe it. And there's been too much time wasted already with this nonsense. If he's got something going with Becky, tell him to break it."

"Tilly!" Lauren exclaimed in shock. "I most certainly will not. I still have a little pride left."

"It's the problem of saving pride that's fed this whole charade for five years. If you want Jason back, go and get him." She waved a hand in the air. "And if Jason's so serious about Becky, I'd be knowin' about it." She pointed her finger lazily at Lauren. "You talk to him—straight! You hear?"

Lauren nodded grudgingly.

"Enough said, then!" Tilly declared. "Now let's break out the cookies, have a cup of tea, and relax a bit."

Dusk was dropping quickly over the cabin when Lauren received Tom's expected call.

"It was a good day," Tom exclaimed about his exam. "Much easier than Saturday's." He paused only long enough to change the subject. "And what about you? How did things go today?"

Lauren was sensitive enough to know this wasn't the time to reveal her recent insights into their doomed relationship. Tom needed a clear mind for his last exam, and she wouldn't spoil that. "There's not been much of a change," she explained, filling him in on only the most mundane of details.

But Tom was more perceptive than that. "Something's wrong."

"There's nothing wrong," she quickly lied, giving a chuckle to prove it. "You worry too much."

"Maybe because there's something to worry about," he said quietly. "Did you know Cassie called me today?"

Lauren swallowed hard. "Cassie!"

"She told me about Tara's phone call," he continued. "What I'm wondering is why you didn't mention it."

Lauren felt trapped! Didn't he understand she wasn't at liberty to say—not right now? Before a proper response could be formed, he continued.

"Maybe I shouldn't have sent you to Piney Point alone," he declared, worry evident in his voice. "It seemed the right choice at the time, but now. . ." He paused. "Maybe I should come up to Piney Point. I could catch the late boat tomorrow after the exam. We could straighten—"

"No!" Lauren cried hastily, immediately lowering her voice. "There's nothing wrong that a good night's sleep couldn't take care of." As tired as she felt, it was as close to the truth as she dared to hope.

"You know I'd come," he insisted.

"I know you would," she said appreciatively. "But let me handle this my way. I'll work it out and be home by Sunday afternoon just like we planned." She left no room for argument, hating the secrecy she knew was truly for his benefit. But the revelation gave her no comfort.

# Chapter 10

Lauren had barely laid the receiver to rest when it jumped to life again.

"Hello, Lauren."

"Jason?" Lauren held her breath.

"Didn't wake you, did I?"

"Nope." Sleep! What was that?

"I hoped you'd still be up."

"Really?" She smoothed her hair nervously. "Something wrong?"

"Not at all," he assured. "It's just that I've been thinking—"

"Uh-oh!"

Jason gave a pleasing chuckle. "It's not that bad."

"Don't be too sure. Remember, I know how your ideas work," she teased, feeling much lighter and inexplicably pleased at hearing his voice. "Should I sit down?" A satisfied snicker on the other end made her wonder what he was up to.

"Depends," he responded happily. "Where you at?"

"Same place as usual when I'm on the phone," Lauren laughed. "The cord only stretches so far."

"You should get a cordless."

"That's not why you called, is it?"

"Guess not." His buoyant banter slipped away. "It's something more important than that."

"Yes?"

Jason let the moment hang precariously in the air. "What would you think about staying the summer on Bay Island?"

Lauren nearly choked. "Stay the summer! What are you talking about?"

"I mean, staying on the island for a while," he answered pragmatically. "I could always use another accountant. We could work something out—"

"I already have a job," she interrupted. Jason was asking her back!

"I know that. Arrangements can always be made with the university. They can live without you a couple months, can't they? And I'd pay for your leave!" he offered, undaunted. "Then, if and when you decided to go back, your job would still be there." He seemed to have the entire scenario mapped out and analyzed. "You can stay right there at Piney Point. The roof and a few other odds and ends need fixing, but I'll get that done tomorrow. The place will be good as new."

This was the old, logical Jason she once knew. The one who thought through every detail, every question, every possibility. All but one question! "Why, Jason?"

"Why, what?"

Lauren rolled her eyes in exasperation. "Why do you want me to stay the summer?"

"It's not obvious?"

"Not exactly." *Say it!*

Silence begged to be relieved before he spoke what she desired and needed to hear. "I don't want you to leave, Lauren." A husky quality crept into his voice. "Seeing you again has just—just made me crazy. I've missed you!" Lauren didn't dare breathe as he continued. "You do something to me, something I can't explain. I'm not wrong in assuming you still feel something, too, am I?"

Tingles ran down her spine. Slowly, she chose her words. "There's still something there," she admitted. "I just don't know what it is."

She heard him give an elaborate sigh of relief. "Stay the summer then! Give us the time we need to find out. I don't want us to live our lives in regret over what might have been."

He made it sound so easy, so possible. "But I can't just make a decision like that so quickly!" she countered guardedly, finally stretching the phone cord far enough for her to sink into the kitchen chair.

Jason acknowledged her concern. "It's a lot, I know." His voice softened. "But it's too important to turn down without serious consideration. Will you think it over? Sleep on it?"

What did the man have against sleep? How could anyone sleep with such an issue on their mind? "Do I have a choice?"

He gave a gentle laugh. "Not any more than I do."

"I'll give it some thought," she reluctantly agreed. "But please don't push me if the answer's no."

What he asked seemed exhilarating, yet impossible, totally impossible. Besides, Tom was expecting her back. And as easily as Jason thought her job could be dropped, he didn't understand the weight of her responsibilities. Supervisors didn't just take several weeks off when the whim hit. And Jason had yet to hear the story of Cassie and Tara's phone call. Would the offer be so attractive when he knew? Would he believe her?

"There's one other thing you should know," Jason said softly, breaking into her thoughts.

Uh-oh! Here drops the other shoe. "Yes?"

"We've been through some rough times. I take full blame for that." Lauren lowered her forehead to her palm, resting her elbow on the table as she listened. "No matter about the unexplained call, no matter about what the future holds—I trust you. I believe in you."

A lump was quickly forming in her throat. She couldn't trust her voice to respond. He'd said it! He believed her, even beyond the odds. Her heart quivered.

"And, Lauren?"

"Hmm?" She barely managed a sound.

"I'm going to pray hard about this. You won't make this decision without a lot of prayer, will you?"

Didn't he know since her arrival, prayers flowed frequently—in near panic? Not since that last glimpse of Bay Island five years ago had she poured her heart out to God in such torment.

"I'll pray."

"I can't ask for more than that." His voice softened further. "And, Lauren—"

"Yes?"

"Sweet dreams!"

The sun woke Lauren early the next morning. For several minutes she lay watching the skittering sunbeams bounce across the ceiling. Tuesday! She glanced at the clock. Jason would be arriving in less than an hour to fix the roof. The thought drew both hope and dread. Slowly she ambled out of bed, showered, and towel-dried her hair, all the while pondering what the day might bring. Could it be there was hope? Into the wee hours of the morning, she'd wondered. But with God all things were possible, right? Would Jason hold true to his convictions of trusting her after she explained Cassie's story? Her thoughts had progressed little more when the phone rang.

"Miss Wright?" asked an unfamiliar voice.

"Yes."

"This is Becky Merrill, Mr. Levitte's secretary."

Lauren stood stock-still. The raven-haired beauty! "Yes?" Her voice now held caution.

"Mr. Levitte," the woman began, "asked me to call and let you know he won't be able to keep his appointment with you this morning."

"Appointment?"

"Yes," Miss Merrill confirmed, her manner unnervingly professional. "He's been called out of state, I'm afraid. He's expected back Friday morning and will reschedule with you then."

Appointment! Reschedule! What was happening? "When did he leave?" Lauren asked.

There was hesitation on the other end. "He hasn't left yet," Miss Merrill answered slowly. "But we'll be leaving shortly to make the nine o'clock flight."

The plural emphasis wasn't lost on Lauren as she looked at her watch in disbelief. It was nearly nine now. "He's flying from Bay Airport!" Lauren stated, rather than questioned, in amazement.

"Yes," she answered. "And I'm really sorry to have to cut you short, but we are running late—"

"Thank you for calling, then," Lauren managed to say before numbly resting the phone back into the base.

Unbelievable! How could it be? And why hadn't Jason called himself? What about their day together, their discussion of important issues he never wanted to regret?

A deep breath escaped. Why should it surprise her? Work had always come first, hadn't it? What made her think things had changed on that front? Lauren gave a snort. She supposed he expected her to sit around and wait for him. And she'd be there! There'd be no accusations of her running out this time—no matter the reason.

She couldn't believe Jason was taking a flight from Bay Airport. He'd never done that before. He hated flying in small planes. And small was all the miniature airstrip on the island could handle.

She also mulled over Becky Merrill's words. Was Lauren no more than an appointment to reschedule? She wondered if Jason had led Becky to believe their relationship was all business. Maybe Tilly had missed the mark with Jason and Becky. Had Lauren misunderstood Jason last night? Her heart shriveled at the thought.

The day dragged endlessly until late afternoon when Lauren spotted Larry Newkirk's police cruiser rolling up the incline toward the cottage. He slowed the car to a stop and stepped out. Lauren descended the steps to greet him.

"Brought your necklace," he announced, unfolding his lanky frame from the car. A smile stretched across his boyish face as he leaned into the car to retrieve a small red bag.

"I can't believe you found it," Lauren gushed appreciatively when he passed the bag to her. The crackling plastic bag fell quickly away as she stripped off the soft tissue paper inside to reveal a shiny cross necklace. She lifted the shimmering chain up for inspection. "I don't know how to thank you."

"You don't have to," he responded graciously, watching her delight. "I was just glad to find it."

Lauren gave him a warm smile. "It means the world to me." She unclasped the chain to put it on.

"Here." Larry quickly took the necklace from her fingers and placed it gently around her neck. "There you go."

"Oh, it's beautiful," she exclaimed.

"Yes, it is."

Lauren looked up at him, his uniform badge flashing a slice of sun at her. "Can you stay a few minutes?" she asked, stepping sideways from the glare.

"Maybe some lemonade and cookies—"

Larry looked at his watch. "Sorry. I'm on patrol this afternoon."

"That's too bad." She fingered the gold cross. There had to be a way to repay this man's kindness.

"But I'm off in two hours," he said, obviously noticing her disappointment. "Maybe you'd like to take an early supper at Phil's? He still has the best show of fish on the island."

Lauren brightened. "That'd be great." The last thing she wanted to do was mope around until Jason returned. "And I'm buying. You can tell me all about how you found the necklace."

He smiled warmly. "Sounds good. How about six o'clock?"

"Six o'clock it is."

---

It was well after midnight before the dark blue truck halted in front of Piney Point.

"All these years I never knew those caves existed," Lauren said in astonishment. "I still can't believe it. They're wonderful."

Larry seemed to share her enthusiasm. "We could explore the caves sometime when it's light if you want."

"Even in the daylight, the openings would be hard to find unless you knew they were there."

Larry had driven her to the island's south corridor after dinner to watch the magnificent sunset. It was then he showed her the deeply recessed caves below a treacherous cliff. Larry knew the less perilous route to get a good view.

"With the openings so well hidden, it was a good refuge for criminals," Larry explained.

"I can see why," she replied, stifling a yawn. "It must be getting late. I'm sorry for keeping you out so long. Guess I didn't realize the time."

"I'm a big boy now," he said with a laugh. "With great company, great food, and great scenery, time gets away, doesn't it?"

After viewing the outer caves, it seemed natural to soak up the peace and quiet. Tourists didn't venture much to the less populated southern tip of the island. Water lapped at the shore as they sat on two large rocks, talking amiably. They spoke of the past and then caught up to the present. Larry had graduated from Ohio State University with a law enforcement degree the year before. He wanted nothing more than to stay on the island all the way through retirement.

Larry stifled his own yawn before hopping out of the truck and circling to her door. She stepped out when he opened it.

"Do you need an escort to the door?" he asked, looking up at the cabin.

Lauren glanced at the dark windows. "No. If you'll just wait long enough to see I'm safely in, that'll be fine."

Larry opened the driver's door. "I had a great time," he said, leaning partially out the window opening, a lopsided grin plastered on his face.

Lauren returned the smile. "I did, too." It did feel good to get out—even in her exhaustion, but for that very reason, she was thankful Larry didn't seem inclined to stick around. "Thank you for the lovely evening."

"Anytime," he returned easily. Lauren gave a friendly wave and was about to ascend the steps when he called again. "I noticed earlier the roof could use some nailing on those gable ends." He was pointing toward the roof.

Lauren looked at the roof, remembering Jason's broken promise. "Well—"

"I'll be by in the morning to fix it," he declared, giving Lauren no chance to protest. "I'm off duty tomorrow, and it won't take but a minute."

"Well—"

"Go on up," he said, giving her a verbal nudge. "I'll see you in the morning."

Lauren gave a resigned shrug as she climbed the wooden steps and finally turned the key in the lock. She switched on the porch light and gave an acknowledging wave after entering. She heard the truck's engine start and watched as Larry threw a wave out the window. He soon disappeared into the darkness.

After locking the door securely, Lauren leaned back against it. Jason had been right about Larry. He wasn't a kid anymore, he was a man. The lanky teenager had become a successful and interesting person. She'd enjoyed his company immensely—a platonic and uncomplicated relationship. It was crazy of Jason to think beyond that. A platonic friendship was a precious commodity right now.

With a sleepy smile, she headed off to bed.

# Chapter 11

By eight the next morning, the rhythmic sound of a hammer penetrated her slumber. Blinking sleepily, she swung her legs from the bed and padded over to look out the window. Larry's truck was parked outside, and an aluminum ladder leaned at an angle against the front gutter. A smile lit on her lips. At least her parents' cabin was receiving a good overhaul during her visit.

Quickly she showered and dressed before heading to the kitchen. With the flip of a switch and new ingredients, the coffeemaker sputtered to life. She set out two mugs and ambled off to the front room. Cool, fresh air rushed in through the open windows when she pulled open the front door. The screen door creaked as she stepped out onto the porch.

Larry peeked over the edge of the roof. "Finally awake, sleepyhead?"

"I'm on vacation, remember?" she retorted with a smile, using a hand to shield her eyes from the bright sun.

He laughed. "Haven't you ever heard 'the early bird gets the worm'?"

"Sorry! Don't eat worms."

"Glad to hear that," he teased. He disappeared for a second, repositioning his legs. His blond head became visible again. "It won't be much longer. I'm almost done."

"Would you like some coffee? It's fresh and hot."

"Won't turn that down for sure," he laughed. "Give me five minutes."

Lauren nodded and stepped back inside as the hammering resumed. Slowly she poured herself a cup of coffee, all the while trying to smother a yawn. She felt exhausted. The past few days of emotional upheaval and the previous night's late hour were taking their toll. After one sip, she stared into the steadily rising steam.

Her thoughts wandered to Jason. Where was he? And why hadn't he called? Not that she'd thought much about it last night while sitting under the stars. The shimmering night sky seemed to snatch each worry into its vastness. God's vastness! But the welcome, temporary respite was gone now. Morning brought with it the unresolved remnants of yesterday.

The sound of Larry descending the ladder jostled Lauren back to the present. Hastily she made her way to the coffeemaker and poured another cup. Propping the screen door open with her hip, she brought both cups out and sat at the picnic table. Larry was easing the ladder to the ground. He glanced her way.

"Smells good," he said, unsnapping his tool belt from the downed ladder.

"Would you care for some toast or something to go with it?" she offered. "I might be able to find a muffin or bagel."

"Coffee's fine," he answered with a smile as she handed him the cup. He nodded toward the roof. "You might want to think about a ridge vent for the roof."

"Oh?"

"I had one put in," he went on. "It does a lot to cool things down." His gaze scanned the massive trees. "But I suppose with all the trees you might not need it."

Lauren also looked up at the trees. "The cabin does stay pretty cool with all the shade." She thought of Jason building the warm fire just four days ago. Jason! Everything reminded her of him. She shook off the disturbing thought. "Does the roof look okay?"

He nodded. "Good as new."

"I appreciate you doing this," she responded with gratitude. "Jason was. . ." She stopped.

He tipped his head slightly and took a nonchalant sip. "When's Jason due back from South Carolina?"

South Carolina! Larry knew more about Jason's excursion than she did. Could she be the only one in the dark as to his whereabouts?

"I think he's due back Friday," she finally answered.

He nodded and seemed to mull over her reply. "Well, I know it's none of my business," he began, then paused for an uncomfortable moment as she waited, "but I think you should be careful with Jason."

Funny! That was exactly what Jason had said about him. "So I don't get hurt again?" she finished for him.

"Something like that." He fidgeted nervously with the coffee cup. "You're a great person. You could get any guy you wanted." A blush seemed to rush up his neck. "Even I wouldn't turn down the chance. . ."

Oh, no! This wasn't good—or platonic—at all. "That's really sweet to say," she finally mumbled, giving serious thought to what she should say. "And I know you're just being kind. No young man would waste his time on an old fogy like me. Too many girls your own age to choose from." Hint, hint!

He took the cue. "Just be careful, all the same."

Lauren quickly changed the subject. "Now, I'd like to pay you for mending the roof."

"Sorry! Your money's no good with me," he stated, setting down his coffee. He picked up his tool belt. "Matter of fact, I can't even stay to enjoy a second cup. I'm headed over to the church to hang drywall."

"But I've got to do something," she protested. What if she'd hurt his feelings? Had she been too rough, sloughing off his attentions?

Larry hoisted the ladder to one broad shoulder and laughed. "I suppose if you insist, you could treat me to some ice cream after church tonight."

Evidently he'd recovered faster than anticipated. What was she to do?

"Don't worry," he called over his shoulder as he tied the ladder to the side rail of his truck. "I know where you stand. I'm too young for you." He flashed a mischievous smile. "Can't blame a guy for trying, though." He tucked the dangling orange rope from the extension between the rungs. "I'm satisfied with being friends if you are."

The tension deflated like an unplugged inner tube. "Ice cream would be wonderful."

Another smile flickered. "Want me to pick you up?"

"I suppose that'd be best," she answered after some thought. It would be illogical for them both to drive. Prayer meeting! She hadn't even planned to go earlier. Not with Jason gone.

Larry opened the truck door and climbed in. "Great! I'll be by to pick you up at six-thirty."

Lauren waved and turned back to the cottage. She hoped seeing Larry after church was the right decision. Even though he seemed to understand and promised to be just friends, she couldn't bear the thought that this might lead to something awkward. Regardless, she was lonely and looked forward to keeping occupied for the evening. Friday was already approaching with enough trepidation. Jason hadn't phoned during his absence, and she wondered if he'd be back as planned. What if he didn't come back before Sunday? Right now it was becoming hard to distinguish between the hurt and anger she felt at his betrayal, for that's what it was—betrayal. He'd vowed to make things up to her! But where was he? Doing business—always business.

The hot sun bore down as Lauren hiked up the narrow trail leading to Tilly's cabin. A cool lake breeze rustled the leaves and kept the temperature bearable. Tilly had called, inviting her for an afternoon visit, quickly reminding Lauren she had yet to visit the familiar cabin she so adored as a child.

The log cabin came into view, and Lauren instantly smiled. The rustic scene blanketed her with its welcome. It was so peaceful and serene. Slowly she stepped up to the covered patio. A white porcelain pitcher and bowl, filled with water, seemed to wait for someone to wash in front of the aging, mounted mirror. The scene took her back to a more pleasant time. A time she wished could be recaptured like an old classic movie tape to be played over and over again.

She tapped the screen door. The wooden frame banged loosely against the doorjamb.

"Tilly?" she called into the screen, her voice echoing back from the windowpane. The scratchy view of the polka-dotted tile floor and well-worn furniture was the same as it was her first summer at Piney Point.

"Is that you, girl? Come on in. I'm in the kitchen."

The door opened easily as Lauren let herself in. The smell of fresh-baked bread immediately accosted her. "Oh, that smells good," Lauren greeted, savoring a deep breath as she watched the older woman pull two loaf pans from the oven.

"You like it, huh?" Tilly chuckled knowingly.

Lauren nodded. A large paddle fan dispersed the oven heat and wonderful aroma, giving her nose a full and delicious assault.

Tilly straightened and plopped each pan on a cooling rack. "Stollen bread!" she announced.

"Tilly!" Lauren exclaimed in disbelief. "You're baking that for Jason, aren't you?"

The older woman gave a mischievous smile. "What makes you say that?"

"Because you know very well how much Jason loves your German breads," she scolded. "Just like his favorite pop and snickerdoodles cookies." She couldn't hold back a small smile. "You're really shameless, you know that?"

Tilly only shrugged her shoulders. "Nothin' wrong with makin' someone happy."

"And Jason's not even here to appreciate all your hard work."

"I know that," she answered gaily. "When's he comin' back? Tomorrow?"

"Friday—I think."

Tilly gave her a sharp glance. "He hasn't called?"

Lauren shook her head. "And knowing him, he probably won't. Not when he's caught up with work." She hoped the bitterness wasn't too evident.

But Tilly missed nothing. "Did you have that talk you promised?"

"We did," Lauren answered quickly.

"Well?"

"He was called away before we finished."

Tilly grabbed a pitcher of iced tea from the refrigerator. "You must have got some things straight, 'cause you're not the same wet-eyed girl I left the other day."

Tilly wasn't about to give up. Lauren knew this as well as anything. "He asked me to stay the summer."

"Really!" The pitcher nearly dropped to the counter. A smile split the woman's wrinkles clear in two. "That's wonderful."

Lauren only shrugged. "I don't know. There's a job to think about, my family—"

"And Jason traipsin' off at the drop of a hat," Tilly concluded. She opened the cupboard and reached for two tall glasses. "And you're upset with him!"

"That's part of it," Lauren admitted, holding each glass in turn as Tilly poured the iced tea. "Jason says he's not married to the business, but he really is." She spooned sugar into her glass, giving it an aggressive stir. "He didn't even have the courtesy to call me personally. His secretary did it." The memory still rankled her. "She wanted to reschedule my appointment. Can you believe that?"

Tilly's eyebrows inched up, and she stroked her chin thoughtfully. "Mighty curious."

"I'm trying to give him the benefit of the doubt, but. . ."

Lauren was still vigorously stirring the iced tea. Tilly patted her hand and said, "You're gonna stir the color right out of it, girl."

"Sorry!" Lauren pulled a yellow napkin from the rooster-shaped holder and laid the spoon on it.

"You know what I think?"

Lauren knew the answer would come regardless of her response. She waited.

"It's time to stop being so self-absorbed." Tilly stared at Lauren for a moment. "Jason is a businessman. He shoulders a lot of responsibility trying to keep his company profitable. A good woman could help him, side up with him—join him."

Lauren stiffened. "What about my dreams? Why can't he side up with me?"

Tilly paused long enough to get two plates, then began cutting one of the loaves of warm bread. Back and forth the knife cut, slowly driving Lauren crazy. Why did Tilly always screech conversations to a halt? One piece of bread fell forward, revealing the colorful fruit inside.

"Butter?" Tilly shoved the butter dish toward her, ignoring her look of frustration.

"Why not!" Lauren knew Tilly wouldn't have her say until she was ready. The butter melted over the thick slice, and she took a bite.

"Do you even know what your dreams are, girl?"

Lauren looked up to see Tilly leisurely buttering her own piece of bread. "I have plenty of dreams."

"Really?"

"Yes, really." She had dreams. Plenty of them. So why couldn't she think of any at the moment?

"Well," she fumbled, "I'd like to be head CPA someday at the university or maybe even teach a couple accounting classes." She racked her brain for more. "It'd be nice to go back to school and get my masters."

"What else?" Tilly encouraged.

"Teach Sunday school again."

"Okay! What else?"

*The woman just doesn't give up!* Lauren smiled. "You know what I'd really like to do?"

"What?"

"I'd like to buy one of those tent trailers and travel to all the state parks." As a child Lauren would sneak over to Uncle Ed's Campground and mingle with the kids at the playground. Food cooking in cast iron pots over smoky fires fascinated her just as much as the tiny houses on wheels. She'd vowed to own one someday yet hadn't thought of it in years.

"What else?"

Lauren laughed. "All those aren't enough?" She thought harder. "I wouldn't mind having a house with enough land for a little garden. Maybe some tomatoes, corn, peppers. . .and some lettuce." She smiled. "And while I'm dreaming, one of those easy garden tillers would be nice."

"Those are nice dreams." Tilly cut another piece of bread. "Now, do you know what Jason's dreams might be?"

Lauren was taken aback. "I don't know. I suppose all his dreams rest on making his business a success. He doesn't have time for much else."

"Do you think it's possible he might pour himself into that business because there's no one to share his other dreams with?" Tilly rested her heavy hand on Lauren's. "He has plenty of capable people who can handle the day-to-day operations. I think he's givin' it a small trial this week, letting go, you know, just to be with you."

Lauren thought a moment. "But he couldn't do it. It lasted a whole day, and he was off and running again Tuesday morning!"

"Maybe." Tilly gave it some thought. "It must have been somethin' mighty serious for him to leave town while you're here."

"He could have called."

A worried expression creased Tilly's brow. "That's the worrisome part. What would keep him from calling? I'm tellin' you, it must have been somethin' mighty important." There was a long silence, and she appeared finished with the interrogation and lecture. "Are you comin' to church tonight?"

Lauren told her of Larry's invitation.

"Nice boy, that Larry is," Tilly said with a nod.

Lauren wanted to tell her that the nice boy had grown into a man but thought better of it. Tilly didn't need any extra ammunition. She was too good with what she already had.

Tilly kept right on talking. "Everything's gonna work out fine. You'll see!"

Lauren wished she could be so sure. Time was running out, running against her. If God was going to remedy the situation, He'd need to act quickly. But she, of all people, knew God worked on His own timetable.

# Chapter 12

The midnight hour pressed close as Larry rolled the truck to a noiseless stop in front of the Piney Point cottage.

"Safe and sound," he announced with a smile, shutting off the engine. "Hope you had a good evening."

Lauren looked over in the darkness. "If anything, it's been memorable."

He chuckled. "I'll take that as a compliment."

"Mr. Edwards will never look me in the eye again." She chuckled quietly, still recalling the gawking look of surprise behind the old man's thick glasses. "I still can't believe you did that."

Larry smirked. "If I'd known the old guy was supplementing his retirement dipping ice cream at the Dairy Barn, I'd have taken you there sooner."

"But you did everything except pull your badge to shame the man into buying my ice cream!" She'd never admit the tiny inkling of satisfaction she felt.

"He owes you more than a double cone, I assure you." He smiled again. "You noticed he didn't argue."

A laughing gurgle escaped from Lauren. "I wouldn't have argued either. Not with a two-hundred-pound police officer breathing down my neck."

She thought of Jason. How would he have reacted upon seeing Mr. Edwards making milk shakes and cleaning tables? She was sure he would have handled the situation differently, with more finesse, more patience. Jason had compassion for people. He wouldn't have painted Mr. Edwards into a corner as Larry had done. But Larry was young and impulsive. She hoped a few more years would smooth out the rough edges causing such direct action. Larry was protecting her honor and didn't seem to care whether he'd squeezed it from the old man willingly or not.

But Jason hadn't escaped Larry's keen sense of protection either. No amount of assurance on her part seemed to clear Jason of his earlier deeds, those Larry thought unforgivable. Of course, Lauren wasn't entirely convinced herself. That didn't help matters. It was good Larry kept more thoughts to himself than he voiced, yet disapproval remained etched on his features.

"I hope you're not mad about it," Larry went on about Mr. Edwards, seemingly genuinely concerned.

"I'm not mad," she reassured. Embarrassed—yes. Pleased—maybe a little. But she suspected God wasn't pleased at all.

"And I've kept you out late again. Guess I owe you another apology for that."

His tone didn't sound the least bit apologetic.

"It was well worth it to see the sunset again," Lauren remarked truthfully. She opened the passenger door and stepped down. "And I appreciate the lift to church—and the ice cream." She'd been careful all evening, especially at church where tongues could wag faster than lightning, to keep their conversation and manner low-key. It wouldn't pay to start another scandal. Keeping her own head afloat was hard enough.

Larry lighted from the truck. "You didn't put the porch light on again," he scolded. "You really should to be safe. It's just too dark without it." He followed her to the steps. "I'll walk you to the door."

"I did turn on the light. But like everything else, the bulb must need to be replaced."

"I can change—"

She laughed. "The bulb I can manage."

"All right," he drawled. "But I'll see you to the door all the same."

Lauren quickly ascended the steps with Larry following close behind. Thankfully, he stayed back a comfortable distance as she opened the screen door. It wasn't a decent hour for the man to linger. But all thoughts screeched to a halt as the solid door slowly swung open before the jingling keys hit their mark. Icy fingers of fear grabbed at her heart. She took an involuntary step back.

Larry seemed to sense her fear and stepped forward. "What—"

The phone inside the cottage blared like a siren, nearly causing her heart to stop. Before she could step back further from fright, there was a loud crash. Suddenly, a tall figure loomed alarmingly close before her. Then Lauren felt the forceful blow of the stranger's body as he forced his way past, sending her flying backward over the deck furniture. Chairs scraped loudly across the wood planks and tumbled haphazardly. She heard a man groan, but whether it was the intruder or Larry she couldn't tell. Thunderous footsteps tore down the steps.

She lay stunned, one leg painfully arched over a wrought iron plant stand. The insistent ring of the phone added to the chaos.

"Are you okay?" called a breathless voice.

Relief rained down as she recognized Larry's voice. "Yes," she quickly answered without thought.

Larry's silhouette stumbled forward. "Stay right here," he ordered. His footsteps treaded heavily down the steps, and he disappeared.

Lauren strained to hear over the unrelenting phone as she tried to disentangle her leg from the plant stand and a deck chair. For the first time, pain seared across her right arm as she leaned precariously. She winced hard and bit back the groan forcing its way up her throat.

Shouts echoed through the trees some distance away. Tilly! The voices came from the direction of Tilly's cabin. Lauren pulled the painful arm across her stomach in an effort to sit up, loosing a cry of torment. Her body fell back again, tears of agony squeezing past her tightly closed eyes.

She knew her arm was badly broken.

The phone stopped! Minutes ticked by as she lay perfectly still, the pain easing slightly. The starry sky seemed to stare down upon her pathetic figure sprawled across the deck.

"Jason," she groaned. "Where are you, Jason?"

Silence greeted her.

"I need you, Jason Levitte." It was little more than a raw whisper.

A rifle blast pierced the night.

Lauren jerked and another spasm of pain coursed through her. "Oh, God, please don't let Larry be hurt." The thought of her own helpless state brought a renewed sense of panic. "I'm scared, Father. Please don't leave me."

An eternity seemed to pass before snapping twigs and the sound of weeds whipping against someone's heavy stride grew ominously louder. Lauren stiffened in fear.

"Lauren?" There was a winded desperation to the man's voice. Larry's voice.

No air managed to squeak past her windpipe. He was okay! He hadn't been shot. *Thank You, dear Lord,* she prayed. Two figures emerged from the shadows. Was danger still afoot? Fresh fear gripped her.

"Sit still," Larry ordered the second figure. "I'd just as soon this woman shoot you."

Lauren swiveled her attention to a third person, several yards away. The dark made it impossible to see who it was.

Larry was noisily taking two steps at a time. "Lauren? Are you okay?" Worried concern saturated his every word.

"My arm's hurt," Lauren sputtered. "I think it's bad." Just the act of speaking drew the throbbing ache to new heights.

Larry carefully moved two chairs aside and knelt close. "Just sit tight," he murmured. "I'm going to see if I can get some light." He quickly left her side and headed for the cottage door.

"You'd better not have hurt that girl," a woman's strained voice threatened.

Lauren turned toward the voice as a flood of light illuminated the blackness. Squinting, she saw Tilly jabbing the point of her rifle toward the darkly clad figure.

"Tilly!"

"It's me, girl," came the reply. "This rascal hurt you?"

Larry was rushing to her side again, his eyes roving over her in quick assessment. A curse spilled from his lips. "You're arm's busted up pretty bad." He didn't touch her but rocked on his heels in contemplation. "Are you hurt anywhere else?"

Lauren said nothing for a moment as she eyed him. "Don't."

"Don't what?"

"Don't curse."

He was silent for the longest time, and she could tell he was wondering if she was coherent. His worried expression deepened. "Did you hit your head?" He didn't wait for an answer as he cautiously examined her head.

"My head's fine." Lauren nearly laughed, but pain kept the impulse in check. "It's just my arm—I think."

He didn't look quite convinced. "First, we need to get you some help," he announced and stood. "Sit tight."

"I'm not going anywhere," she answered.

"You doing okay, Tilly?" he called, making his way down the steps. He paused only long enough to see her head nod.

"This scoundrel ain't goin' nowhere." Tilly jabbed the rifle at the figure again for emphasis. "Is Lauren hurt bad?"

Larry pulled a cell phone from the truck, angling the keypad to the light. "Looks like one arm took the brunt of it." He dialed the numbers, and his voice lowered. "She might have taken a knock to the head."

His voice wasn't low enough to keep Lauren from hearing, and Tilly's responding grunt certainly echoed loudly enough. Only a snippet or two of the phone conversation, however, reached Lauren. Waning strength drew her interest away anyway. She gave a long and weary exhale, drawing Tilly's attention.

"Tell 'em to get here and quick," Tilly demanded.

Larry stuffed the slender phone into his back pocket. "Help's on the way!"

Jason arrived on an early-morning flight and didn't bother to phone before driving to Piney Point. He parked beside Larry's dew-covered truck, his gaze lingering only a moment on the sight before turning toward the cabin.

A wobbly Lauren stepped sideways out onto the deck, her tall frame leaning heavily against Larry. Her beautiful brown hair was mussed and disorderly—a rarity for Lauren. He'd have found it endearing and attractive if not for her behavior. The pair pivoted toward the steps. It was then Jason saw that her right arm was bandaged and in a sling.

Larry frowned when he saw Jason, then turned his attention back to Lauren. "Just take it slow. That pain medication has you higher than a kite."

Lauren gave an easy, slow smile. "Yeah."

Larry shook his head and glanced at Jason.

"What day is it?" Lauren asked.

"Thursday," Larry answered. "Look, Jason's back a day sooner than expected."

"Oh!"

"Whoa," Larry warned, pulling her back from the top step. "You're going to take a tumble."

Jason didn't wait an extra second before quickly climbing the steps. "What happened?" he asked, looking at Larry first and then Lauren.

"It was terrible, just terrible," Lauren slurred. She broke from Larry's grasp and lurched heavily into Jason's arms, practically knocking him off balance.

Jason looked at Larry in alarm.

"Her arm's broken in two places. It happened during a break-in last night." Larry glanced toward the front door. "We surprised an intruder, and she got knocked down hard."

*We?* Jason wondered.

"I'm fine now," Lauren murmured, smiling up at Jason, apparently oblivious to the serious nature of the conversation.

"No, you're not," Larry countered, then looked at Jason. "She's on some heavy drugs. The urgent care doctor gave her a whole arsenal full." He looked at his watch. "We were just on our way to Mercy Hospital on the mainland where the orthopedist should be waiting to set her arm. That first dose of pain medication will be wearing off soon. Hopefully, it'll last long enough to get her there."

Jason repositioned his bearing as Lauren leaned more weight on him. "I'll take her over."

Larry looked about to argue but shrugged his shoulders instead. "Take her to the emergency room. They're expecting her to check in there. Her insurance card is in her wallet, in case she's still fuzzy when you get there."

Both men helped her into Jason's car.

"Are there any papers from urgent care I need to bring?" Jason asked.

Larry shook his head. "They didn't give me any. Evidently, the doctor already faxed over what they needed."

Jason climbed into the car and rolled the window down. "Did you catch the guy?"

For the first time, Larry smiled. "He's sitting in the tank as we speak."

Silence lingered a moment until Jason spoke again. "Thanks for taking care of her, Larry."

"Yeah, well." Larry seemed at a loss for words.

"Hey, Jason," Lauren interrupted happily. "Larry here made old Mr. Edwards give me ice cream."

Jason frowned at her in confusion before looking back to Larry.

"It's a long story." Larry leaned close to the window and gave Jason a meaningful look. "Better get to the ferry before the drugs wear off. This happy side is no comparison to her pre-drug condition."

Jason nodded and turned the ignition key.

"Call me on my cell phone when she gets into surgery, and I'll fill you in," Larry said, nodding toward the deck.

He gave Larry a quick wave and let the car coast down the slight incline.

At least the early hour would benefit their travel time.

"It was cookies and cream," Lauren began talking again. "You know I like cookies and cream."

"I know." Jason looked in the rearview mirror at Larry's lone figure.

Lauren kept right on talking. "And did you know there's hidden caves on the island?"

"No, I didn't," he humored, still troubled. "Now, why don't you just lay your head back for a few minutes and rest?"

"But I have so much to tell you," she said wistfully.

Jason looked over at her. "Close your eyes and rest. You'll need all the strength you can muster."

It was going to be a very long journey to the mainland.

# Chapter 13

An annoying insect threatened to ruin an otherwise perfect nap. Lauren gave it a halfhearted slap as she burrowed her head deeper into the scratchy pillow. She felt so heavy, so sleepy.

"She's coming around," a garbled voice announced.

Couldn't a body get some rest? Lauren forced one eyelid slightly open, but exhaustion quickly dropped it back in place. Sleep, sweet sleep. Approaching awareness, however, drew notice to several uncomfortable sensations. Her throat felt parched, for one, and the pesky bug just wouldn't quit.

"Lauren." The dreamy masculine voice definitely caught her attention.

Lauren ventured another peek. With effort, the double image slowly drew into focus.

"Jason?" she croaked hoarsely, finally recognizing his face so near. The familiar scent of his musky cologne seemed to kiss the air ever so lightly. For one short moment she basked in his presence before questions began to surface. Where was she, and why was Jason with her? Her head twisted uncomfortably to get a better view. Unfamiliar surroundings created further confusion.

"You're still at the hospital," Jason explained, his hand grasping hers through the side rail opening. "Dr. Lazero set your arm, and everything's fine."

Lauren swept her tongue across dry lips. "Hospital?" Snatches of memory began to leak through the cracks of consciousness. The intruder, her fall—the pain. Her eyes closed in reflection. It was coming back. And Jason had arrived early at the cabin, but she hadn't expected him. Not that she'd cared much at the time. Just seeing him seemed to make everything fall into place, all nice and tidy. All she'd wanted was to be held by him. Had she really thrown herself into his arms? That short memory clip seemed clearer than the rest. But the memory faded from there. "What day is it?"

Jason smiled indulgently. "It's still Thursday morning. You've only been out for about half an hour."

A rustling movement sounded from the other side of the bed. "Can you wiggle your fingers for me, Lauren?"

For the first time Lauren noticed the uniformed nurse, a shiny, green stethoscope hung about her neck. "Huh?" She looked down at the white cast hidden under the blue sling. Pale, swollen fingers protruded like tree stubs. She moved them slightly and with great reserve.

"That's good," the nurse encouraged. "The fingers will be stiff for a while, at least until the swelling goes down." She bent closer for observation, pinching each fingernail. "Are you having any pain?"

Lauren shook her head. "But I could sure use some water."

"Let's start with some ice chips," the nurse responded, taking the chart from the nightstand. "Be right back."

*Ice chips? No, no, no! I want ice water—supersized.*

"Thirsty, are we?" Jason asked, watching her frown.

Lauren shifted her gaze back to him, and the frown lifted slightly. "Yes, we are."

"What's this *we* stuff?" He laughed. "You got a mouse in your pocket?"

She couldn't help but smile. He hadn't used that line on her for ages. It always made him laugh, the delightful laugh she'd so missed. "What time did you say it was?"

He looked at the wall clock. "I didn't say, but it's ten-thirty." His chin rested squarely on the rail. "They said you could leave as soon as the twilight sleep wore off."

The effects of the anesthesia were quickly wearing thin, she could tell. She didn't feel giddy at all, not like she had on arrival. But at least the pain had vanished—a definite blessing after the terrible night she had. And what a night it'd been. She glanced at Jason. Judging by the look of his disheveled hair, the dark circles under his eyes, and his shadowy beard, he hadn't fared much better.

"You really look terrible," she observed, wondering if he'd gotten even less sleep than she.

His chin dipped further over the rail, and he gave her a lopsided smile. "Thanks! I love you, too."

"Funny!"

"It was meant to be." A yawn escaped as his smile deepened.

Despite his tousled appearance, his good humor remained unaffected. And he seemed so innocent and appealing with those compassionate eyes. But caution was needed. She hadn't forgotten his abrupt departure two days before or his failure to call.

"When did you get back to the island?"

He stretched and arched his back like angel wings. "Flew in early this morning." Another yawn.

"Did you fly into the island airport?"

"Yep!"

"But you hate those planes."

"Yep!"

"Why didn't you take the ferry from the mainland then?"

He studied her closely before answering. "Because Lauren Wright was waiting on the island and flying all the way saved a lot of time, time that couldn't be wasted." Suddenly he laid his hand on her good arm; his fingers felt warm on her skin.

Lauren felt a strange thrill of joy accompanied by a surge of perplexity. Had Jason disregarded his own safety in order to be by her side? Had he even known of her need? She remembered crying Jason's name during the most frightening moments of the ordeal as she lay helpless under the dark sky. Yet it made no sense. Why should he rush back to her side when he hadn't even called during his absence?

Such thoughts were abruptly halted when the nurse sauntered into the room with a large cup of ice.

"Dr. Lazero has written your discharge papers," she announced. "We'll see how you do with the ice, and if you feel awake enough, we'll get you signed out." She extended the ice-filled paper cup and a spoon to Lauren. "Take it slow to start," she cautioned.

Lauren accepted the cup and unconsciously looked over at Jason. The nurse's well-put advice, she thought, could apply to more than just the cup of ice.

"The horse-pills are three times a day," Jason read, holding the brown prescription bottle in one hand and balancing the list of hospital instructions against the steering wheel of his swaying car with the other. "Those are the anti-inflammatory drugs."

An abrupt horn blast from the ferry broke loose, giving Lauren a start. She stretched her neck to see past the hood to the churning blue water. They were almost to the island. "I'm to take them on an empty stomach, right?" One eyebrow went up in deliberation. "Or was that on a full stomach?" Oh, she'd never remember anything after those mind-boggling drugs the night before.

"The bottle says to eat something before taking the medication to prevent stomach upset," he answered, turning the bottle on end to read the red vertical pharmacy sticker.

"What's in the other bottle again?"

Jason dropped one prescription bottle into the white paper sack and retrieved another. "These are the pain pills." He gave a mischievous smile. "Not as potent as you're used to, though, I'm afraid."

She ignored him. "And what about the other discharge instructions?"

"Use cold compresses as needed and follow up with Dr. Lazero on Monday."

Lauren glanced over at him. "Cold compresses? Over the cast?"

"Guess so." Jason shrugged. "I didn't even think to ask when she rattled off all those directions."

"And the appointment's Monday?" Surely her mind must have flown south to miss the implication of timing that presented. She would be due back at work on Monday.

"Monday at one o'clock," he confirmed, glancing her way before absently asking, "Is the time a problem?"

"Yes," she answered with a sigh. The boat bumped against the dock with a slight jolt. "I'm supposed to be in Cincinnati by Monday."

He turned toward her, his gaze raised candidly to hers. "I know we haven't fully discussed your staying the summer yet, but I thought with this latest development, you'd at least stay until you're well enough to go back."

With the oddest little thrill running up her spine, she gazed back. It all seemed so simple the way he presented things. Yet it wasn't simple at all. She'd almost considered his offer—until the raven-haired beauty called. Ever since, the pendulum of decision couldn't quite find its center mark. "It's just a broken arm. It'll heal just as well there as here," she reasoned.

"It's not just a broken arm," he argued. "You actually broke two bones and damaged part of a tendon." He looked at her sling with hard speculation. "Not to mention the fact you're right-handed. Work will have to wait either way. And you can't drive while you're on that pain medication."

Her gaze fell to the sling. Jason was absolutely right. "And it also means I can't work for you either," she countered.

"I'll find something for you to do," he assured with a wave of his hand. "Staying at Piney Point solves all your problems. It only makes sense, Lauren." He ticked off three fingers. "You're temporarily out of service for working on a computer, I'm providing the perfect substitute job, and there's someone here who can take care of you."

Trying to examine the situation dispassionately with Jason by her side was impossible. "I don't exactly need to be taken care of," she muttered. "I can still function."

He eyed her dubiously. "That may be true, but will you feel totally safe at the cabin? What about tonight, tomorrow night?"

Lauren felt the color drain slightly from her face. "Well, Larry did catch the guy," she began unconvincingly, trying to gain a momentum of assurance, more for herself than Jason. "He wasn't even an islander, but a drifter, an oversized juvenile looking for something to steal. It was only a fluke. It won't happen again." But how would she feel when darkness dropped its cloak tonight? Would she feel so safe then? "I suppose I might be a little jittery," she finally admitted. "Who wouldn't? But I'm sure it'll be fine."

The boat ramp dropped loudly against the concrete, and Jason gave her a penetrating look as he started the car. "I'm staying the night, regardless."

"You can't do that," she gasped, growing restless under his gaze. "It's not appropriate."

"Protecting you is quite appropriate." Without looking at her, he steered the car off the ferry. "You weren't alone last night."

Lauren could feel color storming up her face. "That was police business. I can't believe you'd even insinuate—"

"I'm not insinuating anything," he answered calmly. "I know exactly why Larry stayed the night, as well he should have, given the situation." He turned the car toward town and glanced her way again. "I called him from the hospital this morning. We had nice chat."

"Oh, really." She gave him a curious look. "Then he told you how the whole thing happened?"

He nodded. "Larry said you surprised the kid at the door and he bolted, knocking you across the deck as he did."

"The phone spooked him," she quickly added.

"The phone? What time was it?"

"I think it was near midnight or a little after," she recalled after a moment of thought.

"That was me calling."

Lauren lifted one eyebrow a fraction but didn't dare look at him. "You called?"

"Well, you were never home any other time," he countered. "I was forced to call off-hours, figuring you'd at least be home by midnight." Was there a note of accusation in his voice? "I let it ring for a long time."

"I know." How could she forget the phone that wouldn't quit?

She'd later learned while fighting off her painful condition during those tense moments, Larry had quickly overtaken her clumsy intruder on the path to Tilly's cabin. Then Tilly joined the confusion, sporting a .22 caliber rifle, ready and willing to shoot the criminal with perfect aim. It didn't pay the intruder to be fooled by the woman's age. Her agility and quick thinking were not to be underestimated.

Jason gave her an odd, level look, his gray eyes unreadable. "I figured you just weren't answering your phone."

Lauren looked up in surprise. "Why would I have done that?"

"So you wouldn't have to talk with me," he answered without hesitation. "It seems to me you might be sore about me leaving the island so abruptly."

"I wasn't," she lied nonchalantly, watching his wary eyes scrutinize her face.

"Maybe, maybe not. But even now you seem a bit reserved," Jason observed after a moment of uncomfortable silence. He maneuvered the car to a stop at the curb across from the public park. "It's been especially noticeable since the drugs wore off this morning."

She felt her cheeks blanch again. "I can't be held accountable for anything I said or did while under the influence." The memory was too humiliating.

He chuckled. "All right!" He twisted slightly in the bucket seat toward her. "But I want to clear up the situation, and I think you'll understand the urgency of my departure once I explain. And I plan to explain right now before we go any further."

"There's no need to explain, Jason." There most certainly was every reason, but she wasn't about to admit how badly she wanted to know.

"I'm going to tell you anyway," he said with determination. "I wanted to call you before I left, but there just wasn't time. We had an emergency at one of the other sites in South Carolina where a dockside shop collapsed."

This drew Lauren's full attention. "A collapse? I didn't even know you had built any other shopping centers."

He nodded and went on. "Two others, actually—Charleston and Fort Myers."

"I had no idea," Lauren responded, then asked with concern, "Was anyone hurt?"

"Thank the good Lord, no," he answered. "It happened in the early morning hours when no one was around except a security guard. But the other stores had to be shut down until the cause could be determined, just in case the collapse was in any way related to the design." Three young children skipped gaily past them, glancing curiously at the idling car before crossing the street toward the park. Jason seemed not to notice. "By the time I got the call, there wasn't much time to locate the job plans, let alone make any phone calls before catching the plane. Nearly missed it, as it was." He let his gaze fall on her. "I didn't have a choice. I had to be there!"

She didn't argue the fact but returned his pointed look. "And what did you find out?" She couldn't imagine the meticulous Jason ever designing anything faulty.

He scowled. "The contractor overran costs and used below-grade materials on the last three shops." There was consolation in his words. "But at least it wasn't the design!"

"I'm glad everything worked out," Lauren responded. She truly felt glad for Jason's sake. Despite her opinion of his workaholic patterns, he deserved better for his hard work. But the raven-haired beauty flashed before her eyes. She'd apparently never get an explanation as to why she was in attendance. Just like she might never know the mystery surrounding the house at Muriel's Inlet.

"I'm just glad to be back," he went on. "And I'm looking forward to the Skipper's Festival this weekend." He threw her a quick glance. "We are still going?"

"Of course."

"Your arm won't bother you?"

"I'm sure it'll be okay."

"And you're not mad about my leaving the island?"

"I told you I wasn't."

Jason's persistence remained as if he detected an unsettled element to their conversation. "Everything's in the open then?"

Lauren hesitated.

"Whatever it is, let's talk about it," he insisted.

"There is something I need to tell you." This was awful. So much had happened; she'd nearly forgotten about Cassie and her admission of guilt—until a few minutes ago. "I spoke with Cassie the other night," she began, pausing long enough to collect her thoughts.

"And?"

Lauren found she couldn't quite look into his gray eyes as the story she'd rehearsed so many times spilled out, every detail she was loath to remember. "I really can't blame her," she finished. "She was just trying to protect me." She watched carefully for any reaction on Jason's part. He gave none. "I know this doesn't look good for me, but it's the honest truth. I had no idea Tara called."

An eternity of silence passed before he spoke. "I'm relieved to know Tara's conversion was real." He seemed genuinely comforted but not satisfied. "And I believe you, Lauren." He paused again in thought. "But there's just one thing I can't but wonder."

"Yes?"

"Was Cassie protecting you from Tara—or from me?"

Lauren thought the question over a moment. "Both," she answered with brutal honesty. "Things were really going well for me by that time, and Cassie didn't want to see me hurt again. She's leery of you even yet."

Jason nodded and fingered the keys dangling from the ignition. "And what about you? Do you think I'm a threat to your stable life?"

Not sure how to respond, Lauren didn't answer right away. "What's that have to do with Cassie and the phone call?"

"Didn't say it had anything to do with the call," he said quietly. "But you've said all along Tara did what she did to protect me—from you. Now you say Cassie's done what she's done to protect you—from me." Even though his voice held steady, Lauren could hear the pain in his words. "I just want to know if you feel the need to be protected from me."

He seemed genuinely taunted by the possibility, and Lauren felt a tug deep in her soul. "In a way, you do pose a threat," she admitted softly. "Just coming back to Piney Point, seeing you again, and facing God's command to forgive have pulled the rug out from under me." Lauren drew in a deep breath. "Just when I think I've come to grips with you and this forgiveness thing, I lose it again." Nervously she fingered the hem of her blue sling. "But I'm learning and coming closer to it than I have in the past five years."

"But there isn't much time now, is there," he stated matter-of-factly. "You're still planning to leave Sunday?"

How could she answer what she didn't know? It made perfect sense to stay on, at least for a short time until things settled. Yet she hadn't even talked with Tom, not about their doomed relationship, nor the chaotic events surrounding her now.

"I can't commit either way just yet," she finally answered, a sudden weariness overtaking her.

"I'll take that answer—for now," he said, putting the car in gear before easing back into traffic. "But I can be persistent."

How well she knew!

# Chapter 14

Several parked cars crowded the area surrounding the cabin at Piney Point, causing Jason a bit of tight maneuvering to press his large car in close.

"Where did all these cars come from?" Lauren wanted to know, alarmed at the sight. Thoughts of the jimmied front door left unrepaired that morning opened several possibilities for disaster.

Jason turned the ignition off, looking perplexed as well. "Larry said some church folks might be bringing food, but it shouldn't take this many people to bring over a casserole or two." He paused at the sound of an electric drill and hammering wafting from the cabin's open door. "Well, at least we know two people are fixing your busted door."

Lauren reached over with her left hand to unlatch the passenger door. "We'd better see who is here." The thought of people, especially church people, milling about inside her cabin rooted an unsettled feeling.

"Wait and I'll open your door," Jason commanded, hopping out quickly. He opened her door. "Can you make it?"

Deep bucket seats made twisting her body difficult without the aid of her right arm. "I can do it," she assured, resolutely rocking her weight forward enough to gain the proper momentum. A slight but audible grunt escaped as she successfully extricated herself. "Could you please get the prescription bag? It's on the floor."

She moved out of the way as Jason leaned into the car and retrieved the white paper bag. He closed the door just as Tilly came bounding out of the cabin, across the deck, and down the steps.

"Where've the two of you been?" Tilly asked happily, gently patting Jason on the cheek before sidling up to Lauren. "We've been waitin' with a fine spread of food." She eyed Lauren's sling. "Did you make out okay at the hospital?"

Lauren nodded, her attention still riveted to the cottage where voices mingled with the sound of power tools. Any hope for a quiet afternoon seemed distant.

Tilly nudged them forward. "Come on! The ladies are fixin' up the place." She looked at Jason, a frown crinkling her brow. "That rascal sure did make a mess."

The cottage had been in disarray after the burglary, but Lauren's euphoric condition hadn't allowed for the least bit of worry. Now the memory of strewn books and overturned drawers drew a troubled sigh.

"Does it look like the guy took anything?" Jason asked as they walked.

"Hard to tell." Tilly started up the steps first. "There was some jewelry, but Larry got it back, probably holdin' it for evidence."

Lauren stopped mid-step, her hand flying to her throat. "My cross necklace!"

"I'm sure Larry has it," Jason reasoned, his light hold on her good arm tightening with reassurance. "But we'll take a look here first to make sure."

Tilly made it to the top step. "Don't worry none about that. Larry nearly turned that scoundrel upside down to empty his pockets. You'll get it back."

Lauren didn't doubt Larry made an aggressive search, but she wouldn't rest until the necklace returned safely to her very own hands.

"Here they come," called a voice from the screen door. Lottie Bon Durant opened the squeaky screen door to let Tilly and the couple in. Wood splinters and dust littered the entryway.

Lauren managed a smile as she passed through. Two church deacons and several ladies, many in work smocks, swarmed the living room. Dishes of food loaded the small dining table like an oversized smorgasbord, and delicious smells permeated the room. Everyone seemed to be speaking at once.

"I don't know what to say." Overwhelmed, Lauren surveyed each hopeful face in turn. "This is wonderful." The place was spotless—with no sign of the disturbance she'd experienced. The welcoming smells of home flooded the place. The kindness evident here soothed her bruised soul. Yet guilt seized her. Those earlier, ungrateful thoughts she held against her brothers and sisters in Christ were straight from the pit of hell, and she knew it. These God-fearing people, like herself, were capable of making errors of judgment and needed her forgiveness as much as she needed theirs. How many times would God need to forgive her before she understood the dynamics of such actions? The thought made her reel in wonder, and she found herself swaying ever so slightly.

Jason put his arm around her waist, steadying her, and took over. "Let's give Lauren a little room," he told the well-wishers with a smile. He turned to her. "Do you need to freshen up and maybe look for your necklace?" She nodded absently, and he turned his attention to the others. "Give us a few minutes, and we'll be back to dig into that great food."

The ladies smiled appreciatively as Jason threaded Lauren through the crowd toward the back hall. Immediately the ladies busied themselves with final food preparations.

"Are you doing okay?" he asked with concern as they entered the back room, his arm still firmly wrapped around her.

Lauren met his eyes. "I'm afraid the effects of the medication last night haven't totally worn off yet." She couldn't tell him his close presence made her head spin much more than any drug ever could, and for the moment she didn't want to think about the raven-haired beauty, his mystery house, or any other unresolved issues. How nice it would be to cut loose those strings and love the man as she had so many years ago, as her heart wanted to do at this very moment.

Jason led her to the white wicker chair situated between the bed and window and quickly brought over the wooden jewelry box. "Take a look and see if your cross necklace is there."

Lauren fingered the latch and slowly lifted the pine cover, drawing a soft gasp upon seeing dirty smudges speckled across the empty red velvet bottom. "It's gone," she whispered. "It's all gone." Weary dismay overtook her. The creep not only took her most precious life mementos but touched her things with grimy hands, leaving a frightening scent of desecration in his wake. In one lone night, her security and sense of well-being had been stripped away.

"Larry probably has your jewelry in evidence as Tilly said," Jason said logically, dropping on one knee beside her. Softly he lifted her chin with his fingers. "I'll make sure you get the necklace back." Gray eyes searched hers. "I hate to see you like this." He pulled her close to his chest, his voice vibrating against her ear. "I'd have done anything to have protected you from this."

Lauren closed her eyes for fear she'd cave in to the growing urge to cry, something she definitely didn't want to do. Her tired mind needed some sleep, and a good shower and afternoon nap would restore the energy needed to keep things in perspective.

"Let's get something to eat," Jason said after several silent moments ticked away. He placed the jewelry box back on the bureau. "I don't know about you, but I'm starved."

"Oh, Jason. I didn't even think," Lauren replied aghast. "You've been up all night and haven't even had breakfast or lunch."

Jason chuckled. "By the looks of the food laid out on your dining room table, it was worth the wait."

"All that food! Can you believe it? It's enough to feed an army!" she exclaimed, still amazed by the women's generosity. She stood, catching a glimpse of her unkempt appearance in the wall mirror. Dark circles accented her wide eyes, and she stared at her pale reflection. Her hair pressed into unnatural waves of dull brown chaos. What a mess!

Jason drew her away from the mirror and circled his arm around her shoulder, his face close. "You're still beautiful to me and to the friends waiting just beyond this door." He waved toward the hallway. "And given a chance, you'd be surprised how loving these Christians can be. You're never alone in a group like this, or with me—especially with me." Lauren felt herself relax into his arms. "I don't want you to leave, Lauren. I need you as much as you need me."

The crushing weight of decision forced its way once again upon her moment of pleasure, smothering any embers of happiness like a drizzling rain. "It's not that easy, Jason."

Jason studied her for a long moment before dropping a kiss on her forehead. "I know." He loosened his embrace and prodded her toward the hallway. "But if you're like me, things are always clearer on a full stomach."

The next hour sped by as Lauren visited with her guests and listened to those eager to catch her up with island news. She finally emptied her plate, awkward as that was left-handed, and laid it aside. Tasting everything at the insistence of others nearly put her stomach over the top. She leaned back into the sofa, noticing for the first time an aching sensation from her right arm. She had no idea where Jason had placed the medicine or the instruction sheet. Certainly one of the pain pills was due. She looked across the room where Jason was busy showering praise on the ladies for their fine cooking.

"Tilly, you've outdone yourself," he exclaimed, taking a huge bite from a slice of Stollen bread.

Tilly blushed and waved him off. "Wait until Lauren gets the recipe. She'll make it even better than me. You wait and see!"

Both glanced her direction, and Lauren rolled her eyes. Jason chuckled, pausing long enough to send her a wink before moving on to talk with the two men examining the repaired door. The medication could wait, she finally determined, finding no appropriate opportunity to disentangle herself from the ladies who kept her occupied in conversation. A few minutes later, Tilly began covering the food dishes with foil.

"It's time to let the girl have her rest," Tilly announced to the group. "Did someone bring more foil?"

The women slowly separated and began the massive job of cleanup, refusing Lauren's offer of help. She watched silently as dish after dish made its way to the kitchen. Tilly placed a full plate of chocolate brownies on the counter, sealing the foil edges as she slid it into the corner. She took a final look about, obviously pleased with the results, and made her way to the sofa where Lauren sat.

"Finally a second or two to talk without interruption," Tilly replied, dropping herself into the sofa. The cushion sandwiched her hips in a deep vee. "Because I have something to tell ya."

The seriousness of her tone gained Lauren's interest. "Is something wrong?"

"Don't know," Tilly answered strangely. "You had a call this morning from that boyfriend of yours in Cincinnati."

"Tom?" Lauren groaned. "When did he call?" She didn't wait for the answer as words spilled over each other in horror. "You didn't tell him about the break-in, did you?"

"Yes." Tilly gave the word a curious stress that sounded affronted. "He asked where you were and what was goin' on. Couldn't lie to him." She used the corner of her apron to wipe a smear of chocolate off her hand.

"What did he say?"

"Nothin' much," she answered in a decidedly strained voice. "Said he'd call tonight. Guess he'd finished whatever testing he had to take."

"That all?" Suspicion pointed to more.

"Well. . ." Tilly hedged.

"Yes?"

"He did ask about the ferry schedule."

"What!" Lauren lowered her voice when Jason shot her a quick look from across the room. "I can't have Tom coming here. Jason's threatening to camp out on the deck tonight." Her mind whirled desperately. "Did Tom say when he was coming?"

"No," Tilly answered. "He didn't say he was coming at all. He just asked about the ferry schedule, that's all." She patted Lauren's knee. "He said he'd call tonight. I'm assumin' he meant from Cincinnati."

Lauren calmed. "You're right! He'll probably call tonight and try to convince me he should come." She bit her lip in contemplation. "He wouldn't just come." *I hope.*

"See! Nothin' to worry about." Tilly lumbered up and out of the sofa. She looked over at Jason, who was still talking with the men. "I'm glad he's stayin' out here tonight. Makes me feel a boatload better. But you're gonna spend the night at my place."

Lauren opened her mouth to protest, but Tilly cut her off. "You and Jason don't need to set tongues wagging all over again. Now, let me shoo these folks outta here so you can get some rest, and I can go make up my guest bed for you."

Jason turned and gave Tilly a knowing smile as if he'd heard. Lauren ran her fingers nervously through her hair, feeling its disheveled condition. She couldn't wait until everyone left so she could take a much-needed shower.

"You can't take a shower with the cast," Jason pointed out logically, pulling back the plastic curtain. "The showerhead's up too high. You'll get everything wet."

"What about using plastic wrap around the cast?" Lauren asked. A good, hot shower was all she really wanted, a daily function she'd taken for granted—until today. Was it too much to hope for now?

Jason only shook his head. "True, wrapping the arm might keep it dry, but just the same you shouldn't try showering until you're no longer woozy." He studied the fixtures. "What's wrong with a bath?"

"I'd never be able wash my hair without breaking my neck," she pointed out. The cast was proving to be more of a complication than she expected. "Maybe if I did my hair first, before the bath, I could lean under the spigot."

"Maybe." He gave a thoughtful glance at the tub. "With the cast on your right arm and spigot on this end, you'll have more than your share of difficulty." His eyes roamed the room. "Well, there's only one thing to do."

"What?" She didn't like the determined look on his face.

He reached over her head for two towels on the rack above the commode. "I'll have to wash your hair for you."

Lauren stepped back. "You can't do that!" she sputtered. "It's not—not appropriate."

"Don't be a prude," he said, ignoring her objections as he draped one towel over her shoulders. "Now, find a comfortable place to lean over the tub edge so I can get the water going." Placing the other towel across the cold porcelain, he moved to her other side.

"Jason Levitte, this is ridiculous," she voiced, clumsily finding her way to the floor. "What will the neighbors say?"

He chuckled, turning the faucet handles. "You worry too much about the neighbors. They're not in here."

"It's not funny."

His smile said otherwise. "There's absolutely nothing wrong with me washing your hair. Male hairstylists do it all the time."

"At the salon, maybe, but not in a woman's cramped bathroom."

"Location, location, location—is that it?" His hand tested the water. "Perfect!" He turned suddenly and left the bathroom.

"Jason!"

Before she could get to her feet again, he returned, brandishing a large pitcher. "Try to turn this way," he said, guiding her cast to rest on the towel. "Lean your head down over the tub. That's it."

He filled the pitcher, and Lauren felt the rush of warm water stream across the back of her neck then pour over her forehead. Jason's hand gently tilted her head to each side, moving her hair until it became thoroughly wet.

"Pull back a little," he instructed, and Lauren heard the familiar wheeze of shampoo being expressed from the bottle. A flowery smell filled the room. "Back a little more."

Lauren did as commanded, her eyes tightly closed. The situation bordered on crazy, but no argument could change Jason's mind once set. How well she knew that!

"I've never seen sparkly blue shampoo before," he said, massaging the suds into her scalp.

"That's because it's a girl thing." She began to relax under the caring, soothing touch of his hands. If she were totally honest with herself, she'd admit how good it felt to be cared for by Jason—even if the pressure of leaning over the bathtub did threaten to explode her head.

"Time to rinse," he announced, smoothly steering her head farther over the tub edge. Once again he repeated the shampooing process, this time in silence. Suddenly he stopped.

"What's wrong?" she questioned, tasting a bitter bubble of soap. His continued silence caused her to turn slightly, eyes still tightly closed. "What is it, Jason?"

Unhurriedly, his fingers began to work again. "I was just thinking about the past."

*Could that be good?* Lauren waited in silence.

"Your hair has always been stunning, Lauren," he continued. "Even short, it's beautiful." All movement stopped for a second time. "I just hope you didn't cut it because of me."

Her long tresses had been his pride and joy. She couldn't help but remember the bolt of revenge each snip embedded in her heart and mind as lock after lock fell soundlessly to the tile floor. But the act never did rid her of his memory. Like her hair which sold for wigs, the memory of his love stayed alive and circulating somewhere unknown.

Lauren tilted back trying to catch a glimpse of Jason through watery eyes. Why didn't he speak? But his blurry image quickly faded into nothing as a burning sensation forced her to duck back under the water. "The soap's in my eyes!"

"Wait a minute," he commanded, quickly rinsing her hair with one hand and wiping her eyes with the other. "Here, use the towel." He drew her back from the water, helping her upright.

Lauren felt a soft towel press into her open hand, and she quickly dabbed her eyes as Jason began using the other to soak up the streams of water spilling from her hair.

Abruptly he stopped.

Water dripped on her leg. What now! Blinking rapidly, she turned, glimpsing the source of Jason's silence.

There in the doorway stood Tom Thurman.

# Chapter 15

"Tom!" Lauren could only stare wide-eyed at the tall figure filling the small doorway.

He was dressed in dark blue shorts and a T-shirt, and Tom's black hair seemed naturally outfitted to the ensemble, harmonizing to fit his usually unpretentious character. Right now, however, his low-lidded gaze was anything but harmonious.

Strained silence hung in the air like morning fog—cold and clammy.

Jason was the first to recover. "You must be Tom Thurman," he greeted, wiping one wet hand across his jeans before extending it.

"And you must be Jason Levitte," Tom replied in a carefully modulated voice, slowly accepting his hand. His gaze lit expectantly on Lauren.

Trepidation suddenly made it hard to breathe. "Why, Tom, I wasn't expecting you."

"That much is obvious," he said dryly.

Lauren was definitely at a disadvantage, crouched uncomfortably on the cold tile floor, water dripping off her nose like a small child. *Why, oh why, can't my life be normal like most folks?* Using the edge of the towel, she quickly dabbed the offending drops. "As you can see, I'm in the process of getting my hair washed," she explained, moving the cast into better view, "and Jason is helping with this seemingly impossible task." She cast a meaningful look at Tom, then Jason. "And I'm finding this situation extremely awkward at the moment. Would you gentlemen mind very much excusing me to finish?"

Tom said nothing but stared between the two as he gradually backed out of the room and walked down the hallway.

Jason stood, offering a hand to hoist her up. "I'll talk to him."

"You will do no such thing!" she responded breathlessly, capturing his arm in a tight grip. "That's the last thing I need." A sudden wave of dizziness overtook her, and she stumbled backward.

Jason quickly steadied her. "The first thing you need to do is get some sleep."

"Stood up too quickly, that's all," she excused, moving from his hold. "Maybe it'd be best if you went home until I've had a chance to talk to him."

"Absolutely not!" He planted both hands on her shoulders, turning her squarely in front of him, and gave her a look of determination she knew all too well. "You're going to haul yourself into the bedroom and get some shut-eye." He cut off all protest. "You're in no condition to deal with anything, much less ex-boyfriends," he added with a whisper. Before she could object to his erroneous conclusion concerning Tom, he prodded her out the door, across the hall, and through her bedroom doorway. "Don't let me see you for at least four hours."

He quickly crossed the hall again, then returned with her pain pills and a plastic cup filled with water. "Open wide," he teased, holding a pain pill in front of her face.

"But I haven't even taken my bath—"

"Later!"

She took the pill from his hand and set it on her tongue, then took several sips of the cool water before handing the cup back to Jason. She tried to protest again. "But—"

"No buts!" he whispered, softly closing the door behind him until it clicked.

Lauren looked about the room, anger welling like a spring as she flung the wet towel from her neck and onto the wicker chair. Of all the nerve! She ripped the bedcovers back. Just what she needed: Jason and Tom holed up in the living room having a tête-à-tête. And Jason thought she could sleep through that. "Ha!" The bitter laugh was nothing more than a chirp.

The bed groaned under her brusque flop, the pillows receiving much the same as she punched them to shape with both hands. Instantly she wished she hadn't as throbs of pain echoed through the broken arm in protest. Fortunately, a few moments of stillness encouraged the pain to subside.

Lauren hadn't expected to sleep, but physical weariness finally overcame her tumultuous and confused emotional state. She awoke to find the late afternoon sun pouring through the open curtains of the back window. Groaning, she turned onto her side, stretching to see the bedside clock. Five-thirty! It'd been less than two hours, and she didn't feel particularly refreshed, a leftover drug haze still plaguing her body. Wearily she flopped to her back, staring at the ceiling, listening for any telltale signs of Jason or Tom. Hearing none, she gradually sat up, willing full wakefulness upon herself.

From the edge of the bed, the wall mirror took in her scruffy appearance, and she moaned. The wet, stringy hair had dried into nothing short of a frizzy bird's nest with unruly tangles.

"Same to you," she mumbled at the offending reflection as she padded over to the bureau to grab the wooden-handle brush.

Clumsily she brushed with her left hand, tearing at the roots as bristles caught every unseen knot. Finally, several strokes later, her hair turned almost manageable. She smoothed out her wrinkled shorts outfit before carefully opening the bedroom door. Cautiously, she peered into the empty hallway. All was quiet. She ventured toward the living room.

Rhythmic ticking from the rooster clock mounted above the fireplace reverberated loudly in the silence. The front door stood open, and Lauren quietly peeked through the screen, discovering Tom asleep in the Adirondack chair, his leather sandals propped on the picnic table. Jason was still nowhere to be seen. Noiselessly she backed from the door and made her way to the bathroom. Finally, the bath she desperately needed. . . Tom could wait. And what Jason didn't know wouldn't hurt him.

Lauren found the hot, scented bubble bath dissolved much of the weariness from her limbs and gave her time to think. Surprise would have been too mild a term to express her reaction to Tom's arrival. Beyond her own worries, she hoped Tom hadn't risked his pastoral exams by coming to the island. He'd no doubt come to her aid with heroic measures in mind, a knight making a chivalrous rescue for his damsel in distress, only to find another man wearing his suit of armor. What a disastrous turn of events, poor timing, and a terrible misconstruing of the facts.

What could she say to Tom? He'd sent her to Bay Island in an effort to save their relationship, an opportunity to get things right with God. Now she had nothing to offer. Nothing! She didn't love him. The first seeds of doubt, planted well before her arrival to Bay Island, had grown into full realization. Even their friendship would suffer inevitable demise when she explained this newfound insight toward their ill-fated romance, when he learned she didn't love him like a woman should. He'd never settle for the brother-sister routine. Even the fact she'd made no commitment whatsoever to Jason would be of little consolation for this ultimate blow. She dreaded the moment of disclosure that was close upon her.

And Jason? Where did he come off assuming Tom and she were through? Never once had she indicated it to be so. She'd never given an answer to his summer request or discussed any real future plans.

A light knock at the door startled Lauren. "Yes?"

"Are you okay in there?" Tom called softly.

"Yes," she repeated, her former nervousness returning. "I'm nearly finished."

"Just be careful." He paused, then asked, "Do you need any help?"

"No. I'm just fine."

"That's good." He sounded relieved.

"Are you alone?" she ventured to ask, repositioning the cast on the tub's edge.

"Yes. Your—friend left awhile ago but said he'd return this evening."

Lauren thought a moment. "I won't be long. If you're hungry, there's plenty in the refrigerator. Just help yourself."

"Do you want me to fix you something?"

"No." She still felt stuffed, no better than a fat Thanksgiving turkey. "But you get whatever you want. I promise not to be long."

A second later she heard him retreat back up the hallway. Quickly she rinsed, stepped from the tub, and grabbed a towel to dry, finding even this effort a most difficult one. She gave an elaborate sigh as the robe sash finally tightened, and she hurriedly glanced out the door before making a mad dash to the bedroom.

Trying to clear one leg at a time into her plaid shorts turned into a major event. Twice she practically tumbled as her toes snagged the waistband first and then the hem. Finally she completed dressing, frustrated but presentable.

Tom stood at the kitchen counter replacing the foil top on a casserole dish. Immediately he looked her way, his watchful and wary consideration evident. "Feeling better?" he asked, crimping the shiny foil securely over the edges.

"Much better." She sensed his apprehension matched her own. "Did you find enough to eat?"

He nodded, gesturing to the casserole dish. "Are you sure you don't want something? I can heat up another square of lasagna."

"No thanks," she answered, wondering just how they were to get beyond the niceties. Hesitantly she extended her good hand toward him. "Can we talk?"

He took this encouraging sign and made his way to her side, grasping her hand in his own. "I'm sorry for being such a cad when I arrived," he apologized straightaway. "I was awfully worried after hearing you were robbed and went to the hospital." A slight smile touched his mouth. "I don't know what I expected to find when I got here, but it wasn't the sight of you sitting on the bathroom floor having a daily beauty treatment—or answering questions about your well-being to some guy on the phone."

Lauren gave a puzzled look. "Some guy?"

"Larry somebody. He called while you were asleep."

"Ah," she acknowledged, leading Tom outside to the shaded picnic table. "That would be the police officer who was here last night." It seemed best to keep things simple. Unimportant facts would only complicate matters.

Tom shrugged as he sat next to her. "I don't think he said."

There was an aching pause.

"Tom?"

"Uh-oh," he murmured, taking a deep breath. "Here it comes."

"Please don't say that," she pleaded, squeezing his hand. The situation was difficult enough without seeing the dejected expression crossing his handsome face. "First I need to know how your exams went. You didn't jeopardize them by coming to the island, did you?"

"No," he answered quickly enough. "The last exam finished late yesterday, and I'm sure I did well."

"You didn't get scores yet?"

"Post-exam interviews and scores were this afternoon. Those I missed."

Lauren digested this for a moment. "I hope it won't look poorly for you. I'd hate to be the cause—"

Tom turned toward her, closing what little gap existed between them. "It wouldn't have mattered, Lauren. With the exception of God, you've always been first, and I couldn't have stayed in Cincinnati, not knowing you were hurt and at the hospital. There wasn't even a question about my coming."

"You're one of the sweetest people I know," she said sadly, caressing his cheek as she stood. "That's what makes this so much harder for me to say."

"This is where the uh-oh part comes in." He paused, eyeing her, then held out his hand again. "Come on and sit down. Whatever you have to say will be easier sitting down."

She looked at him steadily, finally taking his hand before she sat down. Tom had always been of a gentle nature, compassionate and understanding when the walls of trouble closed in about her. His rock-strong approach had steadied her more than once. He wasn't headstrong and absorbed with life like Jason or impulsive as Larry, just firm and solid. A girl couldn't hope for more. So why did her feelings of love fizzle like a wet firecracker with the man? She knew the answer might elude her for life, but the recognizable truth it produced could not be ignored or pushed aside.

Gathering courage, she met his gaze straight on. "Tom, you sent me to the island hoping I'd find the path to God, to serve Him fully again. I think that's happening." Abruptly she stood again, finding the need to pace and maintain space between them. She moved behind a lawn chair, one hand braced on the frame. "The first thing I've discovered is the beginnings of forgiveness. What I'd called forgiveness before wasn't forgiveness at all. There's a big difference between real forgiveness and the ability to file away the problem and the feelings associated with it. When I came back to the island last weekend, the file came back out, the very same file I'd stashed away five years ago, and it was still stuffed with every hurtful memory and allegation."

Tom leaned forward listening intently.

"I'm still learning the essence of this forgiveness, but I believe God is finally getting the message through this thick skull of mine." She tapped her temple for emphasis. "The second thing I discovered is that God isn't calling me to foreign missions." She waited for a reaction.

His unreadable face told her nothing. "Go on."

"In that same light," she continued, "I've also discovered I'm unworthy of your love and devotion." She met his blank stare. "Although I love you dearly, it's not the type of love you ought to have from a future wife." Suddenly she moved to his side. "It wasn't supposed to turn out like this—it just did."

"Poor Lauren." Tom touched her hair lightly for a moment. "I can't say I'm happy to hear the news, but I've suspected for quite awhile."

"You knew!"

"I knew something wasn't right," he answered. "I didn't know if the problem rested in your relationship with God, with me, or both."

Lauren drew a weary breath. "But now it's gone sour, hasn't it—for both of us?"

"It's never sour when God makes the plans," Tom reminded. "This wasn't perhaps what I'd originally intended when you came to the island, but. . ." He seemed momentarily without words. "And Jason? Are you still in love with him?"

Lauren colored. "Yes," she said after a momentary hesitation. She shifted uncomfortably under his penetrating stare. "But there are still unresolved issues, and I'm not sure what hope, if any, exists." She spread out her left hand helplessly. "I haven't a clue what to do. Jason's asked me to stay the summer, to give it a chance, to see what might happen."

"What did you tell him?"

"Nothing."

"Nothing?"

"I'm not sure what I should do," Lauren said miserably. "There's my job and apartment to consider."

"Have you prayed?"

"A lot!" She sighed. "Sometimes I just wish God made phone calls, especially when there seems to be no answer to the question."

"He does answer," Tom remarked in all seriousness. "He just doesn't use the phone."

"What?"

"Take time to mediate on His Word, and He'll speak to you."

That she knew. "Tom?"

"Hmm?"

"You need to know my feelings for Jason in no way affected my decision about our relationship."

"I know." Warmly he took her outstretched hands. "And Jason's head over heels in love with you. You know that, don't you?"

"What makes you say such a thing?" she asked, puzzled, her voice giving a slight betraying quiver.

"We talked a little bit."

She frowned, her brow pinched. This couldn't be good.

"Don't worry." He laughed. "He didn't reveal any deep, dark secrets. It was his demeanor, his actions which told me. He's very protective of you. I'd only hoped my initial impressions were wrong, but his asking you to stay the summer confirms the notion." His smile waned. "And I give you my blessing, whatever you choose."

Lauren blinked. She was frankly taken aback by his calm acceptance. Not that she wanted him heartbroken, but there should have been some reaction. "What will you do?"

"Go to the mission field as planned," he announced with certainty. "Now that I know how things stand at home, I'll move forward with those plans."

"I feel terribly miserable about this, Tom."

"Don't!" He gently rubbed her back as he'd done so many times. "Be thankful God's given us the answer. Trusting God means trusting His answers whether we like them or not."

Lauren gave an understanding nod. Tom was right. He'd always grasped the intended spiritual parallel of life's situations, the parallels she so often missed. "What are you going to do right now?"

"Well," he began, "that funny friend of yours, Tilly, offered me a place to stay tonight. She said one of the nearby cabins is vacant this week."

"Tilly? You met her?"

"I've had one busy afternoon while you napped. Tilly came visiting with another woman not long after Jason left."

"Oh!"

"Anyway, she's going to show me to the cabin as soon as Jason gets back, and I'll go home in the morning." Both looked up as a large black car came up the road slowly approaching the incline. "And it looks like my relief is here."

# Chapter 16

"A bit of fresh air will do you good," Jason told Lauren as he wheeled her open golf cart onto the main road. "It'll help clear out the cobwebs."

Lauren was busy looking at the lakeshore. "I suppose." The episode with Tom had left her completely exhausted and relieved at the same time. In retrospect, the separation gave her freedom, some open space to grow—and a feeling of sadness. The fact her life must irrevocably change seemed more than a little unsettling. A small part of her wanted to cling to her old life like a suction cup clings to the window, gradually loosening, gradually breaking the seal with dryness until the complete detachment is ready and expected.

She remembered similar feelings while attending camp during her eleventh year. The exciting week of new friends and new bonds came to an end way too soon. For the first time, she'd felt the emotional pull between the old and the new, between the home she knew and the world she'd discovered. She'd learned how impossible it was to maintain both without taking in one area in order to give in another.

This juncture had presented itself again. She'd released Tom to follow the path set before him, forcing her to find a path of her own. But her own passageway was fraught with options and less than concrete facts with which to make wise choices.

"Hey, there!"

Lauren looked up, startled at Jason's laughter.

"I thought you dozed off there for a minute." His disarming smile nearly took her breath away. "Not very good for my ego, you know."

Lauren laughed with him. "Sorry!"

"I think you'll find the spot up ahead will do wonders for your wandering mind." Jason made a narrow turn onto a graveled back road. "Besides pizza, I know your other vices, cookies and cream being one of them." Amusement crept into his voice. "I believe you mentioned ice cream earlier this morning."

The man wasn't about to let her forget the state he'd found her in that morning, Lauren thought with chagrin. What Jason found to be endearing, she found most awkward. Never in her life had she felt so euphorically out of control as she had during that time.

"Here we are!" Jason announced, steering the cart to a stop between freshly painted yellow lines in the half-full parking lot.

To her horror, she immediately recognized the Dairy Barn. Visions of Mr. Edwards filled her head. The event seemed miles away in time, but in fact, it'd only been last night since the obligatory ice cream cone ordeal.

"Surprised?" he asked, obviously misinterpreting her expression for one of pleasure. "It's much bigger and nicer than the building they had at their old site. I think the new look and location's been good for business." He quickly slipped out his side and circled to her. "Come on." His hand extended to hers.

Lauren hesitated only a moment before accepting his grasp. She couldn't very well refuse to go in. What would she say? No, she could only hope the old man wasn't working tonight. With her hand still firmly in Jason's hold, she followed him through the double set of clear, heavy doors. The sight of Mr. Edwards' gray head and slim figure behind the counter quickly dashed her hopes.

"Hello, Van," Jason called in greeting as they neared the ice cream case. "You remember Lauren!"

The owlish face turned her way, eyes narrowed in deliberation behind the thick glasses. "Yep, I remember." He finished giving change to another customer before his glance lit on her again, focusing on the sling first and then her face.

"Hello, Mr. Edwards," Lauren returned clumsily.

Jason gave her a smile. "I bet you didn't know Van now owns the Dairy Barn." He turned to Mr. Edwards, his smile never wavering. "What do you recommend this evening?"

Mr. Edwards used a thumb to push his glasses up a notch on his bulbous nose. A moment of hesitation followed before he spoke. "Might I recommend the flavor of the week: cookies and cream?"

Lauren thought she'd drop straight through the floor into the basement.

Jason seemed oblivious to the tension and gladly ordered. "Make it two in waffle cones." He pulled money from his wallet.

The old man slowly slid the curved glass cover back and reached deep into the crevasse with a wet silver scoop while she looked on. Jason had called him by his first name. Van! Lauren couldn't ever remember hearing the man referred to as anything but Mr. Edwards. She wasn't even sure until this very moment he had a first name. Certainly there were people who knew him on a first-name basis, but his gruff exterior kept most at bay—everyone except Jason, that is. Leave it to Jason to break through.

Mr. Edwards handed one filled waffle cone to Jason, who in turn passed it to Lauren. Gingerly she accepted the cold treat and waited patiently as the old man began filling the second cone. Silently she looked about, watching the many people who sat at the parlor-style tables. Jason had been right. The place did look clean and bright, evidently thriving under new management. But where were the workers? Thinking back, she couldn't recall any staff on duty the night before, either. Surely he didn't run the place by himself.

"There you go, young man," Mr. Edwards said, handing Jason the second cone.

Jason thanked the old man as he made change from the cash register and dropped the clinking coins noisily into his pocket.

"Let's go to the tables outside," Jason suggested, snatching several napkins as he passed the condiment table. He opened the door for her.

Lauren followed him to the farthest concrete picnic table under a large oak. Nestled next to a man-made pond, she watched two ducks clamber out of the water toward them in hopes of a handout. A warm breeze rustled the leaves, and she took in the sweet air.

"I think you're right," Lauren began. "This property is so much nicer than their old place. It's so picturesque and quiet."

Jason nodded. "The Dairy Barn was given a fair price for their land, and the option to set up at Levitte's Landing or here. When management saw this piece of land, they took it right away. After a year, though, they sold the business. I'm not sure how or why Mr. Edwards acquired it. It was a closed-door deal."

"He seems a little bit over his head trying to work the counter and the tables. I noticed he doesn't have much help." A drip of ice cream plopped onto her shorts.

Jason dabbed the spot away. "He can't keep his staff." He threw her a mischievous smile. "Some think he's a little rough around the edges. Imagine that!"

"Really?" Lauren laughed with mock surprise.

They lapsed into a companionable silence. One duck ventured close enough, and Jason broke a piece from his cone to toss at the waiting mallard. Lauren's thoughts returned to Tilly's advice. *It's time to stop being so self-absorbed. Jason is a businessman. He shoulders a lot of responsibility trying to keep his company profitable. A good woman could help him, side up with him—join him. Do you know what Jason's dreams might be?*

"Jason?"

"Hmm?" He tossed another crumb at the lingering bird and turned toward her.

"Have you ever thought about where you want to be in ten years?"

His eyebrows inched up with uncertainty. "You mean with the business?"

Lauren shrugged. "Not necessarily." Two more ducks began to congregate at their feet, and she tossed the rest of her cone toward them. "Certainly your business plays an important part in who you are and what you want, but there must be other dreams apart from your work."

"Like what?"

"You know! Dreams like. . ." She waved her hand about as if trying to pluck words out of the air. "Like being cast for the lead role in the summer theatre production of *Fiddler on the Roof,* or maybe taking a white-water rafting trip."

"Well," he hesitated, a smile tugging at the corners of his mouth, "I can safely say I've never had the urge to be an actor or to risk life and limb on an oversized rubber raft."

Lauren took a steadying breath. "Then what would you like to do if time and money were no object?"

"You really want to know?" He seemed cautiously surprised, abandoning his former teasing mood.

"Yes."

"First and foremost, I always want to be in God's will no matter where I am or what I do," he answered in all seriousness. "And one of these days I'd like to take a more active role at church, maybe the office of church deacon or trustee. They never seem to have enough men willing to run for either office."

"You'd make a good deacon," Lauren commented, knowing how needed and beneficial a compassionate spirit would be in that position. "I'm surprised they haven't asked you." Lauren abruptly hurried him along. "What else? What other things would you like to accomplish?"

He laughed, his eyes twinkling impishly. "Well. . .," he hesitated, rubbing his hand across his chin in thought, "there are several places I'd like to visit around the country. I always thought it'd be interesting to go across the country by train or maybe take a steamer excursion trip." A wistful look crossed his face.

Jason had never expressed an interest in trains before. Had she been too self-absorbed to bother with his ideas as Tilly suggested? "I didn't know you liked trains."

"Been hooked on them since I was five and got my first electric train." He laughed, obviously finding the memory a happy one. "I have several boxes of those trains packed away in the attic, and one of these days. . ." He paused, his expression pensive. "One of these days, I'm going to set up every one of those trains in the living room like we used to at Christmas. I might even try my hand at garden railroading." His smile widened. "All I need is a garden."

Her own words came back. *I wouldn't mind having a house with enough land for a little garden. Maybe some tomatoes, corn, peppers. . .and some lettuce. And while I'm dreaming, one of those easy garden tillers would be nice.* "Those are nice dreams, Jason."

Jason leaned toward her, his head tilted quizzically as he released the crumpled napkins he held on the table. Gently he took her hand. "What's this all about?" His voice, like his touch, was a caress.

He smiled down at her so tenderly, she lowered her gaze. "I'm just realizing how very little I really know about you." This insight accompanied another revelation; she wanted to know everything there was to know about the man beside her.

"Don't you know you're the only person who really does know me?" He met her stunned amazement with a hint of laughter in his eyes. "It's true. You know how I think and operate. You already know how bullheaded I can be."

Yes, that she did know. Firsthand! Yet she didn't know what made him tick on the inside, outside his business dealings. Could it have been because the business commanded his every minute during those early years, or because she couldn't see past the demanding force his business implied? Or a combination of both? She'd loved him beyond what she thought capable back then, never once dreaming anything could pull them apart—even the business. Then the unthinkable happened, destroying everything in its path, a mudslide of turmoil and hurt washing an entire five years away.

And she still loved Jason. Just one tender look from his gray eyes or the touch of his hand melted her insides to jelly. Even now, her heart ached to be held by him, to feel his breath on her hair. Yet she couldn't rely on her emotions! Jason had yet to explain why he built her house or what role, if any, Becky Merrill played in his life. Either of the two could easily change their future course of events.

"Lauren!" She looked up at his teasing eyes, laughter lurking in their depths. "Do you know just how beautiful you are when you're thinking too hard?" Gently he drew her head against his shoulder, lowering his clean-shaven cheek against hers. "Tell me you'll stay the summer," he murmured.

Lauren basked in the moment, nearly throwing all caution to the wind as she looked up. He lifted her chin gently and, lowering his head, placed his lips tenderly on her own.

"Jason," she responded breathlessly. "I—"

The moment burst quicker than a pricked balloon when his cell phone rang. Both stiffened and remained still. He made no immediate move to answer it, but the interruption had already caused the damage, breaking the mood—and her spirits. The phone persisted, and Lauren slowly moved from his embrace. She heard Jason sigh as he reached for the phone clipped to his belt.

"Yes," he answered brusquely into the phone, annoyance coating the edge of his voice. He remained silent a moment as he listened, turning slightly from Lauren before he stood.

Lauren sensed his want of privacy and swiveled to face the other direction. Yet his low voice carried.

"Now, Bec, this is something Anderson could have handled." His voice lowered another degree, now barely audible. "I'm with a client. . ."

The remaining words drifted off into oblivion as he reached the bank of the pond. Client! He'd told the caller she was a client. No doubt the caller, Bec, was none other than Becky Merrill. Lauren's hands trembled, and her stomach tightened. Not once, but twice, he'd told the beautiful woman a lie concerning her. The deceit could have only one purpose, a means to keep both women in the dark. Still she was hesitant to believe it. Jason wasn't perfect, but he'd never intentionally hurt anyone.

But she'd heard the incriminating words from his own lips, the very same lips that had but a moment ago sealed their kiss. Her mind reeled with possibilities. Maybe he'd committed himself to the other woman, never dreaming Lauren would ever return to the island, and suddenly found himself in a tight spot. But how long did he think the charade could continue if she stayed the summer? Panic filled her as she realized just how close she'd come to agreeing.

Hurt threatened to explode her heart.

Giving a hard stare at his turned back, Lauren stood with as much dignity as she could muster and brushed the fine dust of crumbs from her lap. At least she didn't have to stay here and watch. Marching off to the golf cart, she plopped hard into the passenger seat, cupping her sling for support. If she had any courage, she'd leave him to walk home.

But she didn't have to wait long.

"I'm sorry for the interruption, Lauren," he apologized the moment he rounded the cart and sat behind the wheel. "I told her not to call me unless it was an emergency." He still sounded annoyed.

"Maybe she didn't think your client was important enough to hold your calls for," Lauren retorted, anger quickly displacing the hurt.

Two perplexed lines appeared between his straight blond brows. "What's that supposed to mean?"

"It means your appointment is over, and I'd like to be taken home." Lauren didn't dare look at Jason but stared straight ahead into the ice cream shop's window. Absently wiping tables and peering at them with interest was Mr. Edwards. She knew Jason saw the old man's curious attention.

"Just what I need," he muttered, turning the ignition, "an audience." His arm brushed against her as he backed the cart up. "And as for you, my girl, when we reach Piney Point, you're going to explain to me exactly what your problem is."

"I'll be happy to," she flung back at him. "I'll make everything wonderfully clear, because when I leave Bay Island this time, it'll be for good."

# Chapter 17

The ride to the cottage grew stiff with tension as dusk fell. Brief but frequent glances from Jason told her his anger simmered close to the top. It was there in the thinness of his lips and the jutting of his jaw, yet he seemed to be exercising great self-restraint and remained silent. Lauren said not a word, her mind whirling ahead to the unavoidable collision due between Jason and herself. Fingering the sling's soft material, she fixed her eyes demurely ahead to the road. It wasn't until they reached Piney Point and he quietly and firmly snapped off the ignition that either spoke. Lauren assumed she'd go first, but Jason snatched the ball in play, his offense strategy ready to take the field.

"Lauren, I don't know what it is you want from me," he began, sounding exasperated as he turned toward her, his eyes probing her face. "Do you want me to quit the business, to sell it off? Is that what you want? Would that finally make you happy?"

"Absolutely not!" Lauren retorted, slightly puzzled. It seemed apparent Jason had erroneously assumed the source of her unhappiness lay with his business. "What makes you think your business has anything to do with this?"

"You've never hidden how much you detest the demands the business places on my time." He gave her a hard stare and continued. "But I thought you understood the reasons for my departure the other day. I had no other choice, you knew that. What would you have had me do?" Lauren would have gladly answered, but he didn't give her a chance. "There will always be times when a phone call needs to be answered or instances when I'm called away or our time together might be interrupted or cut short. That's part of the territory, Lauren." He took a deep breath as if readying himself to wind another pitch. "I've done everything I could to bend over backward this week to spend time with you, including the delegation of my work to other associates. The demands aren't as great as they were years ago, but there are responsibilities that still require my attention. I don't see why you can't accept that."

She took advantage of a slight pause. "I understand the demands of your job perfectly," she told him firmly. "I may not like them, but I understand them." Not once had she voiced a disparaging remark to him about the business since arriving on the island, and his callous acceptance of these accusations hurt deeply. What kind of woman did he take her for? "Your business responsibilities are not the problem."

Jason drew an impatient breath. "Then would you kindly tell me what is?"

"It's about trust and respect, Jason." She raised her chin militantly. "I don't like being referred to as a client or an appointment so you can—can schmooze it up with your secretary."

"What!" His voice boomed in disbelief as he stared at her in amazement.

Lauren raised appealing eyes to heaven. The man was going to deny it. "Was the phone call tonight from your secretary, Becky Merrill?"

He paused briefly before answering. "Yes!" Then more slowly, "Why?"

"When she called, you told her you were with a client." She waved off the protest she saw brewing, her voice calm but icy. "I had to ask myself why you would do such a thing." She now waved her hand carelessly in the air. "I might not have thought anything of it, except for the phone call your secretary made to me the morning you left the island for South Carolina. At that time, I was your appointment!" Disgust overtook her voice. "She asked me to reschedule our meeting time. Granted, you might not consider fixing my roof a date, but it certainly wasn't an appointment."

He looked puzzled. "Lauren, I haven't a clue what you're talking about."

"Are you denying the fact you told Becky Merrill, just minutes ago, I was your client?"

His surprise seemed genuine, but Lauren refused to be moved.

"Yes, I'm denying it!" His gray eyes narrowed in thought. "I'm trying my best to think back to exactly what I did say." He rubbed the back of his neck, a motion Lauren found oddly defenseless.

But she didn't let up. "And did you lead your secretary to believe I was your appointment the morning you were called away?"

"Definitely not!" Something in his defensive tone spoke of momentary bewilderment. "Why would I have done either? It just doesn't make sense."

Lauren swung herself from the cart. "Five years is a long time. It wouldn't be so unexpected to find you might be—be committed to someone else. But I don't expect you to lead me on in one direction when you're not free to do so—deceiving some other poor girl in the process. It's unconscionable."

"Let's stick to one accusation at a time, shall we?" he flung back, his face grim. "You're flying all over the place. How's a person expected to defend himself when you keep changing the charges?"

Lauren didn't move, her cheeks flushed with indignation. How could Jason try to skirt the real issue when faced with the truth? "How indeed!" In anger, she marched to the steps.

But Jason raced ahead, barring her way, frowning heavily. For several palpable moments they squared off glances.

"There must be some explanation, and we're not going anywhere until we discover exactly what that explanation is." A muscle moved at the side of his mouth as he silently appraised her, and she guessed the inward struggle he was having to get himself under control. "Frankly, I'm getting a little tired of these misunderstandings."

"Well, if there's an explanation, I'll be glad to hear it," Lauren responded in an expressionless tone. There could be no possible explanation, no matter how much she longed to think there might be.

"Sit down a minute and let me think," he demanded, rubbing his neck again.

Lauren sank willingly onto the wooden step and waited. "I'm listening."

In the waning light, his face bore a haggard look, and Lauren felt her heart lurch. Instantly, her mind returned to another time, a time when the tables were turned. She was the accused and he the accuser. Persuasive proof convicted her then, even as later evidence proved it wrong. Could she have misjudged this situation in much the same way?

"You say Becky asked you to reschedule our appointment the morning I left?" he asked, and Lauren nodded. "I suppose that doesn't surprise me since Becky knows nothing of our relationship."

Lauren winced. "I see." A chilling sensation coursed through her at the thought of Jason and Becky together.

"You're jumping to conclusions again," he accused, frowning deeply at her. "Becky knows nothing of our relationship because I haven't said anything to her or anyone else about us. If she knows anything, it'd be from gossip, not me. I've been trying to preserve your privacy—our privacy." He leaned hard on the post. "When I asked her to call that morning, she wouldn't have known what kind of a meeting we were having. It seems plausible for her to guess it to be an appointment."

Lauren had to agree this might be true. "And tonight's conversation?" she asked, lifting one eyebrow slightly. "You told her you were with a client. That's hardly letting her come to her own conclusions."

He looked doubtful. "I don't recall telling her where I was or who I was with."

"But I heard you!" she insisted, gently rubbing away at the increasingly noticeable ache in her right arm. "I wasn't trying to listen in, but I couldn't help but overhear." A sad quality overtook her voice. "I truly wish I hadn't!"

A strange look flickered in his eyes. "I'm trying my best to figure this one out." His weight shifted from one foot to the other in thought. "I don't know how a call about thermostat covers comes even close to my calling you a client."

Curiosity got the better of her. "Thermostat covers?"

"I had locks put on the thermostat covers at the office this week," he explained. "It's one of those inherent gender difference problems. The guys keep turning the air conditioning up, and the gals keep turning it down. It was driving me absolutely crazy, so I had automatic thermostats installed and locked covers put over them." He rubbed a hand across his jaw. "But I'd forgotten about Ina from the cleaning service. She likes the air on full blast while she's working, and she called Becky when she couldn't open the cover." His eyes clouded in deliberation. "I remember telling Becky that Bill Anderson could have handled the call. He would have known to tell Ina the climate control. . ." The sentenced dropped off into nothing, the still night snatching the unsaid words.

Lauren's eyes widen with intense interest. "What?"

Jason didn't answer right away. Instead she could hear his laughter, softly at first and then more audible.

"What?"

"You don't get it?"

Her brow wrinkled in consideration, annoyance slowly creeping in. "Get what?"

"How the mix-up occurred!"

"No!" Nothing struck an answering chord.

"Do the words 'Ina the climate' mean anything to you?"

Lauren's eyes squinted in thought. "Ina the climate?"

"That's evidently what you mistook for 'I'm with a client,' " he reasoned. "Although I do have to say it couldn't have been done without a good deal of slurring and a drawl."

She looked up at Jason worriedly, thinking over his words. His explanation seemed exasperatingly possible, and much more than that—probable. All indications pointed to her own guilt and stupidity. She paused long and hard before speaking. "It seems I owe you an apology."

He dropped onto the step beside her. "Yes, you do!"

Something about the way he said the words made her pause again. She studied his face as he calmly waited. His hard expression had faded, replaced by an unreadable look. "Jason, I. . ." The words stuck in her throat. "I'm really sorry. I—accused you unjustly."

Jason took her hand in his. "Apology accepted." His steady gaze fixed her. "And this is where the rubber meets the road, so to speak."

Apprehension filled her. "What do you mean?"

"What I mean is, real forgiveness means total amnesty," he replied. "No-holds-barred amnesty." The sigh accompanying those words made Lauren wince. "Although our memories can't really forget the way we've been mistreated, how I was wrongly accused tonight or how badly I treated you five years ago, we do have control over how those memories are used. As far as I'm concerned, what happened tonight," he paused and snapped his fingers, "it's gone. I don't plan to discuss it again or ever use it against you, no matter the circumstances."

"Total forgiveness?"

He nodded. "Total forgiveness!"

"Just like Jesus," she added, her voice barely a whisper. The thought nudged her heart with guilt. How many times had she claimed forgiveness for Jason, only to bring his past shortcomings to the surface, letting them gasp for air before taking a dive under again? God's forgiveness wasn't anything like that, and He didn't tolerate it among His children. And the sins God had forgiven her were mountainous in contrast.

She felt Jason stir slightly beside her as he said, "I've given you my forgiveness freely. Now I want your forgiveness, Lauren—real forgiveness this time. The problem tonight stemmed directly from your unwillingness to forgive what happened five years ago. You're still waiting for the other shoe to drop. I want a clean slate!"

Night sounds grew louder as tree frogs chorused together in the darkness. Lauren wrinkled her forehead in thought. Of course she must forgive Jason and with true forgiveness, a total pardon. God wouldn't honor anything less.

"Jason," she spoke, her voice full of emotion, "I do forgive you and promise to file away those memories permanently." She paused. "And I'll try, with everything in me, to not let the past influence our today."

Jason stood and pulled her to her feet, looking into her face in a way surely meant to melt her heart. "You don't know what that means to me." He drew her close to his chest, gently cushioning her sling. "I know you must be awfully exhausted after last night and the hospital trip this morning, but I need to know one more thing."

Lauren drew back slightly to see his face. "What's that?"

"Are you willing to give God the chance to show us what He wants?"

"You mean about my staying the summer, don't you?" she asked, her voice trembling slightly.

"Yes."

She drew back completely to fully view him. "I need to know something before I can even begin to contemplate the possibility."

"Anything!"

"Are you in any way committed to someone else?" she asked bluntly. If he wasn't free, there was no use pursuing their relationship further. She didn't want a repeat of their last love story—it'd be like watching a bad film through for a second time.

Jason gave her a considering look before answering. "I'm a perfectly free man!" A smile crept over his face. "Is that all you needed to know?"

"And Becky?" She needed total assurance.

"Becky?" He looked perplexed for a moment before smiling again. "Becky's my secretary—nothing more! There's never been anything between Becky and me. Scout's honor!" He held up two fingers.

"It's three," Lauren said.

"What?"

"Three fingers—that is if you were a Boy Scout. Cub Scouts use two." Lauren drew his third finger up.

"Don't change the subject. And you?"

"Me?"

"Yes, you! While we're playing truth or dare, I'd like to ask you the same question. Are you committed in any way to Tom or anyone else?"

Sadness tugged at her again at the thought of Tom. Tomorrow he'd be gone from her life for good. "No."

"Then you'll stay the summer?"

There was a slight pause and a cautious answer. "Maybe!" She gave a sigh. "But it's not up to just me. I have a job to consider, an apartment standing empty, church duties—"

Gently he laid a finger to her lips. "All these things can be dealt with. Do you trust me enough to let me handle them?"

"You?"

"Yes, me!"

Lauren thought a moment, not sure what to say. She loved Jason and knew he was quite capable of getting his way when put to task. Even her employer might bend to his will. "All right, Jason. If God enables you to work things out, I'll stay the summer."

"That's all I needed to hear." Jason's eyes danced a jig. "And you, young lady, need to head up those steps and get your beauty sleep. It's been a long day for the both of us."

Lauren looked anxiously toward the dark cabin and instinctively cradled her good hand under the sling.

Jason followed her gaze perceptively. "It's all right! I'm going to be right outside the door all night long. You'll be quite safe."

"Tilly insisted I spend the night at her place. You can stay in the cabin. I don't think I can make up a bed for you, though," she stated with concern.

"Not to worry," he assured. "I've come prepared with a sleeping bag." He laughed at her whimsical look. "When you're ready, I'll walk you to Tilly's. Now up the steps."

Lauren yielded to his touch as he guided her toward the deck. She waited as he entered the cottage, giving it a thorough search before he'd allow her to enter.

"Everything's in dandy shape," he announced at last.

"Thank you, Jason." Instinctively she drew her hand to her throat, immediately remembering her missing necklace. "Did you talk with Larry about my necklace?"

A worried expression crossed his face. "Yes, I did. The cross necklace wasn't on the boy."

"It's lost again?" she noted in despair.

Jason drew an arm around her, his face close. "We'll find it. The boy must have dropped it somewhere here at the cottage or on the trail to Tilly's. We'll look for it tomorrow."

"Tomorrow's the Skipper's Festival," she reminded. "You won't have time."

"There's plenty of time." He moved her to the door. "You just get your things and let me worry about everything else." Lauren felt sure he was going to kiss her, but he drew away.

Lauren closed the screen, leaving the main door open. Finally, she collected her things. Glancing out the window, she watched Jason pull a dark sleeping bag from the trunk of his car.

# Chapter 18

Lauren awoke suddenly, opening startled eyes as she lifted her head from the pillow. Sunlight flooded the bedroom floor through the small window, and she quickly turned toward the bedside clock. Ten-thirty! The late hour quickly brought her to a sitting position. How could Tilly have let her sleep so long? Hastily she threw aside the covers and raced to the window, cupping the heavy white cast as she did.

A satisfied smile slowly spread across her face. For once she relaxed in the knowledge of Jason's nearness. It felt so right! She dressed quickly, then grabbed her blue fleece jacket, carefully wove the cast through the loose arm opening, and headed for the hallway. Very much to her surprise, she felt refreshed.

Tilly had left a note on the kitchen table saying she had an errand to run before she headed for the Skipper's Festival, so Lauren gathered her things and left, locking the door securely behind her.

Inside her cabin, the aroma of coffee greeted her, and she quickly glanced about. An empty cup sat next to the coffeemaker, and a half-filled carafe remained on the hot plate. Lauren drifted noiselessly back to the screen door and peered out. She hadn't seen Jason when she arrived, but now she noticed him crouched close to the deck floor on the far right, his back to her. Her eyes opened with the mildest flicker of interest as she watched his hand sweep back and forth across the deep gouges caused by the patio furniture during her unfortunate fall. His gaze seemed to intensify as he leaned closer. Then, as if sensing her presence, he slowly turned and met her stare. His face creased into smiles as he stretched up to his full height.

"Good morning," he greeted. "You're looking much better."

Lauren didn't know how he could judge through the hazy screen, but she took the compliment to heart anyway. "Good morning," she returned, taking note of his fresh clothes. "Have you been home this morning?" Even as she said it, the word home struck a peculiar chord. His home was really her house—the one unanswered question yet to be addressed.

"Nope!" He seemed to find amusement in her confusion. "I didn't think you'd mind me using your facilities. It's the least one could offer a man willing to risk his life guarding her home."

"I suppose," she said with mock indignation, leaning casually on the doorjamb.

"And good help is so hard to come by these days. Guess I'll have to keep you happy with occasional perks."

His eyes twinkled. "And don't you forget it."

Lauren's eyes widened slightly, and she smiled at him. "Would it be too much to ask the help to fix some breakfast?" She chuckled, adding, "Or brunch—or whatever people have when they don't get up until the day's nearly half spent."

"That'll be extra, I'm afraid."

"Oh, really?"

"Of course." One brow rose upward into the blond thatch over his forehead, an impish light making his eyes gleam. "Especially if you want any more salon treatments."

Lauren blushed slightly. "I don't think that will be necessary."

He laughed and opened the screen door. "Go and get yourself ready for the day then. The Skipper's Festival starts this afternoon, and you don't want to miss my performance for sure." When she didn't move right away, he prodded her forward. "Hurry up now, or you'll be even later than late getting your medicine."

Slowly Lauren made her way to the back hall, reluctant to break away from Jason. The feeling of freedom she felt with him seemed so novel, like a new toy one didn't want to part with. She hadn't realized the burden unforgiveness had placed on her heart for the past five years, not until it was lifted. Even the air seemed easier to breathe. A tickle of anticipation coursed through her. God had something wonderful ahead, she just knew.

A cool bath, fully brushed hair, and fresh clothes did wonders for her morale. The hard tasks of yesterday seemed easier today, something she attributed to her rested condition.

"Need help with the sling?" Jason asked, watching her adjust the blue folds without success as she entered the kitchen.

Lauren tried to move the back knot to one side. "It's making my neck hurt this morning."

"Let's see." Jason lifted the material slightly, examining her neck. "I can see why! The sling's rubbed a sore." She could feel his warm fingers move across the sling and the weight shift to the other side of her neck. "A bandage should fix the problem. Do you have any first aid supplies?" Lauren nodded, explaining their whereabouts, and a moment later Jason returned with the white box.

He gently applied an antiseptic and soft covering. "Better?"

"Much." She threw him a mischievous smile. "You're not only a good security guy, cook, hairstylist, and overall handyman, but you provide nursing care as well. Quite talented, I'd say."

Filling her cup with hot coffee, he motioned for her to sit. "I only need to win the Skipper's title today to make complete the set then, eh?" Lauren could see the amusement behind his serious gaze. He sat opposite her, his left ankle resting on his right knee as he quietly sipped his own coffee. "I spoke with Paul Waggoner earlier this morning."

Lauren's head snapped up to meet his gaze, the movement almost spilling her coffee. "You talked with my boss?" She didn't quite know what to expect from Jason's announcement the night before about taking care of things back in Cincinnati, but she hadn't quite expected this.

"He's a pretty nice guy," Jason answered back, nonplussed. "But you were right. He doesn't seem so inclined to let you go for the summer. I think he wants you back, broken arm and all."

Lauren's heart plunged straight to the floor. "Oh." Hadn't she told herself things weren't as simple as Jason presented? Yet she couldn't deny the disappointment all the same.

"Not to worry," Jason said with a shrug, watching her closely. There was total nonchalance in his voice. "I'm not multitalented for just any reason. This is only round one."

Lauren couldn't be so confident, but she said nothing.

"Hurry up and eat," he teased, "or we'll miss the festival."

The Skipper's Festival was crowded. Hoots and screams of delight filled the air as Jason and Lauren passed through the midway.

"Can't interest you in riding the roller coaster, can I?" he asked, half laughing and pointing to the four-person car swooping down at an alarming rate along the steep rails. He squeezed her fingers in shameless teasing.

"You know very well I'd faint on the first drop." She laughed.

He smiled down at her. "Guess we'll have to stay with tamer activities. How about some midway games?"

Lauren nodded in agreement. Jason seemed different, more carefree. Had he experienced the same release of guilt and emotions she had? This emancipation was so new, she hardly knew how to handle it.

For an hour, Jason dragged Lauren by the hand from booth to booth. Twice he'd won unusable souvenirs by knocking down stacked milk cans and making baskets through small hoops. Finally, he seemed to tire of the games and went in search of the food booths.

"What's your pleasure?" he asked as they surveyed the line of vendors.

Lauren smiled and grabbed his hand, pulling him forward. "It looks like McDuffy's stand is here this year."

"Should have guessed," he laughed, easily following her lead. "You never could resist their corn dogs, eating more than any other girl could ever hope to."

She playfully slapped at his arm. "You love their corn dogs as much as I do, and you know it," she told him, stopping at the open serving window.

Jason only laughed and motioned the woman for two foot-long corn dogs.

"I haven't had one of these in years."

"Then you're due!"

"I'm due for a lot of things after five years," he said, throwing Lauren a meaningful glance. His eyes sparkled, and she found herself holding his gaze.

"Your change, sir," interrupted the woman, handing Jason his money and then two perfectly browned corn dogs.

Jason laced each with a stripe of mustard before happily handing one to Lauren. "Let's sit over there," he instructed, guiding her to an empty bench.

"These are wonderful," Lauren gushed, then took a second bite.

He laughed. "I must say you're right. I'd nearly forgotten."

"Told you so," she cried triumphantly.

Lauren couldn't believe the completeness she felt at Jason's side. Like old times, she assumed her starry-eyed role, but with totally new features and directions. Jason and Lauren were together again. A week ago she wouldn't have believed it possible.

"Come on," Jason urged, snapping her from a state of reverie just as she'd swallowed her last bite. "It's time for me to sign in." He led her to the registration table at the edge of the sandy beach, giving her a contagious smile. "Find me a couple of skipping stones, will you, while I fill out this paperwork?"

"You don't have your stones picked out yet?" she asked incredulously.

"Nope," he answered with a laugh. "Always pick them out just before the contest."

She pulled a face at him. "No wonder you never win."

He only chuckled. "Just find me a lucky stone."

Lauren did as bidden, carefully stooping and scouring the sand with one hand. She examined and discarded several stones.

"Got it!" she announced just as Jason joined her, proudly displaying the perfectly flat rock before him.

Jason scrutinized the stone she laid in his hand and gave her a nod of approval. "This year I'll win for sure," he declared.

"If you say so," Lauren teased. She watched as Jason concentrated on the stone, tumbling it over and over again with his fingers as if memorizing each facet.

The loud squawk of a bullhorn interrupted her thoughts. The skipping competition was about to begin.

"You'll cheer me on, won't you?" he asked.

"Of course. I'm your biggest fan."

He reached over and took her hand, raising it briefly to his lips. "I'm holding you to that."

Lauren could feel herself color. "Just make sure you skip that rock like it's never been skipped before."

Jason let her hand drop after a brief squeeze and mingled with the crowd. Twenty-two contestants drew their lottery and gathered in line. Jason was difficult to miss, even in a crowd, with his blond hair looking almost white in the brilliant sun. He'd evidently drawn next to last, the reigning three-year champion right before him and an unknown behind.

"Nervous?" asked a teasing voice from behind.

Lauren turned to face Larry Newkirk, a smile immediately coming to her lips. It was then she saw his young female companion. "Hello, Larry," she greeted warmly. "And who's this with you?"

The fair-haired woman smiled engagingly as Larry made introductions. He looked at Lauren's arm. "I see you're doing okay."

"Yes," Lauren agreed. "Thanks to you. I never did get a chance to properly tell you how much I appreciated all your help. Who knows what would have. . ." She shuddered to think of it.

The young woman nodded. "Larry's very brave."

Larry only grinned. "All in the line of duty." Then his expression turned solemn. "Jason did tell you; I couldn't find your cross necklace."

Lauren nodded with a sad smile. "I suppose it wasn't meant for me to have after all."

"Ah, don't worry," he encouraged. "It'll turn up again."

"Sure." Yet she knew it wouldn't happen.

Larry and his date soon wandered off, and Lauren immediately turned her attention back to the contest. She watched in anxious anticipation as each competitor stepped up to the line to throw his or her stone, some far, some miserably short. Halfway through, she saw Tilly and waved her over.

"I see Jason's got himself almost dead last," Tilly said cheerfully, her broad, plump face full of smiles. "That'll give the other chaps something to worry about."

Lauren chuckled. "What about the woman contestant?"

"What!" Tilly instantly scrutinized the group, her brows scrunched into wrinkles. "Well, if that don't beat all. That'll be a first." She snorted. "It'll do the boys good to have some real competition for a change."

"Yes, but we're rooting for Jason, remember," Lauren playfully rebuked.

"Of course, girl. Who else!" She eyed Lauren closely. "I take it to mean things are patched."

Lauren nodded, finding it hard to keep from smiling.

"That's the way it should be." Tilly watched the next contestant complete his throw before speaking again. "I saw your Tom off to the ferry this mornin'."

Lauren slowly nodded again, remembering the errand Tilly mentioned in her note. "I appreciate your taking care of him." Although his inevitable departure caused sadness, she'd made the right choice. It was Jason she loved. She'd been in danger of mistaking loneliness for something deeper with Tom. "Did he seem okay?"

"He'll be right as rain soon enough," the older woman assured.

Both women shifted their attention as the reigning champion stepped up to the line. Silence fell among the multitude. Seconds seemed to drag before the stone finally took flight.

"Forty-three skips," announced the record keeper. "New record!"

The crowd broke out in claps of excitement.

Now Jason stepped up to the line in the sand, and Lauren clenched her hands nervously together. A small prayer escaped her lips, immediately followed by a request of forgiveness for such a selfish petition. But it seemed important Jason should win—to win at something—anything.

"Come on, Jason," she whispered.

Tilly didn't say a word.

Jason closed his eyes briefly before rolling the stone carefully in his hand. Then he drew his arm back and threw the rock low and flat. The stone skimmed the water, tapping the surface lightly several times, hovering low, never sinking. Forty-one, forty-two, forty-three—Lauren held her breath—forty-four—forty-five!

The announcer barked over the speakers, "Forty-five! It's another record, folks!"

The crowd went wild, and Jason threw a victorious arm in the air. A knowing smile crossed his lips as his gaze locked with Lauren's for several seconds. Then the trancelike moment broke as he was forced to move on, letting the last contestant forward. She watched the tall, thin man step up to the line. A hush fell over the spectators once again as the man began his windup pitch, snapping the stone hard against the water. The rock went airborne but immediately tumbled perilously on the water's surface, sinking deftly after only ten skips. The crowd exhaled a sympathetic coo for the man, but cheers heartily resumed again when Jason was announced winner.

Lauren nearly choked on her happiness, coming quite close to it as Tilly turned to her, squeezing what little breath she had left in a bear hug.

"It's enough to make an ol' woman cry, it is," she squealed, wiping her wide thumb under her eye.

"Go ahead and have a good cry, Tilly," Lauren laughed with unconcealed enjoyment. "You deserve it! We all do."

She watched as several well-wishers patted Jason on the back as he threaded his way through the crowd to her.

"Congratulations," Lauren yelled excitedly over the roar.

There was great delight in his voice as he hurried forward. "I'm the happiest man in the world, Lauren Wright!" He caught her by surprise as he scooped her up in his arms, planting a kiss firmly on her lips. The crowd hooted.

"Jason!" Her face had to be cherry-red. Had he gone stark-raving mad?

"What?" he shouted happily, giving her a catching smile.

Lauren looked aghast at the mob of watching faces and again at Jason. He was grinning down at her, his gray eyes slightly narrowed. She felt her face being tipped closer as he landed another kiss on her lips.

"Jason Levitte!" she exclaimed.

This brought more hoots and whistles from the onlookers.

Jason leaned close to her ear. "I've never been happier," he announced, the warmth tickling her ear. "And I'll not let you spoil it by ever leaving Bay Island again."

Lauren looked up in confusion. "What?"

"You'll find out soon enough," Jason told her obscurely, his dimple deepening with his widening smile. "I have plans—"

"Come on, Levitte," intruded a voice at the microphone. "Up to the podium."

"Don't go anywhere," Jason instructed before sprinting off to the platform.

Lauren moved her arm in a helpless little gesture. What had Jason meant? What plans? What had come over him?

Tilly only shrugged her shoulders, a silly smile transfixed on her face, evidently pleased beyond belief. "Whatever it is, I'm sure it's worth waiting for."

# Chapter 19

It seemed forever before Jason finished his acceptance speech and joined her again, this time with a trophy under his arm. Tilly had discreetly disappeared.

Lauren suddenly felt anxious. What had he meant about his plans? She would surely die of curiosity if the answer didn't come soon.

Jason lightly grasped her arm, and a smile spread across his face. "Let's go."

"Where to?"

"Your home!"

Distress spread over her. She hadn't quite expected to leave the festival for Piney Point just yet. What was the man up to? But Jason seemed oblivious to her quandary as he led her to the car, their footsteps deadened by the soft grass. He opened the trunk and threw the trophy haphazardly inside, then slammed the lid.

"Jason," she cried. "You'll bust the thing before you even have a chance to display it."

He opened her door. "It's only a trophy."

"Only a trophy!" she scolded as soon as he seated himself behind the wheel. "You've tried for I don't know how many years to win that precious trophy. What's gotten into you?"

"Shush and be still." He laughed, much to her disconcertment.

They traveled in silence as Lauren's mind continued to somersault. "You missed the turn, Jason," she announced when the car veered from the usual route.

"I know," Jason said calmly. "I'm taking you to the house." He turned to look at her. "It's time you knew the truth."

Lauren swallowed hard. Wasn't this what she'd wanted all along—to know the truth about her house? Then why was her heart screaming for him to turn back? Jason edged the car up the long drive and parked neatly in front of the large white garage door. Quickly he hopped out and opened her door.

"This way," Jason instructed, guiding her around to the front porch. Slowly he swung the wide French doors open.

Lauren stepped gingerly inside the great hall, nearly gasping at the beauty she saw. It was exactly as she'd pictured, every mental image coming to life. Even the beautiful cherry woodwork and stately light fixtures were hauntingly familiar. Lauren ran her hand across the shiny banister and a lump formed in her throat.

Jason wouldn't taunt her, would he? Not with her dream house.

"Jason." She nearly choked.

"Shush!" he whispered softly, letting one finger slide gently over her lips. "I want to show you the tower." He led her up the carpeted steps.

The tower door opened into a spaciously windowed room. The breathtaking view drew Lauren to the glass. "It's beautiful!"

"It's yours," Jason said, his voice so low she could barely catch it. "I made this tower, this house—for you." He stood beside her, looking out the large window toward the lighthouse in the distance.

"For me?" she asked, her voice but a bare whisper.

"I began building it after Tara confessed." He turned toward her, taking her hands in his. "When the truth of your innocence came out, I nearly died—from shame, from my stupidity. But then there was hope—hope you might come back, and hope you'd forgive me. I built this house—your house—on that hope."

"And then came Tara's phone call," Lauren finished sadly.

"Yes," Jason concurred, shaking his head. "The infamous phone call."

"But this tower," Lauren began after a moment's silence; "it was never part of the plan."

"No," he agreed. "I added it for me." He pointed toward the lighthouse. "It's to remind me, to keep me from forgetting that God's my lighthouse." His gray eyes deepened. "If I'd kept my eyes on His light to begin with, you would have never been forced to leave Bay Island." Lauren sensed his raw pain. "When Tara made that call to you, it squeezed the last drop of hope from me. I knew then the house was a wasted effort; you were never coming back." He sighed. "But the house was nearly complete, so I finished it. Then everywhere I turned, the house kept reminding me of you, torturing me about what a hardened person I thought you'd become—what I'd made you become." A smile slowly crept over his face. "But God's told me there's a second chance for us."

Lauren drew her brows together in deliberation. "God told you that!"

He smiled again. "I asked God to show me. And He has!"

"How?" she asked warily.

"I asked God for a sign. If you were meant to stay with me, I'd win the tournament." The crooked smile deepened. "And I won! It was a sign."

"You asked God to do that?" Lauren cried, her own smile forming as she suddenly remembered her own little prayer.

"And I wouldn't ask—not ordinarily," Jason conceded. "But there was so little time, and I knew God's hand was in it." He smiled triumphantly. "I've never skipped a stone that far in my life. It had to be God's hand." But Lauren gave him a wary look. "And there's something else."

She drew in a deep breath. "Yes."

Jason reached into his back pocket and produced a white handkerchief.

"I found something that belongs to you." Slowly he unwrapped the creased fold, finally revealing a glittering piece of jewelry.

Her eyes widened. "My necklace! But how—"

"I told you, God's hand was in it." Gently he lifted the delicate chain like an entranced cobra and slipped it around her neck, centering the cross. "It made sense to trace the path the thief took, and sure enough—"

"Where I fell?" She suddenly knew, recalling how Jason had examined the deck that morning.

"Actually," Jason began, "the necklace fell between the deck boards where he collided with you. He must have dropped it in the scuffle." He smiled. "It wasn't easy fishing it out, I can tell you."

"You didn't crawl under the deck, did you?" she asked in horror. "There's poison ivy and snakes. . ." A shiver coursed down her spine.

He laughed easily. "No, I'm not that foolish. I fished it out through the deck boards with a hanger. Not an easy task, but doable."

"Oh, Jason," she murmured. "How can I ever thank you? Losing it again was nearly as unbearable as losing it the first time. Now, it's like a second chance for a second chance."

"And I believe in second chances." He drew his finger reflectively across her cheek. "I can't bear the thought of hurting you again, and I don't want to wreck the life you've finally built for yourself." He seemed to be struggling again. "But I love you, Lauren—I've never stopped, and I can't live my life without you."

Lauren's heart stepped up a beat. "You really love me?"

Immediately Jason embraced her. "Of course I love you!" He looked down at her. "Is that so hard to believe?"

"Not anymore. It seems so real right now."

"I plan to spend my life convincing you just how real it is." Jason clasped her chin and drew her face close. Their lips met. "Now what do you say?"

Lauren smiled stupidly. "I say you need a shave, Jason Levitte."

Jason rubbed his jaw. "I already know that." He smirked. "What I want to know is what you think about us." His gaze held hers. "Is there an us?"

"Your methods of finding God's assurance and blessing for us is shaky—at best," Lauren teased. "But I do still love you, and I do believe in second chances, too. And you know what?"

"What?" he whispered.

Lauren looked up, smiling. "Since my boss won't let me have temporary time off, I'll just have to make it a permanent time off. Know of anyone looking for an accountant?"

He grinned. "Let me check around. I'm sure there's a suitable employer for you somewhere on the island." Drawing her close, he whispered, "You will stay, won't you?"

Lauren nodded. "I must warn you, though. God's not through with me. I still have a lot to work though—forgiving Tara, forgiving the church—"

"You're not alone," Jason replied, pulling her nearer still. "This time we'll work through the problems together, including my work schedule. We'll set the priorities straight—God first, then us—then work."

"Sounds good so far." Lauren nestled closer.

"Do you want to see the rest of your house, then?" He pulled her back just enough to see her face clearly.

"You mean our house, don't you?" she teased.

"Not just yet it isn't," Jason replied seriously. "But I plan to win your heart back, lock, stock, and barrel. And when you finally say 'I do,' then it'll be our house."

"If you insist," Lauren razzed.

Jason answered her with a kiss. "I insist."

# Epilogue

It seemed only fitting for the sun to splash its color and consequently spill criss-cross shadows through the trellis and into the gazebo. Lauren's beautiful gown seemed to reflect the light and illuminated the space with brightness. There was a chill in the spring air, but she didn't mind a bit—not today. Today was her day. Jason's day.

Jason smiled down at her, squeezing her hand. She detected his excitement as they turned to the waiting crowd. Loud applause greeted them.

"Was it worth the wait, Mr. Levitte?" Lauren teased.

"It's the hardest winter I've ever endured on this island," he whispered back with a mischievous grin. "But I would have waited longer if necessary. You know that don't you, Mrs. Levitte?"

Lauren shrugged. "Possibly. But I don't think I couldn't have waited a moment longer."

"Thought so," he mocked with a smug grin.

"Oh?" she laughed, her eyebrows rising in challenge. She twisted the gold band around her finger. "I could give it back."

"That, my dear wife, you will never do." Much to the delight of the crowd, he kissed her soundly. He pulled back slightly, turning his gaze to the house, the crowd, and then her, bringing his lips close to her ear. "You belong here now—with me and your own special made-to-order house."

Lauren smiled knowingly. "Our house!"

"Our house," he repeated in agreement. He brought her close and drew a deep contented sigh. "Welcome home, Lauren. Welcome home!"

# Thunder Bay

# Dedication

My husband, Ellis, and children, Jessica and Erica, are my greatest assets. Thanks for being patient while I tapped away at the computer and drifted off to Thunder Bay for long periods of time.

If there were an honor badge for courage and dedication after having a stroke, my father should be awarded such a medal. You have taught me to forge triumphantly on when life gets tough and God allows the pressure cooker to heat up. This book is for you!

A special thanks to my good friend John Pierce. I could never have made it without your endless and talented hours of editing. You stuck by me, knowing I'd never in a million years understand the meaning of a dangling modifier.

For Becky Rickard who is a great encourager and editor who can find those pesky mistakes plaguing all writers. God knew what He was doing when He reunited two old friends last year at Christian camp.

Thanks to Bill Crothers for giving his great expertise on water heaters.

To my good friend Becky Nelson for having the knack for finding errors only seasoned readers would see. She's done a great service for those of you bugged by story inconsistencies.

Appreciation goes to Columbus police officer and friend Charlie Sutherland for sharing his knowledge of law enforcement to make this book authentic.

# Prologue

*Move now! There's no time!*

Becky Merrill pulled frantically against the force of the heavy-handed American consulate aide as he gripped her arm tighter.

"Just one more minute!" she pleaded, not daring to take her eyes from those gathered in the room.

The man grunted a negative and proved the point by hustling her through the crudely made doorway into the night. Her luggage bag, clenched tightly in her sweaty free hand, skipped hard across the dirt, the wheels barely touching.

She resisted once more. "I only want to say good-bye—"

"There's real danger, miss." The strong, middle-aged guard paused long enough to fasten his bright blue eyes on her with an accusing light. "I don't particularly want to engage in battle with these commandos, and if you had any sense, you wouldn't either."

"But why the Americans?" she asked in desperation. "We're here to help!"

As soon as the words were out she knew the question to be inane. Hadn't she heard anti-American rumblings at the marketplace just last week? But the people! Her work! How could she leave?

She twisted painfully to see behind as anxious black faces stared back with outstretched arms. Her long black hair pulled across the guard's arm. She hadn't even had time to ponytail the mess in the midnight raid. Tears trickled hot against her cheeks. The heartache of the raw farewell forcing her to leave the Congolese women she'd come to serve threatened to overwhelm her.

They stopped at the army-green jeep, and she took the opportunity to appeal again. "When will it be safe? When can I return?"

She had to wait until her bag was thrown haphazardly into the windowless opening in the back of the jeep before the reply came. The guard turned back to her in a show of tight patience. "You're going to Germany tonight where you and other Americans will be sequestered before flying back to the States. Don't hold your hopes out," he warned. "It could be next month—it could be never!"

The answer seared like a hot poker to her chest. Was it possible she might never return? How could it be? God had placed her in the Congo. Of this she was sure. How could she abandon her post?

All thoughts were rudely interrupted as her five-foot frame was hoisted unceremoniously into the front passenger seat.

"Get in the back," the man commanded before shutting the heavy door. "And keep down."

With resignation Becky crawled to the back, her leg scraping hard against an unseen object. Blood trickled untended down her thigh as she propped herself on both knees to look out the back. The lump in her throat threatened to choke her. These people needed her.

"That's it!" yelled another guard as he hopped in the seat she'd just vacated. "Let's go!"

The jeep came to life, and the sound of worn, coarsely grinding gears tore through the night.

The driver heaved an audible and impatient sigh. "Will you get her down?" he ordered the other. "We're not in the clear by any means."

Becky felt a gentle hand tug on her shoulder.

"You won't do those people any good if you get yourself shot," the passenger guard reasoned. "Curl up in the seat and keep your head down."

His gentle tone drew a nod as she complied. He was right. She must protect herself for the Congolese people, to be ready to return.

But for now the missionary must go home to the States. Just the thought drew another weight onto her already heavy heart. She had no choice. She'd return to the last place she called home—Bay Island!

# Chapter 1

Becky Merrill watched the dangling keys drop into her hand.

"Are you absolutely sure?" Becky asked, her left eyebrow arched in question.

"Absolutely!" Lauren Levitte answered. "I'm finally off on my honeymoon in two days. And I don't need the cabin when I return, do I? You can even use my car for as long as you need it."

Becky relaxed under Lauren's smile. "I'm sorry your honeymoon was delayed by a week, but I'm sure glad you were available when I needed you."

"And I'm happy I was here for you." Lauren gave a genuine smile. "I was disappointed, of course, by the hotel mix-up, but God always knows best and I'm learning to live within His plan instead of mine."

"It's a lesson we're all learning," Becky responded. "He's been so good to work out the details so fast and make Piney Point available at just the right time." She gave a contented sigh. "What a beautiful place to come back to." Both women turned to look at the four-room cabin surrounded by majestic pine trees. The cool spring breeze coming off the lake stirred the heavy branches. Bay Island was once again in blossom after a cold, hard winter. The promise of spring and wedding happiness washed over the inhabitants.

"It seems too good to be true." Becky fingered the warm keys in one hand and straightened the straw hat on her head with the other. "When they rushed me out of the Congo without notice, I literally had no place to go. Bay Island is the only home I've known for two years."

"Bay Island has been a refuge to many," Lauren replied, casting Becky a mischievous look as she held up her wedding ring as proof.

Becky found herself smiling at the other woman's radiance. The islanders had almost given up hope for Jason Levitte and Lauren, the now happy newlyweds, until Lauren's return last year. Maybe hope would resurrect itself for her, too.

It wasn't just being ousted from the mission field. She was truly and totally alone, ostracized by her family and forgotten by her childhood friends. Suffering from a dysfunctional family might be a newer term, but it was old hat to Becky. Her parents were well-to-do and revered in public. Life changed, however, when the front door closed.

Becky was their one embarrassment. She couldn't muster the grades for the Ivy League school or present the polished grace they demanded. Finding God at a community college only widened the chasm. When she announced her decision to enter missions, they called her everything but a drug-smoking hippie. In their minds she'd entered the cult world. A right-wing Jesus freak, they had said.

Although never spoken aloud, Becky knew she was no longer worthy to be called a Merrill. Rejected, she replied to a job advertisement and traveled far from California to a small island on Lake Erie. Genuinely on her own for the first time, circumstances had cultivated her faith and prepared her for the mission field. There was Michael Petit, though, to consider.

She thought about Michael, still peeved at his behavior at the airport two years ago.

"Come on, Beck," he'd pleaded, planting both hands deep within the pockets of his finely tailored pants. "Why run halfway across the country to work in a sweaty office?"

"It's not a sweaty office," exclaimed Becky indignantly. "Jason Levitte is a reputable architect, and I'm a proficient bookkeeper."

"But it's all unnecessary," he argued, his right hand suddenly grasping hers. "Your father will come to his senses soon. You just have to know how to work him. Religion is good in small doses. It's only that you need to stop being such a fanatic about the whole thing."

Becky felt her mouth drop. Would no one side with her? Michael had been her soul mate at the private high school they'd attended. He was good-looking, wealthy, and amusing. He'd made an immediate hit with her parents. Yes, he was made of the right stuff, they told her.

Their college courtship met with her parents' approval, but finding God changed everything. From that time she could feel the added weight of the chains being woven around her. It became evident she must either break free or succumb to their relentless pressure to become what they wanted. She knew God wanted her life totally, not the Merrill leftovers.

"I'll talk with your father," Michael finally said in exasperation. "He's not against religion. Really he's not." Becky watched him roll his tongue thoughtfully around his front teeth and move it away with a smacking sound before he continued. "Maybe you should be a tad bit more delicate in how you come across with your religious beliefs, that's all."

"If that's all there is to it, then why are you so nervous?"

He shook his head. "Not nervous, just concerned."

"Nervous!" she announced. "I've known you long enough to catch every nervous habit you have, and tongue clucking is one of them."

He had the decency to look surprised. "If I do have a nervous habit it's from distress, not nervousness."

"Over my leaving, of course."

"Of course!"

"Then why didn't you stand up for me in front of Father if you were so distressed?" she murmured, steadily meeting his gray eyes. The question seemed fair enough.

Giving her a searching stare, he patted her arm in an almost clumsy gesture. "You know as well as anyone, your father has to be handled with kid gloves. He can be won over, but not with the hit-and-run approach."

"It was hardly hit-and-run, Michael." Becky swallowed the ache in her throat. "What you really mean is that you think I should cater to Father and let him think the matter is dropped—a sort of out-of-sight, out-of-mind approach." She felt a fresh pang of grief. "Then I'm supposed to let him think I'm on a year-long trip to France when I'm actually in the Congo doing missionary work. Isn't that how we've always handled my father, with deception and lies?"

Michael flushed. "Your father necessitates a little creative handling."

"Amen to that!" Becky replied. "But I refuse to make Father happy with lies anymore. He may not be pleased with my choice to be a missionary or my decision to leave California, but at least he knows the truth. When it comes to pleasing God or my father, I have to choose God."

Michael seemed resigned to lose the argument and raised both hands in surrender. "What about us? How are we going to handle living on two different coasts?"

A pent-up sigh escaped her lips. "I don't know."

"Just don't board that plane," he whispered ardently, drawing her into his arms. "I'm afraid of what will become of you."

"Could it be anything worse than what I've endured at home?" she asked softly.

He pulled her back slightly, giving her one of his sweeping looks from head to toe she found disconcerting. "Don't be like that. You'll wrinkle your beautiful skin scowling at me so hard."

Beautiful. Yes, she did have beauty. Her long raven-black hair was the envy of many, and her porcelain skin shimmered like flawless glass. It was hard not to be noticed with the flowing grace that a ten-year commitment to ballet had brought. She often wondered why Michael and her family noticed only the outside appearance and couldn't see the beauty within, the beauty they were crushing with every verbal blow they heaped upon her.

"Michael," Becky said with a sigh, "I'm leaving on the plane. I will work as a lowly bookkeeper for a year until the mission board has my financial support in order. I will be going to the mission field." Her dark eyes considered him again. "Can't you understand my need to do what God wants?"

"No, I don't understand," Michael replied decisively, suddenly willing to take up the battle once again. His arms dropped from her. "How can you know for sure God wants you overseas? Tell me that! Maybe God wants you to stay home and perform your honor-thy-parents duties." His brow smoothed. "I could even pull some strings and get you a job at the church in Turnstile. With five thousand members they'd pay what you're worth. What could be godlier than working in a church—right here in California?"

Becky shook her head in resignation. An unbeliever wouldn't understand. "You've been a good friend to me. I know you don't comprehend, but I'd hoped you'd give me your blessing." Her throat grew dry. "I need your support."

Michael's silence gave his answer. Yet another rejection.

"Flight 157 to Cleveland is now boarding at Gate 12."

Becky shifted to move, but Michael grasped tightly onto her hand.

"Don't go," he begged. "Please."

She knew the plea was hard for him. He'd never pleaded for anything.

"I'm going to be late." She turned away, letting his hand drop heavily to his side. "I'm sorry."

For palpitating moments they measured glances before she quickly walked toward security screening. She recalled her feelings of sheer relief when the plane finally reached for the skies and Bay Island waited with a new life. It seemed like ages ago.

"Hey." Lauren laughed, waving her hand before Becky's eyes. "Are you going to daydream all day or let me help you with the luggage?"

"It seems like only yesterday when I came to the island for the first time," Becky replied with a smile, shaking off her memories. It did little good reliving the past. Michael had kept in touch for only six months. No doubt he'd forgotten her by now. It was time to focus on the future.

Lauren must have sensed her mixed sadness and gave her a light hug. "It's good to have you home."

Becky thanked her and moved to open the trunk of the rental car. The lid slid open noiselessly. One bare bag lay in the compartment.

"That's it?" Lauren asked softly, shifting her eyes back to her.

Becky flushed. "That's all they let me escape with."

Lauren quickly recovered. "No problem. You can share my clothes." Her gaze hurriedly assessed Becky's petite five-foot figure. She tapped her finger across her lips. "Then again maybe we'd better go shopping at Levitte's Landing."

Shopping! Yes, indeed, it was good to be back.

Becky jerked herself up on the bed, her elbows sinking into the comforter. What was that sound? Her skin prickled at the possibilities. The red glow of the night-stand clock read 2:15. It was her second night in the cabin. Jason and Lauren would now be enjoying a gorgeous view of Niagara Falls from their honeymoon suite.

Slowly Becky shoved the smooth covers aside and let her feet sink quietly to the floor. The soft hem of her gown encircled her ankles. She shivered after the warmth of the bed. A small stream of light from outside sprayed a glow across the floor.

Her ears strained to hear the sound of the watery hiss. Several knocking thumps interrupted. Becky moved her feet forward to the hallway where the sounds grew louder. She peeked around the corner into the dark and empty hallway. No one would call her a weak female when it came to nighttime sights and sounds, and she'd hardened even further on the mission field; yet she felt a small sensation of alarm at that very moment.

*Shish! Ping, pang, pong.*

The cool hardwood floors in the hall creaked slightly under her weight. Her hand skimmed the painted walls to steady her tense body as her head cocked toward the contained clatter. At the kitchen she stopped and felt for the light switch. With one flick the room was bathed in light. Trickling water-like pings continued uninterrupted from beyond the kitchen and into the unlit utility room.

Becky took a steadying deep breath before crossing the cool linoleum floor of the kitchen. Her hand paused momentarily over the knife block before moving on. No, a knife was never good protection when an intruder could easily turn it upon his victim. Past the refrigerator, she stopped again to listen. It was a definite watery sound.

She crept forward. Warm wetness greeted her bare feet before she reached the utility room. Startled, she stepped back. *Water! Plenty of it!* Gathering her senses, she tiptoed forward warily across the wetness to find the light switch of the room. To her relief the water didn't appear to be getting deeper as she paused long enough to feel the walls. *On the right or left?* Nothing but smoothness greeted her hand. As her eyes adjusted slowly to the room's darkness, she saw the white string hanging from the bare bulb.

*Click!*

Light flooded the room.

Becky drew in a breath at the sight. The forty-gallon water heater hissed and spit water from its base across the floor. The thirsty drain in the center of the small room slurped the clear fluid.

Mildly inclined toward mechanics, Becky could be handy in the house—much to her father's chagrin. Yet she had never dealt with water heaters. She eyed the white monster, letting her gaze drop to the control knob. Bent over to see the markings, she snapped the gray knob to the off position. Still the water hissed across the floor.

Water pipes. There had to be a shutoff for the supply pipe somewhere. Becky gazed up and tilted her eyebrow. She traced the pipes coming and going before finally finding the shutoff lever. Her hand trembled slightly as she reached up toward the lever.

"Four inches short," she snorted aloud in disgust. "I'm always four inches too short."

A glance about the room yielded a yellow ten-gallon bucket, which instantly became the perfect perch when turned upside down. The lever yielded to her touch. Water splattered across her feet as she stepped down. In silence she watched. It took nearly ten minutes before the guzzling water burps slowed to a stop.

Twenty minutes later Becky propped the mop against the wall. Although the floor still gleamed with wetness, it would dry soon enough. In the morning she'd call neighbor Tilly Storm and see about a new water heater. If anyone knew what to do, it would be Tilly. For now, she planned to plop herself, prune-like feet and all, back into bed.

Larry Newkirk rapped on the wooden screen door and waited. His cleanly pressed police uniform felt stiff this morning as he looped one finger inside the collar to give it a stretch. His hand rested over his black gun holster, and the leather creaked with familiarity when he shifted his weight.

"Yes?" A raven-haired beauty suddenly peered at him from the other side of the screen door.

Larry took off his police hat and tucked it under his arm. "Tilly called and said you might need some assistance." He watched her closely, remembering the bookkeeper now. It had been awhile, and she hadn't been an islander long before leaving last year. "I believe she said you had a water heater mishap in the night."

There was a small intake of air before she answered. "She sent the police?"

# Chapter 2

Larry Newkirk had to smile at the woman. The screen cast odd shadows across her face, but he could tell she was beautiful. Tresses of shimmery long black hair encircled her face and the surprised look planted upon it.

"Tilly didn't exactly send the police." Larry chuckled, his head tilting her way. He could feel the sun bouncing off his blond, military-style crew cut. "Besides being a police officer I'm an island handyman of sorts for the church folks." His eyes twinkled. "And when Tilly says jump, I jump."

The woman laughed in return, and a shy smile blossomed. "Please come in." She pushed the door open. "I'm Becky Merrill." She offered her hand.

"Larry Newkirk," he returned, taking her hand. He stepped over the threshold, letting the screen door close behind with a soft bump. "We attended the same church some time ago, but I don't think we were ever properly introduced."

Once again her smile seemed to light the room. "My schedule was busy during that time. It seemed as if I was visiting one of my supporting churches on the mainland nearly every weekend. I'm sure I know several folks by sight but never met them."

"Tilly said you're a missionary to the Congo."

Her smile faded slightly. "Political unrest made it necessary for me to leave. It's just for a little while." She swiveled her look away from him and nodded her head toward the kitchen. "Coffee?"

"No, thanks." Larry sensed the change in subject. "It'll only take a few minutes to look at the water heater. From Tilly's description it sounds like you'll be needing a new one."

Becky instantly motioned him to the utility room. "It's dry now," she explained, "but the tank was spewing water halfway across the floor in the middle of the night. I'm thankful the room has a drain."

He followed, laying his hat on the dining room table as they passed. "The liner might have split," he offered. "It's a good thing you woke up."

When they reached the utility room, Larry bent on one knee and felt under the tank. Wetness greeted his touch. The gray thermostat cover slid off, and he peeked inside with the penlight he pulled from a black holder attached to his belt. Slowly he pushed himself up. "You'll need a new water heater," he told her matter-of-factly.

A worried expression creased her face. "Lauren's on her honeymoon, and

I don't exactly have enough cash at the moment to pay for a new water heater."

The woman's air of vulnerability gave his gut a strange twinge. He was much too sensitive for his own good, he knew. "I think we can find a way to replace the tank now and settle with Lauren later." Withdrawing a small notepad from his shirt pocket, he penned several specifics from the tank label. "Harvey's Hardware might have a tank in stock. If not, we'll get one from the mainland by tomorrow."

Becky's expression looked hopeful. "You'll be able to install the new water tank by tomorrow?"

"By tonight if Harvey comes through," he assured her. He had to smile at the look of sheer delight crossing her fair features. She looked ready to burst. Maybe she'd kiss him right on the lips as Mitzi Trammell did when he unclogged her bathroom sink. Being a hero did have its benefits. Although he knew he didn't need any new complications in the world of relationships. His pride still felt the sting of losing Lauren to Jason last year. Well, he didn't really lose Lauren; he'd never had her in the first place. It was all a dream on his part. But still. . .his love life never quite achieved the serious level he'd envisioned.

Larry snapped the notebook shut and stuffed it back into his shirt pocket. "I'll call you by three this afternoon to let you know."

She followed him from the room. "You're an angel sent from heaven."

"Hardly." He laughed pleasantly, taking his police hat from the table. Once again he tucked it under his arm. He stopped and turned when he felt her light touch on his arm.

"It's true," she said with such seriousness. "You can't imagine how God keeps taking care of every difficult detail." Her eyes twinkled. "God's given you special talents. I can feel it. You've probably saved as many people as a handyman as you have by being a police officer."

Larry could feel the heat of embarrassment creep up his neck, but he gave a lopsided grin in response. "I'd hold off judgment until you have hot water again."

"Oh, I have faith," she declared, looking him squarely in the eyes. Her wide eyes opened wider still. "I'm what you call a dreamer. If it can be done, there's always a way. Do you have faith in what God can do through you?"

Silence reigned for a moment, and when he did speak his voice dropped low. "I have a down-to-earth kind of faith," he answered. He didn't want to begin a discussion on the virtues of reality. Let the young lady hang on to her dreams. Most dreams crumble soon enough. This much he knew in his line of business. "I'll give you a call."

She thanked him profusely as he walked out the door and down the wooden steps to his white cruiser. He gave a quick wave of his hand before nudging the car forward.

"Don't get any ideas, Newkirk," he said aloud. "Most women are trouble, and that woman is no exception."

"He's absolutely wonderful," Becky announced to Tilly Storm that afternoon during a visit to her cabin. "He thinks he might even have the new water tank in by tonight."

Tilly gave a hearty laugh, her ample-sized bosom heaving with each chuckle. "So you fell for his charm. Most gals do." She poured more iced tea for Becky. "Larry's one of the finest officers we have on the island. A real gentleman, too."

"I'm not interested in that way," Becky volleyed, holding up both hands in defense. "There's no place in my life for men. I'll be back in the Congo before long."

"Maybe," Tilly said noncommittally. "It never hurts to keep your options open. Why, you can't let yourself mope around Lauren's cabin and do nothing. You never know when a handsome man at your side might come in handy."

Becky glanced at Tilly warily. Tilly was well-known for her matchmaking schemes, and her success rate seemed astounding. "I'll find plenty to keep me busy. There's no room for moping either."

"Glad to hear it," Tilly responded, using even strokes of the knife with her beefy hands to cut the freshly baked bread. Slice after slice fell in perfect order. "I just might have a proposition to keep you busy."

Instantly alert, Becky experienced an odd moment of apprehension. "Am I about to get shanghaied?"

"Absolutely not!" Tilly looked shocked, but Becky didn't miss the devious smile she tried to hide. "Aren't you at all interested in knowing what the proposition might be?"

"Do I have a choice?" she said with a laugh. "What's this plan you've cooked up?"

The motherly woman sat down and served Becky a slice of bread before placing a slice on her own plate. She buttered her piece. She seemed in no hurry, and several seconds passed before she let her gaze fall on Becky. "The church is lookin' to start a Christian camp here on the island. They need a strong leader, a director who can devote some serious time to the project. I think you're that person."

Becky took a sip of her iced tea, listening. "What kind of Christian camp?"

"The camp would be mostly for kids in the summer and a mix of ages for retreats during the fall and spring," Tilly answered. She lifted her slice of bread and pointed toward the window. "Once the lake freezes, though, the camp would be shut down for the season."

How well Becky knew what a harsh winter meant to the island. "So it would be run like most camps where one group of kids stays a week with a speaker and a program? The next week might be the same with a different age group?"

"Yep," Tilly said with a nod. "The camp committee has more details, but you've got the basic gist of things."

"Where do they propose to build the camp?"

"They're lookin' at Thunder Bay."

Becky tilted her head in surprise. "The old Union landmark site?"

"The very one."

Intrigued, Becky asked, "Can you build on a landmark?"

"There're over fifty acres," Tilly explained. "We only need twenty-five to do the job. It's convincing Kelly Enterprises that it can be done without disturbing any delicate historical value."

"Tell me about it."

Tilly seemed pleased with Becky's interest and set the butter-smeared knife across her plate with a clank. "The church has wanted to build a camp for as many years as I can remember. They had their sights set on Frank Ludlow's north shore property, but he sold it to a developer for thousands more than the church could give."

"North Shore's condominiums?"

"Yep," Tilly answered, her lips pursed in disapproval. "Nothin' we could do once city council approved the zonin'. Oh, Ludlow was right sorry after all was said and done. They've ruined the north shore, tramplin' the place with all their litter and whatnot. And they've not held up their end of the bargain with noise curfews." She gave a snort of disgust. "But that's all water over the bridge now. Church folks thought the camp idea was doomed until Jason started lookin' into Thunder Bay. Most of the land is unused. He thinks it can be done."

"He's talked with the owner?" Becky could feel an unexplained excitement grow within. The idea of a Christian camp on the island was perfect. Even if she could only give a few weeks to the project, it would give her purpose.

Tilly nodded her peppery-colored head. "Kelly Enterprises told him it couldn't be done without disturbing the landmark. But Jason's right smart. He's drawin' a plan to show how it can be done. We're hopin' it will do the trick."

Becky took a bite of the warm German bread. "How do you think I can be of help?"

"I knew you'd come on board." Tilly nearly yelped with joy.

"Whoa," Becky chirped. "There are several things to consider. First I have to talk with the mission board about my financial support. They have to be in agreement. It's possible the churches might decide to cut my support if I find another so-called job. They might think I'm not planning to return to the Congo."

Surprise overtook Tilly's face. "It's none of your doin'. You'll be doing missionary work of a different sort, that's all."

Becky smiled at how easily Tilly moved problems into neat boxes of logic.

Too bad logic didn't rule everywhere. "It may be a form of missionary work, but it's not the work the supporting churches sent me to do. But don't fret." She laid a hand on Tilly's. "I'm interested in finding out more about this camp. If God opens the door, I'll walk through it."

A knowing look came over Tilly. "It's a done deal. Trust me."

The decisive thud of a truck door brought Becky to the wooden screen door. Larry Newkirk was already unstrapping a large cardboard box from the bed of his red pickup. She watched unobserved as he made quick work of the strong twine.

He was handsome in his own right. Maybe twenty-six or twenty-seven. She guessed him to be at least six feet tall, and his super-short blond hair gleamed against the sun. He looked quite different in straight-legged jeans and a blue T-shirt; yet she sensed he was at home in work clothes as well as a uniform. When he'd phoned earlier, his deep voice could have melted butter. It was easy to see why Tilly was eager to matchmake with the man, but it was ludicrous to think Becky would fit the bill.

What could she offer a man at this point in her life? At best, her plans were short-term. And what man would stick around once he'd met her family? She couldn't ignore the unruly clan forever. One visit with her parents and any sane man would turn tail and run. Only Michael seemed immune. What good was that?

"Hello!"

Becky focused her attention back to Larry, who now stood at the bottom of the wooden porch steps. She stepped outside the door and smiled. "I'm certainly glad Harvey came through with a new water heater."

"Your dreaming must have paid off this time around," he said with a returning smile. He motioned directly behind him to the large box strapped to a silver dolly. "It was the last one in stock."

Her tennis shoes thudded softly across the wooden boards as she moved to the edge of the landing. "That's wonderful. I have to tell you again how grateful I am you're doing this."

He seemed to watch her closely. "That's why they call me Handy."

"Who does?" Her eyebrow lifted fractionally.

"All the women, of course," he laughed. "Haven't you ever heard the saying that if women can't find a man handsome, they should at least find him handy?"

Becky smirked. She wasn't about to tell him he was both.

He only laughed at her expression and grabbed the red rubber handles of the dolly. "Get the door—would you, please?"

Becky obeyed, standing back to clear the entrance. The large, awkward box caused the dolly to slap loudly against each step as he pulled the heavy tank backward with even timing. With certainty he rolled the box through the door. Becky followed him to the kitchen where he let the dolly come to rest.

She watched him enter the utility room. He made his way to the corner. The rhythmic squeal of the old valve let her know he'd found the main water shutoff. Suddenly he reappeared.

"Let me grab my tool bag, and I'll be right back."

Becky only nodded and waited patiently. He reappeared a moment later with a small but heavy duffle bag. Without fanfare he dropped the bag on the floor. The zipper gave way with a loud groan as he split the bag open. Several tools were placed in order on the hardwood floor.

Larry stopped rummaging and looked up. "I brought some old towels. Would you mind getting them from the backseat of the truck?"

"Sure," Becky answered, glad to be of help. "Be right back."

Gravel crunched under her feet, and a light wind seemed to sprinkle the air with the scent of pine. Becky took an appreciative breath. In many ways she was glad to experience the familiar smells and sounds of home. The Congo was so different. She had come to appreciate the smallest of things she'd taken for granted before—running water, flush toilets, and even carpeting. One month on the mission field and she'd realized how rich her American home truly was. Excess! After managing on so little, the endless amenities she now experienced seemed like excess.

Becky opened the driver's door to Larry's truck. The four-by-four rested high above the ground, causing her to stretch to reach the loose towels on the backseat. The inside of the truck was as she'd imagined. The leather seats were creased from comfortable use, but not worn. A light spicy aroma enveloped the interior. A pair of work boots lay neatly on the mat behind the passenger seat. His police hat sat positioned on the backseat as if placed with care. The gray carpet was clean except for small pebbles of rock and dirt on the driver's mat. Somehow she found the scene calming. This man was methodical and in control.

She gathered the worn towels and held them close. Even these frayed and tatty towels would be a luxury in the Congo. God had blessed her so much throughout her life, and she'd never realized what privileges He'd given her. She'd made a pledge never to forget God's wonderful gifts. Now God had provided a Christian man to fix the water heater. The thought nearly brought tears. Even in her fierce fight for independence, it felt so very good to be on the receiving end of someone else's care. This sudden realization brought both joy and emotional turmoil. How she longed for those in her village to experience such care. A poignant tiredness enveloped her.

"Is something wrong?"

Larry stood less than ten feet from her. She'd been too engrossed in her thoughts to notice his approach. She could feel a warm tide surge into her face.

"I'm sorry," she apologized with a grimace. "You've caught me daydreaming." Once again she hugged the towels close and firmly shut the door of the truck.

He looked unconvinced and inched closer. "From the expression on your face I'd say it's more than daydreaming. Are you missing your friends in the Congo?"

Becky locked her gaze to his. "Am I that obvious?"

"What's wrong with that?" he said with a shrug of understanding. "From what Tilly tells me, in the past week you've not only been forced to leave the people you've come to care a great deal about, but there've been long flights, layovers, and delays." His gaze stayed with her. "Not to mention a lack of sleep last night from an ornery water heater."

She laughed suddenly, caught up in the absurdity of the moment. The man was absolutely right. "You're not only a policeman and handyman, but an observant counselor as well."

"Oh, please," he answered with mocking chagrin. "Don't start that rumor, or they'll have me working overtime trying to rehabilitate criminals. I can hardly keep up with catching the offenders and scheduling all my handyman jobs."

A smile lit her face. "I promise not to tell."

"Good!" He held out his hand for the towels. "We'd better get back to work if you want hot water sometime today."

Becky gave him the towels. She noticed the roughness of his callused hands and sensed these hands also knew how to be soft. Her lips pursed together in consternation. She had no business with those thoughts. God had sent the man to do a plumbing job, nothing else.

"Ready?" Larry asked, waiting patiently at the foot of the stairs. He directed her toward the steps.

"Ready as I'll ever be," she countered, taking the lead. *But not ready enough!*

# Chapter 3

"That looks mighty fine, it does," said Tilly as she gave the new water heater the once-over. She planted her hand on the doorjamb and leaned back enough to be heard in the kitchen. "What did I tell you about Larry? He does good work."

Becky glanced at Tilly again and pulled two dry plates from the dish drainer. "It's incredible how quickly he disconnected and reconnected everything. The man's amazing."

Tilly smiled at her. "He's a good man, Becky Merrill. They don't make too many like that one."

"He's certainly efficient." Becky opened the cupboard and slid the plates into place on the stack.

"Efficient!" Tilly harrumphed. "Is that all you can say?"

Becky smiled and let the cupboard door close softly. "Handy, too."

Tilly gave a *tsk*. "You'll be findin' out soon enough just how much you'll be needin' his handiness."

"What's that supposed to mean?" Becky narrowed her eyes.

"It means you'll be needin' him to help with the camp project," Tilly explained. "You do realize how much his expertise will be needed?"

Becky wagged her finger in Tilly's direction. "First of all, Larry seems to be a man with enough irons in the fire. He might not have time to help. Second, I haven't given an official okay to directing the project. And third," she went on, "actual building of the camp may be months away. And. . .the committee will have to agree to your assessment that I can do the job. The meeting is tomorrow night, right?"

"That's nothin'." Tilly waved off her protest. "I'm bettin' on you. Not that I'm a bettin' woman, mind you. It's just that you're perfect for the job—and available."

"I've agreed to talk with the committee, but I'm not promising anything," warned Becky. "Besides, there would be several people needed to help, and as I said, Larry may not be interested."

"Oh, I think he'll be interested," said Tilly with a casual nod. "Didn't I tell you Larry's the head trustee of the camp committee?"

A long pause ensued. "No," Becky finally murmured with constrained patience. She shifted her weight to the other foot as she reached across the counter for another dish in the drainer. "I believe you left out that one important detail."

Tilly's lips curved into a smile. "I'm sure I mentioned it earlier. Matter of fact, I called Larry before coming over tonight—you know, just to see if he'd gotten around to your water heater." Her innocent look deserved an award. "I told him you were interested in helping with the camp project. He seemed very excited."

"I'm sure he was," Becky noted with doubt. "What else did he say?"

"Oh, that's all. I told him how much you looked forward to working with him." She held out her hands in a helpful gesture. "Then again I thought you already knew he was chairman."

Becky pulled herself together with an effort and managed a smile. She wondered how she could remain so calm. So far, Tilly had arranged everything from the water heater repair to the camp committee in an effort to push Larry her way. Becky hadn't even been on the island more than a few days. If she didn't know better, she'd suspect Tilly of sabotaging the water tank to set the events in motion.

"I told him to give you a call," Tilly went on. "It would be a good idea for Larry to take you over to Thunder Bay to see the place. That should give you a better feel for the project."

Becky eyed her calmly. "And what did he say to that?"

"He'll call you, of course."

"Of course!" Becky moistened her dry lips. What good would a protest do? Tilly had a one-track mind, and Larry knew Tilly as well as anyone. He probably had a good inkling of the situation.

"I'd better skedaddle. He'll probably call anytime." The woman donned her jacket and rubbed both large hands together with a finishing touch before producing a flashlight from her pocket. She stepped out the door and turned. "Lock the door, you hear?"

Before Becky could oblige, the shrill ring of the telephone interrupted.

"Go on now," Tilly instructed. "Lock up quickly and answer the phone." She ambled off, but not before Becky saw a satisfied smile erupt across Tilly's lips.

Becky smirked and firmly shut and locked the door before making her way to the phone.

"Becky?" began the familiar low rumble of a male's voice as soon as she lifted the receiver. "This is Larry Newkirk."

"Good evening," Becky began, feeling more than a little awkward. She took a steadying breath. "Tilly told me you'd be calling."

"Yes." He cleared his throat. "I think it was more of an order."

Becky flinched. Yes, Tilly had done it now.

"Seems she wants us to discuss the Christian camp," Larry went on. "I must say she had me puzzled about your interest in helping with the camp since you didn't mention it earlier this afternoon."

"It must seem confusing, but Tilly just let me know about your involvement with the camp committee."

He chuckled. "No explanation needed. Where Tilly's concerned, there's more going on than either of us knows."

Relieved, Becky let a laugh escape. "Tilly has several ideas, and the camp is only one of them. She did ask me yesterday about helping with the camp; but she failed to mention you were on the committee, or I would have spoken with you about it today."

"Are you genuinely interested?" he asked with what she could only guess to be concern. "Tilly can be quite persuasive when she wants to be. If you're interested, that's great. We can use the help. But if you're not, you can be honest. My feelings can take it."

Becky gripped the phone tighter. "Actually I am interested and would like to learn more. The camp sounds like a great idea." She paused. "I'm planning to attend the meeting tomorrow."

"Tilly suggested we visit the proposed camp site," he said. "That might be a good idea. It would certainly give you more background into the venture. Would you be interested?"

"I don't see why not."

He seemed pleased. "Great. The meeting starts at seven." A thoughtful silence followed. "There's no sense in both of us driving. How about I pick you up at six to see the property and then we can go to the meeting?"

"All right." She almost finished with her usual banter of "it's a date" but stopped herself. With Tilly's matchmaking schemes she needn't give any encouragement, innocent or not, to fuel the fire. The situation was embarrassing enough.

There was another moment of silence, and Becky felt sure Larry wanted to say more. Evidently he must have thought better of it for he rang off after repeating the time he'd arrive for her the next evening. Becky dropped the phone back into the cradle.

For the next two hours she puttered about the cabin then settled into reading a mystery book Lauren had on the shelf. At last she made her way to the bedroom.

In her room, however, a strange restlessness overtook her, and she finally donned the terrycloth robe left hanging on the hook of the door. The front door unlocked easily, and she pushed open the screen. Her bare feet crossed the cold wood of the deck, and crisp air encircled her ankles. The light wind held a whimsical chill. Leaning against the picnic table, Becky lifted her face upward to drink in the beauty of the night, listening to the stray sounds of an early cricket. In the quietness she could almost hear the muted sounds of a band playing at the

Curry Party House near Levitte's Landing.

The moon was rising to fill the cosmos with a silvery light. Looking to the heavens, Becky sent up a prayer for the Bantu-speaking people of her village. By now they were rising for the day. She should be rising with them. A long and slow breath gave way to a heavy sigh. *What's Your plan for them, Father? I can't help but feel it was a mistake for me to leave. I'd just begun to gain their confidence. So many of the women were asking the right questions about You. Who will give them the message now?*

Only silence greeted her, and she drew the bathrobe closer.

*Please protect them and give the new Christians courage and hope. Send someone to help them.*

A sudden groan escaped her lips. Why did it feel as though she were leading two lives? Becky the missionary, and Becky the ex-bookkeeper of Bay Island. Would she take on a third identity as camp director? When she went to the Congo she desperately missed those on the island. Once back in the States she desperately missed her village. Nothing seemed certain anymore. She'd anticipated many things happening on the mission field or at home, but being yanked out of the country in the middle of the night wasn't one of them.

Minutes ticked on as she intermingled musings, questions, and prayers until she had to rub her arms vigorously against the cool of the night. Finally she yielded to the chill and went inside. The warm robe slipped off easily. She slid between the sheets, exhaustion finally having its way. Sleep overtook the night.

Larry rested his hand across the steering wheel as the nippy island wind tunneled through the half-opened window.

"Cold?" He looked over at Becky, who sat beside him, her hands clasped loosely in her lap.

She turned her attention from the road ahead and flashed him a smile. "Not at all. It's absolutely wonderful. The cool weather is a welcome change."

Still, Larry nudged the electric window up several inches. "I'm guessing the weather in the Congo is warm."

She nodded. "We average in the seventies and eighties year-round. Some days are just plain hot. Warm and rainy is an apt description."

"Seventies and eighties sound good right now. Add plenty of sun, and I'm a warm-weather kind of guy."

"Me, too," she agreed. "I'm not used to Midwest winters."

He cocked his brow. "Where you from? South or West?"

A definite look of reserve crossed her features. "Out West."

Larry watched her shift uncomfortably in the seat and changed the subject. "We'll look at the east side of Thunder Bay first so you can see how much property we're proposing to buy."

The palpable tension eased, and he saw her shoulders relax. "Tilly mentioned the owner might not be willing to sell."

Larry flicked the turn signal. "Kelly Enterprises is what I'd call a mysterious and secretive company." He glanced left before turning. "It's one of those foundations where the owner or owners like to remain anonymous. All of our communications have been by written letters to a post office box, not even e-mail. Since we haven't personally talked with a representative, it's difficult to plead our case. But the landmark is obviously the perfect place for the camp."

Seemingly intrigued, Becky tilted her head. "How long has this Kelly Enterprises owned Thunder Bay?"

"I believe"—he hesitated, thinking—"Kelly purchased Thunder Bay some fifty years ago from another foundation that went belly-up. From what I've heard, the place nearly went to ruins. One thing I do know: Kelly Enterprises had the funds to restore the dilapidated buildings and maintain the landmark since that time."

"That's interesting." She halted then asked, "Do you think Kelly's owned by a family on the island?"

Larry grinned. "There's no one that rich on this island. The foundation owns at least three other Civil War landmarks. Whoever they are, they're a big player."

"Big player?"

Larry gave her a quick look, noting her cautious tone. "Kelly Enterprises carries clout on Bay Island. When the foundation opposed a zoning variance for an alcohol drive-through carryout more than a mile from the landmark, the mayor and trustees promptly nixed the motion." He slowed the truck and pulled into the gravel parking lot. "Needless to say, the island bends over backward for Kelly Enterprises."

She shifted her eyebrow in comment. "From your tone you obviously disapprove. Which bothers you more—the carryout or interference from the foundation?"

"Both." Larry eased the truck to a stop, shifting the gear into park. "I don't like the idea of additional alcohol sales on the island. It makes my job that much more difficult, especially during tourist season. Alcohol generates more disturbances and complaints than any other problem." He gave her the full benefit of his blue eyes. A coldness edged into his voice. "But more than that, I have a greater distaste for talking money."

He heard a slight but sudden intake of breath on her part, but a glance revealed no telltale facial expression on her part. Curiosity caused him to await her response. The moment gave him time to note just how striking the woman looked with her sleek black hair pulled back in a long ponytail. Clad in dress slacks and a long-sleeve blouse, she looked at ease, yet fashionable. Her light complexion probably stayed year round, he reasoned, watching her dark eyes widen at his stare.

She stirred restlessly and shifted her look to the Thunder Bay sign. "So this is the old Civil War site."

"This is it!" He gave her a wry smile. The abrupt change of conversation was apparent. The discussion was over. But why? He'd obviously touched a nerve, not once but twice during their ride. "Let's take a look around."

Both stepped out and met at the front of the truck.

"This way," he instructed, cupping her elbow with his hand. He steered her toward the pebbled path leading beyond the grove of ornamental cherry trees. Maybe the sooner he gave the tour, the better.

"Absolutely gorgeous," Becky said with awe, touching an early pink bloom of a nearby branch. She turned to Larry. "I've passed this way so many times and never stopped."

Larry smiled in understanding. "I think tourists appreciate Thunder Bay much more than our residents." He pointed ahead. "Just beyond here is a refurbished weaponry building."

The path opened into a large, freshly mowed field. Larry inhaled the earthy smell of the green cuttings. His gait slowed to match hers as she scanned the site.

"What's that building?" With her finger she directed Larry to a rough stone structure with barred windows. "A Union jailhouse?"

"Actually," Larry answered, "that's the treasury. Union money was stored here. The building is nearly indestructible and, from what I understand, one of the few that didn't need major repair."

He turned his attention to three log cabins sitting beyond the treasury. "They dismantled almost every piece of wood in those cabins to rebuild the structure to its previous glory." He cast his look back to her. "I might have been eight or nine years old when the work began."

This seemed to interest her. "You grew up on the island?"

"Born and bred!"

"You're not only knowledgeable but loyal to the island as well." She smiled.

"Very loyal."

"Loyalty is a wonderful thing." A brief shadow crossed her face and disappeared. Suddenly she laid her hand on his arm, her fingers cool on his bare flesh. "Is that the property beyond that line of trees?"

Larry nodded and followed Becky as she made her way toward the break in the trees. It was he who had a difficult time keeping up as she steamed forward. Finally they walked into the clearing, and he could hear her light, quick breaths from the lively jaunt. A large, square piece of acreage framed by trees on all sides lay before them. Sunbeams sparkled off the small and irregularly shaped pond to their left.

"This is just one portion of the property we propose to buy," Larry announced, breaking the silence. "Come with me." He led Becky across the field until another opening could be seen.

"Another large field," she exclaimed, completely turning around to view the surroundings. "Look at the shoreline!" The site obviously met her approval.

"It's perfect," he agreed.

"It's also separate from the landmark buildings. I can see why your committee is trying to buy this land." They walked to the shore, and her smile widened. "Eventually you could add sailboats, skiing, and almost any water sport here."

He smiled. "Like I said—perfect."

As they walked back, Becky continually stopped and mentioned potential buildings and possibilities until Larry laughed and held up his hand to stop the onslaught.

"Those are all fine ideas," he admitted, "but not practical."

Becky stopped. "Like what?"

Larry noticed the questioning of her uplifted face. He towered over her, but her enthusiasm seemed to inch her closer up toward him. "The buildings, for example, will need to be built in the first field, not by the lake."

"But why?"

"We need close access to electric, potable water, and to sanitation."

She seemed to digest the information. "Why not run the electric lines further to the back field?"

"Electric is the least of the obstacles," he pointed out. "There's no village water or sanitary system out this far, and it's impossible to dig a well through the limestone near the lake or to find suitable ground for a leach bed."

"What about closer to the tree line?" She seemed unwilling to give up her idea of lakeside cabins as her gaze panned the collage of tall pines, oaks, and maples.

He flicked an amused glance her way. "The deep limestone doesn't level off sufficiently until the second field."

From her expression he could tell she wasn't satisfied. As they walked back into the first field, she continued offering possibilities. He watched her facial features alternate between consternation and hope. *Right-brained! Definitely right-brained.* He hated popping her dream-bubble again and again, but idea after idea just didn't fit reality. All she seemed to see was a perfect setting. Reality rarely provided such luxuries.

"Your suggestions show plenty of thought," he finally said. "We just need to find a match of ideas with the resources we have."

"I suppose the pond can't be used for swimming," she challenged in response, as they edged near the greenish-colored water.

He sensed her frustration. "Not everything is impossible."

"Isn't it?" She blew a puff of air between her tight lips. "Every idea has an obstacle." She paused. "I don't know. Maybe I'm not cut out for helping with the project. There's a great deal to consider when building a camp. My skill level might not be of help."

Larry drew his eyebrows together. "As I said before, you have plenty of good ideas. But reality is hard. Dreams are great as long as they stay grounded with realism."

She began walking toward the pebbled path but suddenly stopped and turned to him. "Are you a half-empty or half-full kind of guy?"

"What?" He threw her a puzzled look.

"Oh, never mind. It was a nonsensical question."

"If you say so."

"I do."

# Chapter 4

Becky snapped her seat belt in with a decisive click. She heard Larry do the same. The trip was informative, but far from productive. She pursed her lips in thought. Larry knew the technical aspects, the bricks and mortar, so to speak, of building a camp. But it was possible, she had to admit, he might lack the ability to go beyond the obvious obstacles.

With such a beautiful lakeside view it seemed criminal not to look at every possible angle to build the cabins near that very spot. With some ingenuity they might overcome those pesky details of potable water and leach beds. It wasn't as if Larry didn't have the skill, she reasoned. He certainly had his facts straight. He just needed to think outside the box. Dream a little!

Becky stole a glance his way. His handsome face had a no-nonsense look, the facts-and-figures presence that made him seem so strong and fiercely dependable. Nurturing, too! Most women would jump at the chance to work with the man. He even had a sense of humor. And who could forget that memorable night a year ago when he captured a burglar outside Lauren's cabin? The entire island talked about nothing else for months, so Lauren had written her. To hear of the residents' endless chatter, he was an island hero. She turned her gaze back toward the window. It wouldn't do to daydream about the guy. An unpredictable future meant an unpredictable life and no room for relationships. Besides, he was a bit of a pessimist.

The red brick church came into view, and the truck drew smoothly to a halt. He seemed as relieved as she was for the drive to end. The same rather strained silence persisted as they entered the side door and walked the long hall to the small multipurpose meeting room. Ten chairs surrounded one lone table. Larry directed her to sit next to him at the far end.

A few members greeted Becky. Church librarian Mrs. Phillips and her close friend Lottie BonDurant brought refreshments and begged Becky to try their best brownie concoction. Others filed in, but none brought anxiety like church elder Mr. Edwards. Now here was a gentleman no one, least of all Becky, wanted to cross. Certainly he did more than his share of work for the church, but he was more than cantankerous as well. Notoriously! And he never missed a business meeting. How well she remembered why a twenty-minute meeting could stretch into eternity. The last she'd heard, he was working at the Dairy Barn running the cash register and cleaning tables. Money was an issue, local gossip whispered.

Most felt little pity. It took only one personal introduction to his barbed tongue to lose the sympathy.

She smiled when Lottie rolled her eyes as Mr. Edwards seated himself opposite Becky. She'd have to keep an open mind. He was, after all, a child of God.

The room hushed as Larry commanded their attention and opened with prayer.

"We have quite a few updates," he began after prayer, still standing at the head of the table. "I'd like to bring the committee up to speed on current finances." Larry circulated copies of a financial statement. "We also have Becky Merrill with us tonight. She's considering the job of camp director for the interim. Most of you heard on Sunday that Becky will be with us until it's safe for her to return to the mission field."

Becky felt all eyes on her, and she gave an acknowledging nod. Lottie patted her hand as Larry introduced each member. He quickly moved on.

"We are still awaiting a response from Kelly Enterprises to our proposal," Larry announced. "As you can see from the financial statement, we can negotiate a substantial offer for the property—"

Immediately a low grumble erupted from the white-haired Mr. Edwards. "Don't know why we have to go about disturbing a historical landmark. I've said it before—it's sacrilegious!" A following *harrumph* punctuated his disapproval.

Both Mrs. Phillips and Lottie raised their eyes to the ceiling in unison.

Larry took in a slow, deep breath, and Becky knew he was keeping his anger in check. "We've already been through this, Mr. Edwards. As we discussed before, the Civil War landmark and the camp can coexist. I was planning to share additional information proving the fact later in the meeting, but since the subject has been brought up I'll discuss it now." He shuffled through his folder, finally producing a typed letter. "The Bay Island Department of Commerce has provided a recommendation for us to use during negotiations with Kelly Enterprises. A recent tourism study indicates a project such as our family-friendly camp on the unused portions of Thunder Bay's acreage could easily generate twenty-five percent or more tourism for the island."

"I'd like to see that letter," Mr. Edwards demanded, holding out his hand.

Larry offered the paper and continued talking as Mr. Edwards brought the print within two inches of his thick glasses. "Allowing the camp to build on the property also predicts a sizable increase in visitors to the landmark itself—a definite benefit for the foundation. Kelly Enterprises has devoted thousands, if not millions, to preserving history and educating the public about the past. What better way to achieve their goal."

"Interesting," said Mr. Edwards, sliding the paper across the table at Larry. His voice conveyed a wealth of intonation in his simple response, and Becky glanced cautiously back at Larry. It would take more than a spoonful of grace for Larry to deal with the inferred challenge.

"It's more than interesting," Larry assured him in measured tones. He let his eyes roam the roomful of members. "No one is more conscious of the importance of the landmark than I am. It's part of our history, the history of Bay Island and our people. That's what makes it perfect. Like other residents I watched Thunder Bay be restored with such historical accuracy that, as a child, I felt as if I were being transported back in time. We would never let the camp infringe on that heritage but protect and encourage others to see God's hand in its preservation. Its resources are too valuable to be lost."

Becky's heart warmed at his short, impassioned speech. It was from the heart, she knew. Maybe a dreamer did lie dormant beneath his pessimistic exterior.

Mr. Edwards seemed moved as well. "It is something to think about, young man."

"With the commerce department endorsing our idea," Larry added, "it has given solid evidence to back our decision. I feel this is an answer from God and an indication we are following the path God would have us to take. We need to give Kelly Enterprises the chance to decide. If God wants the camp at Thunder Bay, God will provide it."

Lottie slapped her palm decisively on the table, causing Becky to jump. "I'm with Larry. This is the best news we've had in a long time. I say we show this letter to Kelly Enterprises and see what God has in store for us."

Becky watched the other members bob their heads in agreement. Her gaze finally rested on Mr. Edwards. His lips whitened slightly from his taut expression.

"I suppose it wouldn't hurt," Mr. Edwards grudgingly agreed.

"All right," Larry acknowledged with a deep intake of air. "I'll contact Kelly Enterprises immediately with the letter. We'll accept God's answer—" He looked pointedly at the white-haired elder. "We'll accept the answer—whether yes or no."

A murmur of approval spread throughout the room, followed by an elongated pause. When Mr. Edwards remained silent, Larry continued.

"The next item on the agenda deals with the position of camp director." He gave Becky a supportive smile. "The job of camp director is outlined on this sheet." Larry raised the duplicates in the air. "Please take a copy and review the description." He divided the papers and handed a set to Becky and another to Mr. Edwards. The papers shuffled noisily down both sides of the table. "The job is currently limited to idea building and coordination of various aspects of design, planning, volunteer staffing, and general duties. At this point the job is on a volunteer basis, although Becky believes the missionary agency will continue her financial support at least through the summer." Larry paused. "There's also the possibility she might be called back to the Congo or financial support might be terminated. We'll cross that bridge when and if we need to. For now, she is willing to give of her time to help with the project." He smiled at Becky. "Becky, you might want to say a few words."

Becky suddenly felt her palms grow sweaty, and she clutched them together nervously under the table. She wouldn't dare look at Mr. Edwards. "If you believe I can be of help, I'd be glad to do what I can as camp director." A slight smile lit upon her lips. "It's different from anything I've done before, but I hope my experiences in accounting and my head for facts and figures will be useful."

Larry nodded in support, but his laid-back features quickly dimmed when Mr. Edwards stood to his feet.

"Does Jason Levitte know about this?" The old man looked sternly at Larry through thick eyeglasses. "He should be here."

"Here we go again," whispered Lottie loud enough for several to hear.

Becky stirred uneasily and risked a glance at the elderly man. This meeting was becoming an emotional landmine. Obstinate would be too kind a word for Mr. Edwards. He wasn't known to mince his words lightly or with congeniality, but this was ridiculous.

"Jason and Lauren are on their honeymoon," Larry responded. He paused; not a muscle of his face moved. "I haven't spoken to him for this reason, but he's worked extensively with Ms. Merrill in the past and will no doubt welcome her help without reservation."

Mr. Edwards squinted his enlarged blue eyes. "But we've never discussed having a woman for camp director. With construction and technical details, certainly it's a man's job."

Becky heard several members gasp in astonishment and displeasure. Her heart turned over. No wonder Larry leaned toward being pessimistic over camp details if every itty-bitty item had to be squeezed through Mr. Edwards's tight grasp. Dragging a ball and chain would be easier. How should she respond to someone so unreasonable? God would have to help her. She was usually even-tempered, and anger didn't come easily; but any minute now she might explode. Desperately she tried to assemble her thoughts into some sort of godly, coherent order.

But Larry was already trying to soothe the tense air. "I'm sure, Mr. Edwards, you didn't mean that to come across as it did—"

"I most certainly did." The old man gave a punctuated sniff. His gravelly voice continued. "This is a man's job! And I say—"

Larry cut him off at the pass. "We've swam these waters before, and unless a new life jacket has been purchased I respectfully suggest this line of discussion be dropped." He was using his police-authority voice Becky knew would stop most in their tracks.

*Good for you.* She silently applauded him. Unfortunately Mr. Edwards ignored the warning and didn't seem inclined to forgo the issue just yet.

"Ms. Merrill has admitted she doesn't have any experience being a camp director," he stated. "Just because she comes free of charge doesn't make it right."

This brought Mrs. Phillips and Lottie bounding to their feet like identical twins with agility beyond their age. Larry's muscular jaw began to work, and he seemed ready to release whatever handle he had on his anger; but Becky was quicker than either.

"Please, Mr. Edwards," she pleaded, praying for calmness and control. "I'm not trying to take over the project." She motioned to the standing ladies and the old man. "Please sit down." Becky glanced at Larry and spoke carefully past a sudden constriction in her throat. "You're right. I don't have experience designing structures, building frames, or putting up drywall, but if someone would show me how, I'd help. Not because I'm a woman, but because I'm God's servant." She had to smile—God made her words sound so good and spiritually sound. "Give me a chance to see if my skills can be used. If not, I'll eagerly hand over the responsibilities to someone better."

"Well. . ." Mr. Edwards seemed to think over the proposal.

Feeling much more confident, Becky continued soothingly, "If it helps, just think of me as Larry's right-hand woman."

The minute the words escaped, her eyes widened in horror. What had she just said? It had come out wrong—so wrong. Even though Larry was smiling, she could see the familiar red climbing up his neck. Mr. Edwards squinted as if it were too much to comprehend, and the two ladies giggled. How she wished she could melt and slink under the table.

Stunned silence continued until Lottie spoke. "We all know what you meant, dear. Now, if Tilly were here, well, you might not be off the hook so easily."

Becky heard Larry laugh softly at that, and after a moment's hesitation she laughed as well. "Before digging myself any deeper, I'll rest my case."

"Wise idea," Larry said low enough to be heard only by her.

The tension-filled room suddenly brightened, and everyone, including Mr. Edwards, grinned.

"May I have a motion to accept Becky Merrill as interim camp director?" Larry asked, obviously taking advantage of the lighter moment.

Unanimously accepted, Becky swallowed her trepidation. Reprieved! She'd defended her position for a job she wasn't even sure she wanted—and won—and managed to embarrass herself in one fell swoop. Only God could orchestrate such an event.

# Chapter 5

Becky coaxed her sleek black hair into a smooth knot at the nape of her neck. Hurriedly she slid her arms into the light blue jacket. Larry had called fifteen minutes earlier with exciting news about Thunder Bay and asked to meet at Jason's home within the hour. He was unusually evasive, but she could tell he was ecstatic. It could only mean Kelly Enterprises agreed to sell.

The honeymooners had returned two days ago, and Becky smiled at the thought of their happiness. She would be glad to see them. It certainly seemed more than two weeks since they'd left. Plucking the keys from the counter, she snugged the door shut and locked the dead bolt. The small car came to life, and Becky descended the short incline toward the shoreline. So much had happened in a week.

The thought brought a groan. Things had gone smoothly until the mail arrived yesterday. If only Larry hadn't been with her at the time. Now she almost dreaded seeing him, to face his questioning glances again.

Larry had visited the day before to show her the results of a preliminary land survey for Thunder Bay. There might be hope for one or two cabins by the shore after all, he'd said.

"The survey is unofficial," Larry warned, sitting down on the top step of the deck outside her cabin. "A friend of mine gave a cursory examination of both parcels as a favor. It might be more expensive but doable. We'll have to wait on Jason to see what he thinks."

Pleased, Becky beamed and sat beside him. "Thank you for believing enough to at least give the idea a chance. That means a lot to me." She felt a tinge of warmth come into her cheeks. "I'm really getting excited about the camp. The initial drawings from Jason you gave me the other day are fantastic. And God's going to come through with the land; I can feel it." She began to peruse the land survey documents. "Have you heard anything at all?"

"We should have an answer any day."

She flipped a page and held it in front of her. "How interesting."

Larry leaned closer to see. "Aerial map of the site."

"Your friend did these?"

"It pays to have friends in high places."

Becky laughed at his teasing and pointed to the map. "Whose land abuts the Thunder Bay shoreline property to the west? That's the only house close by."

"That would be Mayor Thompson's place," he answered, continuing to look over her shoulder. He pointed to the faint outline of a boat dock on the property. "Mayor Thompson used to let us dock our family's boat during the summer at his place. He's a good guy, almost like a second father."

Astonished, Becky asked, "He's been mayor since you were a kid?"

"Yep." There was a laugh at her expression. "Twenty-seven is not *that* old."

She lightly slapped his arm. "That's not what I meant, and you know it. It's just unusual for people to stay in a public office that long. People don't usually hang around in one place for any length of time."

Larry seemed to ponder her statement. "So you've said before."

"What?"

"Oh, I don't know," he answered with care. "You've mentioned on occasion how hard it is to find people devoted to their roots." He paused a little before continuing. "Did your family move around a great deal when you were younger?"

The seemingly innocent question put Becky on full alert. How could she tell him how her family progressed steadily from lower class to high class, buying bigger and better with every move? How her father moved heaven and earth to provide what he deemed to be deserved? It didn't matter who stood in his way; they were merely stepping-stones providing a way to the prize. It was always move on and move up. Perhaps her parents had moved on and up again during her time in the Congo. There had been no contact since she'd left California.

"Does talking about your family make you nervous?" His gentle voice, however tender, increased her anxiety to new heights.

"I don't have much family to speak of," she finally responded, rubbing her hands together in apprehension. What would he say when he discovered she was disowned? Her head swam with the knowledge. She wasn't to blame, right? But her heart wondered what kind of disappointment she must be to cause a mother and father, dysfunctional or not, to stoop to such measures.

"Do you want to talk about it?"

She risked an upward glance. "Maybe someday, but not today."

"Sure?"

"There's not much to tell." She turned her gaze to the tall pines, knowing her words weren't true. "It can wait." Her heart ached to tell someone—someone like Larry. How easy it would be to lean close and tell him how her heart burned in humiliation. But she wouldn't. She was already dangerously close to enjoying Larry's company more than planned. It just wouldn't do. She was confused and vulnerable—hardly a worthy state of mind when making decisions about a relationship, especially one she wasn't free to give. His caring demeanor, however, touched her heart as nothing before, and she feared this might be her undoing. And he was available—too available, too close.

"I'll be here when you care to talk." His hooded look stayed with her. "I'm a homebody and not going anywhere."

She raised her head again and saw his face was quiet and grave, his blue eyes unfathomable. "I believe you. You're so much a part of this island."

"Born and bred!"

"So you've said before." She repeated his previous line.

"That's why this camp project is so important," he went on, shifting the subject matter back to safer ground, much to Becky's relief. "The church has tossed around the idea of a camp for so many years; it seemed more like pie in the sky than reality. It's hard to believe the time has come, and it's actually approaching fruition. We're so close."

Becky instinctively laid her hand on his arm. "You've worked so hard on this project. God will bless you for it."

"He already has." He laid his other hand over hers.

She glanced up and locked her gaze with his bright blue eyes. He meant her! It was written clearly across his face. He liked her, was interested in knowing her better. It was all there. The revelation warmed her very core—yet trepidation still lay heavy on her heart. How effortless it would be to fall for a man such as Larry. In the few days she'd known him, he'd been attentive to her needs and those of others. What else could she say? He was a man of character, exactly what she would want—if she were looking.

The sound of an approaching mail truck broke the silence and drew their attention to the road. The flag went up on the mailbox at the end of the drive.

"I've got mail," she whispered with obvious distraction, unwilling to break the moment. Then the thought hit her, and she sat straight up. "I've got mail!"

"That would be an echo."

Feeling suddenly lighter, she laughed. "You don't understand. I've been awaiting word from my people in the Congo. Maybe a letter has finally come."

"Want me to fetch the mail for you?" he asked lazily.

She shook her head. "Let's go together."

As one, they descended the steps and walked the long pine-covered drive. The emotional tension had since evaporated, and Larry seemed back to his usual self. Laughing, he feigned an attempt to reach the mailbox before she did. Becky sped past him.

"Keep your scratchers off," she teased, opening the box. "This is only my second time to get mail since arriving on the island. I can't afford to miss even one letter." One letter did lie in the box, and she snatched it, laughing as he tried to see it. "Back off, Buster!"

He playfully retreated, both hands up in surrender. She held the letter mischievously within sight but out of his reach. Her good humor, though, suddenly took a dive when she saw the Sacramento postmark.

"Something wrong?" Larry asked, his voice immediately filled with concern.

Becky was silent. Unbidden memories returned to her mind. Michael! A letter from Michael. How did he know she was on Bay Island? She hadn't even told her family. Her past rushed upon her, and a shiver of anxiety coursed up her spine. Complications! Always complications. And Michael Petit was one big complication.

Larry held open the front door and greeted Becky and immediately helped her slip out of her light blue coat. "Jason and Lauren are in the sunroom," he announced, pointing to the back room.

She nodded and thanked him as she pulled several wisps of stray hair away from her rosy cheeks. "I rushed over as soon as I could." Her features became animated. "It's Thunder Bay, isn't it? We have the property!"

He laughed. "Sorry, but you'll have to wait. Jason wants to break the news." Steering her across the formal room, he felt his leather boots sink into the deep pile of the honey gold carpet. "Everything okay?" he asked in a low voice.

A shadow crossed her face, but she smiled. "Just fine."

*Liar!* From her expression it was evident all was not well, and it had to do with the letter she'd received yesterday. It was postmarked from Sacramento; at least he'd seen that much before she hurriedly stuffed it into her pants pocket. Whoever sent the mail caused the woman to clam up faster than a criminal claiming the fifth.

"Becky!" Lauren immediately accosted Becky as they entered the room.

Larry watched for several moments as the two hugged and exchanged updates. Some of the strain seemed to leave Becky's face. He'd give his eye teeth to find out about that letter. A deep and frustrated breath filled his lungs. That was his trouble. Something drove him to be the white knight, rescuing lost souls and feebly attempting to fix the world's problems. And Becky was his worst case. Since laying eyes on her anxious face the day he'd arrived to fix the water heater, he'd thought of nothing else. He wanted to help, to know her better, but she purposely kept him at arm's length.

"Take a seat."

Larry turned to look at Jason and smiled. Jason shrugged his shoulders and with a knowing grin pointed to the table and tall wooden stools set next to the window. "They might be awhile."

Larry perched himself on a stool and hooked the heel of his boot on the cross bar beneath. "Don't mind if I do."

"Heard you took care of a water heater problem at the cabin while we were gone." A note of amusement filled Jason's voice.

"A Tilly referral."

Jason burst into laughter. "Ouch! What did that cost you, and I don't mean the labor? Are you engaged yet?"

"I was on duty that morning, and poor Becky thought Tilly had sent the police over to help." Larry chuckled, trying to keep his voice out of range of the ladies. "And you know Tilly. I'm almost certain the woman knows everything that goes on. She probably had a hand in putting the water heater out of action."

"Did it work?"

"Well, let's see," Larry began. "We're working together a couple of times a week on the camp project and on the phone even more often. I'd say Tilly's in her glory."

Jason seemed to find the whole ordeal innately funny. "Oh, before I forget," he said, reaching into his pocket and handing over a check. "Here's the payment to take care of the water heater expenses. Will that cover it?"

"Whoa! Too much." Larry passed the check back. "The tank was only—"

Jason pushed the check toward him. "Doesn't matter. I'm taking into account your labor and short-notice availability." When Larry didn't budge, Jason stubbornly shook his head. "I'm not taking it back."

Reluctantly Larry folded the check and tucked it into his wallet. When he slid the wallet into the pocket of his jeans and looked up, Becky was at his side, obviously seeing the check exchange.

"I hope it was okay about the water heater, Jason." Becky looked anxiously from Jason to Larry. "I didn't know what else to do. And Larry did such a good job—"

Jason patted her arm. "You did exactly what we would have wanted."

"Are you sure? I can pay you back."

"It's fine, Becky," Lauren reassured her. "Actually I'm the one who feels bad about this happening to you. It must have scared you to death in the middle of the night. I should have changed the tank last year. It was older than Methuselah."

Larry could still see Becky's apprehension, her vulnerability surfacing again. Obviously she wanted to pay for the water heater but was embarrassed not to have the resources to do so. It was preposterous, really. As a guest at Piney Point, she must know maintenance items wouldn't be her responsibility. Hotel guests didn't change burned-out light bulbs or loose towel bars, did they? He wouldn't count the time he fixed the broken showerhead on his last trip to Dallas for a conference. Chalk that up to compulsive behavior on his part—hardly normal for the general public. Yet, from the look on her face, she was equating her situation with a handout.

This gave Larry some thought. Maybe she came from a family who worried over money, a tight income. Could this be the reason for her hesitancy in talking about her family? She did seem disturbed when he discussed the issue of talking money. Still it didn't make sense. Even in the short time she'd known him, certainly she knew he wouldn't look down on one's financial status. Money wasn't everything!

Another thought hit him. Maybe she came from money! He looked at Becky again and quickly dismissed the idea. He'd seen his fair share of rich folks during tourist season, and Becky didn't fit the bill. She'd never fit in. No, he'd have to give another path of thought more time to form. Right now, though, it seemed as if their small group was ready to assemble.

"Shall we talk about Kelly Enterprises?" Jason asked, motioning for all to sit around the table. "God has pulled off the most remarkable feat, over and beyond what we even prayed."

"I knew it," Becky exclaimed excitedly, already seeming to set aside her previous problems. "Kelly's going to sell."

"Better than that!" Jason gave Becky a neatly folded letter. "Kelly Enterprises is donating the land."

Becky unfolded the sheet and read the letter carefully, her face radiating joy at the news. "This is unbelievable! How did we go from the foundation showing no interest to a land donation?"

"It's a God-thing," Larry offered. "I think this fits under the oh-ye-of-so-little-faith category. And you realize what this means—"

Clearly the others knew, but puzzlement crossed Becky's face. "What?"

"It means," Larry continued, "the monies earmarked for the purchase of the land can be used for building. Jason has the first-phase designs nearly completed, and once an official land survey is conducted and permits obtained, we can break ground."

"How soon?" Becky seemed breathless.

"A month, maybe two."

Becky clapped her hands together. "This is fantastic!"

"And a reason to celebrate," Lauren chimed in. "That's why we wanted you to come over. Jason's treating us to dinner at the Landing tonight. Please tell me you're both free." She looked at Larry and Becky. "Jason will bring the designs, and we can set the plans into motion."

Larry gave a shrug. "Don't see why not."

"Absolutely!" There was no hesitation on Becky's part.

Pleased, Lauren gave Jason a kiss on the cheek. "I'm starved. Can we go now?"

"I'll get the car," Jason announced, already standing.

Outside the sun pleasantly warmed the cool air. With an even stride Larry walked behind Becky, his boots sounding heavy against the concrete walk. He opened the back door of the black sedan and helped Becky, her coat draped over her arm, climb into the backseat. He slid in next to her. She turned and gave him a smile.

He leaned toward her. "Did you bring the aerial maps? Jason will want to see them."

"Yes," she answered, digging into her purse. "I put them in my purse right away after you called so I wouldn't forget." The small packet slid out easily, and she handed it to him. Another object landed in the seat between them.

Larry recognized the object as the letter she'd received the day before. She rushed to grab the letter from the seat and jam it into the middle compartment of her purse. Then with great effort she tried to close the zipper, but her clumsy attempt only wedged the zipper into the material.

"Let me." Larry reached over and worked the zipper until it gave way and closed.

"Thank you." She managed a smile, an impish one at that. "Rescued again."

"No problem."

Oblivious to the charged atmosphere, Jason began to engage them in a discussion about Thunder Bay. Becky participated with vigor. Larry, however, didn't miss the slight change in her demeanor. Something powerful lay within the envelope now tucked safely inside her purse. But for now he could only wonder at its contents.

Becky kept a tight grip on her purse, her face growing warm under Larry's scrutiny. It took all of her courage to meet the gaze that regarded her so intently. Of course the letter had to fall out of her purse. What rotten luck. It wasn't as if she could forget the note, even if she'd tried. Michael's words were memorized, emblazoned within her mind.

*My dearest Rebecca,*

*News has reached home about your hasty and dangerous departure from Africa. I contacted the missionary board who gave me your forwarding address, but of course I had hoped you might call. The gentleman wouldn't give additional information on your welfare. Are you all right? Your parents are sick with worry. Please call me when you receive this letter. We can work out our differences enough to be friends, can't we?*

*Lovingly,*
*Michael*

Becky would have to make the call soon; that much she knew. Michael wouldn't go away without an answer. The letter was already a week old, and Michael was not a man known for his patience. She'd make the call, but right now she wanted to concentrate on Thunder Bay. God had exciting things in store for the project.

# Chapter 6

It took a long time for the island sun to rise up over the peak of the trees in the morning, and yet to Becky it seemed as if it was down again before one knew it, slipping and sliding behind the cabin. She was thankful daylight hours were steadily increasing with the warmer temperatures. She stretched languidly in the comfortable bed, aware the sun was pouring in through a gap in the curtains. It most certainly was late in the morning. Her brain refused to shut down during the night, and now she was feeling the tiring effects.

It came as no surprise when after lunch she plopped down on the porch lounger ready for an afternoon siesta. The first unseasonably warm day since her arrival lay in wait, and she plumped the cushion with her hands until the firmness felt just right, contouring perfectly to her exhausted body. In the distance the faint blare of the ferry horn blended with hundreds of seagulls squealing their call, no doubt looking for the bounty of fish brought near the surface from the churning propulsion of the boat. The vision brought a smile to her lips. Home never sounded so good. She took a satisfied breath and reveled in the sun's warmth against her skin as it released the fragrance of tropical coconut from the sunscreen she wore. Slowly she felt her eyelids grow heavy.

Becky knew she must have slept, for she awakened with a sixth sense telling her she wasn't alone. Slowly her dark eyes opened, and her head turned almost of its own accord.

"Don't look so unbelieving," said the man beside her. "It's really me." He laughed at her wide-eyed look. "I'm not the bogeyman."

Becky felt her face pale. "Michael!"

"Yes?"

She sat up. "What are you doing here?"

"At the moment," he said, "watching you sleep." His full lips twitched. "Is life so easy on the island you can laze away the day sleeping on a chaise lounge?"

Becky could only stare at him. He was sitting on the picnic table bench within a foot of her, watching closely with his intense gray eyes, his dark curly hair exactly as she remembered. His expensive, dark blue sports jacket opened wider as he leaned back with his elbows on the table.

"You didn't answer my letter, Rebecca," he chided.

Becky's lips parted silently. If she could have found something to say, though, Michael didn't wait to hear what it was.

"Don't look so chagrined. It's your own fault I'm here, having to travel across the country to find out if you're in one piece. Your father is in a true snit."

Becky found her voice. "But I was going to call tonight."

"Really?"

"I was!" she said almost resentfully. "I'm very busy working on a project."

"So I see!" His eyebrows lifted then suddenly smoothed. "Let's not argue. I've crossed enough miles in one day to drain a person. Then there was the awful ride in a rental car from Cleveland—only to find out I couldn't bring the car across on the ferry. Who knew the island restricted motor traffic to those with lodging reservations? And now"—he motioned to the white golf cart on the gravel drive—"I'm reduced to renting an archaic Flintstone mobile. I should think after all that I deserve a better welcome."

"I'm sorry," she managed, desperately collecting herself with effort. "You've shocked me, that's all."

He laughed, a deep, hearty laugh, his teeth a brilliant contrast of whiteness against his dark tan. "I can only hope it's a good shock." He looked at his gold wristwatch. "A major portion of the day is already wasted, and we have a great deal to talk about. Now be a gracious hostess—get up and fetch us something cold to drink. I'm dying of thirst."

"Of course." Obediently she swung her legs over the side of the chaise.

Michael had changed little in appearance or behavior. His handsome features were somehow deeper, sharper. . .more mature. Yet his smoky gray eyes still held their usual mesmerizing quality, which sparked to life just before the flash reached his lips. Becky became keenly aware of his masculine cologne assailing her nose as he leaned across the space between them.

"Come on," he said, offering his hand. "I'll help you up."

Flustered, she waved him off. "I'm all right." She stood to her feet. "You might as well come inside." Leading the way, she held the door until he took its weight and advanced to the kitchen. She opened the refrigerator. "Juice, cola. . ."

"I could really use a wine cooler." Michael had pushed his hands into his tailor-made pants pockets, regarding her in an enigmatic fashion.

"Sorry!"

"Beer?"

Becky frowned at him. He was testing her, knowing good and well she wouldn't have alcohol. "Sorry."

"Oh, very well, I'll have a cola."

She pulled two cold soda cans from the shelf and rinsed the tops in the sink. "Glass and ice?" Without awaiting his nod she opened the cabinet door and produced a tall glass. Michael never, ever drank from a can. The snap of the lid followed by the clinking of ice rang loudly in the silence; even the fizz of soda seemed to reverberate in the room. "Here you go."

Michael accepted the glass, leaned against the kitchen wall, and took a long drink, never letting his gaze waver from her direction. "You've changed."

"I suppose we both have." Becky took a sip from her can, not missing his slight wince as she did so. "Two years is a long time apart."

"Too long!"

She returned his stare in silence. "You said Father's upset," she managed to say, trying to break the spell. "How are Mother and Father?"

"Heartsick." He motioned her to the living room. "Shall we sit?" When Becky followed and sank into the sofa beside him, he continued. "You really have been negligent in contacting them. You must have known they would hear about the evacuation and be worried."

Heat flooded her face. "That's hardly fair, Michael. When I left two years ago Father made it clear there was no turning back. He severed relations with me, and. . .it hurt deeply. They expressed their wishes to hear from me only if I gave up this"—she drew quote marks with her curved fingers—"absolutely horrid cultlike fixation."

"I think they've softened," he offered.

She shook her head. "That doesn't seem likely. Neither of them has attempted to contact me here or abroad."

"Some developments recently have changed that."

Startled, she looked at him, aware of a sudden tremble. "Something has happened? They aren't well?"

Michael's face became grim. "Your mother suffered a slight stroke nearly three weeks ago." Upon seeing her distress he took her hand in his. "She's okay—truly she is. She suffered no permanent effects, and the doctors have her on a powerful drug therapy. Nevertheless they asked me to contact you in the Congo, and that's when I heard the news."

"How awful." Becky looked anxiously at him. "Are you sure she's all right?"

"Positive."

"I'll call them tonight." Her hands grew clammy at the thought. "Do they know you've come to Bay Island?"

He nodded. "They asked me to come."

Becky sat woodenly for moments. Everything was happening too fast. Michael—her parents. Emotions exploded within her—anguish, anger, trepidation. Disjointed sections of her life were colliding together, and the result could only be an explosion; she could feel it in every painful breath.

"And I'm going to need a place to crash tonight," he added, giving her a hopeful look.

"You're staying?" she exclaimed in disbelief.

"You didn't think I would travel almost three thousand miles for a twenty-minute conversation, did you?" he answered with a wry smile. "I plan to stay a few days. Do you have an extra bedroom?"

She shook her head violently. "You can't stay here, Michael!"

"Oh, it's like that, is it?"

Becky's heart went cold. "Yes, it is like that."

He lifted her chin with one hand and looked down at her, his gray eyes amused and hardly repentant. "I didn't mean to offend. I'm sorry if I did." He stood up. "Maybe you can direct me to a hotel." He paused. "They do have a real hotel on the island, I presume?"

"We have two hotels," she answered in distraction. "There are also condos and several bed-and-breakfast establishments to choose from. Being midweek, I'm sure you'll have your pick."

"One of the hotels will be fine." He reached into the inside pocket of his jacket and brought out an electronic date book. Quietly he worked the screen before finally speaking. "We'll have dinner tonight and discuss the next couple of days."

"Days?"

He cocked his brow at her, and she knew without a doubt he was laughing at her. "Yes, I believe we just had that discussion." He laughed. "You look shell-shocked, my dear. Maybe you need to finish that nap of yours once you escort me into town to find the hotel."

How easily he manipulated his requests to make a polite refusal impossible. He'd evidently perfected the skill during her absence and wasted no time using it to his advantage, but to what purpose? What was his agenda?

"You can follow me in the cart," she suggested, trying to gain some control. When he didn't argue, she gathered her purse and swung it over her shoulder. The keys jingled nervously in her hands.

He was already to the door. "Lead the way."

She stepped out into the sunshine, and he followed. Leaning past him, she locked the door. "I think you'll like the Baymont Hotel, and it's not very far. We'll be turning right onto Shoreline Drive," she explained, pointing to the barely visible road. To her dismay she saw a familiar police cruiser turning off that very road toward Piney Point.

"I'll just follow you." He was already moving to the steps.

But Becky stood stock-still, and with butterflies in her stomach she watched Michael go down the stairs with nonchalant grace before glancing back at the road again. "This can't be good!" she said quietly.

Suddenly he turned. "Are you coming?" Obviously seeing her distraction, he slid his gaze to her line of vision then back to her. "Ah, your local gendarme. Promise—I'm clean." He laughed, pointing to the golf cart. "The little hootenanny's paid up."

Becky finally sprang to action and made her way down the steps. She'd better head off Michael. Who knew what Michael might say? She blew out a sigh. This was inconvenient. Not that she thought she could shuffle Michael off the island in a few days without anyone taking notice. Reports of the newcomer would spread far and wide before nightfall. It might be just as well to have Larry meet him first before the rumors had time to touch ground.

The white cruiser braked to a stop beside the four-seater cart, and Larry stepped out, his tall frame barely clearing the door opening.

"Good afternoon!" Larry greeted them both, but Becky could see his attention was focused on Michael. He left the engine running and made no move to close the door but leisurely moved toward them.

"Officer." Michael boldly stepped out and shook Larry's hand. "Michael Petit."

"Larry Newkirk," Larry responded with a pleasant but reserved tone, his facial expressions imperceptible as he peered from Michael to Becky.

"Larry, what a nice surprise," Becky managed, stepping forward. "What brings you by this afternoon?"

This seemed to prompt Michael to continue. "So you know each other then. What a relief that is," he said with a charming smile. "For a moment there you had me going." Becky could tell from his tone he hadn't been worried in the least. "Rebecca's kindly invited me to stay on the island for a few days."

Larry arched his eyebrow but said nothing. Becky flung Michael a warning glance only to receive a grinning, challenging look. Plainly he was enjoying the scene and, having sensed her distress, planned to make the most of it. This concerned her further. Had he always been like this? What she remembered as hard strength and decision—could it have been control? Had she been so immersed in her perceived love for him that she overlooked the obvious signals? Well, she determined, if he thought he could barge back into her life and easily maneuver her and those around her, he would soon find out otherwise.

"Larry," she finally said, pushing an easy smile to her lips. "I'm glad you stopped by so you could meet Michael. He's a dear childhood chum who decided to visit at the last minute." Her confidence rose a notch, and she reveled in the sudden start in Michael's face at her contradiction. "Matter of fact, I was just getting ready to escort him to the Baymont so he could find a room. But you know what?" She paused for the right effect and smiled at Larry. "Since you're making rounds, would you mind giving him an escort?"

"I wouldn't mind at all."

She turned to Michael. "You wouldn't mind, would you, if Larry took you in?"

Michael seemed speechless.

Larry gave Becky a knowing smile. "We're always glad to have new tourists on the island, and the Baymont is our finest hotel."

Becky could have kissed him. "But where are my manners?" she continued her charade. "You came here for a purpose. Is there something I can do for you?"

"I stopped by to remind you of the camp meeting at seven."

"Oh, I almost forgot," she remarked truthfully and after a moment turned to Michael. "I'm sorry, Michael, but we'll have to postpone dinner—unless you care to eat early." One thing she could count on—Michael never ate before seven.

"No, that's all right," he answered with resignation.

"Maybe tomorrow night. I'll call you." She turned to Larry. "Thanks for seeing him safe and sound to the hotel. You're a gem."

"No problem."

"See you at seven then?"

"Seven o'clock."

She turned to Michael, finally giving him some attention. "Have a good evening, Michael." She gave him a charming smile, but their gazes met and clashed. She would be in for a bad quarter of an hour once he was free to talk with her. She'd turned the tables on him, and he wouldn't like that one bit.

Michael pulled out his hundred-dollar sunglasses and casually slid them on before plopping himself into the golf cart. Larry took the cue and made his way back to the car.

Becky didn't move until Larry had pulled the cruiser out and Michael turned the golf cart around to follow. They disappeared into the distance. It was several minutes before she turned and made her way up the steps. Still shaken by Michael's sudden appearance, she wondered what his visit would do to her already unsettled life. One thing she knew: Michael would not be given a length of leash to lead her about. She was no longer the same woman, and in some sense she was no longer alone. She had Larry!

# Chapter 7

Larry shifted in his seat and settled in to listen as Jason Levitte spoke about possible dates for the Thunder Bay groundbreaking ceremony. His mind, however, kept drifting to the raven-haired beauty sitting next to him. Her silky black mane, pulled into a smooth ponytail, hung lightly over the back of the chair, and her loosely balled fist propped her delicate chin. She seemed quite absorbed by the topic and oblivious to his unfocused attention or frequent glances.

Having come late to the meeting, she'd successfully dodged any conversation beyond a nod of greeting. Not that she'd be inclined to talk after the meeting, especially if it concerned the unexpected arrival of her male friend to the island. Off limits! She might not say it in so many words, but he knew. She didn't talk about family, and she most certainly wouldn't be disposed to converse about the man she seemed so anxious to pawn off earlier that afternoon. He just hoped the new visitor wouldn't keep her from their needed duties. Once the date was set for the groundbreaking, they would have more work to do than either of them could handle.

"May first then?" Jason asked, and the room grew quiet.

Looking at Jason and then to the rest of the committee members, Larry realized they were waiting on him to answer. "May first?" he repeated, flipping the page of his planner over a month. "I'm on patrol in the late afternoon, but during the day it looks clear."

"What about the May Day celebrations?" It wasn't surprising Mr. Edwards's first contribution to the meeting was a question. His modus operandi was to begin with a question before an onslaught of biased opinions. "No, sir, that date won't do. There will be the parade and all those newfangled carnival events. Why, the island will be crawling with people."

"That's true," Jason remarked. "You might have missed the earlier discussion about the May Day celebration and how we can use the events to our advantage."

Of course Larry bristled. They'd discussed the May Day celebration earlier. Mr. Edwards was too busy yakking in Culliver's ear to hear the discussion. Culliver was as deaf as they came, and neither seemed the least bit disturbed that the others had difficulty hearing over their loud voices. But Jason was cool as ever, and Larry wondered, not for the first time, why Jason hadn't gone into law enforcement instead of architecture—other than the fact he was a top-notch designer and easily pulled down four times as much income. Yet it wasn't the brilliant designs or ample bank accounts Larry desired; it was Jason's patience. He had a way with people. Larry had worked hard over the past year to develop more staying power and tolerance—to use these enduring life skills not only at work but in his personal life as well.

He tapped the pen between his fingers lightly on the table. His patience would always be a work-in-progress as long as Mr. Edwards stuck around to stretch his reserves.

"If we schedule the groundbreaking for eleven o'clock," Jason continued, "we'll be able to catch the crowd before the noon kickoff. This will be a good boost not only for the camp but for the landmark itself. As a committee we should do everything we can to promote the landmark in appreciation to Kelly Enterprises." He looked around the room at the other members. "The church calendar is clear, and most, if not all, committee members are available."

"I could work on setting up a booth for free refreshments," Becky chimed in. "If we want to attract as many islanders and visitors as possible, refreshments are a general magnet." She penned a flurry of notes in her notebook. "I'll see about helium balloons for the kids. Flora at the Balloon Boutique might be willing to donate several dozen."

Larry watched the hopeful expression on her face with some amusement. "Good idea!" he encouraged. "There's a canvas canopy tent in the church garage we can use and an old but working helium tank if we need more balloons. Harvey can fill the tank for next to nothing." He looked to Jason. "We should also have fliers about our camp to pass out."

"We'll work on that!" Lottie BonDurant looked at Mrs. Phillips, who nodded in agreement.

"Thank you, ladies," Jason responded, smiling at the duo.

"Let's have a vote on the date," Larry proposed. "If Becky believes we can pull this together in three weeks, I say we go for it."

Becky turned slightly to see him. "We should be ready!"

Jason looked over at Mr. Edwards. "What's your call?"

"I suppose." Something short of a growl accented his reluctant approval.

Mr. Edwards never gave in easily, but Larry was glad he'd agreed without a twenty-minute dissertation. Jason followed with a vote, and the meeting adjourned. Larry watched as Becky closed her notebook and stood, sliding the heavy leather chair back into place. He heard the arms of her chair thud against the table as he began to rise. Their gazes met.

"What do you think about having the high school pep band perform at the opening?" Becky was asking him.

He lifted his eyebrows in thought. "The marching band is usually in the May Day kickoff, and the pep band members are probably in the marching band."

Before she could think him a pessimist again, he agreed to ask the school. "Don't be disappointed if they aren't able to come. There can't be more than twenty-five band members as is, so separating the pep band won't be an option."

She appeared satisfied and walked quietly beside him as they exited the building. "I hope you didn't mind showing Michael to the hotel this afternoon. Afterward I thought it was awfully pushy of me."

"I was glad to do it," Larry responded. "He isn't a very talkative fellow, though, is he? He did manage to say he was from Sacramento." He slid a look her way. "Hope he's settling in all right. He didn't seem quite satisfied with the hotel." He paused. "I get the impression the simple Baymont wasn't his usual style."

"He'll get over it!"

Something in her tone prevented him from pursuing the matter. She'd say no more; that much he knew. As predicted, this friend of hers was off-limits. Larry would risk his badge the newcomer from Sacramento was the author of the letter she'd received the other day. The correspondence had troubled Becky before she'd even opened the envelope and could account for the less than warm reception her childhood chum had been given. And the man had all the marks of a rich jet-setter. This was yet another puzzle piece of her past she seemed unwilling to discuss. There would be no more talking tonight.

Then she surprised him.

"You want to go for an ice cream at the Dairy Barn?" she suddenly asked.

"Okay," came his slow answer. What he really wanted to do was go home and hit the sack. The extra hours and rotating shifts were taking a toll. He perceived, though, that Becky's spur-of-the-moment invitation entailed more than an enjoyable outing. Avoidance perhaps? And if so, who else but her visiting friend could be the cause? The question begged to be answered—why should she want to avoid this Michael character?

They stopped at her borrowed car, and Becky threw her purse across and onto the passenger seat. "I'll meet you there."

Larry gave her a salute and walked to his truck. Less than a mile later he pulled into the lot and parked next to the small car. Falling in step beside her, they walked into the shop.

"What's your pleasure?" he asked her as they peered over the concave, clear glass to the wide array of ice cream tubs. "The pecan-and-praline looks good."

With her lips pursed in contemplation she edged toward the second bin. "Well," she said, "what about the monthly special?"

Larry looked at the marked tub and wrinkled his nose. "Are you sure?"

"Heavenly Surprise is too intriguing to pass up," she said with an amusing smile. "Have you no sense of adventure?"

"Adventure, yes—death wish, no."

She laughed. "Chicken."

"Foods with the words *surprise* or *mystery* are generally named that way for a reason." He nodded to the clerk. "One scoop of pecan-and-praline, please." Unknown mixtures were right up there with chocolate cheese and pickled green beans.

Becky rolled her eyes at him before turning to make her order. "Make it the special for me."

"Ever heard the saying, 'better safe than sorry'?"

She laughed again. "What about, 'no pain, no gain'?"

"About midnight you'll be recalling that very saying, I'm sure." Larry took his napkin-wrapped cone and passed it to Becky while he reached for his wallet.

"Oh, no!" she protested. "I asked you out for ice cream."

"What are you going to do about it?" he responded, pointing to the cones she held in each hand. "Someone on the camp committee has to treat you right so you don't quit from a lack of appreciation." He took the change and slid the coins into his front pocket.

She frowned at him as he took his cone from her hand, but he could tell she was pleased. "Next time, my treat."

"I'm glad to hear it. Next time I'll order a triple."

They walked outside and sat on the red-painted bench of a picnic table.

She twirled the cone and murmured her approval as she took a 360-degree swipe of ice cream. "A triple it is—as long as you order the special. It's really good." She tipped her cone toward him. "Want to try it?"

"Absolutely not!" he exclaimed, playfully holding his hand over his chest. "What if you have tuberculosis or whooping cough—or something worse? You trying to kill me?"

She shook her head. "Oh, I can't afford to lose you. Who else will keep my feet grounded on the camp project? Besides, we have those issues of water and electricity to work on." She looked at him. "And your ice cream's melting."

Larry could feel the cool, sticky wetness dripping across his fingers. "It's all your fault," he announced, quickly taking in the drippings. "If you hadn't chosen that awful flavor and then offered to kill me with it."

"Has anyone ever mentioned you're hopeless?"

"Hopeless?" He tilted his head. "Not lately. But I'm sure if I stick around you long enough, the term will come up now and again."

She smiled. "I don't doubt it."

They ate their cones in companionable silence for several minutes. Conversation turned to the May Day groundbreaking before their dialogue dwindled into nothing. Larry wadded the wet and sticky napkin into a ball and looked up. Dusk had overtaken the sky.

He took a lungful of the night air. "Ready?"

"I guess." She made no attempt to move.

Larry altered his position to look at her more, instantly sensing her reluctance to leave. "Do you need me to see you home?"

"No, thanks."

"Is everything okay?"

She nodded and turned her gaze to the emerging stars above. "I'd probably better go back to Piney Point before it gets too late. I have a few phone calls to make." There was a lack of enthusiasm in her voice.

"Come on," he urged. "I'll at least see you to your car." He stifled a yawn.

She gave him a pained smile and said softly, "I'm sorry." She stood to her feet. "You're probably bushed and have to be up and about early in the morning. Here I am keeping you out late listening to me ramble on about nothing."

"I don't need much sleep." He wanted to kick himself for letting her see his tiredness. "If you're not ready to go back. . ."

"No, I'm ready," she said with what he would call resignation.

They walked side-by-side to her car. The warmth of the day had lifted, leaving a clammy cool in its place, and he saw her give a slight shiver. Her pale, bare arms reflected from the overhead light, and he wished he had a jacket to give her.

"Thanks for the ice cream." Becky lifted her head and regarded him steadily. "I owe you one."

"I won't let you forget."

She stopped by her car and gave a half smile. "I'm sure you won't."

He opened the car door and firmly closed it when she settled into the driver's seat. "Buckle up and be careful," he warned then backed away. He waited until she pulled out of the parking lot before climbing into his truck. Her reluctance set his mind to wondering about her Sacramento friend. Was he the cause of her hesitation? Did she worry he'd be waiting for her?

He pulled the truck out of the lot and made his way around Shore Lane, slowing as he passed the road leading to Piney Point. In the emerging moonlight he could see her parked car and no other vehicles.

"Help the young lady out, God," Larry spoke aloud. "I don't know what's eating her, but she looked worried tonight. Show her Your peace."

Satisfied, he drove home and welcomed a night of uninterrupted sleep.

Becky twisted her hands together as she paced in front of the unlit fireplace. Her eyes shifted to the silent phone, and she shook her head. No, she wasn't ready. It would take a few more minutes before her nerves would settle enough to make her move.

Becky thought back over the night. Larry had been such a gentleman. To be honest she didn't think he really wanted to go for ice cream. What a knucklehead she'd been. Of course the man was exhausted. She'd seen the barely concealed yawn. He worked a full-time, stressful job between offering his handyman services, and added into the mess was the camp business. Since Jason's return the two of them had been busy with permits, zoning, and variances.

A smile lit her lips. If possible, the man was becoming better looking every time she saw him. The well-shaped head on wide shoulders; the laughing blue eyes, piercing and intelligent; the firm jawline and well-defined mouth told her he was made of strong stock. She might even let her mind dream a bit—no, no, and no! Her time and resources were limited and unknown. What if she let herself fall for him? Or worse—what if he fell for her?

The abrupt *clang* of the ringing phone caused her to jump, knocking the chair into the table at her side. With a pounding heart she stood still staring at the offending noise. She wouldn't answer it! Most assuredly it was Michael. The phone had rung off and on all afternoon, and she hadn't answered it then—she wouldn't now. She was in no mood to listen to what she knew was coming—his predictable ranting about his earlier dismissal. She needed all her energy to prepare herself for talking with her parents.

The phone finally grew silent, and she gave it a dubious look.

The thought of lifting the phone receiver and dialing the familiar number nearly made her nauseous. It was ridiculous really! She was a grown woman after all. They were her parents and no longer could lord over her, unleashing their venom, unless she gave them permission to do so. She'd overcome many obstacles in life. God had strengthened her during her time in the Congo, teaching her more in a year than she could have understood in a decade in the States. She was a woman of God, not a woman of fear.

Taking a deep breath, she marched to the phone and lifted the receiver. With determined fingers she punched the numbers in quick succession. A brief pause followed by ringing—and ringing. Eleven, twelve, thirteen—no answer. Holding the receiver briefly to her chest, she dropped it back into place, letting a relieved breath escape as she dropped herself against the wall. Reprieved! Not even the dreaded answering machine to do business with. The firing squad was disbanded for yet another day.

Hoisting herself away from the wall, she switched on the kitchen light. Suddenly she was hungry for a ham and cheese sandwich. Tomorrow would deal with itself. After a good night's sleep she would have the strength to deal with Michael and her parents.

"You are the remarkable God who makes the weak strong!" she announced toward heaven with certainty.

She opened the refrigerator and peered inside at the wide array of food before slowly letting the door close. A refrigerator! What an amazing appliance. What a shock to adjust to life without one. But she had done it.

A sudden and overwhelming sentiment caused her heart to lurch. She didn't want to be here in a warm kitchen with a full refrigerator when the ones she loved were living without. Contentment seemed so fickle, so relative to each person's wants. Even the small grocery store on the island, the one mainlanders called quaint, represented a bonanza-style of offerings never, ever seen by the Congolese people. When she first came to the island, she remembered with shame how she'd complained about the lack of variety compared to the megastores where she'd shopped in California. *God, forgive me! What a spoiled lot Your people have become. Contentment isn't relative to my life or those around me, but to You. The fullness of life's blessings can only be enjoyed when shared with others.*

Her heart ached. How she longed to be back in the Congo.

Becky slid to the floor, feeling the slickness of the wood cabinets against her back. What if God didn't let her return? Would she ever feel whole again?

"You've given me so much," she prayed aloud. "I'm having a go at it trying to adjust back to the status quo, but You don't want me there, do You? I want to appreciate everything You've given me and not take for granted the blessings which never stop." She laughed. "Even the ice cream tonight was such a treat. I wish I could have shared it with Yelessa and Regine."

A tear trickled down her cheek. "I'm worried. Why hasn't word come yet about their well-being? You will protect them, won't You? I know You can. But what I'm really asking is—will You?" She shook her head. "No, what I'm asking for is their protection, if You can be glorified through that. What an awesome God You are. Teach me. Show me what You want from me. Make it clear. Sometimes I'm too dense to see Your path. Give me the simple version—the God's-Will-for-Dummies version."

Why did she feel so emotionally overwhelmed? It wasn't big setbacks or problems making her loss feel more acute, but the small, insignificant things of life—the smell of a woodburning fire, the ratty towels in Larry's truck, or the taste of tropical fruit. She'd listened to other missionaries speak about the emotional turmoil associated with reentering the United States, leaving behind one culture for another. But she'd only been in the Congo for a year. Surely she could adapt for the short time she would be here. At times she felt normal; then a sudden, overpowering sensation would strike her very being, driving her mind back to the people she loved while her body remained trapped, chained to the life she now lived.

Yet. . .she enjoyed Bay Island and working with Larry. What a confused mess she was!

Becky drew up her knees and rested her chin. Was she going crazy? How could her mind and soul be split between two lives at the same time? Adding to the heap, Michael's arrival on the island with messages from her parents caused a collision of yet another culture.

She was emotionally spent. Yet she knew God could and would renew her spirit—starting with a good night's sleep.

Grabbing the countertop, she pulled herself to standing. A deep sigh seemed to drain the last of her energy. Abandoning the plans for a ham and cheese sandwich, she switched off the light. Her feet padded down the hallway and into the bedroom. Changing into a gown, she collapsed into the bed, closed her eyes, and let her burdened heart drift into sleep.

# Chapter 8

Becky toyed with the toast on the blue-flowered china plate. Although she slept deep and hard, morning arrived much too soon. In a daze she watched the warm, narrow shaft of light skitter across the counter and spray light through her water glass, refracting tiny rainbows of colors on the toast.

A knock at the screen door broke her sleepy trance.

"It's Tilly here," announced her neighbor loudly through the screen. "You up for a visit?"

"Coming." Becky sauntered from the kitchen to the door with a smile and unhooked the latch. "Come on in."

Tilly stepped inside. "Don't mind if I do."

"You're around and about early this morning."

"Just checkin' to see how you're doing." She stopped and gave Becky a sharp look. "And I'd say you look as though you've not been sleeping too well."

"I'm sleeping okay," she answered. "It's taking awhile for my body to adjust to the time change." She waved Tilly to follow her to the kitchen. "How about sharing some toast for breakfast?" Popping two more slices of bread in the toaster, she pointed to the coffeepot. "I can make some if you'd like. I'm not much of a coffee drinker, but this morning a cup might give me the jump start I need."

"That new young fella keep you out late?" Tilly asked without fanfare, eyeing her. "And, yes, I'd like some coffee if you're makin' a batch."

Becky hesitated a moment before sliding the carafe from the coffeemaker and walking to the sink. "Now how do you know about a certain young man?"

"Fred at the Cart Corral, of course," Tilly answered. "That new fella asked after you when he rented the cart. Said he was a close friend of yours, he did. Fred didn't like 'im too much, though, and wouldn't tell 'im, but his wife, Mirabelle, couldn't help herself and told 'im anyways."

Becky remained silent as she went about pouring water into the coffeemaker and stuffing a white filter into the brown bucket.

"I see you're not sayin' much." A smile broke out on Tilly's round face. "Couldn't get much out of Larry either."

The mention of Larry's name grabbed Becky's attention, and she stopped midair with a scoop of coffee crystals. "Larry?"

"He's on early patrol this mornin'," Tilly was saying. "I flagged him down to see how the camp project was comin' along. He's real talkative about the camp but tight-lipped as can be about your visitor."

Becky dropped three more scoops into the basket. "A discreet cop! I knew there was something I liked about Larry." In went another scoop. "What did he say about the camp?"

"Quite an earful actually." Tilly stopped and pointed to the coffeemaker. "You keep it up and both sets of our eyeballs will be rollin' back into our heads."

"Oh!" Becky halted and looked into the nearly full basket. She scooped out several spoonfuls. "So what did he say about the camp? Is he happy with the project?"

"Tickled pink, I'd say," she replied. "He did say old Edwards was givin' you a hard time. That's another reason why I came over—to make sure the old coot doesn't scare you off." She tossed Becky a look. "Plus Larry asked me to check on you."

"Check on me?" This alerted Becky like a prod in the ribs.

"I'm only tellin' you what he said." She shrugged her large shoulders. "He's a caring body, that's for sure." Several more praises followed until Becky thought she'd laugh aloud.

"It's useless, Tilly," she murmured, trying to hide her smile. "I know Larry's a great guy. The problem is, I'm not available."

Tilly drew her brows together in concern. "It's that young fella who came yesterday, is it?"

"No." It wasn't any of Tilly's concern, but Becky took no offense. She knew the motherly woman meant no harm. In some ways it felt comforting to know someone cared enough to notice even the small particulars of her life. There was a reason why Tilly was well loved by the island residents—her own love of people.

"Someone else?"

"There's no one else," she assured Tilly. "And before you start pairing Larry and me together, it's only fair to tell you he's not interested in me that way. We're working together, that's all."

"Uh-huh," Tilly grunted. "I've been around the block enough times to know when a fella's interested in a woman. And he sure does ask about your well-being enough to make a body wonder."

Becky tossed Tilly a dubious glance and poured two cups of coffee. "He might be worried that I'm offended by Mr. Edwards, as you said before. But Larry can stop worrying. It's okay—really it is."

This seemed to derail Tilly from her matchmaking mission for a moment. "Old Edwards is a real sweetheart down deep."

"Really?"

"Really!"

Becky took a sip of coffee and felt an instantaneous jolt. Her eyes began to water. "You might need some sugar and cream for this coffee," she pronounced at once, scooting over the sugar bowl and shoveling in several teaspoons. "Wow!"

"Just right!" Tilly said, taking a big gulp without flinching. "But like I was sayin', Van can be a real softie once you get to know him."

"His name is Van?" This tidbit amazed Becky. "I don't think I've ever heard him being referred to by his first name. Like Mrs. Phillips, it's almost as if they don't even have first names." She shoved the overpowering coffee cup to the side. "Mr. Edwards seems to be passionate about the camp project, but at times it's difficult to know whether he's for or against the camp. He resists nearly every move that's made. Surely he can see how God has provided in ways we could never have expected."

Tilly smiled. "He's from the old school. But if you can prove your point of view with facts that make sense to him, he'll be behind you one hundred percent. And he's one good ally to have."

"You seem quite fond of him."

To Becky's surprise the older woman blushed a light pink. "He's been at the church for more years than I care to remember, that's all." She smoothed the folds of her light blue checked dress with her hands. "He can come off being a bit harsh, and I'd hate to see you takin' it the wrong way—hard feelings and all."

"I'm not the one he needs to worry about. Lottie almost decked him the other night," Becky proclaimed with some amusement. "He started an exposition on the roles of women versus men."

Tilly shook her head. "It'll do him no good gettin' Lottie all riled up." She drained the last of her cup. "I might call the old coot and have a heart-to-heart with him. Someone needs to keep him in line."

"If anyone can do it, it's you." Becky laughed.

Tilly winked at her. "I'm takin' that as a compliment.

"Such is the spirit in which it was said."

Tilly stood. "I'd better skedaddle and get to my chores." She gave Becky a level look. "And you'd better get you some sleep. Don't let that young fella keep you out to all hours gallivantin' across the island. You look a might peaked and need your rest."

"Yes, Tilly."

"I can have Larry check on you later if there's something you need—"

"No!" Becky nearly shouted. "I'm fine! Really." She had her hands full enough dealing with Michael's presence; she didn't need an audience—especially Larry.

"All right then." Tilly made her way to the door. "Take care of yourself now, and call on ol' Tilly if you need anything."

"I will."

Tilly clomped down the outside steps, and Becky latched the door before making her way back to the kitchen. She dumped the coffee in the sink and moved the toaster back into place. It was then she saw the untoasted bread sitting idle in the machine. It did little good to place bread inside the appliance if it wasn't plugged in.

The neglected bread was much like her, she reasoned with some anxiety. If Tilly knew about Michael, then so did half the community. What a thought that was. She'd better keep Michael unplugged from the local gossip—or she'd be toast.

Becky watched as Michael strolled up the narrow walk to the café. The small bell above the entrance jingled as he opened the door and breezed through the opening. He searched the room until their gazes met and quickly weaved between the tables until he reached her.

"Why are you sitting so far back?" he asked, taking off his sunglasses. "Any further back and we'll be doing dishes."

Becky motioned for him to sit across from her. "It will give us some measure of privacy so we can talk." She wouldn't dare let him know the back booth would also limit the prying eyes she wished to avoid at all costs.

"I don't know why we couldn't have met at the hotel," he insisted as he slid across the maroon vinyl seat. He gave the room a cursory look. "The hotel restaurant is more than a step or two above this joint."

Becky took two menus from the holder at the end of the table and extended one to him. "They have good food. You won't complain, I promise."

He cast her a skeptical glance before looking over the menu. Both decided on soup and a sandwich. He frowned when the waitress informed him the establishment did not serve alcoholic beverages. Brusquely he ordered a mineral water and said nothing until the waitress returned with their drinks.

"You know," Michael finally began, resting his arm on the back of his seat, "I'm not exactly happy with the stunt you pulled yesterday. Being made to look like a fool wasn't in the plans for our happy reunion." He took a leisurely swallow of his cold drink. "You have something going on with that police guy or what?"

Becky watched the turbulence made by her spoon as she stirred her iced tea. The action gave her time to think, time to pray for guidance. Much-needed ground rules would have to be set. "Michael," she finally began, drawing a deep breath, "you can't just plummet from the sky after two years and expect me to drop everything. I am glad to see you. Truly I am." She hesitated. "But I can't let you take over like you're used to doing. I'll try to be as flexible as I can while you're here."

He looked both surprised and hurt. "That doesn't seem quite realistic. When have I ever tried to take over?"

She had to smile at his naiveté. "You've always been a leader, Michael. And up until two years ago I deferred to your judgment of where we should eat, where we should go, or even which college classes to take."

"That's hardly taking over," he said, drawing his brows together.

"Don't be offended, Michael," she gently pleaded. "I didn't mind back then. You always took good care of me. But things are different now."

"Different?" He gave her a long, steady look. "In what way are things different?"

Becky pushed back her hair. "It's hard to explain."

"Try me!"

"My focus in life has changed drastically in the past two years. The Congo is incredibly different from anything I've ever experienced."

"Because they're impoverished?"

She nodded. "That's part of it, I suppose. These people live, and have lived their whole lives, without anything we'd call of worth. I had to adapt to their way of living. It was difficult to adjust at first—to change how I dressed, how I ate, how I slept—how I related to people. Most of all I had to adjust to being alone with God. Here in the States I'd come to depend heavily on my job, my bank account, and even my friends. But when that's all stripped away, what do you have?" She spread her hands out. "God!"

"Certainly they didn't send a single woman out in that wilderness alone?" He seemed taken aback by such an idea.

"No," she answered, flustered that she couldn't adequately describe her experience of faith. "Another missionary couple was serving in the next village to help me. What I'm trying to say is, I'm different because God has let me rely on Him without the aid of my usual safety nets."

Michael gave her an uncomprehending look. "I'm sure such an experience would broaden one's view of the world, but what does that have to do with you and me and my visit?"

"For one thing," she said, "I'll be returning to the Congo once it's safe again."

"Safety is a fickle thing in those countries. It wouldn't be wise to go back for a long, long time." His brows drew together. "You don't already have a date set to return, I hope!" he exclaimed with a flash of alarm in his eyes.

"No." She shook her head. "It's a wait-and-see situation right now."

"That's good—very good." He thoughtfully rubbed his chin. "So what you're telling me is that God has shown you how to be selfless and how to make a difference in people's lives." Michael's face broke out into a smile. "That can't be much different from the Becky I knew before." He reached across the table and took both her hands in his. "You never had a selfish bone in your body. Don't you know it was your selflessness that attracted me to you in the first place? If this God-thing improved your attributes I'm all for it, because it's only made you better, not different."

Other people were drifting into the café. They cast interested glances toward them, and Becky lightly pulled her hands out of his grasp.

She tilted her head back. "Can I ask you a question?"

"Of course."

"Why did you come to Bay Island?"

He seemed bewildered. "I think you know the answer to that question—to talk with you." His eyebrows lifted. "Why does that surprise you?"

"You could have phoned to talk with me."

He nodded. "I suppose that's true. It wouldn't have taken much effort to get your number." He shrugged expressively. "I wanted to see you in person."

Becky's heart turned over. "But why?"

"When I heard you might be in danger, it did something to me. I don't know." He paused a moment. "We didn't part on the best of terms when you left, and I'm afraid I must take responsibility. I shouldn't have pushed you." He leaned forward. "As I said before, I came to talk with you about your parents; but I suppose I've also come to see if anything was left of our relationship."

Becky could feel the blood drain from her face. She'd never seen Michael so humble or brutally honest. And she was confused. "You realize the same issues still exist, Michael? My life is dedicated to doing what God wants of me. We don't share that same dedication."

"Cutting right to the chase, aren't you?" His gray eyes narrowed in deliberation. "I can live with your convictions about God. Do I have to believe exactly as you do? Not everyone is as gung ho as you are. We could learn to accept one another's positions."

Becky shook her head slowly. Michael was trying so hard, but he didn't have a clue what it meant to follow God. His idea of Jesus was limited to the making of a good story. He had no personal interest. "I know this is hard for you to understand, but God makes it clear that I can't seek a serious relationship with someone unless that person's focus is the same. It's more than having different tastes in furniture."

Michael flicked his glance over her face. "That's so. . . intolerant."

"God is intolerant at times."

He laughed. "That's the most absurd notion I've ever heard."

"Did God let the Israelites worship other gods?" she asked. "He did, but they suffered the consequences. God is jealous of anything that keeps us from doing what He wants."

"And you don't think a few thousand years has made a difference?" There was frustration in his voice.

"For both of our sakes, I hope not."

"And that means. . ."

"God doesn't change. His Word doesn't change," Becky continued, softening her voice when she noticed the rejection in the depths of his eyes. "God loves you, Michael Petit, and He wants you to accept Him as the driving force for everything you do. He sent His Son to die on the cross so you could have a direct connection with Him. But you have to make the move—not to please me, but to please God. It's not about church attendance or pledging money to the church—it's about you and God. He doesn't want your tolerance. He wants you!"

A painful silence followed until Michael straightened in his seat. "How did we move from exploring our relationship to preaching?" His mouth twisted into a half smile, but his eyes were determined. "I'm only here for a couple of more days. Can we spend some time together for old times' sake? I promise to be good if you promise to stay out of the pulpit."

"Well. . ."

The waitress arrived with their lunch, and Michael took the opportunity to move their conversation on. "Did you call your folks last night?"

She drew back, disappointed. She'd muffed it again. Would Michael never understand his soul was at stake?

"Well?" he prompted.

"I tried."

"Did you leave a message?"

"The answering machine never picked up," she explained. "I'll try again this afternoon."

He took a bite of sandwich. "You're not trying to avoid calling, are you? Your mother might not be in immediate danger, but she is extremely worried."

"I did try calling," she repeated. "Have you spoken with them since yesterday?"

He seemed reluctant to answer. "Yes. . .last night. I also tried calling you, but no one answered."

"I was at a planning meeting until late."

"With that police officer?"

"He's the head of the committee."

"That's convenient." Michael's egotistical behavior seemed to be seeping back.

"What's that supposed to mean?"

He gave her hand a quick, friendly squeeze. "Nothing at all. Let's not talk about your police friend anymore. How about we plan something for tonight? Would you like to take in a movie this evening?"

Becky shook her head. "We don't have a movie theater on the island."

"Then what do you do for fun around here?"

"Well," she began, "we're a little too old for the arcade, and it's too early in the season for midweek entertainment." She smiled. "But I could show you Thunder Bay."

"Thunder Bay?"

"It's an old Civil War site," she happily explained. "Property has been donated to build the camp on part of the land. I'd like you to see what I'm working on."

"All right," he said.

"How about six o'clock? We'll have plenty of light left in the day to see the place."

"Are you driving, or do you want me to pick you up in the hootenanny?"

She thought about this. Which would draw less attention? "We'll take your hooten—I mean your golf cart." What a mess! He had her talking like him.

He laughed. "I'll be there."

She smiled back then sobered. While she planned to share a visit to Thunder Bay with Michael, it was Larry who now drifted into her mind. It was Larry who shared her enthusiasm for the camp and her work. It was Larry she wanted to be with. Was her heart heading into dangerous territory without her permission? If Tilly was right in her observations, Larry might be in the same boat. The thought warmed her heart and yet made her head swim. Between Larry and Michael she was headed for trouble. What had she gotten herself into?

# *Chapter 9*

Larry opened the door to his cruiser, grabbed his hat and ticket pad, and swung his long legs out. The leather of his black holster creaked when he stood, and he paused long enough to fit the police hat firmly over his crew cut. When would Walter Burchell stop parking his worn-out Cadillac across the street from the Schooner's Surf and Turf—right in front of the fire hydrant?

"I've parked in the same spot for thirty-some odd years," he'd said over the last ticket, "and I don't plan on changing."

It didn't matter to Walter that city water had been placed along Pelican Avenue ten years ago or that fire hydrants were a natural and welcome outcome. Walter insisted he'd been there first, not the water, and that was all there was to it.

Larry flipped open the citations book and thumbed through the pages until he found the next fresh sheet. Slowly he walked to the two-tone blue car and withdrew a pen from his shirt pocket. How many tickets would this make—nineteen, maybe twenty? It was as if the guy enjoyed personally funding the city coffers. He'd pay the ticket every time with plenty of lip service and behave for a short time, but it wasn't long before his car would find its way back to the usual spot. Just like now! Good thing parking tickets didn't rack up points against a driver's license like moving violations. Otherwise Walter would be walking.

Leaning over the windshield, Larry copied the vehicle identification number from the metal tag on the dash. *I should have it memorized by now.* It took a short time to fill in the remaining information. Finishing the sheet, he tore off the top copy and placed it snugly under the driver's side windshield wiper blade. He looked at his watch before heading back to the white cruiser. The leather bottoms of his shiny black uniform shoes ground against the small stones on the street. Only forty-five more minutes and he could call it a night. He'd agreed to cover an extra three hours for another officer, making for a long day. Seven o'clock couldn't come too soon.

His walkie-talkie radio came to life. "Dispatch to one-ninety-four."

Larry reached for the handheld mike clipped to the cloth epaulet on the left shoulder of his starched white shirt. Depressing the lever, he turned and leaned his head close to the mouthpiece. "One-ninety-four—Pelican and Ferry Avenues."

"One-ninety-four," announced the professional-sounding female voice coming across his walkie, "please respond to a ten-thirty-eight at the Thunder Bay Civil War Landmark, at six-two-five Runaway Bay Road. Meet caller at the rear of the property."

Larry felt a shot of adrenaline surge through his body. He squeezed the lever again. "Do we have a caller's name?"

"That would be an affirmative. I'll check the report." There was a brief silence. "The caller is a Becky Merrill."

"I'm on it! E.T.A. four minutes." Larry tossed his hat inside the cruiser and climbed inside. He didn't know what Becky Merrill could be doing at Thunder Bay at this hour or what property damage might have occurred, but he didn't like the sound of it.

"One-ninety-four," the dispatcher's voice continued to crackle across the line, "do you need a backup unit for that location?"

"Negative," he answered. "I'll check and advise."

Larry put the cruiser in gear. His foot felt heavy on the gas pedal as he pulled onto the road and made an immediate U-turn. He could hear stones hitting the undercarriage of the car as he accelerated. His mind computed the information given. Property damage to Thunder Bay would most certainly be related to one of the Civil War buildings, but he'd been directed to the rear of the property—the camp property.

The shoreline scenery passed, and he glanced at the speedometer. The digital numbers corresponded precisely with the posted speed limit, and he once again focused his attention and energy to the destination at hand. Soon Thunder Bay came into sight, and he pulled the cruiser to a stop at the entrance. He stepped out and twisted his hat back on. Laying a hand over the butt of his gun in a subconscious move, he strode up the path toward the outbuildings. Nothing looked amiss.

He pressed on toward the break in trees to the first back lot. He spotted two figures standing close together with their backs turned. It was Becky who turned first as he neared the couple.

Becky left the other figure and moved toward Larry with alacrity, greeting him with what he could only call relief. "Larry. I'm so glad you were still on duty. I thought you'd left for the day."

"What's the problem, Becky?" His glance diverted from her concerned face to the other person joining them, the man he now recognized as Michael from Sacramento. He acknowledged his presence with a polite nod before bringing his gaze back to Becky. "The dispatcher said you reported some type of property damage."

Becky touched his arm. "Come with me." She led him to the spot she'd just left. "Look at these." She made a wide sweep of her hands toward the area in front of her. "There are dozens of holes dug throughout this part of the field. I'm sure it's not the work of an animal, but I can't imagine who or what it's from. I don't understand it at all."

Larry bent down and sat on his haunches to examine one of the holes. He pulled the heavy-duty flashlight from his utility holder, leaned on one knee, and shone the light into the dark depths. His black tie fell forward, touching the ground. The hole was only eight to ten inches across, but a good two feet deep. On closer inspection he could see and feel the distinct ridges made from what he'd guess to be a posthole digger. Piles of fresh earth lay in a heap to the side.

"What do you make of it?" Becky was asking him.

Brushing off his hands, he stood. "I'd say someone's looking for something buried in the field. How many holes did you say there were?" He turned in a circle looking over the area, noticing several similar cavities and mounds of dirt.

"I'm not sure." She stood quite still, her voice sharp with distress. "Maybe thirty or forty of them."

"I'd say more like twenty-five," Michael offered, speaking for the first time.

Larry turned to look at him. "What time did the two of you arrive?"

"Not more than twenty minutes ago," he answered, flitting a glance at Becky. "Wouldn't you say that's right?"

"I suppose," she agreed with a nod. "I was showing Michael the land for the camp, and all of a sudden we noticed these holes." She was backing up to point behind Larry. "They start over there—"

Larry immediately shot his hand out and latched firmly onto her arm. "Watch it there." He pulled her forward from the yawning opening behind her. "You could easily break an ankle stumbling into one of these holes."

Startled, she turned to see the dark opening just inches from her feet. Even in the waning light Larry could see the light hue of pink highlighting her cheeks as he released his grip. She seemed breathless. "You're right, Larry. These are very dangerous. We'll have to fill them in tomorrow."

Larry nodded. "The two of you stay here and let me count the holes." He surveyed the area, counting exactly twenty-five, just as Sacramento Michael had said. "Have you been over to the field next to the shore?" he asked Becky when he rejoined them.

"We didn't see anything there," she responded. "We went to the back property first. It wasn't until we came back this way to see the pond that we found these holes."

"What do you think the person was looking for?" This question came from Michael.

Larry let his full gaze fall on the man beside Becky. He was the same height as he was but with a much different, stocky build and dark complexion. Not for the first time he wondered what relationship the two shared—or had shared.

This much he noticed—Becky seemed almost to ignore her friend while fretting over the mysterious damage.

Finally Larry spoke. "My first guess would be the vandals are looking for old war relics since the holes are deep and narrow. If the person was looking to find a spot where several relics might be, they would pepper the area." He let his eyes scan the field. "There's almost an organized pattern."

Michael looked in the same direction. "You're probably right. The holes would have to be deep to find good Civil War items."

*The man is smarter than he looks.* "I'm working the afternoon shift tomorrow," he said to Becky. "I'll stop by early tomorrow morning and see what I can do about filling in these holes so someone doesn't get hurt. For now, I'll get my police tape and rope off the area."

"What time do you think you'll be here?" she asked. "I can meet you here."

Larry saw the frown creep across Michael's face, but the man said nothing. "I'm thinking about eight o'clock."

Becky nodded. "I'll be here."

"Why don't I pick you up?" Larry didn't know what prompted him to offer, but the suggestion must have been appreciated for he was rewarded with a big smile from Becky. "I'll walk you two out to the parking lot. I want to get the police tape put up before it becomes any darker."

The three made their way to the nearly vacant gravel lot. Larry noticed the lone four-seater golf cart parked near the entrance and surmised it belonged to Becky's friend.

Suddenly he felt a warm hand on his arm. Becky was looking up at him. "Do you need help with the police tape? I could help."

"No. I'm fine." He looked at the golf cart again. "You'll be wanting to get back to Piney Point before dark settles in." Golf carts made great transportation—in the daytime, not at night. He could see Michael was already settling behind the wheel. "Make sure he uses the headlights."

"He will," she agreed after much hesitation, seeming reluctant to leave. "About a quarter till eight?"

"Quarter till eight," he repeated. "And don't worry about the holes. We'll take care of them tomorrow. It's probably a onetime deal. I doubt the vandals will be back."

"I sure hope so," she said in a low whisper.

Her worried tone caused him to give her a deeper look. "It will be okay," he assured her, giving her hand a light squeeze. "Trust me. You go on now and make sure you get a good night's sleep."

Becky nodded and gave a wave before heading for the golf cart. Larry opened the trunk of the cruiser and reached for the roll of police tape and four stakes.

"I thought we had breakfast plans in the morning," he heard Michael say after the white golf cart started and backed up several feet.

The cart moved away before Larry could hear Becky's response. He shut the trunk and walked back to the field. Placing the stakes and winding the tape around the irregular square perimeter gave Larry plenty of time to think. He couldn't put his finger on the problem, but Becky and her friend seemed—well, the closest he could describe was—uncomfortable. That was it. The two seemed uncomfortable. Becky didn't appear afraid, angry, or upset, but ill at ease. Much like last night when she asked him out for ice cream. He didn't know how concerned he should be or how involved he wanted to become. Tangling with females and their emotions could very well resemble a real minefield. Did he really want to go there?

Larry tied off the last of the tape. He supposed it was a good sign Becky liked to be with him, a point proven with her quick acceptance of a ride in the morning. Behind her bubbly, dreaming brain, however, were turbulent waters. Being yanked from the mission field could account for much of her troubles; yet his instincts told him there was much more. Something about Becky tugged on his sense of chivalry, and knowing her better would be a good thing; but she kept sending mixed signals. He didn't mind playing the white knight in shining armor as long as the damsel in distress wanted to be rescued. Having to drag a reluctant woman to safety put a genuine damper on the process.

Dark fell quickly, and he used his flashlight to navigate back to the cruiser. He sat behind the wheel and flipped on the interior light. It would take a few minutes to complete the report. He reached for the car radio mike, unclipping the mouthpiece from the holder. The coiled cord stretched easily.

"One-ninety-four to dispatch."

"Go ahead, one-ninety-four."

"The thirty-eight will be a code one."

"Copy."

"I'll be clear and code four and heading back to the station."

"Copy, one-ninety-four, and good night."

Larry looked at his watch. Seven forty-five! The police chief would have something to say about the overtime—again. Maybe he could bargain some comp time instead. He needed the time more than the money with the camp project moving forward on the fast track. Yes, the chief might be obliging. Anything to keep the dreaded overtime off the books.

# Chapter 10

Becky sat stoically in the passenger seat, thankful for the warmth of her jacket as the cool wind whipped at her face and hair. Michael was angry with her. It was as though he believed she'd concocted the deep gopher-like holes as an excuse to avoid having breakfast with him.

She risked a glance at him. He sat beside her, his hands gripping the wheel of the golf cart while he gazed ahead as if seeing things beyond her vision. His profile, etched against the waning light, sent an odd shiver along her nerves. Suddenly he turned his head toward her as though aware of her scrutiny.

"Sure you won't reconsider breakfast tomorrow?" he asked for the second time. "I think your police friend could handle the job by himself. He looks strong enough. Besides, that type of manual labor isn't women's work. Any man worth his salt wouldn't let you help, let alone encourage your participation."

Becky only shook her head at his question and was relieved to see they were nearing Piney Point. Michael's mouth was pressed into a disagreeable line, and she'd about had enough for one day. He raced the cart up the incline and parked near the deck stairs then shut off the engine.

"What would it take to get you to California for a few days?" he asked abruptly, his gray eyes piercing her own.

Becky gave him a perplexed look. "California?"

"I want you to return with me to California," he explained. "Your parents are worried about you, and frankly I'm worried about you. This whole camp project—" He waved his hand in the air. "This camp project is stressing you out. I can see it in your face. What you need is some rest and relaxation."

"I can't just leave my duties, Michael. There's work to be done, and the groundbreaking ceremony is just around the corner." His suggestion was ludicrous at best. "I'm going to try calling Mother and Father again tonight. They'll calm down once I let them know I'm all right."

"And when they find out their little girl is shoveling dirt—then what?" was his crisp reply. "Now tell me—what would it take to relieve you of these duties for a while? Ten thousand? Twenty?"

"Michael!" She couldn't believe her ears.

"Thirty?"

"Michael, stop it. I don't want your money."

"I wouldn't be giving it to you," he reasoned. "I'll donate the money to the camp so they can hire some island goon to dig trenches and backfill holes. There'd be enough to get someone else to do the piddly work they're running you ragged with."

Becky felt the air leave her lungs. Michael was being obstinate and unreasonable. He acted as though she didn't have the sense of a child. Did he believe throwing money at every problem he encountered would make the world a better place?

"Michael, the answer is no." She glared at him indignantly and stepped from the cart. "I don't want to go back with you to California. My home is here. And I don't want your. . .bribe money." She held onto the roof as she peered inside. "I like my job, and I'm good at it. Hard work never hurt anyone. There's no shame in manual labor."

Michael leaned over the passenger seat and stared up at her. "I'm not getting down on you, darling. I just care about what happens to you."

She drew back sharply. Darling? The endearment brought back memories and at the moment sounded contrived. "It's time to say good night, Michael. I'll call you sometime tomorrow."

"I won't be here."

"What's that supposed to mean?"

"I'm leaving after breakfast tomorrow," he announced. "I'd like you to come with me, but since you seem determined to work on this camp project, I'll just have to come back—with reinforcements."

Becky's hands shook. "Reinforcements?"

"When's this groundbreaking ceremony?" he asked, ignoring her startled gaze. "May first, is it? I'm not going to give up yet. Take care of yourself, Becky."

He started the engine and without further argument drove off, leaving Becky gaping after him. What nerve! She could hardly believe the audacity of the man. Reinforcements indeed! Who did he think he was? He couldn't just barge back into her life and take over.

With fervor she tromped up the steps and let herself into the cabin. Her keys clattered as she dropped them to the counter with more force than necessary. What impertinence! Her heart pounded in agitation, and a parallel, pulsating sensation could be felt above her left temple. It took several minutes to calm sufficiently to attack her next problem—her parents. Slowly she lifted the phone receiver and dialed the familiar number.

"Hello?" Her mother's voice came across the line, and Becky nearly buckled.

She held the phone tight to her ear. "Mother. . .it's Becky."

"Becky?" came the surprised gasp. "Is it really you?"

"Yes, it's really me."

"Are you all right?" her mother asked. "We've been extremely worried, you know. Is Michael there with you?"

Becky sank into the dining room chair. "I'm fine, and, no, Michael just left to go back to his hotel." She paused. "Michael told me you had a small stroke a few weeks ago. Is everything okay?"

"It was really nothing. The doctors have me on a blood thinner, and I have to watch my diet—that sort of thing." Becky could hear a sigh come across the line. "I think the stroke was more stress related, you know. Your father and I have been sick with worry about you since we heard about them pulling out the Americans. But what can you expect when you're living among savages? Who knows what could have happened to you?"

Becky set her teeth. The guilt-trip voyage was about to begin. "I was not living among savages, Mother."

But her mother wasn't listening. Becky could hear her talking to someone, and then her father's voice came across the line.

"Becky," boomed her father, "it's about time you gave us a call. Didn't Michael tell you how anxious we were? It's really inexcusable to keep us in such a state."

Becky rubbed one temple with her free hand. Michael said her parents' attitude had changed. How wrong could he be? It was as if their conversation picked right up from the day she left—their offensive attack, her defense.

"Daddy, I don't want to argue with you," she said gravely. "Michael said you were concerned and that you wished for me to call. I tried calling last night and this afternoon, but there was no answer and no answering machine to leave a message."

"We were home the entire evening last night," he said sharply. "Your mother could have been lying on her deathbed for all you care. Are you sure you weren't out all night with that police fellow Michael mentioned?"

This was going to get ugly. The old feelings of anger and disgust were rising like helium in her burning chest. Time had only scabbed over the wound, which refused to heal. If she didn't intervene, the old injury would break wide open.

"I won't argue with you, Daddy. You'll just have to take my word that I did call."

"Where's Michael?" came his crusty reply.

"At the hotel."

"You have him give me a call tomorrow," he demanded. "I want to talk with that boy."

"He's leaving in the morning," she answered. "If you want to talk with him, I suggest you give him a call tonight."

"Leaving?"

"That's what he told me a few minutes ago."

"Are you coming back with him?"

Becky felt constriction in her chest. Uncertainty clouded her voice, for a humiliating suspicion was taking form. "No."

"And why not?"

Coming back to California must have been her parents' idea, not Michael's. That had been the plan all along, but something caused Michael to make his move earlier than expected. This annoyed her immensely.

"No, I'm not coming back with Michael." She sat straighter in the chair. "I'm twenty-five years old and capable of taking care of myself. I'm not sure what Michael has told you, but I'm working on the island as a camp director until I have news on my position in the Congo. I realize you don't approve of the path I've chosen, but you must learn to accept who I am."

Her father grunted into the phone. "They've brainwashed you. That much I know."

"As I said before, I don't want to argue. I called to find out how Mother was doing. Can't we have a normal conversation?"

"You never did listen to your mother and me," he charged, and Becky could imagine the large vein on his forehead was bulging by this time. "You've always been strong-willed and difficult to raise. We've tried our best, and this is how we're rewarded? Your brother has a full-time job with a nationally known company and is earning what he's worth. If you had kept up your grades, you could have entered Stanford and by now—"

She interrupted his tirade. "Father?"

"What?"

"I do love you," she responded more calmly than she felt. "Tell Mother I love her, too. Thank you for sending Michael out to check on me, but you can stop worrying. I'm doing fine. I'll check on you and Mother again soon. Take care of yourselves, okay?"

With that she gently replaced the receiver. She'd taken control and stopped the vicious cycle she knew her father would have continued. God had given her the strength to bring the verbal abuse to an end. Then why did she feel so horrible? And why did she wish Larry were here to make things better. He would have known how to calm her father.

Larry! It was becoming more difficult to remain detached from his strengths—and his charms. He was solid as a rock and seemed to have a knack for fixing everything from water heaters to vandalism. Nothing moved him. Why then shouldn't he be an expert in fixing broken and tired hearts? And she was tired. Tired of fighting. Tired of setting down a path of dreams and finding the path blocked. Tired of her parents. Tired of worrying about things she couldn't control. Larry would be the kind of man who could look at each problem with objectivity and help forge a plan of action. She needed his objectivity, and he could use a good dose of dreaming beyond static reality. What a combination they could make!

But she had the threat of rejection to consider. What would Larry say once he knew she came from the dreaded "talking money" background he detested?

Or, worse yet, discovered her full-blown, bigger-than-life dysfunctional family was alive and well—and ready to interfere? It might be difficult for him to understand her family dynamics since she imagined his family to be idyllic.

There were so many ifs. *If* he was even interested in her. *If* he didn't turn tail and run when he found out about her family. *If* she were to remain on the island. *If* God didn't call her back to the Congo. *If* she could choose wisely. Hadn't she always heard women chose men who resembled their fathers? Oh, please. Don't let it be so!

And what did she know about men? She was too shy in high school and college to date anyone other than Michael. Her parents had said he was the right one for her and encouraged her to look no further—so she never did. That's what made it so laughable when Lauren had believed sometime ago that Becky and Jason were an item. Becky was working as Jason's bookkeeper when Lauren returned to the island. The whole thing was a big misunderstanding. If only Lauren had known the so-called beauty queen she feared was dateless and unavailable. Neither paid enough attention to realize.

Now there was Larry, the first man she'd felt comfortable with and the first man she'd consider sharing life experiences with. It scared her spitless.

*God, give me wisdom to know Your path for my life. Life is hard, but I know You are good. Thank You for sending Larry. He's been a blessing. But I need help in navigating the waters—big time. Show this mixed-up woman what You want. Without You I'm toast!*

Larry pressed one heavy-duty boot back and forth over the freshly packed dirt. "That should do it."

"Wonderful!" Becky dusted the knees of her jeans with her hands and leaned on the shovel. "Let's hope whoever had the sudden urge to use this field for digging practice doesn't return."

"I'll make sure a few cars patrol this area regularly. It's unlikely the person or persons will return, but we won't take any chances." His look turned cautious. "Don't come out here alone, and if you're going to show it to your friend again, let me know. I don't want you to meet up with any intruders."

"Michael's already left the island."

Larry detected a tone—of what? Resignation, relief, or agitation? "I thought he was staying a few more days."

"Guess he had other things to do." She shrugged her shoulders. "It's just as well. I'm going to be busy this week setting up for the May Day groundbreaking."

Unfolding the blue tarp next to the cooler, he directed Becky to sit. "Let's take a water break before we clean up the tools."

Becky sat near the far corner. "Have you made much progress with the zoning variance?"

Larry rummaged through the cooler, took out two water bottles, and extended one to her as cold water dripped off his fingers. "Council said there wouldn't be a problem. It's not like bigger cities where it takes an act of God to change zoning and obtain permits. Building will begin sooner than most of us could have hoped for."

"In some ways I'd like to be around to see the entire project completed," she noted with a wistful longing in her eyes. "It's going to be magnificent."

"It must be hard for you wondering what's going to happen from day to day," he returned, hearing the crackle of plastic as he loosened the cap. "Have you heard anything definite from the mission board?"

She shook her head. "On Monday they called to say the Congo was still unsecured for Americans and could remain so for several months. They still haven't heard from those in my village. They're the ones I'm concerned about."

"What made you decide on missions and going to the Congo?" The idea of missions intrigued Larry, and he had a deep respect for those who answered the call.

Becky smiled and fingered the lettering on her bottle. "It started a few years ago. Did you know I found Jesus only three years ago?"

He shook his head, surprised at the revelation. For an unknown reason he thought she grew up in a Christian home. Maybe her strong and hopeful faith led him to wrong assumptions.

"I met several students in college who were part of a Christian collegiate organization and decided to attend their meetings." She tilted her head and gave him an intent look. "Several weeks later I realized my previous views on God were all wrong. Being the best I could in life wasn't the ticket to God—Jesus was. I made a decision to follow Jesus in my life shortly after. Almost immediately I knew God wanted me to tell others about what He did for me—how He changed my life."

"That's when you decided to go overseas?"

"That's hard to describe." She took a sip of her water, seeming at ease speaking about this part of her life. "I guess I'd always been concerned about people from other countries who were in need. Now I knew how to help them not only physically, but also spiritually. My pastor encouraged me to talk with one of the missionary boards our church supports, and I suppose the rest is history."

"And the Congo?"

She laughed. "That was the hardest part. Every time they showed a presentation of a field in need of missionaries, I wanted to go. There were so many places in need and so few people willing to go. It was hard to make a decision. I wanted to go to all of the places. But what made my decision was the missionary couple in the next village who specifically asked for a single woman to work with a small Congolese women's group."

"And you liked the work?" Larry asked, leaning back on both elbows. He enjoyed watching Becky blossom.

"Oh, yes." Another smile spread across her face. "It took a lot of adjustment on my part, but God was able to use me in ways I'd never dreamed. The women were beginning to open up. Things were going well until I was awakened from sleep that terrible night and hustled out of the country." Her dark eyes regarded him solemnly. "It was awful!"

"I'm sure it was." He studied Becky intently for a moment. "And I'm sure you're worried about the people you left behind."

She nodded. "I'm praying for God to take care of them."

"It's a good thing you serve a God who has the power to make the impossible happen." He turned on one elbow. "Just like Kelly Enterprises donating the land. We were prepared for a long struggle haggling over the price—if we could even convince them to sell. And then—they donate the land. If that's not a miracle, I don't know what is!"

"God is amazing," she agreed, her face taking on the familiar glow he'd come to recognize.

"What does your family think of your missionary work?" he asked, watching her very closely.

Their gazes met for a timeless moment before tension slowly crept into her features and the glow dissolved like a water-drenched candle. "They weren't quite as supportive as I would have hoped." With that she put the water bottle down and brought herself up on her knees. "I suppose we should head back. You wanted to stop at the church, remember—and the secretary will be leaving for lunch soon."

He had no doubt in his mind: Becky's family was a source of anxiety. But why? Could she and her parents be estranged? It would be difficult to believe. Dreamers needed people and were generally close to their families. One thing was true: Something was deeply wrong.

Becky was already gathering their tools when Larry finally stood, grabbed the tarp, and folded it into a nice, neat square. Silently they walked to his truck and loaded the shovels and cooler into the back.

"Do you want to drop in at the Dairy Barn for a hot dog after we finish at the church?" he asked, hoping to revive her previous mood.

"Okay," she acquiesced quickly as if their earlier discussion was long gone from her memory. "Are you going to try the special today?"

He turned in time to see the teasing glint in her eyes. "I told you before." He chuckled. "I don't do mystery specials. Living dangerously will kill you!"

"And police work doesn't qualify as dangerous living?" she challenged with amusement written across her delicate features.

"I have a firearm for protection on my job." He laughed. "What defense do

I have against an unknown blob of ice cream?"

"It wouldn't do any good to shoot it."

"You've proved my point."

Both laughed as Larry pulled out of the parking lot. The trip to the church was a short one, and they quickly exited the truck. Larry opened the glass church door for her.

"Hello, you two," Tilly called out, shutting the office door behind her and coming toward them.

"Hi, Tilly," Becky returned. "What are you doing here? Searching for more volunteers to help plant flowers in the box out front?"

"Just droppin' off food for the pantry." Her eyes grew curious. "Heard some vandals went about diggin' holes in the fields of the camp property."

Larry nodded. "We just finished filling them in. Someone's probably trying out their metal detector looking for Civil War relics."

"Could be a specific Civil War relic they're lookin' for," Tilly replied mysteriously. She put her hands on her ample hips. "You do know what I'm speakin' about, don't you?"

Becky looked as confused as he felt. "I'm not sure if I'm following you, Tilly."

"You don't remember the stories about the Union gold believed to still be buried on the island?" Tilly's mouth pulled to one side as she glanced between the two. "Legend has it that Union money was kept on the island, buried somewhere on Thunder Bay." She leaned forward. "They buried the money when some renegade Confederates were approachin' the island. They'd come to break out the Southern prisoners supposed to be held here. There's no way of knowin' if they knew about the secret Union treasury post, but the Yanks weren't takin' chances. They hid the money."

Larry rubbed his hand across his short crop of hair. "I do remember the story now, but it's never been proven to be factual. Most people discount it to great campfire tales."

"Plenty of island people are still believin' the story," she said. "It might be somethin' to consider. Whether the story is true or not, if someone believes—" Suddenly she gave them a wave. "I've got errands to run. Don't you kids work too hard now, ya hear."

Becky and Larry exchanged comical glances as Tilly breezed past them and out the door like a whirlwind.

"Come on," Larry said, walking to the office and opening the door. He let Becky walk through before closing it. He smiled at the secretary. "Good morning, Judi. Do you have the notarized forms for city council?"

"Of course," Judi responded, her eyes bright. "Signed and ready." She handed a white folder to him then picked up an envelope. "Something else arrived by courier for the camp this morning."

Larry scanned the official-looking envelope. “What’s this?”

Judi only shrugged.

Becky looked over his shoulder. “There’s no return address.”

“Guess we’ll just open it.” He leaned over the counter. “Do you have an opener?” Judi reached into the desk drawer and produced what he needed. He slit the top and spread the sides open. “Looks like a check.”

“A check?” Becky was stretching her neck to see.

Larry pulled the cashier’s check and a short, typed letter from the envelope. He gave a low whistle. “The letter says the check is to be used for building materials at the camp. The donor wants to remain anonymous. What do you make of that?” He held it out for Becky to see.

Becky grew very still at his side. “Thirty thousand?”

“Thirty thousand!” He drew the check back and stared at the figure. What a wonderful show of God’s support. Becky would no doubt add this miracle to her collection, reveling in the credence it gave to her dreams. He waved the check before her again. “Can you believe it?” He waited for her delighted squeal but instead watched her eyes grow wide and her face pale. His smile slipped. “What’s the matter?”

She only shook her head before pushing past him and out the door. Judi’s face mirrored his own surprise. He stuffed the check into the envelope then into his back pocket.

With a hurried stride he exited the office and out the side door. He stopped and scanned the parking lot for several seconds before glancing at his truck. A pair of white tennis shoes could be seen underneath the truck. It was time Becky and he talked, and there was no better time than the present.

# Chapter 11

Becky leaned her back against the cool sturdiness of Larry's truck, digging the toe of her sneaker into the gravel. Her thick mane of hair was unquestionably cleaning the fine layer of dirt from the driver's door, but she didn't care. Unbelievable! Michael or Father—or both—had managed what they thought to be thirty thousand reasons for her to return to California. Bribe money! Her chest hurt to visualize the check with the endless zeros mocking her very existence.

And she'd made a fool of herself in the church office, which all but required her to give an explanation. When would she learn to control her emotions? To match her mood, she heard the distant rumble of thunder and gazed up at the approaching dark clouds. Marvelous! Just marvelous!

The sound of approaching footsteps caused her to stiffen. Her heart gave an unpleasant lurch, and she looked to see Larry standing at the front edge of the truck. He said nothing for a moment then approached her. Silently he leaned his back against the truck beside her.

"You'll be wanting an explanation, I suppose?" she murmured softly when the silence became unbearable.

"That would only seem logical," he answered briefly but firmly.

A warmth surged into her face. "It's rather difficult to explain."

"I suspected as much."

Becky closed her eyes and drew a deep breath. She felt his gaze upon her, and when she turned and opened her eyes, she met his intense stare. Oh, this was hard. "I know who sent the check!"

Surprise registered on his face. "You know the anonymous donor?"

Numbly she nodded. "It was Michael, the man you escorted to the hotel and met again last night on the campgrounds."

"Michael?" he repeated with a measure of skepticism, his eyebrows cocked in thought. "You believe Michael can afford such a large sum?"

"I have no doubt he has the resources to post such an amount and much more if necessary." She let her gaze drop to the police insignia of his worn black T-shirt; she knew what she would see if their eyes met, and she wasn't ready to face his contempt. The echo of "talking money" still haunted her thoughts.

"All right," she heard him say. "Let's suppose Michael did donate the money to the camp. It obviously upsets you to believe this to be true. Talk to me about what's going on."

Becky took a deep breath and looked up at him, noticing the power of his perceptive blue eyes. "I'm upset because it's bribe money!" Just saying the words caused her body to shudder.

"Bribe money?" His voice was acute, and she felt him straighten. "That's a serious allegation. What kind of bribe money do you believe Michael is offering?"

"He. . .and my parents want me to return to California."

Larry looked stunned. "And they're willing to part with thirty thousand dollars for you to go? That doesn't make sense, Becky. Why should they offer money to the camp in exchange for a visit home?" He tilted his head in deliberation. "Did you make some type of agreement with your friend Michael?"

Becky whirled to face him. "Absolutely not!"

"Then what?" he asked. "You said he was a 'childhood chum' if I remember right. Is there something else you need to clarify? Something else I need to know?"

His look and manner were too intense for her to pretend she didn't understand. Running her tongue over her suddenly dry lips, she slumped back against the truck's exterior. "We were college sweethearts," she began to explain. "I broke off the relationship when it became evident he wouldn't—or couldn't—share my new faith. My parents were devastated, of course, with my decision concerning Michael and then with entering the mission field. They carried on as if I'd joined a cult."

He seemed to give her explanation a frowning consideration then nodded. "Go on."

"They pretty much disowned me, both Michael and my parents," she continued, each word feeling like a hammer blow to her heart. "I hadn't spoken to either for nearly two years—until Michael wrote the letter and arrived unannounced two days ago. My mother suffered a stroke a few weeks ago, and he'd come to convince me to call my parents—or so I'd thought. His—or my father's—real intentions, I believe, were to have me go back home."

"Why would he assume it would take thirty thousand dollars for you to travel back to California?" His gaze was very still upon her, level.

Becky had to take a deep breath to curb the breathlessness she felt. "Michael and my parents are accustomed to gaining what they want with money. They're not used to being denied their wants." She paused long enough to gain a glimpse of Larry's reaction. When his expression remained unreadable, she continued. "They believe if the camp is given enough money you'll hire a new director to do my job, leaving me with nothing to do but come home."

"You're saying your parents and Michael are trying to manipulate you with money?"

The charged atmosphere crackled with tension. "Yes!"

"Answer me this," he asked, his warm hand suddenly grasping hers. "Are you positive the money is from Michael or your parents?"

"Reasonably sure." She pursed her lips. "He insinuated the offer last night, and the amount—well, it fits."

Larry's fingers released hers as he reached into his back pocket and pulled out the envelope, holding it in front of him. The check slid out easily. "The cashier's check was obtained at a bank on the mainland two days ago. If we're to suppose the check is from your friend, it means he visited the bank the same day he came to the island." He paused. "And following that same analogy, it means he would have anticipated making you the offer before talking with you." He shook his head. "Why go to the trouble of making out such a large check without knowing whether you'd object to traveling home? You hadn't seen or spoken with him in two years, right? As far as he knows, you might have wanted to go home."

"True."

"And," he continued, "he'd have to know you were working with the camp. The check is made out to the camp, not you. How would he have known?"

"True." His words were a cool breath of sanity she ought to welcome.

"Could it be the check might be from an entirely different donor?"

A smidgen of doubt entered her mind, but she shook if off. "I just can't believe the check is a coincidence."

"Maybe it is; maybe it isn't." He slid the check back in the envelope. "Why don't you let me look into the matter and see what I can come up with?"

Larry moved to place the envelope back into his pocket, but Becky reached out, gripping his arm with all her strength. She felt his hard muscles move under her hands as he turned to her. "You won't—won't tell anyone about what I've told you, will you?" She let her hand drop. "I couldn't bear it if people knew. And if one person finds out, it will be all over the island in five minutes."

Something akin to uneasiness crossed his face, and a muscle twitched at the corner of his mouth. "I'll be particularly discreet."

She summoned a smile. "Thank you. I know this entire situation must seem very peculiar to you. It's been extremely embarrassing to explain."

"I appreciate the fact you confided in me," he answered and then leaned close. "Is there anything else I should know? Anything which might be important?"

She hesitated, unsure of herself. "He did say one other thing."

"Go on."

"Before Michael left, he said he would be back." She paused. "With reinforcements."

He didn't respond at once but seemed to mull over her words. "Do you interpret his words to be meant as a threat?"

"I don't think so." She shook her head slowly. "It could mean a variety of things. Maybe he'll come back with a bigger offer of money. It could mean he's bringing my father to the island. It's hard to tell."

"It could be harmless," he offered, rubbing his thumb thoughtfully on the curve of his jaw. "Has he ever shown signs of being possessive or controlling in the past?"

"Possessive? Controlling?"

"Possessive and controlling as in constantly wanting to know where you are or who you're with," he explained. "Making you account for your time. Possessive and controlling as in discouraging your friendships with others and wanting you to spend all your time with him. Has he ever exhibited any of these signs?"

"No, never," she said, appalled at the thought. "He is strong-willed and likes to lead—you know, to take control of some decisions. But I've never felt threatened—annoyed, perhaps, but not threatened."

"You believe his remarks about reinforcements are harmless then?" he asked.

"I can't imagine what else they could be." A deep sigh escaped. "But I do believe he will be back, and if he gave this money"—she pointed to the envelope Larry still held—"he'll expect something in exchange."

"I can imagine this thought alone bothers you a great deal," he observed, his unwavering stare holding steady on her face. "As I said before, I'll make a few inquiries and see if we can clear up the matter."

"Discreetly!"

"Of course," he promised, tilting his head in the familiar way she found appealing. "I'll just need a small amount of information from you to help me begin."

"I'm sorry for being such a bother," she said with regret, letting her gaze drop. "I'm supposed to be helping you with the camp, not giving you more work."

"You don't have to explain further." He pushed himself away from the truck. "Come on," he directed, cupping her elbow to lead her around to the passenger door. Reluctantly she consented. "I promised you a Dairy Barn hot dog." He opened the door and waited until she settled into the seat. "I don't want you fretting about the check. I'll get to the bottom of it."

From his grim look Becky didn't hesitate for one moment to believe him. And although the thought of a hot dog squeezing past her constricted throat seemed impossible, she wasn't about to argue with the man who just climbed into the truck beside her. He was about to save her hide again.

Larry leaned back in the captain's chair waiting for the computer to process his request. "Is NCIC having trouble today?" he asked the lieutenant sorting reports at the next desk. "It's taking forever."

The lieutenant shrugged. "Everything's slow today. I ran a LEADS report earlier, and it took awhile."

Larry blew a puff of air from his cheeks. The National Crime Information Computer was becoming more and more vital to the department. They needed to invest in new computers with a faster connection.

A crack of lightning suddenly flashed light across his desk, and Larry glanced out the window as a deep roll of thunder made the pane vibrate. Large droplets of rain were beginning to ping-pong across the outside ledge, and he glanced to the heavens. Dark clouds were moving quickly northward, but the promise of blue sky could be seen in the horizon. The rainstorm would pass quickly.

The sound of computer noise caused Larry to turn back from the window. Finally! The computer screen came alive, and he leaned forward to type in Michael Petit's name, date of birth, and last known address. Moving the mouse, he clicked several fields before sending the information off for analysis. The desk phone rang.

Larry scooped up the receiver. "Officer Newkirk."

"Got your message," the male caller responded. "What's up?"

Larry smiled and leaned back in the chair. The speaker's voice was unmistakable—fast, clipped, and as usual, to the point. "Yes, Robert. I'm fine—thanks for asking. And you?"

"All right, so I'm a little short on manners today," Robert returned with a gurgling smoker's laugh. He coughed. "Can't blame a guy for being on edge. The only time you call is when you need something. And why do I get the feeling you're going to cash in on the favor I owe you?"

"Because your feeling is right," Larry answered his old college friend. "I need your services."

"Ah," came the voice. "Personal or business?"

"Both."

"Spill it then." Larry could hear Robert ransacking his desk for a pen. "What can this PI do for you? Missing person? Bail jumper?"

"No." Larry tapped his finger on the check before him. "I need you to track down the owner of a cashier's check."

"Cashier's check?" Robert repeated. "That won't be easy, you know. What's the story?"

"I'd like to find the origin of an anonymous donor who has given money to the new church camp we're planning to build on the island," Larry answered.

"Yeah?" He hesitated. "You want to give the person a cigar or what?"

"Just need a name, that's all." Larry gave a brief account of the check. "Do you think finding the donor is possible? I know a cashier's check is hard to trace, especially if the person went to great lengths to remain anonymous."

"Yeah, but it's hard to move thirty grand and not be noticed," Robert pointed out.

"So you can do it?"

"If it can be done, I'm the one to do it." There was no arrogance in his voice, only confidence. "Is the check local?"

"First Community in Cleveland."

"That's good. Very good." More rustling of papers. "When do you need the information? Yesterday, I suppose."

"It wouldn't hurt to put some gas under the burner," Larry answered. "I'd appreciate anything you can do."

"I'm not saying my methods will be conventional, if you get what I mean."

"I don't want to know," Larry replied, knowing full well Robert's methods circumvented the law more often than not. He could use tools and gain information never available to law enforcement. But he was highly effective.

Robert only laughed and coughed again. "All right, buddy. Fax over a copy and let me check it out. As soon as I find something, I'll give you a jingle."

"And I need the inquiry to be discreet," Larry added.

Robert seemed to find this funny. "I'm the pillar of discretion," he said. "We'll be even after this matter is settled. You know that, right?"

"Right!"

"Is that all then?"

"One other thing."

"Yeah?"

"Give up the cigarettes, friend," Larry warned. "You're too young to be sounding like an old man with the croup. A guy of your talents needs to stick around for a long time."

"Sinus cold." Robert chuckled.

"Yes? And my badge is made of pure gold."

"Better keep it polished then. I'll give you a ring soon." The phone went dead.

Larry eased the chair back to an upright position and let the phone drop back into the cradle. Robert would put the matter to rest—one way or the other.

Becky's revelation had come as a total bolt out of the blue. What he expected her to say he didn't know; but it certainly wasn't a theory about the exchange of thirty thousand dollars for an unorthodox manipulation scheme. He wasn't sure which amazed him more: Michael offering the money, or the fact that Becky came from money—evidently lots of it. He prided himself in reading people well. He'd missed this one by a mile. He never figured her for a rich girl.

He plucked Robert's business card from the desk and scooped up the cashier's check. Making a copy, he went to the fax machine and punched in the mainland phone number. The second-long dial tone was followed quickly by the high-pitched digital melody. Several seconds later he walked back to his desk with the copy and confirmation in hand.

Glancing at the computer screen, he noted the requested results beginning to formulate. He scrolled down through the information. Nothing! No outstanding warrants. No felony convictions. Not even an evil twin with the same name to prompt a follow-up lead. Larry folded his arms across his chest. He could call the Sacramento department and run a check for anything local—motor vehicle violations, littering, or even spitting on the sidewalk. Larry drew a deep breath. No, he'd wait to make the call after hearing from Robert.

"Hey, Newkirk!"

Larry turned to the lieutenant. "Yeah?"

"Line two. Sounds like a looker."

Waving off the remark, he punched the blinking red light on the phone. "Officer Newkirk."

"Larry!" Becky's voice came across the line. "They've done it again. The holes are back, and there're twice as many."

"Where are you?" Larry asked, picking up his hat from the corner of the desk.

"At the camp."

"You're not alone, are you?" he asked with concern. "I told you not to go to the camp alone."

"Tilly's with me, and she's very upset," Becky said, her voice sounding troubled. "A nice gentleman who is touring the buildings is with us, too. He loaned me his cell phone to call you. What should we do?"

"Sit tight," he instructed, pulling the cruiser keys from the clip on his belt. "I'll be there in a few minutes." He replaced the phone and walked to the dispatch room. "Nora," he called to the uniformed woman sitting in front of the police computer, "mark me code one at Thunder Bay."

# Chapter 12

Larry's on his way," Becky told Tilly as she closed the cell phone and handed it back to the gray-haired man. "Thank you, sir."

The man acknowledged her thanks with a nod. "Hope you find out who's doing this," he said, looking over the field.

"Foolish kids," Tilly responded, her hands on her hips. "That's what they are."

The man shrugged. "I'll let you women go on about your business. If you need the phone again, I'll be visiting the buildings."

"Thank you again," Becky answered with a warm smile and watched the man wander back to the opening in the trees. She turned to Tilly. "This is getting to be ridiculous. It'll take forever to plug all these holes."

"Enough to give a body indigestion," Tilly agreed, pressing her hand across her chest. She pulled a roll of antacids from her front dress pocket and unraveled the wrapper until two pink chewables dumped into her hand. She threw them in her mouth and grimaced. "Horrible tastin' things."

"What are we going to do, Tilly?" Becky asked, watching Tilly jam the roll back into her pocket. "Whoever did this had to be brazen to come in broad daylight. We just filled the south field holes this morning."

Tilly seemed to think over the problem. "It's gotta be kids skippin' school. They're after the treasure—I'll bet my loafers on it. They're thinkin' they'll strike it rich after listening to them ol' tales about Union gold. Some of these island kids don't use half the brains the good Lord gave them."

"Is there any truth to the story?" Becky asked as she turned to glance at the grove of trees in hopes of spotting Larry. "You'd said Union money was kept in the camp. Is it possible there *is* buried money?"

"The treasure *was* buried—that's for sure," Tilly agreed. "But it was dug up quick enough when the Confederates failed to make it ashore. There's nothing sayin' any was left behind."

Impatiently Becky patted the side of her leg and glanced at the trees once more. Still no sign of Larry. "Do you think it would help to have the newspaper do an article to debunk the tale? Maybe it would stop whoever's doing this."

"Mercy, no," Tilly answered. "You'd have every Tom, Dick, and Harry out here diggin' holes." She sighed. "Nope! We're gonna have to stake out the place to catch them rascals."

Immediately alarmed, Becky shook her head. "Absolutely not! Larry would have our hides. And besides it wouldn't be safe. Who knows what kind of person or persons are crazy enough to come out here and dig these holes? It might not be kids, but some lunatic."

"Never met a lunatic yet who didn't sober at the end of a twenty-two," Tilly pronounced with a grunt. "And Larry ain't got time to waste watching this place all the time."

Becky stared wide-eyed at Tilly, remembering the last time Tilly used her twenty-two rifle to pin down a thief at Piney Point. Lauren had just returned to the cabin when she noticed the open front door. The burglar bolted and ran toward Tilly's place with Larry in pursuit. Tilly jumped into the fray just in time to help Larry capture the man.

Becky had no doubts about Tilly's ability to fire a rifle with more accuracy than Miss Marple. And right now she wasn't about to give her the chance. Larry would have a royal cow. "You'd better keep the twenty-two under lock and key and let Larry handle whoever's doing this."

"We'll see," Tilly said noncommittally.

"You don't think—" Becky began then stopped. The idea taking form was too crazy.

"What?"

"It's nothing."

"How do you know it's nothin' if you don't say it?"

Becky blinked once, again passing the idea around in her head. "You don't think Mr. Edwards could be the one digging the holes, do you?"

Tilly let loose with a laugh that nearly shook the ground. "Van Edwards? Now why on earth would an old coot like him go breakin' his back diggin' holes?"

There was no offense on Tilly's face, but Becky wished she'd kept the question to herself. Of course Tilly would defend the man Becky suspected she might be sweet on. But there was no backpedaling now. Tilly would demand an answer. "It's just that he's been against settling the camp at Thunder Bay. What if he wanted to put the scare into the committee by digging these holes—you know, to stop any building?"

Tilly laid her hand on Becky's shoulder. "If you knew Van like I do, you'd be knowin' he wouldn't do that. He does everything legal-like, always above the table—never below. And he's good enough at the above-table approach not to need another approach."

How well Becky knew. And Tilly's answer did have some logic. Besides, the old man would probably keel over within minutes—still hanging onto the posthole digger. With a sigh she glanced back to the trees. Movement caught her eye.

"Help has arrived," Becky said with relief, watching a tall figure emerge through the opening in the trees. "Larry will know what to do."

"He's lookin' mighty fine in his uniform, don't you think?" Tilly's glance darted between Becky close by and Larry in the distance. "Mighty fine!"

"Behave yourself, Tilly!" Becky chided without rancor then smiled. Tilly was absolutely right. Larry did indeed look handsome in his uniform from the starched black pants to the ironed white shirt and dark tie. The shiny badge on the front of his police hat bounced shards of sunlight with each step. Pride swelled within. Larry might not be a dreamer, but he knew how to protect and preserve the dreams of others. He took his job seriously. That thought alone gave him a high rank in her book.

"Ladies," he greeted them as he came within speaking distance. In one hand he held stakes and in the other police tape. "More holes, huh?" His eyes scanned the field.

"Tilly wanted to see the grounds today, and this is what we found," Becky answered, sweeping her hand out toward the holes.

"Did either of you see anyone around?" he asked, looking from Becky to Tilly. "Anyone suspicious?"

Becky shook her head. "Only an elderly couple was touring the buildings. No one was here in the fields that I could see."

Larry walked over to the first hole and bent down to look at the ground. He let his fingers roam over various areas of the dirt. "They must have left right before you came. There are shoe prints in the mud here and here." He pointed to several places on the mound of wet dirt. "Whoever it was, they were here when we had the brief rain."

"They?" Becky asked, moving over to see the prints.

"Two sets of prints." Larry stood and moved over to another mound of dirt. "Maybe three."

Tilly followed the pair. "Kids?"

Larry looked up at the older woman. "Possibly teens." His attention went back to the mound of dirt. He traced a finger above one imprint then another. "I'd say a man's size eleven here and a possible ten there." His hand moved to the opposite side. "This print is much smaller. Possibly a woman's or girl's shoe."

"Can you tell what kind of tread or brand of shoe?" Becky asked, pulling her black hair back from her face as she leaned forward to see.

"The rain, however brief, also obliterated any fine details on the shoes." Larry straightened. "Let me tape off the area. I'll have to come back in the morning to fill the holes." A concerned look crossed his face. "And I'd feel better if the two of you didn't come here alone." He pinned a look at Becky. "Call me if you want to see or show the property."

Heat rushed into her cheeks. "Of course!" In turn she gave Tilly a warning glance.

Tilly ignored the look and grunted.

"That means you, too," Larry returned, throwing a look Tilly's way. Becky couldn't help but wonder if he, too, wasn't thinking back to the burglary incident at Piney Point.

"We both understand," Becky announced, giving Tilly another warning glance. When Larry turned his attention back to the field, she touched his arm. "Pick me up in the morning? It will go faster with two of us."

"Good idea!" Tilly chimed in with a satisfied smile before Larry could respond. "I'd help y'all, but you know this ol' hip of mine's been actin' up." She patted her ample hips as proof. "I'm sure Becky is well qualified enough to be a good helper and partner."

The look on Larry's face nearly made Becky choke. Tilly didn't mind being obvious, and the red creeping up Larry's neck didn't deter the older woman one bit.

Tilly fluttered a hand in the air. "We'll help you get the tape up, and then we'd better get goin'. I've got chores to do."

The three worked together in silence and had the stakes and tape in place in a short amount of time. They walked back to the parking lot.

"Same time tomorrow," he said to Becky. His look drifted to Tilly. "Remember what I said."

Tilly only smiled sweetly and waved him off before opening the door and plopping herself in the passenger seat of the car. Becky moved on past the car and followed Larry to his cruiser.

"I've made an interesting observation," she whispered, keeping her voice low and out of Tilly's hearing.

His brow lifted slightly. "What kind of observation?"

"Have you ever noticed Tilly's twang becomes more pronounced when she's scheming?"

"Is that so?" A warmth and gentleness had crept into his voice.

"It's true!" She watched the funny, indulgent smile light on his lips. "Sometimes she drops her *g* endings, and sometimes she doesn't. Listen closely and you'll see what I mean." She leaned nearer. "Her twang's thick right now, and that means she's scheming."

"I'll keep that in mind." Then his blue eyes darkened, and he gave her an intent look. "You're very perceptive. Just make sure you don't get caught up in any of her schemes. That dear woman has the entire island wrapped around her pinky and could convince the mayor himself to go along with one of her cockamamie ideas."

Becky smiled. "I promise." She had no desire to stake out Thunder Bay or see firsthand how good of a markswoman Tilly could be.

Larry opened the door to the cruiser and glanced over to her car. "Be careful, and make sure you get Tilly home before she has time to get herself in trouble."

Their eyes met in a flash of understanding, and Becky gave him a nod before walking to her car. Seating herself behind the wheel, she gave her companion a dubious look. "Comfortable?" she asked, knowing full well Tilly's hip complaint was much too convenient. "You're hip's not hurting with these seats?"

Tilly gave a hearty laugh. "In these small cars bad hips aren't the problem. The trouble with these bucket seats is that not everybody has the same size bucket."

Becky chuckled. "Oh, Tilly! What would this island do without you? I hope in thirty years I have your sense of humor and energy level."

"Old age isn't all it's cracked up to be," Tilly said with a wide, toothy smile. "Energy is all relative. The only thing I do with more frequency now is attend funerals and go to the bathroom."

Becky laughed again and started the car. "I'd better get you home before you have me in tears." In the rearview mirror she could see Larry sitting in his cruiser writing on a clipboard. His presence alone warmed her heart, making her feel safe in the midst of chaos.

"As long as they're happy tears, Becky." Tilly gave her a meaningful glance and popped two more antacids between her lips. "Always happy tears."

Becky flipped off the living room light switch, and the cabin plunged into darkness. For several moments she stared out the front window taking in the soft glow of the moon on the trees. Her heart felt content for the first time in weeks. Even the mysterious holes at Thunder Bay or thoughts of Michael and her parents didn't intrude. It came to her in a sudden blaze of understanding as she traced the windowpane with her finger. The camp's success was important to her because it was important to Larry. God had used Larry to fill much of the void left in her heart caused by the uncertainty of her future.

What if God chose not to send her back to the Congo? Wasn't He God enough to know and care for her Congolese friends in the best possible way? And if He chose to send her back, wouldn't He be God enough to fill the void she knew would exist from leaving her newfound rescuer? Yes, she could be content whatever God chose to do.

The faint sound of crunching gravel caused her attention to swivel to the road beyond. A small golf cart passed in the darkness, and Becky narrowed her eyes for a better look. If she didn't know better, the driver looked like none other than Tilly Storm.

She watched the small lights of the cart bob as it made a right turn onto Shore Lane and sped out of sight. Tilly didn't usually go out after dark, and it could mean only one thing. Becky glanced at the clock. Eleven thirty! If she hurried, she might catch Larry before he went off his shift. Carefully threading her way around the furniture, she found the lamp and switched it on before continuing past the dining room table to reach the wall phone. Using her finger as a guide, she scanned the small notepad with several handwritten phone numbers. Finding the right number, she dialed the police station.

"Sorry," the answering female dispatcher informed her. "Officer Newkirk has already left for the night. Would you like to speak with the midnight watch officer?"

"No, thank you," Becky politely declined and rang off.

Once again she picked up the phone and dialed from memory, this time to Larry's house. After several rings the answering machine with Larry's no-nonsense greeting came on. Disappointed, she let the phone rest back in its cradle. What should she do? Did she know if the driver was Tilly? The darkness didn't allow for good visual acuity.

Besides, what could she do anyway? Larry wasn't home, and he wasn't at the police station. Even if she left a message on his answering machine, she had no guarantee he would return home right away. After several minutes of deliberation she decided to wait and talk with Larry in the morning. It wouldn't hurt to pray for protection over the driver and the campgrounds for added insurance, though—just in case Tilly had a foolish idea of staking out Thunder Bay.

"You didn't get a good look at the driver?" Larry asked the next morning as he rounded the turn into the parking lot of Thunder Bay.

"It was dark," Becky explained, her face solemn. "But it could have been Tilly."

He took a deep breath. "I wouldn't put it past her. She's tough as nails, Becky, and apt to take matters into her own hands, quite successfully the majority of the time. I'm more apt to be worried about the people she encounters, not her. They'll be the ones who will be sorry."

"I don't know," Becky said after a moment. "Maybe I should have left a message on your answering machine. It's just that you don't have much downtime between your police duties and the camp project. I didn't want to burden you with what I saw, especially if it turned out to be nothing. It might not have been Tilly."

He turned and gave her a smile. "Let me worry about my workload. You call any time you need me." He pulled the truck to a stop and put it in park. "I was probably on my way home from the station when you called. You can always leave a message."

"I appreciate knowing that."

He shut off the engine and turned to her. "Frankly I'm worried about you."

"Me!" There was shock in Becky's voice.

It was true. The camp project was taking on aspects he'd not bargained for, and Becky must surely be feeling the added stress of Mr. Edwards, suspicious donations, and the mysterious holes rapidly materializing across the camp property. And now, with good reason, she was worried about Tilly and her twenty-two rifle.

"A lot has been going on the last couple of days," he finally answered. "I'm afraid the work and circumstances are beyond what you might have expected for the job. I don't want you to feel the least bit responsible for solving all the problems or putting yourself in danger."

"Oh," said Becky, and she grew thoughtful. "Are you saying you don't think I can do the job?"

He saw a shadow cross her face and immediately scolded himself for failing to get his message across. He was much too concrete for his own good. "I'm not saying that at all," he replied gently. "I'm saying I don't want you fretting or losing sleep over the problems of the camp. You need to enjoy the island—maybe spend some time with Lauren and go shopping."

Becky frowned then. "I'm not fretting—I promise. I believe God will handle the problems." Her calm assurance almost challenged him to disagree. "I'm stronger than I look."

"I'm sure—"

She interrupted, her dark eyes widening. "God is my *total* strength."

His gut tightened. The fire in her eyes and assertive tone left him feeling strangely slighted. It was as if his own faithlessness was being bounced back to him by her very words. What was she trying to say? She didn't need anyone? She didn't need him? She evidently shared a close relationship with God that surpassed his own, for he did experience weakness and was known to fret over the details of life from time to time—well, maybe quite a few times. The thought caused him to draw back in his seat.

Had he read too much into her previous gestures and actions? Was this dreamer more self-sufficient than he'd first realized? If true, he would do well to prevent making a fool of himself. He'd had full intentions of asking her out for a nice, leisurely dinner at the Wharf that evening in hopes of exploring the possibility of knowing her better. Maybe it was time to squash the idea.

"Is something wrong?" She looked up with sudden gentleness in her face, her dark eyes concerned. "Have I said something to offend you?"

"Not at all," he said much more quietly.

"Sure?" Her eyes were a little apprehensive.

"Positive." He managed a smile then opened his door. "We'd better get those holes filled if we want to finish before noon."

"All right," Becky agreed slowly, opening her own door.

Puzzlement showed on her face, and Larry could have kicked himself for letting his heart become involved. Hadn't he warned himself the first time he laid eyes on her? How could one man be so good at giving advice and make a muddled mess of his own affairs?

# Chapter 13

Becky walked out of the Balloon Boutique and into the early afternoon sunshine. The balmy air pushed her hair back as she lifted her face to the wind. Beautiful weather dominated the last week, and the island seemed to come alive with happy tourists ready for the weekend. She tucked the papers Flora signed into her purse. One more duty finished and ready for the groundbreaking ceremony. They would have only a few more days to prepare.

Quietly she walked the wharf and let her hand trail the heavily twined rope fencing. Her soul felt restless. Since the morning Larry and she worked together to fill those dreaded holes the week before, something changed. Larry changed!

Becky sighed and leaned over the ropes to watch a large family of ducks crowding near the pier in hopes of food. After a moment she reached into her pocket and deposited a coin into one of the numerous feeder machines lining the dock. Dozens of tan pellets poured into the mouth of the machine when she turned the crank. Cupping her hand under the opening, she lifted the lid and shoveled the food into her hand. The bobbing ducks grew noisy at the sound of the metal trap door opening, and Becky had to smile. Poor, pampered birds! She leaned over the rope again and tossed several pellets to the scurrying birds, watching as the pill-sized pieces dropped onto the surface of the water, dipping up and down with the light incoming waves. Dozens of openmouthed fish surfaced to the top for a chance at the floating food. When her supply finally diminished to nothing, the ducks continued to peck at the water, frequently glancing up at her.

"Sorry, guys," she called to them, stretching her hands out as evidence.

Then they caught sight of a young child several yards farther along the pier tossing handfuls of the alfalfa rations. The entire group of ducks paddled away without a backward glance.

With the momentary distraction gone her thoughts once again returned to Larry. How many times she'd gone over the scene of their last visit again and again, only to come up short. Everything had been fine until he suggested she might not be quite up to the job of camp director. Oh, he hadn't come right out and said it, but she knew what he'd meant. No doubt he was concerned about the vandalism and Michael's interfering donation. He was afraid the job was too much for her to handle. She tried her best to convince Larry she was up to the challenge—with God's help, of course, but the conversation fell apart shortly thereafter. What she didn't know was why.

Recalling Larry's earlier words about not falling for any of Tilly's schemes made her wonder if Larry hadn't been giving her fair warning to disregard Tilly's notions about any serious relationship between them. At the time she thought he'd meant Tilly's idea of staking out Thunder Bay. But in light of his swift and obvious withdrawal she couldn't be sure.

As a matter of fact, Larry hadn't spoken more than a few words to her all week, keeping any and all phone calls about camp business to a sterile minimum. He'd made no mention of his "inquiry" into the donated money either. Maybe he'd found something about Michael and her family. She didn't know how far or how deep Larry would probe into the money matter or what he might find. But if he discovered the truth about her family, it couldn't bode well for her. The thought caused her to shudder. What man—even a good man—wouldn't run when he discovered her dysfunctional past? Becky blew a lungful of air past her lips.

And worst of all? Her job as camp director had suddenly become duller than a last-period class on the mathematical principles of graphing parabolas and hyperbolas. Without the closeness she'd previously enjoyed with Larry, the new and exciting duties fell flat. What kind of godliness was that? She was supposed to be working for the Lord, not for the pleasure of Larry's company.

*Tell my heart that,* she moaned inside.

Now more than ever she desired to return to the mission field where at least her stimulating adventures weren't clouded by a man's presence. Everything seemed so complicated on the island! And her newfound contentment of waiting upon God for direction was slowly eroding. Larry's nearness and friendship had bolstered her faith and come to mean more to her than she'd realized. Without him, living and working on the island didn't cut it anymore. And she'd only been on the island for what—not even two months? Yet the distance she felt between them penetrated her very being with a deep and chilly coldness. Like an addiction, she'd come to rely on something or someone she never needed before.

*God, what can I do to restore my relationship with Larry? He's a strong and godly man, and I like being around him. I like sharing my ideas and dreams with someone who really listens. Certainly You sent him to me—I mean, why else would he be around every time I've needed him? If I've done something to offend him, show me how to make it right. I don't want to lose his friendship. Yes, Lord, it does seem out of character for me, but it's true. I—Becky Merrill, the woman who has never needed a man—need Larry.*

Becky leaned on the wooden support as she peered into her watery reflection. In all her years with Michael she never felt the same emotions Larry brought to her heart. She really, really liked—and missed—Larry. How could she have messed up the relationship before it even had time to begin? Somehow she had to fix what she'd damaged—if only she knew what she'd broken.

Larry slowed his cruiser as he came upon Levitte's Landing. Tourists were beginning to trickle in for the weekend. Tonight and Saturday promised to be busy for the department, but he didn't mind. It was good to have the island up and running for the season.

He let his eyes roam over the shops and people before finally resting his gaze on a lone female standing on the pier. Without a moment's hesitation he knew the woman to be Becky. No doubt she had been visiting Flora at the Balloon Boutique to secure the balloons for next week's groundbreaking.

Gliding the cruiser to a stop near the entrance of shops, he straightened in his seat, never taking his gaze off her. Their strained relationship had an unnerving effect on him, and he found it plenty difficult to keep his distance from her. He felt drawn against his will. Yet she'd made it clear.

"Dispatch to one-ninety-four."

Larry stretched his mike closer and depressed the switch. "One-ninety-four—Shore Lane and Levitte's Landing."

"You have a mainland call. Would you like the call dispatched to your mobile?"

"That's affirm," Larry answered. "Send it through."

"Dispatching now, one-ninety-four," responded the female voice.

Larry's mobile phone rang, and he picked up the receiver. "Officer Newkirk."

"It's Robert." The raspy, no-nonsense voice was unmistakable. "I've got some information."

"Great! What do you have?"

"The thirty-grand check traces back to a Hague and Sullivant law firm in Cleveland," Robert began, clearing a loose gurgle from his throat. "I'd like to fax you a list of their clients to look at. Maybe you'll recognize a name." Larry could hear him drag on a cigarette. "Then give me a jingle, and I'll dig a little deeper if you find something."

Larry thought a moment. "Give me five minutes to reach the station and send the fax to the number I gave you earlier. I'll get the list from there."

"Will do!"

The line suddenly went silent. Larry took one last glance at the pier, but Becky was already gone. Probably a blessing for him, he reasoned. Looking at her only needled his gut with unpleasant sensations. Slowly he made his way back into traffic and to the station. He was anxious to see the list. He didn't care to know how or when Robert obtained a list of clients. All he knew was it was time to put the matter to rest.

A few minutes later Larry locked the door of his still-running cruiser and fingered the extra car keys dangling on his belt clip. More than one officer had locked themselves out of their cruisers, and he didn't plan to join their ranks. At one time officers didn't worry about leaving their running cruisers unlocked. But those days had passed.

He sprinted into the station and headed straight for the fax machine. Flipping through the tray of incoming faxes, he found the cover sheet and waited as two more sheets came through to be printed.

Rolling the papers into a nice cylinder, he walked to the corner cubicle to read them in private. Slowly he scanned the extensive list of corporations and individuals, drawing his brows together in concentration. Nothing looked familiar in the first column, and the second didn't look promising until his eyes stopped abruptly at a name near the bottom of the page. His mouth parted slightly in disbelief, and he withdrew a pen from his shirt pocket to circle the name. Interesting! More than interesting.

Several names later another prospect seemed to jump off the page. He circled it as well. An idea began to form as he looked at the mismatched pair, and he wondered at the ethical implications he might face if Robert continued the search. The results weren't what he expected—not at all. But what in life was? Gaining additional information about the names in question wouldn't evoke change, only enlighten a confusing situation.

Larry rubbed his chin in deliberation before resolutely picking up the phone to call Robert. He'd already come this far; he might as well finish the job. Whatever the result, let the chips fall where they may.

Becky threw off her covers. How could she sleep when her brain kept swimming with thoughts about her family and Larry? Her father had called that very evening in a tirade about the virtues, or lack thereof, of women who handled dirty shovels in manual labor. His response might have been delayed enough to catch her off guard, but he made up for it in fervor. She would have drowned soon enough if she let herself dwell on the scene many more times.

With resignation she walked across the room and pulled her robe off the door hook. She might as well get up. It was only midnight. For sure, sleep wouldn't come anytime soon, and it made little sense to force what wouldn't budge. Her bare feet padded down the hall and into the living room. Out of habit she stopped at the front window to stare at the peaceful scenery that usually calmed her frayed nerves. The task seemed impossible tonight.

She'd seen Larry in his cruiser at Levitte's Landing earlier in the day. He seemed busy with police work and hadn't noticed her on the pier. She made a quick exit before he spotted her. It was stupid really. Why did she have to avoid or hide from him? It was a nervous and infantile response to her emotions. Receiving the call from her father only added the icing—and a plump cherry—and a few caustic sprinkles—to her already ragged bravado.

The tall pines seemed to sway in response to her disposition. A sudden but dim pair of lights on the road caught her attention. The same golf cart she'd seen several days ago once again bounced down the road to Shore Lane. This time she was sure of the driver—Tilly Storm. It didn't take a rocket scientist to know where she was headed. There'd been no more disturbances at Thunder Bay since the day she and Larry filled the last set of holes, but Tilly had mentioned worrying about the weekend when police patrols would be occupied in town controlling the tourist crowds and drinking establishments.

Without hesitation she turned on a light and dialed the phone. Something troubled her more than usual about Tilly and her escapades. She had to contact Larry at the station. A woman picked up the phone.

"I'll dispatch you through to Officer Newkirk's mobile," she responded when Becky requested to speak with Larry. Becky waited, nervously twisting the curly phone cord around her finger.

"Officer Newkirk," Larry answered, his strong voice coming across the phone line.

Just hearing his voice caused her legs to quiver. "Larry, it's Becky. I'm glad I caught you. The dispatcher said you're pulling extra duty."

"Becky?" he repeated. "What's wrong?"

"Tilly left again in her golf cart a few minutes ago," she explained. "I'm almost sure she's headed for Thunder Bay. She thinks the vandals are going to strike again this weekend. Will you be able to check the camp property and see if she's there?"

"I'm on the other side of the island," he answered, "but I'll make my way over to the site. How long ago did you say she left?"

"Not more than five minutes."

"All right." She could hear him sigh. "Sit tight, and I'll call you once I see what's going on."

"Larry?"

"Yes!"

"Be careful!" A strong sense of disaster washed over her. "Something's not right, and I can feel it."

He was silent for several seconds. "I'll be careful."

The line disconnected, and Becky replaced the phone. She trotted to the bedroom and shed the robe and nightgown for a pair of jeans and a T-shirt. She wouldn't stick around the cabin waiting for a call. Not that she planned to interfere with Larry and his work, but she felt—no, she knew—God was telling her—Tilly needed her help.

*God, protect Tilly and her crazy attempt to save the camp from harm. Watch over Larry and keep him safe. He needs all the wisdom You can give him.*

Locking the door behind her, Becky scampered down the deck stairs to the car. She only hoped her gut feeling was wrong. Nonetheless she felt God directing her course. How could she not follow?

When she came upon Thunder Bay she saw Larry's empty but running cruiser sitting in the parking lot with its high-beam headlights illuminating the grounds and buildings in the distance. She stopped her car several yards away, turned off the ignition, and cut the lights before slowly opening the door. An eerie quietness enveloped her when she stepped out from the car and silently scampered into the shadows across the parking lot. It was then she saw Tilly's cart partially hidden under a grove of trees. So Tilly was here! The thought gave her no comfort. She proceeded on, stopping several times to listen in the stillness for any telltale sound, only to hear the pounding of her own heart. Then a faint and remote sound seemed to skip lightly across the wind. Voices! She could hear voices.

She had to stop and think. If she continued to creep about in the shadows, Larry might mistake her for a criminal and jeopardize both of them. Not smart! If she exposed herself in the lighted parking lot, she might become a walking target. Also not smart. She'd sit tight as Larry previously suggested and wait. Something would happen soon enough even if it was Larry returning to his cruiser with nothing more than wet shoes from the dew.

In the darkness the swishing and thudding sound of someone running grew steadily louder, and Becky backed deeper into the shadows. Two silhouetted figures dashed into the semilighted clearing then back into the wooded area until the sound of their steps faded into nothingness. The brief dim light, though, had been enough for her to make out the runners as the two teenagers who worked at Beckette's Souvenir Shop.

She stood glued to her spot. Were those two boys responsible for the holes? Why were they running? And where was Larry? Why hadn't he surfaced? Where was Tilly? The dilemma of what to do raged inside. Truly she was in a pickle. Either way danger for her or others might lurk.

More voices! Becky strained to hear the new voices and shook her head in frustration. She couldn't decipher where the voices were coming from, let alone who was talking. Cautiously she proceeded in the darkness until the voices grew louder.

"Ain't nothin' wrong with me," came the breathless voice she recognized as Tilly's. "Stop foolin' with me and go on and catch those kids."

"Not a chance!" This time it was Larry's voice.

"So you're keeping me against my will, are you?" Tilly retorted, her voice labored.

Becky finally drew close enough to see Larry standing over a crouched figure. Tilly? A glance around revealed no one else. What was Tilly doing hovering near the ground? The uneasy feeling returned full force. The only way she'd know or be able to help would be to make her presence known—without startling either.

She straightened. "Larry? It's Becky," she called. Her voice, very low, sounded strained and unfamiliar to her own ears.

"Yeah!"

Relieved, Becky relaxed her aching, clenched fists and moved from the shadows. A twig snapped as she stepped into the clearing. In one lightning motion Larry turned toward her, gun drawn, and she nearly sucked her lungs inside out.

"Police!" he shouted. "Stop right there, or I'll shoot!"

# Chapter 14

Not one of Becky's six-hundred-plus muscles moved as she fixed her gaze on the black handgun entrenched in Larry's grasp. Time drew to a sure and paralyzing stop. When she heard slight movement from behind, her muscles constricted tighter still, and she feared they might burst from unabridged fear.

"Police!" the menacingly deep voice announced slow and hard from behind her in the dark. "You're covered in the front and the rear. Just put your hands up real nice and easy."

"It's me." She barely squeaked the words past her lips.

Larry's gun didn't budge. "Do as the man says!"

"Boys—it's Becky!" Tilly shouted, her words cut short with a groan of pain. "Put them guns down before you hurt her. Can't you see it's Becky?"

"Step out where I can see you," Larry demanded, ignoring Tilly, the black gun tilting ever so slightly. "Hands up and show yourself!"

"Nice and easy," warned the voice behind.

Becky forced her frozen limbs to obey, and she held both hands up and in view. "It's me, Becky," she said again, scarcely able to force enough air past her vocal cords to be heard. "Please put your guns down."

Slowly she watched Larry lower his gun, but he didn't relax. "What are you doing here?"

"I wanted to help," came her feeble response. She wondered if it sounded as dumb to him as it did to her at the moment. Had she misread God's cue? Even in the darkness she could see the stern and disapproving look firmly planted on Larry's face.

"Between the two of you, you're going to kill me with your help!" Larry snapped, slowly shoving his gun back in the holster. "It's all right, Kirk. She's clean." He pointed his finger in her direction. "Now move over here and keep out of the way," he ordered.

Becky immediately complied and moved toward Larry. Suddenly she caught full sight of Tilly kneeling on the ground and rushed to drop down at her side. "You're hurt! What's happened?" She tossed an anxious look at Larry and then back to Tilly.

"Nothin's wrong!" Tilly answered through clenched teeth. "It's overreaction, plain and simple. I'm fine as a fiddle."

Larry seemed exasperated as he hunkered down beside the older woman. He glanced at Becky. "Your supersleuth has bought herself a heart attack if my diagnosis is right." He felt for Tilly's wrist.

"Have not!" Tilly looked stubbornly at Larry, shaking her wrist loose.

"Chest pain, profuse sweating, and nausea. Need I say more?"

"Have you called the emergency squad?" Becky managed to ask Larry, placing her hand over her own thundering heart. The faint bellow of a siren seemed to answer.

"I almost had 'em," Tilly said, breathing with difficulty. "Those kids!"

"Stop talking, Tilly," Becky ordered. "You're only upsetting yourself, and that can't be good." Her own unsettled thoughts felt as clammy and cold as the wet grass penetrating the knees of her jeans.

The squad siren grew louder, and her gaze slid to Larry, who looked up at the other officer. "Signal them in with your flashlight," Larry said. "They'll need to come to us. We'll never get her to the parking lot." Larry stood and reached for his walkie. "One-ninety-four to dispatch."

"Go ahead, one-ninety-four."

"The ten-twenty-four's on the scene. Please advise them to the back field location."

"Do you copy, medic two?" the dispatcher asked.

"Medic two copy and en route to back location."

Kirk moved forward and faced Larry. "You said two escaped north and one toward the lake?"

"Dropped their posthole digger where they stood when Tilly confronted them." In the moonlit darkness Becky could see Larry turn briefly to scowl at Tilly.

"I saw two teenage boys run into the woods," Becky interrupted with what she hoped to be helpful information. "It's the two who work at Beckette's."

"I know," Larry responded, clearly unimpressed. "It's the Johnson boys."

Kirk nodded with no impression of surprise. "What about the other one?"

Larry shook his head. "A girl, probably not more than fourteen, I'd say. She took off for the lake." He rested his hands on his hips. "I didn't recognize her, but once we round up the Johnson twins we'll find out who she is quick enough."

Kirk nodded in agreement then glanced behind him. "There they are!" He stepped out into the open field with his high-beam flashlight and began signaling the squad toward him with the steady advance and backward pitch of the light. Becky turned her face against bright headlights now bearing down on them through the field. The large box-unit truck bounced heavily across the uneven ground. When the fire department medic unit finally came to a rough and noisy stop, three men lighted from the truck, and Becky instinctively clutched Tilly's hand.

*Give these men wisdom, Lord, to help Tilly in the best possible way.*

Within seconds two of the medics had each grabbed an end of the heavy stretcher and unloaded it from the back of the truck. The third met Larry. He walked them over to Tilly, who was talking with the taller medic.

The tall one turned to Becky. "If you could let us in here, we'll take a look at this young lady."

Becky quickly moved back, but Tilly groused at him. "Young lady, my foot. I used to change your diapers, Milton Douglas Skaggs. Changed your mama's diapers, too!"

The young medic only laughed and after a cursory assessment directed the other two to bring the stretcher closer. With a flick of a lever they dropped the metal frame and cloth-covered mattress within inches of the ground. Seconds later and with quick precision they placed her on the stretcher, snapped it into high position, and rolled it over the short, coarse distance before hoisting her with great effort into the brightly lighted truck. Larry hovered by the opened back, hooking one hand over the top of the bright red door. Becky hung back and watched from behind as one medic took Tilly's vital signs and another attached white electrodes to her chest. Fear gripped her heart when the men's banter turned more serious.

"She needs to be med-flighted to Cleveland," the tall one told Larry. He stretched the EKG paper out like a scroll. "The sooner she gets treatment, the better."

"I ain't been sick a day in my life," Tilly protested, pulling her arm away from the dark-haired fireman attempting to tie a tourniquet on her upper arm. "I don't need one of them IV jobbers."

"Just settle down, Tilly," the tall medic gently told her. "Your condition is life-threatening, and unless you want to be pushing up daisies you'd better let us do our job."

Tilly grunted once more. "I should have left you in those diapers, Milton Douglas. Mighta taken the spunk outta you. Pushin' up daisies, my foot!"

But she didn't protest again, and a flurry of IV bags, tubing, drugs, oxygen, and beeping monitors took over the next several minutes.

"We have her stabilized," the tall one announced at last. "We're going to meet the chopper at the airstrip. They'll airlift her to the Cleveland Heart Hospital." He backed out of the box and shut the doors of the truck with a decisive bang. He shrugged his broad shoulders at Larry. "Says she doesn't want anyone called. I'll leave that up to you, big guy."

Larry nodded, a grim look still set on his face. Becky felt drained and panicky inside. Larry wouldn't help her this time. He was too angry! The heat of his wrath might not be visible, but it would be a gross understatement to deny the fact that his fury was unquestionably burning a hole in her back at that very moment.

"I'm going to the mainland to be with Tilly," Becky finally said to Larry as the medic truck slowly made a U-turn and bumped out of sight.

"There's no ferry running this late," he told her, his voice still rigid. "It's well after one in the morning. You'll have to wait until the first ferry starts up at seven."

"At seven!" she repeated incredulously. She had to think. "What about the Express Boat Line?"

He looked as if he might not answer but finally shrugged and turned to Kirk. "Do you know how late the express is running tonight?"

"Probably did its last run at midnight," Kirk answered, his gaze fixing on Becky. "What?" He turned to Larry. "She wants to go to the hospital tonight?" When Larry nodded, he continued. "She won't catch a ferry out of here tonight, but I did see Tony Edwards at the Pizza Shack not more than an hour ago. He flew in today in his Cessna."

"Mr. Edwards's grandson?" Larry asked, seeming more than hesitant. "No, I don't like it. Even if he's willing to fly out tonight, he's been at the Shack. Too risky!"

Kirk shook his head. "Tony doesn't touch the stuff. Just like his granddaddy."

Tired of being ignored in the conversation, Becky finally spoke up. "Where can I find this Tony Edwards?"

Both men exchanged glances until Kirk spoke. "I suspect he's still at the Shack. The worst he can do is turn you down." He turned to Larry as if he had nothing more to say on the matter. "I'm going to make a visit at the Johnson home. Are you doing the honors for the paperwork?"

"Sure," Larry conceded. "Why not?" He looked at his lighted watch. "I'm already pressing the clock for several hours of overtime."

"The chief will be thrilled." He patted Larry on the back. "All right then. I'm shoving off. Don't forget to get a few digitals and maybe some prints on the posthole digger. You never know what the prosecutor's going to want." With that he turned and flicked a salute, leaving the two alone in the field.

A heavy silence hung between them as they faced one another in the moonlight. And sure as rain, she knew the explosion of thunder was about to unleash in a torrential downpour upon her aching head.

"I could have shot you," Larry said in a low, controlled tone.

Becky nodded, tucking a few stray wisps of hair behind her ear. "I'm sorry, Larry. It's just that I felt God was telling me something wasn't right. I didn't mean to interfere. I'm really sorry."

His eyes narrowed. "God does lead us in certain directions, Becky, but I sincerely doubt He asked you to sneak out here and scare me witless. I could have killed you. Do you understand the ramifications of what that means? Do you realize Kirk could have nailed you in the back? What possessed you to jump out like that in the dark? Either of us could have mistaken a shadow or a shirtsleeve for a weapon."

"I didn't *jump* out at you in the dark," she defended in a strained calmness. "And I did call out to you. I thought you said yeah, that it was okay."

"Well, I didn't hear you, and it wasn't okay! I was answering Tilly, not you."

Stung to the core by his venomous tone, Becky stepped back, holding at bay the misty tears threatening to come. "I don't know what else to do, Larry, except to say I'm sorry again. It felt as if you and Tilly were in trouble—"

He stopped her midsentence. "I live in the real world, and so should you. You need to stick with what you know and can see, not feel and dream." He pointed his finger at her. "Real life has real consequences. Traipsing through the woods in the dark while I'm on a police call is serious business. What if I'd shot and killed you?"

How many times would he keep saying those horrible words? Undoubtedly she'd given him a terrible fright, not so unlike the one she'd received, but she hadn't intentionally tried to make his way difficult. Yet his words burned her like liquid fire. Did he purposely gain satisfaction by impaling her with as much pain as he could hurl? Another realization hurt even more—he'd just admitted his detestation of her ideas, her dreamerlike view of life. How could she have misjudged his openness so badly? Every time he'd patiently listened to her ramblings or praised her innovations, his recognition was nothing more than a farce. He'd never believed in her. Never! There was no mistaking his contempt.

Well, she thought with determination, she preferred to stick to her ideals even though someday, she was convinced, they would be blown sky-high. Maybe that day had finally arrived—for right now there didn't seem to be a scrap of any dream or hope flickering about within her bruised heart.

"I'm sorry. . . ." Her voice trailed off when she saw his unbending expression and slightly lifted chin. How many times could she keep saying she was sorry? She threw her hands out in frustration but found herself at a loss for words. There would be no convincing Larry of her intentions, not tonight or anytime soon—

Maybe never. He was too cool. Too in control. With a shake of her head she turned and walked to the break in the trees, not caring that her tennis shoes were soaked through with dew or that her bones ached with the rough jarring of her stride. No sounds followed, and she knew Larry had no intention of pursuing her to ease his judgment or her excruciating pain.

*Why didn't You leave me in the Congo, God? The physical danger there doesn't even compare with the emotional danger I'm facing on Bay Island. My faith is faltering, big time. Be with Tilly. . .and Larry and keep them safe. And keep me out of trouble! I know—that's a full-time job in itself!*

Larry opened the cruiser door and threw his clipboard across the seat with more force than intended. Of all the asinine things for Becky to do! His hands still shook at the thought. Just reliving the moment, his gun pointing straight at her, his finger cocked and ready, made him want to explode with—what? Anger, terror, disbelief—possibly all three. Yet he was torn to shreds by the expression of hurt on her face. But how could he make her understand with mere words the gravity of what could have happened? There were no idioms or words in the English language to express how deeply the matter could have affected life itself. Becky and her touchy-feely dream world nearly brought disaster to them both.

Now she was off to see Tony Edwards. And he would fly her to Cleveland. All she'd have to do would be to bat those long black lashes of hers and the man would be putty. But right now he didn't care. He was too mad to care what she did. He was even too mad to pray. Maybe he was partly mad at himself for not recognizing her, but at that moment. . . . It would be a wonder if the two of them would be able to smooth out their differences enough to manage the camp business for the next several weeks. That could only spell trouble! Her bubbly imaginings would believe their opposite views could still work together, but he knew better. After all he was a realist, something Becky didn't understand. How could her virtues of unleashed faith lure him like a magnet, yet drive him crazy at the same time? He wouldn't have a bean left in his head if she continued to rattle him at every turn. Something had to be done! And soon!

Becky took another tight-lipped sip of the terrible coffee as she watched the sun rise between the skyscrapers. The hospital's large plateglass windows needed to be washed, but the dirt didn't detract from the beauty of the yellow ball expanding against the orange and red backdrop. She turned to look at old Mr. Edwards slumped in the lobby chair next to her, his eyes closed in a semiconscious sleep. Lopsided glasses rested awkwardly across the bumpy bridge of his nose.

What a night it had been!

Tony Edwards had agreed to fly her to Cleveland, but not before his grandfather insisted on climbing aboard the Cessna after hearing the news about Tilly. She'd never seen the elderly man move so fast. He was truly distraught over Tilly.

Tilly made it through the night, but she wasn't sure if the same could be said for the staff. Tilly fumed and fussed at the doctors and nurses with such fervor that Becky knew the brunt of her medical storm was past. Nothing, not even coronary disease, could beat Tilly when she set her mind to something.

Becky stood and stretched, feeling the soreness of her cramped muscles with every motion.

"How's Tilly?" Mr. Edwards asked groggily, straightening himself in the chair. He pushed his glasses up on his nose. "I didn't mean to fall asleep."

Becky gave him a small smile. "It's okay. Tilly's been resting for the past couple of hours. She's going to be fine."

"The doctors say so?" he questioned forcefully.

"Not in so many words," she answered. "I can tell, though. She's going to be fine."

He flashed her a disbelieving look and stood to his feet. "I'll go see if there's anything new to know." He limped off slowly as if every joint had yet to wake up and join the human race.

Becky turned her attention back to the blossoming sunrise. Even Mr. Edwards couldn't muster enough faith to believe her. Just like Larry! Larry's accusing words still burned raw in her heart. Maybe she'd missed the boat somewhere. It was one thing when her unbelieving family chose to mock her faith and dreams, but coming from those who knew God—well, this was a new ball game, something she needed to think through.

"She's doing fine," Mr. Edwards announced, coming back around the corner and into the deserted lobby. "Nurse said the doc's going to do the heart catheterization this morning." A smile lit his face. "Tilly's in there giving them what for. She wants her breakfast."

Becky instinctively reached for his hand and gave it a gentle squeeze. "God's going to bring her through."

To her surprise he returned the grip. "I'm sure it means a lot to her that you came."

His words, the first kind words she'd ever heard from the man, were like a balm to her hurting soul. She only nodded and turned her eyes back to the window.

Tilly's heart would pull through this ordeal—of this she was confident. Too bad her own heart had no such guarantee. Her future was more uncertain than ever, and although Larry never physically fired his gun, he'd nailed her head-on with emotionally charged bullets. Now her wounded heart felt too riddled with gaping holes to hope for healing. She only hoped God would give her adequate faith and direction to keep going.

# Chapter 15

Larry balanced the hot casserole dish, cornbread pan, fruit bowl, and dangling bag of cloverleaf rolls in one hand and rapped lightly on the door of Tilly's cottage with the other. Hastily he brought his hand back to steady the tall tower of provisions. The church secretary had asked him to drop off the food when he'd stopped by the church earlier that morning. So here he was—Judi had called him an angel of mercy—delivering the homemade lunch to Tilly to aid in what they hoped would be a speedy recovery.

He had to smile. Angel of mercy! In his case the words might be synonymous with all-around good guy or church gopher. Whatever he was, his actions were quickly becoming popular with the women, young and old alike. He'd never enjoyed such notice. Once word circulated about his role in the apprehension of the three kids responsible for the mysterious holes at Thunder Bay, his reputation with the single women at church skyrocketed. He'd even managed to find time to take two of them out on dates this week and received one whopper of a kiss—right on the lips—from Mitzi Trammell again. And this time he didn't even have to unclog her bathroom sink to earn it. Not that he had much time to squander between the police overtime and camp duties, but the distraction of their company helped him cope. For while his status soared with the other church members, one person remained aloof and blasé.

"Hello, Larry!"

The sound of Becky's voice brought his attention front and center. There she stood on the other side of the screen door looking at him through the haze of wire mesh. The unreadable expression on her face caused him to tense.

"How are you, Becky?" he asked politely, shifting the weight of his packages ever so slightly. He should have known she might be helping Tilly on her first day back.

"I'm fine," she answered with generic civility, propping the door open for him. "And you?"

"Fine." He stepped past her, but not before he caught a whiff of her light and summery perfume. "Where would you like the food?"

"On the kitchen counter," she instructed, not bothering to move away from the door. "Right there is fine." She leaned lightly against the doorjamb, obviously finding no need to proffer assistance.

Larry struggled to let go of the plastic bag holding the rolls but managed to set all three dishes down without spilling. "How's Tilly?"

"I'm fit as a fiddle," Tilly broke in with a broad smile as she came through the back door and around the corner of the kitchen with Mr. Edwards in tow. She looked at the food and clucked her tongue. "Ain't no need for all this fuss. And look—Judi's even sent some of her famous fudge."

Larry walked over to her and planted a kiss on her cheek. "The ladies at the church are providing you with lunch and dinner over the next several days. So for once enjoy the pleasure of receiving instead of giving." His gaze pivoted to Van Edwards, and he extended his hand. "Mr. Edwards."

Mr. Edwards took his hand. "I never had a chance to thank you for taking such good care of Miss Tilly the night of her heart attack. You probably saved her life."

"Just doing my job!" he answered modestly and immediately wondered if he should mention Becky's role in the rescue. After all, she was the one who alerted him, and without her call who knew what might have happened. He shot a glance Becky's way and doused the idea. Her impassive expression, however innocent, was colder than the frozen waters of Lake Erie in January. Instead he said, "I'm just glad to see Tilly's up and around."

"Not that them doctors and their medical finaglin' aren't gonna kill me," said Tilly with a huff. Pulling out a kitchen chair, she plopped herself down. "Do this; do that. No salt, no fat—no taste. Lose weight—eat right, exercise, rest! Why don't they make up their minds?"

Mr. Edwards pushed his glasses up like an old schoolteacher and wagged his finger at her. "And you'll listen to the doctors. They know what's good for you." He patted her arm. "Now I'd better be going, but I'll be back again after dinner to walk with you. We'll only go as far as the birch trees this evening and maybe the big maple for tomorrow. We'll have your strength built up in no time."

"Don't leave on my account," Larry insisted. He couldn't be sure, but he thought a tinge of pink was beginning to show itself on Tilly's cheeks. "I've stopped only long enough to drop off the food, and then I'm off to run errands for the groundbreaking ceremony tomorrow morning."

"Groundbreakin's tomorrow?" Tilly exclaimed in surprise, standing straight to her feet. She ambled to the calendar hanging on the side of her refrigerator. "Today's the last day of April." She turned to Larry then Becky. "Neither of you has time to lollygag around with an old woman. Both of you shoo out of here!" She flicked her wrists at them. "Now go on. There's a lot of work needs done for that groundbreakin' ceremony. I won't have ya sloughin' off from the job on my account."

Larry smiled and held up his hand in defense. "I'm moving."

"Take her with you!" Tilly demanded, pointing an unwavering finger at Becky. "There's nothin' for anyone to do now. I'm gonna eat and rest." She gave

Becky a razor-sharp look. "Now y'all go on, and I'll call ya later. Van will be here later to look in on me."

Becky looked taken aback but gave Tilly a hug and promised to check on her after dinner. All Larry could think about was the amount of slang Tilly was using, and he knew she was conniving to bring Becky and him back together. Judging from the expression on Becky's face, she knew it, too.

Mr. Edwards stayed behind when Larry trailed Becky out the door. She stopped just short of the stone walkway.

"I'll be at Thunder Bay by nine tomorrow to make sure the balloons and refreshments are situated under the canopy," she said matter-of-factly. "Is there anything else you'll need?"

Larry rubbed his thumb over his forehead in thought. "All the ground-breaking tasks are on schedule, and no more help will be needed this afternoon." He paused and stared at her—hard. "But I do believe we have some unfinished business from last week which I'd like to discuss."

She raised her eyebrows at him and stared back. "I'm not sure what else you could say," she said softly. "You made yourself perfectly clear." Her chin tilted. "And for the record I don't find fault with you for speaking your mind the other night, but we do have to work together—at least for a little while—and I'd like to put any hard feelings aside during that time."

Her clinical tone matched what he'd encountered over the past week when they'd spoken on the phone. More disturbing was her ready agreement to anything he'd suggested. There was no debate. No fancy ideas or proposals of her own to interject. While he should be happy with her compliance, the change disturbed him. He knew he'd hurt her with his abrasive words, and though justified he had been too harsh. And now looking into her large dark eyes, he could see the once glowing light of excitement in her eyes had been replaced with detached determination.

"Let me walk you back to Piney Point," he proposed, taking note of a fresh spark of resistance in her eyes. "I'm not going to sound off on you, if that's what you're thinking. I just want to talk with you—and to offer an apology."

"Why not?" she said with resignation after a long moment. "It's not as if I have a choice." She turned and walked past him toward the wooded path.

"Wait a minute!" He stepped forward and caught her arm. When she stopped and looked up at him, he placed his hands lightly on her arms until he had her full attention. "I'm not your parents, and I'm not Michael. With me you'll always have a choice in what you want to do and whom you choose to be with."

"Is that so?" There was no anger in her statement, just skepticism. Without moving she let her gaze drop and linger on his hands, which were still gripping the striped cotton sleeves of her shirt. Slowly she drew her focus back and met his blue gaze with challenging force.

"Sorry!" Larry abruptly released her.

"All right," she said, gesturing with her hand toward the path. "You have my attention—let's talk."

Larry fell in step with her. "I behaved rudely the other night, and I want to apologize for my harshness. What I had to say could have been said with much more grace and tact, and I know your feelings were deeply hurt by my insensitive handling of the situation. I reacted off the cuff and am without excuse."

She turned and looked at him. "Yes, you could have been gentler, but you did speak the truth. I shouldn't have come to the field that night when you told me to stay. I put you in a bad situation, and for that I'm sorry."

"It's hard to convey the adrenaline push and life-preserving fear that comes over a police officer when that gun is pulled, cocked, and ready for action." Just talking about the episode sliced his gut like a fresh wound. "I've only had to draw my gun three times, and unless you've been there and done that, it's impossible to understand the depth of emotion behind that very act." He inhaled deeply. "It is unthinkable to contemplate, Becky, what could have happened that night. If Kirk or I would have. . ." His voice trailed off.

Becky shook her head. "You don't have to make any excuses for your anger, Larry. I accept full responsibility." Her delicate shoulders lifted lightly. "I suppose in a way it was good for you to lay out what you thought."

"No, it wasn't!" he protested.

She moved forward, reaching out to push back a branch extending into the path. "You said things that needed to be said, and you were right! I need to stop envisioning myself as someone who can save the world and everyone in it with my lofty ideals. I need to start living in the real world."

"Whoa!" He touched the sleeve of her shirt again, and she impatiently turned and stopped. "Under no circumstances should you try to dismantle who you are. I never, ever meant to give that impression." He took a deep breath and sent up a wordless prayer for wisdom. "You are a lovely woman inside and out. What I tried, ever so badly, to say the other night was that you need to use discernment with the gifts God has given you. God has given you insight into people—how they think, how they function, and what they need. He gave you insight the other night that Tilly was in trouble, but that didn't mean He wanted you personally to rescue her."

"But—"

Larry shushed her. "God doesn't expect you to go it alone. That night He gave you another person to handle the rescuing." He tapped his finger to his chest. "That someone was me. You need to accept not only His gifts, but His provisions, as well."

"Why is it so complicated? All I want is to do what God wants me to do!"

"Then do it!"

"That's the problem. I don't know what I'm supposed to be doing." She began walking the trail again, her words still strangely distant and uninvolved. "Last year I thought my life's work would be spent in the Congo. Now it doesn't look the least bit promising that I'll be able to return. And this camp project? I'm not sure I'm cut out for it. Mr. Edwards might have been right from the start."

"In what way?" he asked, continuing to feel unsettled by her demeanor. Her words were far-reaching but uncharacteristically dispassionate.

"I'm the stick between the spokes that makes the wheels stop rolling."

"Explain to me what that means."

"It means that what I have to offer you and the camp is more detrimental than helpful."

"I'm not sure how you came to that conclusion, but it couldn't be further from the truth." Larry had to think a moment. "Sure—there are times when certain ideas and plans won't pan out. But just because some of your ideas fail, it doesn't mean the entire program won't work."

Becky shrugged as she continued walking and didn't appear ready to answer. Larry tried again.

"For instance, take your idea about building the cabins near the lake. Jason has worked out a blueprint to make at least one of those cabins work." As the path widened out near Piney Point, Larry pulled up beside her. "Now me—I'd already written off the possibility of building on that portion of the parcel. Being the concrete-type person I am, the obstacle didn't seem to be worth the effort. Now you—you had the dream, and without your persistence the idea wouldn't have become a reality."

At this, Becky halted and swiveled toward him. "And without me it wouldn't be costing the camp another seven thousand dollars to make it work," she said in frustration. "And the camp wouldn't need a thirty-thousand-dollar check from Michael."

"Ah!" Sudden understanding dawned upon him. "If that's still bothering you, you can stop worrying about the money," he assured her. "Neither Michael nor your father sent that check!"

This seemed to catch her attention. "How can you be sure?"

"I can't tell you right now. You'll just have to trust me that it's true."

Her lips pursed and tilted to one side in wariness. "If the check didn't come from Michael or my father, then who did donate the thirty thousand?"

"I can't tell you that either."

Something akin to a ladylike snort escaped her lips. "Top secret?"

"In a way—yes." Larry expected news from Robert any day to confirm or disprove who he believed the donor to be. Even then he wasn't sure whether the information would be of a sharing nature. "I promised to look into the matter, and I did. I didn't find anything to suggest that your friend Michael might be a physical threat or that he was the author of the generous donation. Beyond that, you'll have to trust me with the rest until I have more information."

"More information?" she repeated.

"Perhaps!"

He could tell Becky wasn't satisfied, but she let the matter drop. "Let's just get through the groundbreaking ceremony tomorrow. I'm having a hard time thinking beyond refreshments and balloons at the moment. Do you think we can work together—at least for the interim until I decide what I'm going to do?"

"You're thinking of resigning the directorship?"

"That's a possibility."

"What would you do?"

"I'm not sure." The question seemed to make her nervous, and she began walking the leaf-covered trail again.

"Fair enough!" With great effort he concealed his dismay and fell in step beside her. "I don't see why we can't make this work. The incident the other night was just that—an incident. We can work together."

"Thank you for understanding."

He understood, but did *she* understand? How could he make her understand what he couldn't comprehend? The thought of her leaving the project and possibly the island sent an odd alarm through his core. In the past two months he'd grown to like her quirky ideas and dreams even if they weren't always feasible. *Tell the truth, Newkirk!* he demanded of himself. He'd grown to like her. Not that he would have admitted it the night she nearly scared him out of his six-foot-two skin. In the clear light of day, however, he couldn't deny the attraction between them.

Piney Point came into view, and once again Larry marveled at the picturesque scene the cabin made against the tall pines.

"Wonder whose car that is?" he heard Becky ask.

Larry caught sight of the full-size burgundy sedan parked just below the property on the narrow road. It wasn't an islander car. He knew every vehicle owned by the locals. As they rounded the side of the cabin to the front deck, he heard Becky's quick intake of air.

"Michael?"

The lone figure standing up top suddenly turned at the sound of her voice. The unmistakable dark curly hair and proud face left little doubt that the man was Michael. But it was the appearance of a man and woman walking near the deck's edge that seemed to make Becky stop dead in her tracks. He watched as every scrap of color left her face.

"Your parents, I presume?" he asked dryly.

Numbly she nodded. "When Michael said he was bringing reinforcements, he should have told me his weapons of mass destruction came in tandem."

# *Chapter 16*

The missing daughter returneth," Michael called down to Becky with a swaggering smile, leaning over the deck as her parents gathered to the edge beside him.

Becky looked up and shielded her eyes from the sun with her hand. "Michael!" she acknowledged softly before letting her gaze rest on the couple. "Hello, Daddy. . .Mother." What a marvelous and wretched development this was. She turned to Larry with a grimace. "You might as well meet the clan."

She led the way to the front and agonizingly drew herself up the wooden steps to the landing. Once at the top she attempted to take in a calming lungful of air. Even the feel of Larry's reassuring hand on her arm did little to quiet her jittery nerves.

Her father was the first to accost them. "So you must be the police officer friend Michael has told me about." He gave Larry a piercing look. "You should have instructed this daughter of mine to invest in a decent lock for this place. A single girl shouldn't be protected with such a flimsy piece of junk."

Becky jerked her gaze to the cabin and felt her hands shake. "How did that door get open?" she demanded, feeling the blood pump into her face.

Michael lifted a credit card between two fingers. "Piece of cake."

Had the man no shame? And right in front of an island policeman. "In civilized circles we call that breaking and entering," she retorted.

"Stop being melodramatic," her father chided, pressing down his wind-ruffled patch of combed-over hair. "Michael's only giving you a visual illustration to make a point. The lock's a flimsy excuse for any security." His eyes once again darted to Larry. "Wouldn't you agree with that?"

Becky felt Larry shift beside her, but her petite mother stepped forward before Larry could respond.

"Do stop all the harping," her mother droned, stroking her father's arm. "I haven't come all these miles to argue. I want to take a look at my little girl." She gave Becky a delicate and stiff hug.

"Mother, you should have called," Becky returned, clenching her teeth with the seething anger building within. Ambushed! She'd been purposely ambushed. Even her sweet-smiling mother was in it for all she was worth. Why couldn't she have a normal family where reunions were a happy affair?

"We decided to come at the last minute," Michael threw out with a shrug.

"Your parents wanted to be here for the groundbreaking ceremony you've talked so much about. We've come to support your work!"

*Liar! Liar! Pants on fire!* she wanted to retort. But kids' games wouldn't work on this crew. No, the three were a formidable force. As if sensing her distress, she felt Larry move closer, his hand now resting on the small of her back.

"A proper introduction is in order, don't you think, Becky?" she heard Larry ask in a debutante tone. "Maybe you could do the honors."

She almost smiled at the scowl blossoming on her father's face. His lack of manners had been glaringly exposed. "Certainly," she answered. "Larry Newkirk, I'd like you to meet my father and mother, James and Lolita Merrill." She waited as Larry extended his hand to both. "And you've already met Michael."

"Yes, it's a pleasure." Larry shook Michael's hand. "I'm glad you found the island worth a second visit."

Michael eyed him shrewdly. "Becky makes it worth it, you understand—and I'm sure you won't mind if we kidnap her for the rest of the day, will you?"

"Of course he won't mind!" her father boomed. "We're her family after all. Mr. Newkirk can understand that." He gave Larry a barbed look before nailing Becky with one. "Especially since our daughter hasn't seen fit to visit us."

Becky nearly popped a cork at their audacity. Something had to be done—and quick. Suddenly she pulled her arm through Larry's and leaned against his shoulder.

"I really hate to disappoint all of you," she began with a smoothness and repentant flare she didn't think possible. "But Larry and I have an engagement tonight which can't be broken—a working sort of deal. I really wish you would have called, and we might have been able to include you in the reservations."

"It is a shame," Larry added without missing a beat, and she could have kissed him. He looked at his watch. "And we're running behind!" She intercepted his look. "We might have enough time to see your parents and Michael to the hotel."

Lolita sputtered. "But, dear, I thought we could stay here with you."

"Here?" Becky feigned surprise, gaining strength from Larry's strong presence. "That's impossible, Mother. There's no room prepared." She leaned forward and lowered her voice. "You know my former employer and his wife are letting me stay here rent-free, and I couldn't impose on their generosity by asking them to fix up another room."

"I never!" her mother exclaimed.

*Maybe it's time you did!* She turned to Larry. "Let me go in and grab my bag. We'll show them to the hotel." She suddenly stopped and turned to Michael. "You did make reservations? It's May Day weekend, and there won't be a hotel room left on the island."

Michael glowered. "Yes, but I reserved only one room—for me."

"Oh, dear," Becky went on. She looked at her parents. "I hope you won't mind sharing a room with Michael."

"Sharing a room?" her father exploded. "No, that won't do!"

"There might be some rooms left on the mainland," Becky offered. "Would you like me to call around?"

Her father worked his jaw back and forth, and Becky felt sure he was ready to spit nails. Although she believed in God's command to honor parents, she knew God didn't expect her to lie like a lifeless doormat for their verbal abuse and power plays. Their last phone call still needled her. Her father asserted that God had proved him right. God never intended for her to go overseas, and He kicked her out of the Congo to get it through her thick and stubborn skull.

And from the looks of it she was about to receive another share of his venomous judgments. Sweetly she turned to Larry. "Would you mind fetching my purse from the cabin? I'd like to have a word alone with my parents." She let her gaze drift to Michael. "Michael, would you go with Larry and help him look?"

Michael looked defiant.

Larry gave her a troubled glance. "Are you sure?"

She nodded and watched with gratitude as Larry approached Michael. Whatever he said to Michael made him compliant. As soon as the two disappeared into the cabin, Becky turned to her parents.

"Now, you look here—" her father began.

"No! It's your turn to listen." Becky kept her voice low, but she felt a deep force and God-given power behind the words that made her father quiet. "I've listened patiently to your words for some time, and now it's time for you to listen to me." She bent her head slightly. "I want to love you and enjoy the relationship a daughter should have with her daddy, but I find it impossible to do so. I've been praying for guidance on how to approach the issue, and I guess my only solution is to deal with the problem head-on." Coolly she tucked several strands of loose hair behind her ears. "You might think it's helpful to offer your opinions, and I'm not averse to accepting constructive guidance; but I can no longer tolerate the verbal abuse."

"What rubbish is this?" her father snapped, and his forehead vein began to budge.

"Be quiet and let her finish!" Lolita demanded, much to Becky's surprise.

She took the opportunity to forge ahead. "I'm offering us a chance to be like a real family," Becky continued. "But we'll need to have ground rules for this to work. I can't function under the stress of being judged, sentenced, and strung up. I want to be treated like a human being and respected as a daughter. In return I'll love you as a daughter should." A thick lump formed in her throat. "If you feel that you're unable to treat me with respect, then—then we'll have to part ways."

"That's the most supercilious—" Her father seemed at a loss for words.

"Now, James," Lolita said, throwing a worried glance Becky's way. "Maybe you should listen—"

"No," he barked. "I won't listen." He stepped toward Becky. "You always were the difficult one. Why couldn't you be like your brother? If you'd listened to me instead of being so mule-headed, you'd be successful—instead of living on hand-outs." He seemed ready to continue his tirade, but she cut him off.

"You need to make a choice, Daddy," Becky demanded, standing firm and straight even though her muscles felt like jelly, ready to collapse in a puddle. "I've tried letting your remarks pass over me. I've even tried tuning you out." She spread both hands before them. "I've tried talking calmly and respectfully with you. I've tried showing you what the love of God has done for me and could do for you." A deep sigh escaped. "You cannot judge and tell me what God wants or doesn't want for my life. You don't even know Him!"

He sneered. "So now our turncoat daughter is too good for her family? Is that it?"

Becky held her ground. "If you cannot continue this conversation without insults, I must ask you to leave."

As if she'd physically slapped him, he stumbled back in a rage. "Then so be it!" He turned toward the door of the cabin. "Michael, come out here!" With a malicious glare he turned back to her. "I'll disinherit you!"

"Then so be it," she repeated. His threat might intimidate her brother, but it proved he knew nothing of her heart. She didn't want his money, only his love and acceptance—something he appeared incapable of giving.

When Michael appeared at the door, her father brusquely motioned him out. "We're leaving." He threw a spiteful look at Becky. "You've been a great disappointment to your mother and me." With that he thundered down the steps and toward the car.

Lolita looked lost and gestured helplessly to Becky. "Your father's only trying to help you."

Becky sadly shook her head. "Love doesn't behave that way, Mother—pride does. And I'm sorry he's chosen pride over me."

Lolita gripped Becky's arm in desperation. "You'll give him a heart attack!"

"You can't lay that at my door," Becky insisted with confidence. "He's doing this to himself. I will no longer take the blame for his behavior or any other physical malady either of you might endure."

Michael came closer cautiously and glanced over the railing as her father swung open the car door and hurled himself in. "Whatever did you say to him?"

Becky turned to Michael. "The same thing I'm going to say to you. I want to be treated with respect and will no longer tolerate contrived impositions, bribes, coercion, or guilt trips." She took his hand and looked him in the eye. "God does love you, and I will continue to pray that you'll one day discover Him. And for what it's worth—I'll miss you. We did have something special."

"You're sounding very final."

Becky nodded. "I think when you talk with Daddy, you'll find it's very final." She gave him a sad smile. "And I know you well enough to know you won't cross him." She turned and looked at her mother. "I'll miss you, too. If you and Daddy change your mind, you know my number."

Michael slowly shook his head and gave her a now-you've-done-it look before taking hold of her mother's arm. "Come on."

Without a word they reluctantly proceeded to the landing and down the steps. Becky watched as Michael helped her mother into the car then took command of the wheel before driving the three out of sight. She didn't move until the soft sound of footsteps from behind caused her to turn. Larry stood not more than four feet away.

She tossed her hands out in a careless gesture. "I'm sorry you had to witness that wretched part of my life." She could feel her brave façade begin to crumble. "But there it is! The good, the bad, and especially the ugly."

He shook his head. "I had no idea."

"Most people don't." What else could she say? There was nothing left. The scene had said it all. She'd done the impossible and stood up for what was right! And the event had played out exactly as she'd imagined—not hoped—but imagined.

"I'm sorry your family put you through that," Larry said, stepping close to open his arms in invitation. "I never knew."

She let herself drop against his chest and be enveloped in the warmth of his embrace. The steady rhythm of his heartbeat gave a numbing comfort. What must Larry think? He'd seen the raw and exposed baggage she called life. In truth she was relieved to settle the matter with her parents even if it went badly. What she hated was the fact Larry had been witness. What man would want emotionally damaged goods in need of repair? And how could God be pleased with her when her biggest concern at the moment wasn't her parents at all, but Larry's reaction to the whole thing? She was a failure as a missionary, unmanageable as a dreamer, and orphaned by necessity. It could only mean the third strike in the bottom of the ninth. But there would be no tears. She couldn't—wouldn't—allow it!

Finally she pulled back. Finding the courage to look at his face, she was surprised to see his eyes were damp. What a pathetic creature he must think she was. She turned away, but his grip tightened around her.

"I'm sorry you've had to endure such abuse from the ones who are supposed to love you the most," he murmured into her hair. "It makes me feel that much more like a heel for treating you so terribly the other night."

"It's not your fault." She drew away. "I regret you had to be here when this happened." She gazed up at him. "I gave my parents an ultimatum, and I'll have to live with the results."

"You did what was right and what you had to do in order to survive," he said.

She gave an unhappy laugh. "Am I heartless to feel such relief from booting my parents off the property? I mean, it's like a heavy weight has lifted from my chest."

"Not heartless," he insisted. "Just human!"

"And alone!"

Larry tipped her chin with his fingers. "You won't be alone as long as I'm around." He smiled down at her. "Why don't you go inside and freshen up? Then we'll go out on this big engagement we have."

"I'm sure you don't feel like going out any more than I do," she answered with a small smile.

"Maybe so," he laughed. "But we've already announced our plans, and I for one don't want to be accused of being a fraud."

She shook her head. "I don't know."

"You don't care that God will hold me accountable for aiding and abetting your failure to keep a date?"

"Well, when you put it that way—" she answered. Not that she felt like going anywhere but to the couch where she could lick her wounds.

"Trust me," he whispered. "When the horse throws you, it's time to get right up and try again."

Becky nodded and walked into the cabin. Why was life so complicated, and when was God planning to let the pieces of her life fall back into place?

# Chapter 17

Larry stroked the light stubble of his beard and pulled his electric razor from the bathroom cabinet. The razor slid over his skin in even strokes. Twice he stopped to feel for rough spots. Today was the groundbreaking ceremony, and he wanted to look good.

He'd also requested the afternoon off his scheduled shift. It was time to cash in on the mounting units of comp time he'd earned. Certainly it was inconvenient to the department with the May Day celebration, but he had more important plans—Becky. She just didn't know it yet.

Larry paused to check his reflection in the mirror then reapplied the razor to a missed spot. When the phone rang he did another cursory look and feel of his chin. Satisfied, he replaced the razor in the cabinet and trotted off to the living room phone.

"Got your information, Newkirk," Robert announced as soon as he lifted the phone.

Larry laughed. "You're awfully cheery for six thirty in the morning."

"Yeah, I know it's early, but I did try calling the office." He coughed. "Thought you wouldn't want to wait until your next duty day."

"What do you have?"

"I might add the information wasn't easy to obtain," Robert continued. "This guy's a real Houdini when it comes to hiding money."

"The man and the corporation are one and the same, aren't they?" Larry said.

"Yep." Robert wheezed and cleared his throat. "Kelly Enterprises is owned by Van Franklin Edwards and the distributor of your anonymous sum of thirty grand."

"I knew it!"

"And we're even, right?"

"Even!"

"Anything else you want will cost you big time," Robert asserted with a quick and watery laugh. "As usual it's always a pleasure doing business with you."

Larry smiled. "You did good work! Come visit the island anytime, and I'll treat you to a real seafood dinner."

"I might take you up on it as long as it's a real restaurant, not some pressed-fish and patty place. As I remember, you were always a big cheapskate."

"All lies!" Larry laughed.

"Yeah, well—we'll see when I really do show up and order the biggest lobster on the menu."

"It'll be my pleasure."

"Whatever!" He coughed again. "I'll let you know."

The phone line went dead, and Larry replaced the receiver. So Mr. Edwards wasn't the destitute Dairy Barn employee everyone took him for. He cashiered and bussed tables in an establishment he probably owned. The news caused him to laugh aloud. The old man had everyone fooled.

And they'd stay fooled!

He had no intention of sharing the secret with anyone, not even Becky. No wonder Mr. Edwards caused such a ruckus at the camp committee meetings. He was practically funding the entire project—as well as other church projects, no doubt. Once convinced the camp project was financially solid and worthy in cause, he'd donated the Thunder Bay property and the anonymous gift of money. The news blew his mind. He chuckled again as he walked to the bedroom.

Larry tucked in his shirt and went to the armoire in search of a thin black belt. He threaded the belt through the loops of his dress pants. Snapping the belt into place, he ran a hand over his cropped and bristly hair. Next came the tie and suit coat. Today would be a good day. Things were beginning to fall into place.

Becky tied the last two balloons onto the end of the table and stepped back to assess her work. Twice she moved the small plates and napkins. Twisting her watch into view she looked at the time. Nine o'clock. Not only had she arrived early, but also the work took less time than anticipated. She wanted the ceremony to be flawless. It might be her last chance to work on the camp project.

She opened the lid on one of the coolers and checked the platters of foil-covered finger sandwiches for the third time. The nervous jitters always made her compulsive. It wasn't as if the sandwiches were going to disappear. There was nothing to worry about. Even the mysterious holes thriller had been solved.

It was all so ridiculous anyway. The Johnson boys were charged with a first-degree misdemeanor, and the neighbor girl who was not more than eleven was doing community service. Tilly hadn't been far from the truth that the youths were seeking treasures. Their distorted version of the Union money tale, however, had the boys looking for silver Eisenhower dollars. Becky shook her head in wonder. An American history lesson might have helped point out the obvious one-hundred-year error in their plan.

Even more bizarre was the change in Mr. Edwards. Since Tilly's hospital episode he'd become Becky's sudden ally, bending over backwards for what she might need. The shift made her leery. It simply didn't make sense. He might be buttering her up for the big slam when he ousted her from her position as director.

When the groundbreaking ceremony was over she'd need to make some hard and concrete decisions. She fingered the letter in her dress pocket and gave it a nervous tap. The correspondence had been delivered yesterday, but she'd only retrieved the mail before leaving early this morning—hardly enough time to think through the ramifications of its contents.

Larry's red truck pulled into the parking lot, and she stepped out from the tent.

"Looks like you have everything ready," he greeted her with a smile, climbing down from the truck. "It looks great!" He slipped around to the rear of the truck and pulled back the canvas tarp. "Want to give me a hand with these chairs?"

"Sure!"

Quickly they set the folding chairs in order.

"Doing okay?" he asked with a playful smile when they met in the middle. "I don't want to wear you out before the ceremony."

Becky watched the edges of his eyes crinkle in amusement, and her heart warmed. "I'm fine," she replied. She'd miss him most of all. Given half a chance, she could easily come to love him. The thought nearly caused her spirit to collapse, and she turned away. Silently she set about finishing the chairs.

Several other church members began to arrive, and the time passed rapidly. When a substantial crowd gathered, Larry edged beside her.

"Ten more minutes," he assured her. "Then you can relax."

She looked over the crowd. "At least my parents didn't show up this morning to cause a ruckus." Then she smiled. "Maybe the Johnson boys will come forward with their posthole digger to help."

"They've already done the honors too many times." He laughed, his smile turning toward her.

She smiled back. Their "engagement" last night had been wonderful—dinner, music, and a walk along the shoreline. She'd cherish the memory forever.

"Yoo-hoo," called a woman's voice.

Becky suddenly spotted Tilly and Mr. Edwards coming toward them.

"Don't go breakin' a leg, you hear," Tilly advised with a laugh.

Mr. Edwards pumped Larry's hand with fervor. "Beautiful morning for the ceremony, don't you think?" He winked at Becky, and she blinked in surprise. "Give it a good shovelful."

Becky shook her head. "I'm not shoveling," she clarified, pointing to the canopy tent. "I'm in charge of the food."

"Nonsense," he growled, and her eyes widened. "All committee members get a dig in."

"Stop teasin' the girl," admonished Tilly. She patted Becky's arm. "You'll do just fine."

When Larry announced it was eleven o'clock, everyone gathered together.

Becky tried to slink back out of the way, but Larry had a sure grip on her arm that kept her right next to him as he stepped to the makeshift microphone.

"I'm glad so many of you were able to come this morning and share with us the extraordinary gift God has given in the groundbreaking of the Thunder Bay Christian Camp." Larry stopped when the audience applauded. "By the generous donation of Kelly Enterprises we will be able to make a difference in the lives of children who visit Thunder Bay. We will have a hand in preparing our next generation." More applause erupted.

"I would like to thank the many people who made this possible." Larry rattled off several names, including Becky's. After a few minutes he gave shiny new shovels to Jason, Becky, Lottie, Mrs. Phillips, and Mr. Edwards. He turned to the older man. "I'd like you to do the honor of beginning the groundbreaking."

Becky watched as Mr. Edwards's round eyes grew bigger behind his thick glasses. Larry gave him a searching glance and a nod. Something passed between them, but Becky was at a loss to explain what it was.

In less than ten minutes, the ceremony was over and the crowd descended upon the tent. Colored balloons were pumped with helium and plates filled as the happy crowd mingled until an hour passed and people moved on their way to the opening parade of the May Day celebration.

Larry came to help put away the last of the leftovers.

"We'll finish this up and head over for the festivities," Larry announced, closing the lid on the cooler. "It's time to relax."

Becky gave a weak smile and glanced about to be sure they were alone. "I wanted to wait until the ceremony was over to show you this." Quietly she pulled the folded envelope out of her pocket and extracted the letter. She handed it to Larry. "I'm afraid I'll have to move on."

Larry drew his blond brows together and looked over the letter. "Your missionary board wants you to choose another mission field?"

She nodded. "The Congo won't be open for at least one, if not two, years. They're asking all the missionaries affected to meet next week at their headquarters and discuss other possible areas." Becky gave a smile. "The good news is that the women I worked with are doing well."

"What are you planning to do?"

"To start over again, I guess."

He folded the letter and deposited it in his own pocket. She was about to protest when he held up his finger. "Are you willing to consider a full-time, paid position as camp director of Thunder Bay?"

"That's not going to happen, Larry," she replied, giving him a pointed look.

"Why?"

"There was opposition enough when I came on board without pay."

He leaned close. "Remember when we first met? You told me all I needed to have was a little bit of faith and a dream." He leaned his blond head her way. "Where's that woman today?"

"She grew up and learned to face reality."

"What if I told you the camp committee has already approved your paid position and the money has been secured?"

Becky shook her head. "I'd say you were crazy!"

"Crazy like this—" He lifted his hand and cupped her face. When he bent his head toward her she knew she was about to be kissed.

"Larry—" Her words were muffled when his lips descended on her own.

Becky couldn't think. Instead she pulled him closer until she thought she might break. Larry Newkirk was giving her a royal, truly genuine kiss, and she wasn't going to waste it—even if it might not last.

Suddenly he pulled her away and gently brushed back her hair and looked into her eyes. "Still think you're too grown up for dreams anymore?"

Wide-eyed she shook her head. "Not if the dreams are like this."

"Think this concrete-thinking man and this dreamer woman could make it as a couple if they tried hard enough?" He stroked her face with his finger. "Are you willing to give us a chance at least to see if we can make it? I know you face a bad family situation that will probably rear its head again. I can help you with that." His eyes caressed her face. "God has provided the camp director job. All you have to do is take it and let life live itself."

"And you want to do that together?" Becky raised her eyebrows in question.

"Is there something wrong with that?"

"Even after you met my family?"

"Yes!"

"Even after scaring you to death that night in the field?"

"So?"

"Even though I dream outside of the reality box?"

"Why not?" He chuckled. "Dreaming's good, isn't it?"

"I think I'm dreaming now!"

"Good!" His lips came down on hers again. "See?"

"I'm beginning to see." She suddenly kissed him with all her heart.

He pulled her back with a laugh. "I think we're making a scene." He nodded to the couple standing several yards away.

"Tilly and Van?" She laughed. "They're smiling like oversized toads!"

"Let them find their own romance," he pronounced, pulling her close again. "I've got my hands full enough."

"That's a good thing?" she questioned with a sparkle in her eyes.

"A very good thing!" With that he planted another kiss on her lips.

# Epilogue

Becky glanced down at the delicate folds of her simple but layered wedding dress and smiled. The serene fall island breeze caught the tips of the wispy hem encompassing her feet, and she felt its soothing motion. Larry squeezed her hand, and she lifted her face to see his warm eyes and endearing lopsided smile. Certainly the handsome, tuxedoed groom was as nervous as she. But all was right with the world today.

The newly built open-air chapel of the Thunder Bay Christian Camp still smelled of just-cut timbers and sawdust. Becky had helped Larry and countless others construct this very first building. What better place to have the most perfect wedding to the most perfect man?

Pastor Taylor cleared his throat and Becky reluctantly drew her attention back to the ceremony. Her hand trembled as she repeated the vows and placed the wedding band on his finger. She could hardly stand the wait as Larry did the same.

Pastor Taylor seemed to sense her impatience and gave a low chuckle. "You may now kiss the bride," he told Larry.

"With pleasure," she heard Larry murmur.

Cheers erupted from those gathered in the chapel, but Becky soon tuned out the clamor as Larry bent down ever so tenderly and gave her the kiss she'd waited for. Unbidden, a giggle escaped, and he withdrew slightly with a puzzled smile.

"What's so funny, Mrs. Newkirk?" Larry whispered into her ear.

Becky couldn't keep from grinning. "I was thinking about the first time I saw you at my door in uniform and how I thought Tilly had sent the police. Turns out, she knew more than either of us about matchmaking."

"I can't argue with her results." He laughed. "I'm sure Tilly's in her glory today over her successful venture."

"Very successful, indeed," Becky agreed.

"And you haven't seen anything yet," he teased.

"Promise?"

"Promise!" Much to her pleasure, he sealed that very promise with another kiss.

# Bay Hideaway

# *Dedication*

Special thanks to Becky Rickard for all of her editing services. I couldn't have done it without you.

Deep appreciation goes to Bill Hedrick, city of Columbus prosecuting attorney, for his legal expertise.

A big thank-you to Pennsylvania State Representative Karen Beyer and her assistant, Maurine Payne, for sharing their knowledge of the Pennsylvania Statehouse.

# Prologue

"Are you absolutely positive?" Nathaniel Whithorne gripped the desk with one hand and sank slowly into his expensive desk chair.

"It's her!" the male voice at the other end of the line answered. "It's your wife."

The leather creaked softly as Nathaniel swiveled the chair toward the floor-to-ceiling plates of glass overlooking the city of Harrisburg, Pennsylvania. The bright sun bounced off an adjacent building, reflecting shards of light into his office. For a moment he was speechless. What could he say? He let the back of his knuckles slide back and forth against the square of his clean-shaven jaw. How could he believe the unbelievable in spite of his suspicions?

"Representative Whithorne?" the voice continued. "Are you still there?"

The spray of light coming through the windows slowly seeped out of the room, and Nathaniel's reflection in the glass began to take form. He stared back. His thick black hair was now peppered with gray—a change his regal mother would say enhanced his already aristocratic features. But his features were more haggard than ever and he knew it. He'd aged more over the past two years than during his entire forty.

Suddenly, he swung the chair back toward the massive mahogany desk. "Where is she?"

"On a small Ohio island off Lake Erie," answered the man. "It's called Bay Island—a touristy type place for summer travelers."

"And you're sure it's Judi?"

"I've seen her, sir!" the man assured confidently. "There's no mistake. She's going by the name of Amanda Judith Rydell, but the islanders call her Judi. There are photos I can send you."

"Where's she living on the island?"

"North Shore Condominiums." The sound of shuffling papers came across the line. "The actual address is 791 Wind Surf Drive, Unit E."

Nathan penned the address onto an ivory writing pad. "And her work?"

"Working as a church secretary, sir."

"Church secretary?" Surprise riddled Nathan's voice.

"Yes, sir!"

"Book me a place to stay and ground transportation for this Bay Island place," ordered Nathan. "I'm leaving tomorrow morning."

"But, sir—"

"Use your name for the reservations," Nathan went on uninterrupted. "Under no circumstances do I want her knowing about my arrival." He paused a moment. "And, Thomas?"

"Yes, sir?"

"I don't think I need to tell you how important it is for you to keep this information under wraps. Do you understand? No leaks."

"Yes, sir!"

"You'll need to cancel my appointments for the next few days." Nathan flipped open his daily planner. "Make my apologies and reschedule what you can."

"What about House Bill 65?" questioned Thomas. "It's due for a vote on Thursday."

Nathan groaned. "See what you can do to stall the vote. I can't miss that bill when it hits the floor."

"Yes, sir."

"And, Thomas?"

"Yes, sir?"

"You don't have to keep addressing me as *sir* in private."

"I know, sir."

Nathan gave a sigh of resignation. "One last thing—hand deliver all the original photos and information you have. Don't make copies."

"Yes, sir."

"Thanks for covering this, Thomas."

"My pleasure, sir. Will there be anything else?"

Nathan tapped his pen on the desk as he thought a moment. "No. If you get my transportation and reservations in order, I'll take it from there." He leaned back in the chair. "I'll call you as soon as I know how much time I'm going to need. It's not a small matter when it comes to raising the dead."

"Sounds gruesome, sir."

"I'm sure it will be!"

# Chapter 1

Judi Rydell casually looked up from the computer screen as the church office door swooshed open. Her fingers stilled, hovering lightly over the keyboard, her finely manicured nails making light contact with the keys.

"Good morning," called the blond visitor with obvious enthusiasm, his tall figure striding purposefully through the doorway and straight to the waist-high, natural oak counter. His smiling, raven-haired wife followed.

"You're both early," Judi commented with a slight smile. "What's the occasion?" She watched in amusement as the man's gaze darted sharply toward the clock above her.

A playful smirk crossed Larry Newkirk's lips. "It's Wednesday and ten o'clock. What more do you want?"

"Nine fifty-nine if you want to be exact."

He consulted his gold wristwatch. "According to my precision-made Swiss timepiece, it's ten to be exact—and hence, a moot point." His mischievous eyes dared her to contradict, and when she only shrugged, he continued. "Got anything for us?"

Judi pushed her chair back and lightly stretched as she stood. "Actually, I do have a fax for you." She turned and plucked a paper from the wire basket next to the printer. "Here you go!" With ease, she leaned over the counter, the ends of her hair sliding forward across the padded shoulders of her milky-white blouse. "Also, the folks from the lumberyard called this morning," she announced. "They'll be on the noon ferry."

Larry took the paper and glanced at the clock again. "Good! I'll meet them as soon as they arrive."

Becky sidled up to her husband and silently scanned the typed information while Judi watched the couple. His military-style crew cut made him seem that much more in command, and she thought, yet again, how fortunate Becky must feel.

Looking pleased, Larry neatly folded the sheet of paper into a perfect square and slid it into the back pocket of his jeans. "The new camp buildings are moving according to schedule."

"Ahead of schedule, actually," Becky corrected with a smile. She turned to Judi. "Thanks to a wonderful secretary who doesn't mind keeping the contractors on their toes."

"Someone has to keep them in line," Judi answered with feigned sternness. "And I'm sure Larry is ready for a full and accurate accounting." She gave Becky a knowing glance and then dutifully looked at Larry expectantly, waiting for the barrage of questions sure to follow.

Larry retrieved a small pad of paper from his shirt pocket and flipped it open. "Did the window orders make it in?"

"Done!"

"Heating and cooling?"

Judi smiled. "Done!"

"Bids for plumbing?"

"One is in and two by the end of the week." She lifted her eyebrows a fraction at his impish expression.

"Is there anything you haven't completed?"

"You act surprised!" She laughed, sitting back in her chair. "Church secretaries are always on top of their game, and in your case, on top of the construction process."

The corners of his mouth lifted into a lopsided grin. "And some secretaries are even known to keep a private stash of fudge."

Becky shook her head and laughed. "Real subtle, Mr. Newkirk."

"Your lucky day; I just happen to have a box." Judi smirked. She reached deep into the recesses of the bottom desk drawer and pulled out the black-and-white checkered box. "You two are the only ones who truly appreciate this delicacy besides me."

Larry procured two pieces from the offered box and passed one to his wife before carefully removing the cellophane from his own piece. "If you'd just tell me where you get this stuff, I'd buy it for myself instead of pilfering from you." With practiced precision, he plopped the chocolate square into his mouth.

"Sorry," she told him with pleasure, unable to count the number of times this particular conversation played out. "It's an old family secret." Carefully, she replaced the box.

"It's not like you make it," he grumbled teasingly. "You buy it!"

"It's all the same to me!"

"What's the name of it again?" he asked.

"Angelic hash!" She gave a mock sigh. "Really, you should write it down."

"I'll remember it next time around," he promised.

Judi knew better. He'd ask again—and again. Becky only rolled her eyes.

"So you're not going to tell where you buy the fudge?" Larry asked again, obviously choosing to overlook their amusement.

"Nope!" Judi reached around the desk and pulled out a large cylinder. "But I will give you this."

Larry caught the yellow cardboard tube she rolled across the countertop.

"It's not exactly fudge, but I guess it will do."

A hollow, cannonlike thump reverberated throughout the room when he popped the top. Tightly rolled drawings spilled out into his hands as he tipped the bottom of the canister toward the ceiling. Judi watched as he unraveled and smoothed out the building plans on top of the extra desk in the outer office.

He was tall and handsome, especially on the days he wore his police uniform. All the women in the church loved him. He was gallant, caring, and most of all—handy. Not just a few women were disappointed, she mused, when he married. Actually, he and Becky were still newlyweds. Judi was happy for them—truly. They were such a good match and seemed to work together well. Since the two began working jointly on the Christian camp project, the idea of Thunder Bay went from dreams to paper to life in remarkable time. Most of all, their romance and subsequent marriage took pressure off Judi.

Larry had asked Judi out twice when she first came to the island, practically producing a spontaneous heart attack each time. It wasn't just their age difference. She had at least five years on the man. No, it had nothing to do with Larry at all. By now he probably thought her a bit odd—and rightly so. Surely Larry must have been puzzled by the contrast of her warm office demeanor versus the social ice queen act she put on to discourage all romantically inclined men.

But it had to be that way.

Judi could never date and certainly could never marry again. She drew a deep and painful breath.

Distrust ruled her life. Like an anaconda, suspicion continued to keep a constricting cord around her throat. It threatened to tighten without warning. Just seeing Larry Newkirk in his police uniform for the first time filled her with such panic she'd thought the church secretary job would have to go. Larry was working on various camp details in her church office at least three times a week. Thankfully, she concluded early on that Larry was completely harmless, saving her the heartache of finding a new job.

Besides, it wasn't just Larry. Even the most innocent probing of the church members into her personal life sent a rush of adrenaline speeding through her veins like a frenzied monster.

Still, she was free! The official documents proved it. Yet, if her mind was convinced, why did her incredibly terrified soul fail to believe? All the bases were covered—twice over. Very few could accomplish the meticulous process required to rebuild a new life, a new person. Not even the federal witness protection program promised as much.

The church phone rang, dragging her thoughts back to earth. The friendly voice at the other end offered the same weekly reminder she'd come to expect.

"I've ordered two dozen banana nut and one dozen blueberry," Lottie BonDurant announced. "Don't let Bette charge more than twenty-seven dollars.

Sometimes she forgets to give the discount."

Judi promised to be diligent in her weekly pickup and quietly replaced the receiver. The ladies' Red Hat Club pickup at Bette's Bakery was the highlight of her week. The trip wouldn't be complete unless she purchased Bette's most delicate of creations for herself—the chocolate éclair. She had to laugh at Lottie. Poor Bette practically gave away the muffins at what she usually charged, but Lottie made sure the price never wavered.

Judi glanced at the clock. Ten fifteen! There was still time to get her morning work done. Situating the computer keyboard just right, she began typing again. The July calendar of events seemed filled to the brim this year, and she took special care to make sure every detail was correct. One mistake and the self-appointed editing patrol of the church would let her know—lovingly, of course. She didn't really mind. They thought their assistance was a service to Judi. Maybe it was! She grinned at the thought and hit the SAVE icon.

Satisfied the calendar was perfect, she copied the file to a disk. She'd learned the hard way about fickle church computers and lost data. Ouch! She wouldn't let that happen again. With three clicks of the mouse, she shut down the computer and gathered her pouchlike purse.

"I'll be back in twenty minutes if anyone's looking for me," Judi called over her shoulder. "Pastor's out for the morning, so lock up if you two leave."

Larry and Becky looked up from the drawings. "Muffin run?" they asked at the same time.

A smile passed between the three. The Red Hat ladies had begun with five women, not one of them less than seventy years of age. It wasn't long before the live-wire set of old ladies had gained half the island within the group—young and old alike.

"A muffin run it is!" she answered back. With a quick wave, she disappeared through the door and into the parking lot.

Nathan Whithorne snapped his briefcase closed, his fingers lingering thoughtfully over the clasps. He took a deep breath and let his gaze stray to the aging metal casement window overlooking the front porch where an old wooden swing bobbed gently in the late-June breeze. The island did hold a certain charm, which he might be inclined to enjoy under different circumstances.

Suddenly exhaustion claimed his thoughts. His stomach churned at the prospect of what lay ahead, a situation he hadn't a clue how to handle. If he'd thought his heart had been ripped into shreds over two years ago when Judi died, it was now minced like crushed glass to think she was still alive. He'd loved Judi with everything he possessed. If Thomas was correct—and it blew his mind to believe it—everything in his life was about to change.

The explosive possibilities seemed mind-boggling.

Another sigh escaped as he grabbed the briefcase and shoved it into the corner. He turned to look over the quaint cabin with its smattering of easy chairs and one small sofa sitting before the dark and empty fireplace. A window air conditioner hummed steadily from the living room, providing coolness throughout the small sitting area, kitchen, and dining room. Another air conditioner was cooling the bedroom.

Nathan hadn't taken the time to look over the cabin when he'd arrived the evening before by a small commuter plane at the island airport. An earlier flight hadn't worked out, and Thomas obviously hadn't been able to secure a decent rental car deal, either. Nathan was just lucky to find any transportation to the cabin. All he wanted was a car, but the place seemed overtaken by golf carts. Traffic control, the portly man had said. But golf carts hardly seemed appropriate if it should rain, even if many of the carts were equipped with snap-on plastic windows. Who was the rental manager fooling? Plastic windows!

The small, two-door rental car he eventually found wasn't much better than the golf carts when it came to squeezing his long legs into the cramped compartment. It reminded him of days long ago when his only method of travel was his younger sister's bike—complete with a banana seat and sissy bars. There's nothing quite like pedaling in the knees-to-chest position on a girl's bike.

Now they were adults, each choosing different paths. His sister, Laurie, was the managing editor for a newspaper in Pittsburgh, and the youngest, Jeffrey, was becoming a very rich computer guru. As the oldest, Nathan had chosen to use his law degree in politics. All his desires revolved around making the world a better place. Easier said than done, he'd soon learned. Politics slowed the course of progress with enough roadblocks to discourage even the most valiant men and women.

Then there was Judi! She'd served as his legal assistant for a year while he worked for a prestigious attorney group, handling the nuisance business law cases no one else wanted. Not long after, he'd acquired favor with one of the partners and landed several challenging cases—and respect within the legal community.

It wasn't the media-covered cases he'd won nor the notoriety soon gained that he remembered most. No, his memory always returned straight to Judi. Within that year, they'd fallen madly in love. Both anticipated a less than enthusiastic welcome from his family, but neither was prepared for their volatile reaction.

"The woman's not of your station!" his mother claimed with all the sensibilities the patrician lady could muster. It didn't seem to matter that their own family hadn't always been so upper crust. Truth be told, they weren't technically wealthy, anyway. Well-off, maybe, but not influentially rich. That was a pipe dream.

Judi, though, had come from a less-than-desirable-lineage, and Nathan's entire family seemed bent on convincing him the mismatched marriage could never work. Even his meek and mild father seemed convinced Judi would never fit into the political circles of which Nathan wished to become a part.

"You've got your sights set on being a congressman, son," his father reasoned. "We like the girl, but she is not made from hearty stock. The press will pulverize her, and you by proxy."

Not to be thwarted, the couple eloped. The strategic move proved to be disastrous—for they might have won the battle with his family, but not the war. Irreparable damage was the result. His family felt betrayed; hers disappointed. No matter what Judi or Nathan did to restore family harmony and blessing, the two did not fit comfortably into either world. Judi's father had been somewhat forgiving, but not Nathan's. A chill prevailed during the Whithorne family gatherings and when given the chance, obvious slights. Even the Christmas spirit failed to relieve the tension. Nathan could still see the hurt in Judi's eyes when the family Christmas card arrived in his name alone with the expensive gold address label pronouncing his family's verdict of judgment.

Judi claimed her faith would see her through and often went to church to find solace. Repeatedly she urged Nathan to come with her and he did, but not regularly. He just couldn't make a connection with God the way she did. It wasn't until her death when he'd felt totally devoid of purpose that he chose to seek God. Then Nathan dove in headfirst to erase the pain of his loss. Between his election to the Pennsylvania House of Representatives and church, he had little time to dwell on what might have been.

Now looking back over the past two days, he had begun to reevaluate what these events meant. For if Judi's death was a farce, maybe this God-thing was a farce as well. Real Christians didn't fake their deaths and leave loved ones behind to flounder in their grief. The woman had a brokenhearted father to consider. The idea of anything so heinous was beyond his grasp.

Even now, like a vivid on-screen movie, he could see the riverbank where Judi often went to read or meditate. That horrible day she disappeared, the only thing left on the bank was a set of house keys, a half-empty bottle of water, and a book, facedown on the pages she'd been reading. Her purse and every other personal possession remained untouched in the house.

Police had noted the area where she slipped in, marking every gash in the mud where her bare feet and clawing fingernails failed to stop the fall. A piece of torn cloth from her favorite green skirt was found snagged on a nearby tree branch protruding from the broken wall of rocks. To make matters worse, several days of rain had produced rising waters and swift currents.

Authorities questioned Nathan concerning Judi's ability to swim. Oddly, he didn't know. He should have known, but the subject never came up and they'd never been in a pool deeper than three feet. Couples in love weren't interested in swimming laps.

Rescue teams dredged the Susquehanna River for two days.

"I'm sorry," the sergeant had said to Nathan. "We've not been able to find your wife."

Reliving those words still caused his chest to burn. The police presumed Judi's body would eventually surface. It never did!

But Judi's presence didn't feel lost. Wouldn't he know if she were dead—wouldn't he sense it? Family and friends assured him the reaction was natural, especially since there was no physical evidence to touch and hold. Healing would come, they promised.

It wasn't until months later when he went through her jewelry that he discovered the missing heirloom brooch. The multistoned ruby pin had been one of Judi's most cherished belongings—besides her 1972 sunflower-yellow Volkswagen Beetle. How they'd argued over that car and the high cost of maintenance the old rattletrap generated. When faced with her death, though, the arguments suddenly proved to be frivolous and stupid. Unable to part with this close link to her life, the car remained unmoved in his garage.

A seed of doubt, however, was planted the day he realized the missing jewelry piece was nowhere to be found. Riddled with suspicion, Nathan eventually asked his trusted aide to make a search. Nathan had to find closure and smother these uncertainties.

Instead, his fears became real!

Nathan glanced up at the rooster clock in the kitchen. Ten forty-five! Time to go. If Thomas was correct, Judi would be arriving at Bette's Bakery in twenty minutes. Pulling the keys from his dress pants, he smoothed his tie and gave one last look around the room before opening the door. Sun spilled into the doorway and he casually slipped on his sunglasses. He was determined not to give in to the dread streaming through his body.

The drive was short to the lakeside shops called Levitte's Landing. Tourists were crawling all over the place, and Nathan found it difficult to find a parking space.

"Plenty of time!" he said aloud, pulling the small car into a tight end spot toward the back of the lot.

Quickly, he made his way up the long aisle, his leather shoes scratching across the hot pavement. Finally, he reached the concrete walkway. Bette's Bakery was straight ahead. One shaded bench beckoned as the perfect perch from which to watch. Nathan slowed his pace and sat down, pinching up the pleats of his pants as he did so. Leisurely, he rested his back against the painted wood and waited.

Several customers entered the bakery, and he almost missed the lady in the bright pink flared skirt and white silky blouse. Her smooth strawberry hair bounced as she walked briskly by the retail shops and headed for the bakery. Nathan leaned forward.

He was tempted to remove his glasses but dropped his hand when he realized she was looking his way, her own hand trying to block the bright sun in her eyes. For a moment she hesitated and seemed to take notice of him but eventually turned away.

Nathan's heart began to pound with full force. It was her! The squeezing sensation in his chest made it hard to breathe. He let his eyelids close tightly for a second and quickly snapped them open again. When he looked up, the door to the bakery was closing behind her, and the pink of her skirt vanished inside.

Several minutes passed and he wondered if time ever crawled as slowly as it did now. Then she reappeared, once again looking his way. He stood quietly and smoothly slid his sunglasses off in one fluid motion.

The eyes of his wife suddenly locked with his.

"Long time, no see," he remarked with impressive airiness. His head tilted defiantly. "Surprise, darlin'!"

# Chapter 2

Judi Rydell tensed and immediately felt her hackles rise when she spotted the well-dressed man sitting on the bench outside the bakery. Plagued by an earlier uneasiness, her level of alertness was rapidly escalating.

Something wasn't right! Prior to entering the store, she had taken time to momentarily scan the crowd of tourists to find the source of her apprehension. What had she seen or heard? Nothing appeared amiss throughout the sun-drenched walkways.

Even the nearby bench had been empty when she'd glanced about—or had it? Panic made her stiffen as she glanced back at the man now sitting there. In a split second, the stranger stood resolutely to his feet, and alarm coursed through her every nerve ending. Her eyes opened wide.

Like fast-drying concrete, her feet abruptly stopped, and the three shopping bags full of boxed muffins slammed painfully against her legs. Her breath stuck solidly between her constricted lungs and throat.

There was no mistaking the identity of the strikingly tall man as he effortlessly removed his sunglasses and spoke. "Long time, no see." His mouth twisted determinedly. "Surprise, darlin'!"

*Nathan!*

The prickle of terror churning within rapidly turned into an outbreak of sweat droplets across her forehead. Paralyzed, she could only stare back at the pair of defiant gray eyes. She stiffened again. *Help me, Lord!* The whispered prayer barely squeaked past her lips.

Nathan stepped forward and she began to jerk back, but her feet remained firmly planted. She couldn't even let go of the bags clenched so tightly in her hands.

"What?" his deep voice taunted cruelly. "You don't recognize your own husband?"

Judi went cold. What she wouldn't do for a trapdoor to swallow her whole. Matter of fact, this would be a fine time to check out of the horrendous situation with an elaborate fainting spell like the heroines in those sappy novels, yet she knew even the most contrived luxury of unconsciousness would never happen for her. No, life would force her to be cognizant of every miserable second.

Unprepared! She felt utterly unprepared. After months of readiness, her preparation for such a moment had been stymied by the calm she'd experienced on the island. His impeccable shirt and tie routine didn't help matters. He always dressed the part when he meant business, and right now the solemn expression on his face indicated every last fiber of his being was dead serious.

Biting back the fear, Judi cast Nathan an anxious glance. "What are you doing here?" she blurted.

He looked stunned at her question and laughed—a heartless, unamused laugh. Then his jaw squared and his eyes turned into chipped ice. "You're unbelievable! I come to Bay Island to find my supposedly dead wife and all you can say is 'What are you doing here?'"

"Yes!" she retorted, suddenly finding the strength to react. "It's a perfectly good question. I don't know how you found me, but it seems counterproductive to what you've always wanted."

"Counterproductive to what *I've* always wanted?" Nathan repeated with contempt. "If you're trying to confuse me, it won't work!" His expression, however, told a different story. Judi knew the compressed lines in his forehead verified the perplexity he felt.

"What did you expect, Nathan?"

His gaze traveled slowly over her. "A good story perhaps. You have no amnesia tale or kidnapping conspiracy to bombard me with? No inconsolable tears of bewilderment?" When she gave no reaction, his face inched closer. "Maybe you do surprise me."

Judi flushed but stood her ground. "You have no right to be here."

"Really!" Slowly his hand reached out and she flinched as he touched her hair. "Red hair with the blended shade of creamy milk and strawberry." When he switched his gaze back to her face she saw anger simmering beneath his cool exterior. "But changing your hair and name does not change the fact that you're still my wife, Mrs. Whithorne. Do you have any idea what you've put me through?" He shook his head at her. "You have a lot of explaining to do—a very lengthy and detailed discussion concerning your death and miraculous recovery." He leaned closer still. "Will it be your place or mine?"

She took a quick step back and felt the strands of her loose hair cascade from his hand. "I'm not going anywhere with you!"

"No?"

"No!"

Both of his shoulders lifted with impatience, and Judi braced herself for his fuming. "That's fine with me!" His voice rose a degree. "We can air our dirty laundry right here." He swept a wide arc with his hands toward the passing tourists. "They don't know me from Adam, but not so for you. How will the good folks of Bay Island react when they learn about your past? And you, a church secretary, too!" He gave her a sharp look. "I could also drag you to the island police station. You're smart enough to know it would take only one call to let this faked-death scam explode all over you."

Looking at his grim face, she knew he would make good on his threat. What she didn't know was why. Why search for her? Why come for her at all? Visions of Pastor Taylor, Larry and Becky Newkirk, and Tilly Storm raged through her tumultuous thoughts. What if she called his bluff? Would her newfound friends understand her previous actions, the acts of a desperate woman?

"Still thinking?" he asked with deceptive laziness.

Judi felt unwell. "I don't want to go with you."

"No big revelation in that sentiment, is there?" His eyebrows shot upward sardonically. "For reasons which only you know, and I intend to discover, you went to great lengths to abandon me."

Fingers numb from the heavy muffins, she shifted the bags slightly. "I can't talk now," she argued. "The ladies are waiting on the muffins."

"Muffins!" he boomed, and an incredulous expression crossed his facial features as he glanced down at the packages. He lifted eyes dark with bitterness and annoyance. "You're up to your pretty little neck in trouble and you want to deliver muffins?"

Judi screwed her lips into a frown. "The ladies are expecting me and if I don't show up soon, they'll send a search party." She eyed him with more courage than she felt. "If you want to talk, we'll talk; but I have to stop by the church first."

He seemed to consider her proposition and finally jerked a nod. "Good enough! But we go together."

What choice did she have? As if to ensure her compliance, she felt his hand lightly guide her arm.

He looked down at her, his voice quite calm. "Where's your car?"

"Cart," she corrected and swallowed nervously. "I'm parked at the far end." She pointed toward the ten-foot lighthouse replica near the entrance to the shopping center.

He said nothing more as she struggled to keep up with him. Her mind raced ahead. What was she to do? She could have easily refused to accompany him or even screamed her fool head off as a means of rescue, but he held a mighty sword over her. Those she'd come to care about, and even love, would be devastated by her deception. The important question remained unanswered—what did he want?

Judi reached her golf cart in a daze and absently pulled a set of keys from the pocket of her skirt.

"Nice set of wheels," he commented, rolling his eyes.

Feeling her face flush, she bit back the retort so close to her lips. What did Nathan know about financial struggles? With great effort, she contained herself. "It's what I can afford."

He lifted one eyebrow a fraction and seemed to consider her. "I'm taking exception to the mode of transportation, not the model." He looked over the golf cart and frowned. "Does anyone on the island own a car?"

"Of course!" Judi countered impatiently. "Golf carts are not only easier on fuel but traffic congestion, as well—especially during the height of tourist season." She placed the muffins in the back compartment and sat in the driver's seat. Immediately she noticed his expression of disapproval. A touch of frustration filled her voice. "I suppose you want to drive?"

For a moment, it looked like he might push the issue, but instead he walked over to the passenger side. "Just be sure to keep this buggy on the road." He climbed in with great effort, ducking his head until he settled into the seat, his peppered hair nearly touching the roof. He turned to look at her. "If you're having any thoughts of running us over an embankment and into Lake Erie, squelch the idea. One drowning in the family is enough, don't you think?"

"Very funny!"

A muscle tightened in his cheek. "It wasn't meant to be funny."

Judi caught his hard, incisive look and her insides quaked. Quickly she snapped on the lap belt and twisted the ignition key forward. The electric engine came to life.

Nathan had aged plenty in two years. Was this the same man she had passionately loved and married? The same man who had soon realized what a liability she was to his cherished aspirations for a successful political career? Their castle-in-the-sky marriage had turned out quite different than she'd imagined. Relentless hostility from his family was difficult enough, but having Nathan turn on her had hurt more than she could endure. He had wanted her out of the picture, and she obliged by leaving permanently—what more did the man want?

"By the way," he asked, holding on to the seat frame as she entered the main road, "do you know how to swim?"

Judi looked sharply at him. "What's that supposed to mean?"

Gravel spewed from under the wheels of the golf cart when she veered slightly off the road and onto the rocky berm. Quickly she corrected the wheel.

He frowned again. "Maybe it wasn't such a good idea to let you drive."

"What did you mean by that last remark, Nathan?" She felt her heart begin to pound. Did he intend to harm her? If he thought she would be a docile lamb going to the slaughter, he had better think again.

He gave a wry smile. "I mean, you should keep your eyes on the road."

"Not that remark!" she cut in.

It seemed to take him a moment to follow her thought. "About swimming?"

"You know very well what I meant."

Sudden enlightenment lit his face. "You think. . ." He paused, a look of skepticism now moving across his features. "You think I'm planning to toss you to the fishes in an ironic gesture of revenge?" When she didn't answer, he gave a grunt. "That's a cheap shot, Judi, even for you. I might be angry, but I'd never lay a hand on you. Never have! Never will!" He made a little move of impatience. "I didn't come all this way to settle a score."

Her face grew hot under his scrutiny. "Then why did you come?"

Silence greeted her inquiry and she drew a deep breath, unable to take her eyes from his lean, attractive face. Again, the wheels swerved off the road and once more she corrected them. She felt his burning gaze on her.

"Pull over!" he commanded with a sigh. "You're going to land both of us in the water or the briars or both."

Judi eased the vehicle onto the stony berm and set the brake. With trembling fingers, she fumbled with the clasp of the seat belt. It refused to budge.

Nathan reached over and with one flick easily unsnapped the belt. "My visit is making you a total wreck, isn't it?"

She let the belt fall over the side and pushed herself out of the seat. "What did you expect?"

They crossed paths in front of the cart, staring at one another as they passed, and took their respective seats.

"I'm not sure what I expected from you," he answered, releasing the brake. "It's not every day a man finds his dead wife." Glancing in the side-view mirror, he edged the cart back onto the road. "We take this road until it comes to Bayshore Drive?"

She gave him a stunned perusal before nodding. "Yes."

His glance seemed to appraise her swiftly before returning to the road. "I made a point of knowing the layout of the island before I came. You know I'm a man of details."

Disconcerted, Judi turned her head away and watched the scenery pass. Although the hot sun bore down on the island, the lake provided a fresh breeze, which now cooled her skin as the golf cart pushed past the shoreline. They rode in silence for several minutes. Nathan claimed he wasn't after revenge. Claimed he wasn't here to harm her. What could he possibly want if it wasn't to even the score or worse—finish the job?

"I believe this is your church." His voice was a harsh intrusion into her thoughts.

Judi looked up to see the redbrick church come into view. Beautiful white shutters adorned the long line of windows on either side of the main doors. The roof gradually swooped toward heaven until it peaked with the church steeple. The vented tower housed a bona fide church bell and an equally impressive heavily twined rope. One pull of the cord and the deep chime of the bell would effortlessly resonate over the entire island. Sadly, a few Sunday morning sleepyheads complained to the city council last year and the bell now remained silent except for special occasions.

Nathan turned the golf cart into the gravel parking lot and deftly parked the machine near the entrance. "Shall we go in?"

She slid out. "You could wait for me here," she suggested, bending down to look at him under the roof.

"Sorry!" He swung his long legs out. "You can't get rid of me that easily—again." Grabbing all three shopping bags, he nodded toward the doors. "After you."

Judi took a deep breath and inhaled the familiar tarlike scent that multiplied tenfold on sunny, sizzling days. The church had recently oiled the stony parking lot to keep the constantly resurfacing dirt from dusting everything in its path during the windy summer months. The odor reminded her of the private swimming pool parking lot she used to cross as a shortcut to the public recreation center as a child. Other children, clad in brightly colored swimsuits, happily disappeared into the pool area through the tall multifingered, moving turnstile. Her father never had the money to afford a pool membership. Occasionally, she was lucky enough to pass through the metal gate herself if she had a dollar and could find a member-friend to vouch for her. The pool was bigger than anything she'd ever seen, its depths clear and blue. Memories now swirled around her; smelling the mixture of chlorine, coconut suntan lotion, and tar; how the bottoms of her blue flip-flops would be black from the oiled parking lot. Several years later the pool closed and a paving company purchased the land, filled in the cavernous indigo pool with dirt, and blacktopped over the entire area. The transition only marked another sad step in the changes she would experience between her youth and adulthood.

"Are you ready?" Nathan was asking, nodding toward the church entrance.

From the look on his face, Judi suspected it wasn't the first time he'd asked her this very same question. The brilliant sun now felt blistering and the breeze nonexistent.

She nodded and without a word they walked to the set of double doors. Cool air shot past her as she opened the door and followed Nathan to just inside the foyer. Judi stopped to push tangled hair, now damp with perspiration, from her face.

"The door to your right," she directed, still pondering what she should do next in a short, quick prayer.

When no answer popped from heaven, she once again opened the door for Nathan. As he moved through the opening, he shot her a palpable glance of caution. She knew what rattled through his brain. He was warning her to be careful with her words, knowing that within the next few moments, the future course of her life could suddenly and irrevocably be changed. She held the next playing card, but he owned the trump. Then why did her focus now haphazardly go to his chin and its vulnerable-looking cleft?

When she finally tore her gaze from Nathan, three pairs of curious eyes greeted the two. Larry Newkirk abruptly stopped rolling up the building plans, and even the robust Tilly Storm silenced herself midsentence from an obviously intense discussion. Only seventy-something Lottie BonDurant seemed unmoved by the interruption, fidgeting about and clearing her throat unnecessarily loudly. Becky was nowhere in sight.

"There she is," Lottie announced, her rail-thin frame suddenly straightening. She moved to tidy the frilly red box hat on her head. "We thought you'd gotten lost on the way to the bakery." Her attention rapidly swiveled to Nathan and she smiled sweetly. "Now we understand why."

Judi felt herself color, a tiny pulse starting in her neck. Perplexed, she looked up at Nathan, who was giving one of his most charming smiles back at the woman.

"Yes, I'm the cause of the delay," Nathan readily admitted to the awaiting group. "I apologize for keeping Judi from her chores." His smile widened as he looked down on Judi and she felt herself grow weak. He turned back to Lottie and held out the bags of muffins. "Hope we're not too late."

"Not at all," Lottie babbled, accepting a bag with one weathered hand and waving him off with the other. Clearly she liked what she saw.

Tilly stepped forward to take the other two bags. "Didn't catch the name," she said, her strong voice taking command. Her graying hair, pulled into a bun as usual, was topped with a ridiculously ornate crimson bonnet. The flowered dress she wore hung loosely over her ample hips and amazingly matched the hat.

Nathan stepped forward and offered his hand. "The name is Nathan and I'm glad to meet you." Judi watched as Tilly let him envelop her beefy hand. "Judi and I are close family, and I'm sure you have it in your heart to forgive us for visiting awhile."

Family! Judi rubbed her bare fingers as her eyes flew to his in amazement. How could he make such a flippant statement without flinching when her heart plummeted at the thought?

Nathan answered her look with mocking amusement. "Aren't you going to introduce me to the rest of your friends?"

Overcoming her momentary speechlessness, Judi began the proper introductions. "You've just met Tilly Storm," she began with a slight smile, giving an inward groan when she saw the spark of suspicion in Tilly's eyes. *Ignore it!* Sometimes Tilly was much too perceptive for her own good. The lovable woman had the ability to save the world one individual at a time, but she could also dig her teeth in like a bulldog when needed. The heart attack she suffered the previous fall did little to slow her down.

"And you've met Lottie BonDurant," Judi continued. "She heads up the Red Hat Club." Lottie also helped in the church library and was the self-appointed muffin-supply coordinator for the Red Hatters. She was sweet and harmless unless a church business meeting ran overtime with the frivolous rantings of one elder. Then she could be quite vocal.

Judi turned to Larry and swallowed back the lump in her throat. "Nathan, this is Larry Newkirk, our very own camp builder, handyman, and local police officer."

Larry Newkirk eyed Nathan with interest as they shook hands. Judi hoped Nathan understood her cue. It wouldn't do for Larry to begin probing.

"How long are you stayin' on the island?" This question was from Tilly.

"I'm not sure." Nathan swung his attention Tilly's way. "A couple of days at least."

Tilly continued. "You're part of Judi's family? Cousins?"

"Actually," Nathan quickly responded, not missing one beat, "we're related by marriage." Judi nearly choked, but he ignored her. Tilly opened her mouth slightly as if to ask another question but clamped her lips closed when he held up a hand. "Trust me; it's too complicated to explain."

"Oh, come on, Tilly," Lottie admonished. "Don't give the poor man the third degree. You don't have time for it." She turned to Judi and Nathan. "If you'll excuse us, we're going to be late for our meeting." Lottie blew a fluttering kiss and ambled out with her bag of muffins. "Come on, Tilly," she called.

"Nice to meet you," Tilly finally said with a look of hesitancy crossing her face. "I'm sure we'll be talkin' again."

The two women exited the room with Tilly looking over her shoulder.

If Tilly said they would be talking again, they *would* be talking again. She never spouted idle words. Judi knew that couldn't be good! Tilly wouldn't rest until she knew exactly what was going on. It wasn't merely a busybody type of wondering, but an uncanny discernment when she knew something wasn't quite right.

Larry Newkirk didn't seem quite satisfied, either. "You must be the visitor who came in on the charter plane last evening. Did you have to travel far?"

"Pennsylvania," Nathan answered honestly. "Have you ever been to the Lancaster area? It's beautiful Amish country."

Larry nodded. "Spent a couple of days there before going on to Hershey. You're right—it's beautiful sightseeing and full of good Amish cooking. I hope you enjoy Bay Island as much." His glance landed on Nathan's tie. "And if you're here on business, make sure you take some leisure time to see what the island has to offer."

"I plan to do just that." Nathan gave an easy smile and looked over at Judi. "Are you ready to get started?"

Suddenly conscious that her hands were gripping the folds of her skirt, she loosened her hold. "I suppose." She turned to Larry. "I'm going to take lunch now, but I should be back in the office sometime this afternoon. Do you need anything before I leave?"

Larry seemed to mull over her words. “Everything seems to be in order for now.” He looked at his watch. “I need to be on my way to meet the lumber truck at the dock. Becky’s already at the camp waiting for us.” Unsnapping his cell phone from the clip at his waist, he opened it and appeared satisfied it was operating. His gaze settled on Judi. “You have my cell phone number if you should need me, right?”

This drew an odd look from Nathan, but he said nothing and Judi tried to ignore the rising panic within. She endeavored to give Larry a natural smile. “If I need you, I’ll call.”

Larry clipped the phone back onto his belt. “Good! I’ll be back this afternoon to finish up some camp work before evening duty. Later you can help me with a few tasks. If I don’t see you, I’ll make sure to catch up with you on my rounds.”

Judi knew Larry was uneasy. This was his way of reassuring her he would be available to check on her. God bless his kind soul! Becky Newkirk was a lucky lady to have him. He cared about everyone. The thought warmed her, and yet Larry’s concern might draw unwanted attention to her predicament. How long she could keep this problem silent was anyone’s guess. Nevertheless, she had to try.

“Thanks, Larry,” she finally responded.

Then Nathan looked over at Larry. “I’ll try not to keep her too long.” A warning glance came Judi’s way. “Depending on how the afternoon goes, we might be seeing you sooner than later.”

# Chapter 3

Nathan couldn't wait for the set of double doors to close behind him. He stood for a few moments on the hot concrete entranceway. What an inquisition! The one called Tilly would bear watching. Even with that silly hat balanced unevenly on her head, determination and authority were clearly etched on her wide, muscular face. Here was a woman who knew what she wanted and evidently was used to getting her way. She'd require special handling, the same type of management he frequently used with those on the senate floor—all with a good dose of strength of mind and willpower. He'd dealt with worse.

The other old woman, the muffin lady, was more interested in blowing kisses to strange men than looking at his dossier. Total pussycat.

The police officer was another matter altogether. He seemed more than a little cautious and a bit too interested in Judi. An unwelcome thought had been niggling at his mind ever since the guy protectively made it clear he would be calling to check on Judi. Was it jealousy?

Nathan shot a glance at Judi. Of all the colliding thoughts assailing him the past twenty-four hours, not once had he considered the possibility Judi might be seeing other men. The thought set his teeth on edge. Presumed dead or not, she was still legally married. He felt blindsided by the torrent of hurt and anger the vision caused. Could she be cruel enough to add unfaithfulness to the growing list of illegal and dishonest acts she'd committed against him?

Judi looked up at him. "Did I perform to your satisfaction?" An unmistakable cynical sharpness laced her voice.

"Brilliantly!" He meant to sound equally sarcastic, but his words came out more poignant than harsh, and her emerald green eyes narrowed in what he guessed to be mistrust. What? Did she believe he was immune to the hurt she'd caused? Recovering quickly, he forged ahead. "Seems like you've made quite a few devoted church friends on the island—especially the police fellow." He drew out his last words, slowly and deliberately.

He knew they'd hit the intended target as he gauged her quick and indignant reaction.

"That *police fellow* happens to be a married man!"

Nathan leveled her with a no-nonsense look. "May I remind you the same can be said about you?"

"Just what are you insinuating?" Two angry red splotches immediately crossed her high cheekbones. "Larry's an honorable man."

"He's not the one I'm worried about."

Her mouth dropped open in protest, but she quickly snapped it shut and began walking across the gravel. Using two fingers to loosen his restricting tie, he followed her to the golf cart. His power shirt and tie had done the trick, but they were nearly suffocating him now. The noon heat cloaked him like a heavy blanket.

When they reached the cart, Judi turned to him. "You do realize," she began, her voice tight and brittle, "that I'm not the only one with something to lose?"

"Really?" What else could he lose? He'd already lost what he had thought was the love of his life and experienced the grim realities of a supposed widower. Did she really think anything else mattered as much?

"Exposing my true identity will cause a widespread scandal in the world of politics," Judi continued with a nod of her head. "It may cost you that precious high-powered career you've worked so hard to build."

Nathan returned her angry stare without wavering. "So what!"

"So what?" she repeated with skepticism before flinging herself into the passenger seat. As soon as Nathan climbed into the driver's side, she continued. "This statement from the man who spent two years living and breathing nothing more than government policy and exit polls? I don't believe your nonchalance for one minute. You're too driven to give up that easily."

"Maybe," he answered evasively. Before starting the engine he rolled his shoulders to relax the muscles that were at that very moment knotting into a solid mass across his neck. He turned to look at her. "Your place or mine?"

"You've turned into a real man of ice, haven't you?" came her bravado response, but he could tell she was shaken.

Man of ice? Hardly! But let her suppose what she wanted, to deem him a man of iron, if it gave him the tactical advantage. Judi was a bright woman and had nearly pulled off the greatest scheme of deception he'd ever encountered, if not for two tiny mistakes he'd been fortunate enough to uncover. Or would that be unfortunate? One thing he knew: She couldn't be trusted.

"Since you can't seem to decide," he went on, "we'll visit your place. I'd like to see how my other half's been living for the past few years."

She paled slightly but made no protest. When he released the brake, her hands quickly grasped the chair bars until they formed into white-knuckled fists.

The electric cart pushed forward with ease when he pressed the accelerator. In silence they sailed past the shoreline again, and he stole a glance at her stoic face. No doubt she was planning and plotting her escape. It would do her no good. No excuse or fancy explanation would make him understand how a woman could discard her husband and family to live an anonymous life.

Did she not realize the cost? Didn't she care about the devastation happening to those left behind? There had been the horrible waiting and the equally horrific conclusion that her bloated and decaying body would never be found in the river muck. Visions of her desperate fight against the currents and the inevitable moment when she would no longer be able to hold back the cold and deadly waters from entering her lungs invaded his nightmarish dreams in the late hours of darkness. Night after night, he'd desperately tried to pluck her from the swirling murky waters, only to be pulled back by an unseen force greater than his own. Her horrible screams gurgled into a deadly silence as the swirling water filled her mouth, her eyes bulging wildly in terror. Down, down, she went, until the fiendish river closed over her.

Even now, knowing she was safe and sound, the terrifying image caused his throat to tighten. He loosened the tie another inch.

Judi must have sensed his discomfort for she looked at him questioningly. Looking at her now, he wondered how it was possible to love and yet feel something akin to disgust and hate at the same time. Exactly what emotion did he feel? Was it the same emotion his mother felt when Nathan nearly died trying to hop a passing train car with his teen friends? The foolish stunt cost him a night in the hospital. When his mother arrived at the emergency room, she cried with relief and smothered him with a mammoth bear hug. Then her love turned into wrath and he endured a tongue-lashing far worse than the accident. His mother wanted to throttle him right then and there—in simultaneous fury and love.

Was that what he felt—the relief of knowing the person he loved was alive and well, yet an all-encompassing anger at the audacity that this same loved one managed to be so? Could he really believe that the woman seated beside him, his wife, was indeed a living, breathing soul? There she was in the flesh, looking quite alive, and still. . .the world believed her to be dead.

She would have liked her memorial service. Family and friends gave her a eulogy send-off unmatched by anything he'd seen. The pastor delivered a moving message; Nathan's sister, Laurie, sang a beautiful, soul-searching song; and Nathan spoke brokenheartedly of their short time together. There was the church-prepared, post-funeral luncheon where friends fondly recalled special moments and laughed at such memories. But even their laughter was shrouded in a weighty sadness that made the mind-numbing day drag on and on.

Returning home was worse. His sister stayed for a couple of days, but emptiness echoed in the halls, as well as his heart. Even though Judi had seemed preoccupied and somewhat distant several months before her *death*, she had still managed to fill the house with her presence. At the time he had been glad when Judi finally found something to occupy her time besides obsessing about his political career. She'd almost become needy. Then she was gone. *Poof!*

The North Shore Condominiums sign came into view and Nathan slowed the cart.

"To the left," Judi directed unnecessarily. Nathan knew exactly which condo she rented. She pointed to the numbered parking spaces. "Pull into forty."

Nathan did as directed.

Taking a deep breath, he clicked off the ignition and turned to her. "Shall we?"

Her expression looked anything but ready, and if he knew her as well as he thought he did, the mix of petulance and dismay meant the woman hadn't come up with a workable escape plan.

Nathan slid out of the seat and joined her on the other side of the cart. Together they walked wordlessly toward the Cape Cod–style two-story building. He trailed slightly behind as they ascended the open but roof-covered steps. Judi stopped at the top to search inside her purse, finally producing a set of keys. She gave him a brief look of ill-concealed dread when he reached the landing, a sort of last-chance-no-clemency-firing-squad resignation. She was right where he wanted her. This should have pleased him.

It didn't!

He just hoped she couldn't read his own apprehension at what lay ahead, his own insides quaking at the results—maybe even more than hers. *Always stay on top of the opponent—or be crushed*, his father had always said. The advice seemed ripe for the picking right now. And at present, he'd need all the help he could find.

Judi tried to still her trembling fingers as they clumsily fumbled with the door key. What was she going to do? She could feel Nathan's bigger-than-life presence right behind her—smell the all-too-familiar hint of his aftershave. How well she remembered the expensive Blue Blood scent he always wore with his power suit. Blue Blood was as much a part of the uniform as the shirt and tie. The rich sapphire, genie-in-a-bottle form sat just to the right of Nathan's solid silver catchall tray on his very masculine, solid oak dresser. Why should she remember the scene so vividly?

She tried to beat down the memories and eruption of nerves assailing her.

The dead bolt lock finally gave way and slid back. With a brief moment of hesitation, she turned the knob and let the sizable white door swing open.

Swiftly she walked through the entry, eager to move away from his nearness and into the safety of her home. The contemporary bright array of two cozy matching chairs, a sectional couch, and mission-style end tables filled the room with comfort. The wild grape scent from a previously burned candle still lingered in the air. This was her sanctuary. Bay Island had certainly profited from the bustling tourist trade, but its popularity resulted in skyrocketing property values. If not for the generosity of a church member, she couldn't have afforded the rent, let alone the furniture, on a secretary's salary.

The front door clicked closed and Judi instantly swung back around.

Nathan was slowly advancing into the room. She couldn't help noticing how tall he was or how his expensive leather shoes sank into the plush carpet. What a silly thing to note when her life was on the line. But it was hard not to be aware of Nathan—it had always been that way. He wasn't handsome in the drop-everything-and-look fashion where one might pick him out of a crowd, but it only took a brief introduction to suddenly transform him into a rugged conqueror of the world and female hearts. Yes, he did have power in that way—and he didn't even know it.

Nathan seemed to take in the surroundings before finally turning his attention to her. He remained silent, his gray eyes holding hers.

Judi frowned, a suffocating trepidation taking over. She quelled the feeling and walked to the sliding glass door leading to the balcony overlooking Lake Erie. Quickly she slid it open and turned back to him. He hadn't moved.

"Let's talk out here," she suggested, stepping out onto the deck. Already the open air made her feel less confined. She waited patiently as he walked slowly to the opening and glanced out.

He took in the sights before coming out onto the deck. With a measure of unnerving determination he slid the door closed behind him. "Whatever you want."

Judi tugged firmly on one of the padded, heavy wrought iron chairs and moved it out from the table. The uneven scraping of the chair's hefty feet across the wood deck cut through the air. She motioned for Nathan to sit. "May I get you a soda or ice water?"

He shook his head and sauntered toward the edge of the deck. She could almost understand his fascination. The condo was a great find with a beautiful view. The deck was rather large and octagon shaped—big enough for patio furniture, a gas grill, and a large stack of wood.

She watched as Nathan rested one hand on the decorative braided rope draped between each deck post, giving it a nautical look. He seemed deep in thought, and she took his distracted moments to calm herself. He might be deliberately stalling to build tension for some dramatic moment he'd planned. For the umpteenth time she wondered why he'd tracked her down and followed her to the island after more than two years.

She could only imagine what was going through his mind as he looked so intently at the rhythmic waves washing partway up the dark, sandy beach. With the glorious summer sun reflecting and sparkling off the lake, it seemed almost criminal to mar the day with such foolishness. Even the weather appeared to be asking for tranquility. As if on cue, a cool breeze wafted across the deck, making the temperature much more comfortable.

Judi brushed back a strand of hair with a shaky hand. And she waited. Finally he turned and his gaze flickered back over to her.

"You've done quite well for yourself," he said with a quick look at the water again. Then as quickly, he turned, walked back to the table, and swept his hand gallantly toward the chair she'd indicated for him earlier. "Why don't you sit here?" He then nodded in the direction of the chair on the opposite side of the table facing the water. "I'll sit over there."

"All right," she agreed, sitting down slowly. Although she knew of no advantage the seating arrangement gained him, there had to be a tactical angle other than a view of the lake. There was always a purpose to everything he did, some strategic gain. It made him a good lawyer and, no doubt, a good politician. Regrettably for her, it also made him a formidable adversary.

The other heavy chair made no sound as Nathan pulled it back—yet another reminder of how much stronger he was than she. He sat down and watched her for several seconds before speaking. Then he leaned forward. "I thought you loved me, Judi."

Judi let go of the breath she'd held in waiting and let herself slowly drop farther back in the chair in wary skepticism. She had readied herself for a diversity of angles Nathan might approach in the forthcoming inquisition, but not this opening statement. Actually, it was somewhat comical under the circumstances, and she almost laughed. "I could say the same thing to you."

His eyes narrowed in obvious thought. "You're saying I didn't love you?" He sat up straighter. "Are you asking me to believe this entire escapade and new life is my fault?"

This time Judi couldn't help letting a bitter laugh escape. "From those little notes you left for me, it seems all but obvious that this escapade, as you call it, *is* totally your fault," she accused, shaking her head at the irony of his words. *Love! What does Nathan know about love?* "What I don't understand is why you've come looking for me now. I did what you asked." She spread her hands out in exasperation. "How did you put it? Oh, yes, the exact term was for me to 'move on.'"

He stared at her in amazement. "Notes?" The look on his face left no doubt he'd thought she had popped a brain cork somewhere along the way. "What are you talking about? What notes?"

Judi wasn't about to be taken in by his astonished look of puzzlement, no matter how innocent. She lifted her chin. "Don't play games with me. I know you were the one who wrote those eloquent but threatening notes. It might have taken me some time to decipher your scheme, but I'm not stupid. And I did as you asked; I moved on. What more did you want from me?"

Nathan lightly rapped the knuckles of his loosely fisted hand on the opaque glass-topped table. Finally he leaned forward. "Let me get this straight." Two perplexed lines appeared between his straight brows. "You're saying that I wrote you some kind of threatening notes and told you to disappear. Is that right?"

Judi stood to her feet. "Don't make it sound so harmless, Nathan. You almost killed my father with your power-hungry greed." She pointed a condemning finger at him to quiet his immediate rebuttal. "And don't give me that what-a-pity-she's-gone-mad look, either. I'm not the same naive, trusting woman you married."

Nathan frowned deeply and folded his arms patiently in front of him. "I will agree with you on your last statement, but as for these wild accusations that I'm some sort of wild-eyed villain trying to kill you and your father. . .well, you'll have to produce a plot more believable than that to explain your desertion." She watched his gray eyes narrow at her. "Nice try!" He flung his hand out lazily. "And if you're the least bit interested in your father's welfare, may I suggest that your *death* almost produced what you've so ridiculously accused me of doing?"

"How dare you!" she said in a voice she hardly recognized as her own. For several palpable moments they exchanged measured glances. Judi moved behind her chair, clutching the cushioned back for strength. "I did what was needed to protect my father from you. Don't come waltzing back into my life as if I'm the bad guy. If you've come to make trouble, I'll go to the police."

"The police?" He moved a hand over his clean-shaven chin. "That might not be such a bad option. What do you think?" He cocked his head questioningly toward her.

"I think you're playing with me." Judi stared down at him. "This is all a game to you, isn't it? You've spent two years living the life you've always wanted and now you've come searching for what you've thrown away. What are you, Nathan, two men?"

"At the moment I seem to be only one—a conniving husband who threatens innocent women and their families."

Judi stared at the man she had loved so long ago and willed her heart to harden. "A statement to which I cannot disagree."

"Then we have a problem."

Something in his tone almost touched her, but she fought any sympathetic tendencies she might develop.

"Then what do you suggest?" she asked flatly.

"Just give me a moment," he replied, leaning back thoughtfully in the chair. "When in a pinch, I always think of something."

# *Chapter 4*

Nathan slapped both hands against his thighs, pushed himself to his feet, and strolled over to the wood railing. This was one fine predicament. Call him a lousy husband. . . . Maybe a negligent spouse. . . But a note-toting madman who schemed to *do in* his wife and aging father-in-law?

What he really wanted to know was how a respectable attorney and successful state representative could suddenly plunge into a made-for-television soap opera—without even trying. Taking a deep breath, he let his gaze wander. No more than three hundred feet away were a cabana house, swimming pool, and a sand-filled volleyball court with all the picturesque quality of a vacation getaway brochure. Hardly a true portrait, though, of the current situation.

Slowly he turned and leaned one hip against the post. Pursing his lips in deliberation, he aimed a probing look at Judi. His eyes rested on her light honey tan, the clearness of her bright emerald eyes, and then on the red highlights of her soft hair. The creamy strawberry coloring would take some getting used to. The pictures his assistant took didn't do justice to the luscious coloring. The high cheekbones and full lips were the same, and if her dress weren't so long, he would probably see that her knobby knees were no different, either. She'd always tried to conceal her knees even though he'd repeatedly told her how cute the bony protrusions were.

Women! What did he know? It was as if a woman never believed a man when he said their so-called imperfections didn't bother him. Could it be they didn't want to be convinced and liked to pick over their flaws?

Take Judi's height. Even though she was beautifully tall for a woman, she was also very flatfooted—another thorn in her side, she'd always said. He wouldn't have even noticed the lack of a proper foot arch if Judi hadn't gone to so much trouble to show him her wet footprints on the front walk of their home one summer day while she watered the flowers. Actually, she thought it important enough to prove it again a few months later at the swimming pool just in case he missed the significance of the first exhibition.

As far as he knew, most men didn't fuss much over their own physical flaws and didn't have the time or the energy to fuss over their wife's flat feet or knobby knees. Whether men were just wired differently to look past such things or if love blinded a poor fellow's senses, Nathan could truthfully say there were more important things in life to focus on.

There was one difference in Judi's appearance, however, he did notice. Gone were those oversized prescription eyeglasses. Most likely the thirty-four-year-old had finally taken the leap to wearing contacts, something he could never convince her to try before—not because of her looks, but for practicality. Contacts were much more sensible and convenient.

All in all, Judi did look so very different and yet the same. But for all his scrutiny, he still had a bitter problem to solve that had nothing to do with Judi's knobby knees or nearsightedness. Too bad her intentions and motives were not as visible and open for analysis.

Did she really believe the nonsense she'd told him, or was the entire tale a clever ploy to throw him off balance? If this was all a ruse, he'd have to give her points for ingenuity.

"I suppose you have proof of these allegations?" he finally asked, watching closely for her reaction. "You do have the notes?"

Indecision flitted across Judi's face. "Do you think I'd show you the evidence if I had it?"

Nathan shrugged. "You've asked me to believe that you faked your death to save yourself and your family from a person who wrote you menacing notes. Since I know that I'm not the one guilty of threatening you, then I have to determine whether to believe what you've said, misguided as it might be, or whether you're handing me a line to save your own skin." He looked at her for a long moment. "Now, will you please answer the question? Did you save any of these supposed threatening letters?"

"I have every one of those letters if you must know!" Then as if challenging him, she shook her head and loosened one hand from the back of the chair to point a finger at him. "And the letters are safely tucked away. So don't get any ideas."

Nathan blew out a frustrated breath between his lips. "Then how do you propose we resolve this problem?" When she remained still and silent, he went on. "You seem to be close buddies with that friendly island policeman. Maybe you would like to have him stand guard while we look at the letters? We could even show the letters to him if you'd like."

Something akin to panic sparked in Judi's eyes, and he could see the conflicting wheels of thought churning across her face. Just as he thought! Her reaction lent credence to his previous theory that his wife was lying. If the letters were true, why hadn't she just gone to the police in the first place? Why pull off such an elaborate charade? Wouldn't the most obvious course of action be to contact law enforcement or someone she trusted? That's what he would have done. And then there was this skittishness, which erupted every time he mentioned the police. There had to be something behind that, too. Maybe she didn't want the truth to come to light.

Or was it this particular police officer? What was his name? Larry something—Larry Newkirk. Yes, that was it. The one who was attentive—too attentive. *Don't go there again, pal,* he chided himself. That line of thought would only serve to agitate the already tumultuous waters and would be of little help with the problem at hand.

It wasn't as if he really wanted the police involved, either. The implications of Judi faking her death would be enough to rock the Pennsylvania Statehouse right off its cornerstone and down Commonwealth Avenue. If Judi publicly accused him of threatening her, there was no limit to the extent of explosion the scandal would cause. This kind of publicity he didn't need.

"Well?" He knew there was a trace of annoyance in his voice. "What do you want to do?"

An insolent light gleamed in her eyes, but he refused to back down and met her stare head-on. He could wait her out—all two minutes of it.

"I'll show you the letters," Judi announced at last, ending the standoff. Her inflection was filled with indignation, but also fear. "I don't suppose you'd be foolish enough to pull anything funny in a bank full of people." She looked at her watch. "Then we'll see what you have to say when the hard proof is right in front of you. With everything in the open, maybe we can have an honest discussion and you'll level with me as to why you're here."

"I'm all for honesty," he agreed, regarding her steadily. "And if these letters really *are* in a safety deposit box, I would like to go read them—right now. Let's put all the cards on the table."

"One condition!" Judi shifted her feet and gripped the chair again.

Nathan drew an impatient breath. The woman was deliberately hedging for time and trying to stretch his endurance. He kept his voice composed and deceptively calm. "And what would that be?"

"You may look at the letters, one at a time, but I won't allow you to take any with you, not even one." She stood poised for a second. "If you try to take anything, I'll bring the bank employees running and blow this whole thing sky high."

"Anything else?" This was turning into nothing less than a stage show.

She inclined her head in silence and did not answer. Not immediately. Instead she looked somewhat lost for a moment before responding. "If I think of another condition, you'll be the first to know."

"Glad to hear it," he returned dryly, walking past her to the sliding glass door. Deftly he slid it open. "Ladies first."

Judi turned a pensive glance to the lake waters before stepping around him and inside. Nathan wasn't quite sure, but he thought he heard a whisper of what could have been a prayer. *Good for her,* he thought; *she's going to need all the prayers she can get if this is all a lie.*

"Hello, Judi," greeted the smiling bank clerk when Judi stepped up to the teller window. "How's your day going?"

"Just fine," Judi answered with a fixed smile, curling her hair behind one ear. After exchanging what she felt to be necessary pleasantries, she cleared her throat. "I'd like to get into my safety deposit box."

"Certainly!" The young clerk first glanced at Nathan before nodding toward another counter to the left near the large gated door guarding the bank vault. "Meet me over by the sign-in sheet." The woman grabbed a large dangling set of mismatched keys that jingled noisily as she slid down from her chair.

Judi smoothed down her full skirt as she walked to the brown-paneled counter, well aware that Nathan was right beside her. He was being unusually quiet and that concerned her. The ride over did nothing to calm the nerves plaguing her since his arrival, and she wondered again if showing Nathan the letters was wise. If she was right, *and she was*, Nathan knew exactly what each note said. But she was safe in the bank. The safety deposit boxes were kept in a barred but partially open room. One shout was all it would take.

Still, she hoped she was doing the sensible thing. A tight little cord knotted in her throat as she reached inside her purse. The tiny manila envelope felt smooth between her fingers as she withdrew it from the inside pocket. Slowly, she tipped the envelope and let the key slide out into her other hand then laid it in front of the clerk.

"Number 243," she told the waiting teller in low tones, tilting the numbered key for her to verify.

Again, the smartly dressed young woman gave Nathan another perusal. "Let me find your card."

Judi scrutinized the clerk as she opened a large box and speculated that this woman was already falling under Nathan's spell—without him even saying a word. How could the man not know how much he affected women?

Several three-by-five cards were flipped forward until the clerk plucked one out and gave it a close look. "This is your first time accessing the box." There was a note of surprise in her statement, but she shrugged and placed the card in front of Judi. "Just sign your name and date it on the first line."

Judi did as instructed and slid the card back across the counter.

"Come on back," the clerk directed, swinging open the half door attached to the counter. "The gentleman will be accompanying you?" she asked politely.

Judi looked up at Nathan's solemn face and gave the clerk a reassuring smile she didn't feel. "Yes."

The clerk turned around, popped a large skeleton key into the lock, and the bolt slid back with a loud clang. The heavy barred door creaked open, and Judi followed the bank teller to the boxes. Finding the numbered box, the clerk stopped to inspect the ring of bank keys, trying three before finding the right match.

"Got it!" the clerk proclaimed in triumph. She took Judi's key and twisted both sets until the little metal door released. "These can be tricky at times." She paused. "Will there be anything else?"

Feeling slightly dazed, Judi just shook her head.

"That will be all for now," Nathan spoke for the first time, picking up the slack. His mouth suddenly softened. "Thank you for your help."

"You're welcome." The clerk flashed him a curious smile before turning back to Judi. "The door will automatically lock behind me. Buzz the doorbell when you're finished and one of us will come to let you out."

Judi watched as the heavy door banged shut behind the clerk and the security device clicked loudly.

Alone!

Judi blinked nervously, feeling the silence envelop her like a sealed tomb. The room suddenly felt chilly.

Nathan's voice cut through the quiet. "Do you want me to lift the box?"

"No." She threw him a swift glance and took a steadying breath. "I can reach it."

When Nathan stepped back to allow her room, she slid the box from the compartment and carried it to the waiting table, her instantly cold fingers resting on the lid. A frigid shiver of apprehension feathered across her skin. She hadn't seen or touched the letters since placing them in the box two years ago. The thought of resurrecting this appalling segment of her past weighed heavily on her mind.

She had hoped to never face the nasty accusations and threats again, but here she was, conscious of the growing and searing pain around her fearful heart. Even the deposit box repulsed and burned at her very being, and her fingers impulsively recoiled in agitation and disgust.

"Are you all right?" demanded Nathan, his hand tightly gripping her arm as he guided her less than a foot away to sit in the worn, straight-backed chair to which she sank like a lead-based bottle. Instantly, he was looking down at her with concern, his anger momentarily postponed. "You're beyond pale and completely white."

"Nathan—" Avoiding his narrow, probing glance, she turned her head and made an effort to move her arm out of reach. "I can't do this." When he slackened his hold, she slumped back in the chair. How she hated the contents of the box that sat before her like an uncommuted death sentence. How she hated her weakness showing in front of Nathan. But rattled or not, she would not be fooled by his contrived concern. She couldn't!

"Judi, what's going on here?" he asked, obviously altering his position to look at her more fully. Suddenly there was realization in his smoky gray eyes. "You really do have some kind of horrible letters in this box."

Judi stiffened. "You know it's true."

He didn't answer right away. He seemed to consider the matter. Without waiting, he lifted the flat lid, ignoring her halfhearted attempt to block his hands, and snatched the folded brown note on top. Quickly he spread out the wrinkled sheet between his fingers.

Judi watched as he paced the room, his eyes flitting across the page he held at arm's length, his brows creased deeply in concentration. He stopped and leaned his back against the flat wall of deposit boxes before looking back at her.

"I don't understand." Nathan was frowning heavily. "What does the note mean?" He began to read the note aloud. " 'I smell a rat. A dirty rat. Have you caught the smell of this rodent in the air? Remember the Olde Village Inn.' " He paused a moment to look at her questioningly before reading on. " 'Move on before this rat's demise is your own.' "

She felt numb, yet her throat ached fiercely and her eyes pricked with threatening tears. That menacing note had been particularly bad. It had come right before Christmas, expertly gift-wrapped with expensive decorative foil paper. Figuring Nathan had left her an early present, she'd eagerly torn off the paper and opened the equally decorative box.

What greeted her when she lifted the lid sent her reeling. A swollen, dead rat, crawling with maggots, lay exposed. The sender had carefully wrapped the rodent in a sealed bag meant to burst open with the box lid, immediately spewing all its filthy, revolting sights and smells.

"Judi?" Nathan's voice drew her back. "What's this letter about? What does the writer mean regarding the Olde Village Inn and a rat?"

Judi drew a ragged breath and closed her eyes as tiny tears squeezed through her already damp lashes. "A dead. . .rat accompanied the note."

When she looked up, he was leaning over her, both hands on the table, his face a mixture of shock and puzzlement. She knew he was waiting for further explanation. When she remained wordless, his mouth opened to speak, but he slowly retreated instead, tapping the letter against his hand. Finally he shook his head and exchanged the note for another in the box.

Once again he paced and studied the letter, thrusting one hand into his pocket. " 'Sugar and spice isn't always so nice—is it?' " he read aloud. " 'Especially when a good Amish girl, her head full of curls, has her hand caught in the till. What a beautiful mug shot!' " Again his brow lifted in bewilderment when he turned to her.

"That was the first letter to come," Judy struggled to explain, her lips trembling, "right after the person filled the gas tank of the Volkswagen with sugar."

"What!" Nathan's glance clung to her like hot oil. "You never said anything about this letter when that happened."

"I tried to tell you it was more than a prank," she reasoned, endeavoring to ignore the confusion and anger battling in his voice.

"Judi," he went on, "don't you think I would have taken it more seriously if you would have shown me the letter? Vandals out for kicks don't leave mysterious notes behind, especially ones sounding like personal vendettas." He quirked an eyebrow knowingly. "So that leaves me to assume that you wouldn't, or couldn't, show me these notes for two possible reasons. Either you suspected—why, I don't know—that I was threatening you, or the author knew something and was holding this information over you—a blackmail of sorts."

Judi couldn't avoid his direct gaze. His quick perception of the situation petrified her. He was right, of course—except in opposite order. She didn't suspect Nathan until later. She closed her eyes in a supreme effort to calm the wild fluttering of nerves racing through her.

"I can see that at least one, or possibly both, of my assumptions are on target," Nathan assessed with annoying self-confidence.

"I tried to make you see, Nathan. . . ." Her voice trailed off nervously. "Then I had proof that you were the one sending the letters."

He stared at her in amazement. "What could possibly make you think I'd sent you these types of threatening notes along with vandalizing your car and presenting you with a dead, vile rat?" He tossed an agitated hand into the air. "First off, the handwriting is nothing more than cursive scrawl. I have flawless print!" Then as if carefully weighing an opening statement in front of a jury, he cocked his head thoughtfully in her direction. "I may not be a poet, but the grammar and hacked prose could be improved upon by a five-year-old. At least give me more credit than that."

Judi struggled to keep a flush from creeping up into her cheeks as he threw a frustrated glance to the ceiling.

"Another thing," he went on, landing his gaze back on her, "if I'm as compulsive about every detail as you've always claimed, I can assure you that I wouldn't be able to create such a cheap product."

A hot protest rose in her throat. "You would if you were trying to disguise your handwriting. So not everything you've said is quite true. You don't *always* print, Nathan."

"What do you mean?"

"There are times when you write in cursive," Judi continued, "and no matter what you claim, your script writing is worse than scrawl. That's why you prefer to print." She lifted her chin. "And the cursive writing matches closely enough to raise a valid question."

"The *only* time I write in cursive is to sign my name," he argued. "How could you match the writing with only a signature?"

Squaring her shoulders, she shifted uneasily under his scrutiny. "Not true! When you paid bills, you wrote the entire check in cursive. Remember? You always said the checks should look uniform and that meant they couldn't be done in print *and* cursive."

Nathan's lips twitched in contemplation, and he leaned back to sit on the edge of the table. He gave a low grunt at the idea. "I suppose you're right! I'd forgotten. I used to write the checks that way." The tightness of his mouth twisted into a firm line. "With the age of electronic transactions, it's no longer necessary to write checks, and it seems like ages ago. Guess I just didn't remember."

"So we're right back to the beginning," Judi pointed out. "The handwriting in those notes does look like yours."

"Now wait a minute," Nathan quickly protested, lifting himself from the edge of the table. He scooped up another letter from the box and scanned it intently. "It's really been a long time since I've written in longhand, but I still don't see the similarity. I mean, this writing is absolutely terrible."

Judi couldn't prevent the wry smile from forming at the corners of her mouth. "So is yours."

"This bad?" His question seemed genuine.

Her mouth pulled knowingly to the side and she nodded. "Yes."

Nathan made a face and she could tell he was fighting the idea. His fingers fidgeted with the paper in his hand and he glanced at it again. Something in the boyish confusion marking his features moved her. A dangerous spark of feeling she thought was well hidden in the depths of her contempt for the man who was her husband was beginning to surface.

Was she crazy?

Nathan gave a sigh. "I still don't see it."

"Look at each *R* and *S*. Look at the swoops on the *L*s and slant of each sentence." She watched him closely examine the style. "Trust me, Nathan. I compared the actual letters and it's close enough to be scary."

*"I didn't write these notes."*

She drew a deep breath, unable to take her eyes off his lean, attractive face. The cleft in his chin seemed to deepen. He looked truly perplexed.

Slowly, Nathan leaned over, imprisoning her hand under his. His face drew close and she had the instinctive feeling he was fighting between anger and some other deep emotion. "You never had anything to fear from me, Judi." There was a pause. "I loved you!"

Judi didn't miss the past tense condition of his words. He *had* loved her. "I don't know what to say," she finally replied, trying desperately to keep her voice level. It was the truth. There were no words to describe the barrenness of her heart and feelings she had at that moment.

I say we should get to the bottom of these letters," Nathan demanded, his voice becoming steely hard. "To do that, you'll have to tell me everything—and I mean everything—you know about these letters and what this person is holding over you."

# Chapter 5

Nathan studied the uneven edges of the creased paper in front on him. This was the last of the threatening letters to be copied. Not a single note made sense—at least not to him. Only Judi knew the implications of the innuendos and the power these words held over her. He rested his gold-plated pen a moment.

For some unexplained reason he believed Judi was telling the truth—as she understood it. Maybe it was the fear in her eyes or the poorly hidden grip of panic lashing out against the contents of the cold metal box. Whatever it was, the woman feared for her life. Now what? He was having a difficult time defusing the fury and resentment he'd spent the last few days building.

If only she had come to him.

Yes, he had been enormously busy with the campaign, almost numb from the frenzied pace of speeches, debates, interviews, and television commercials. But he would have dropped everything if he'd known the gravity of Judi's dilemma. She should have known that! She should have trusted him.

It would be hard to calculate the emotional, legal, and even criminal consequences of Judi faking her own death. His own inattentiveness was partially to blame. Even now, he knew the enormity of the situation was beyond his own comprehension.

"We'd better hurry, Nathan," Judi whispered across the table. "That bank teller keeps looking in. I think someone else is waiting to get to their box."

With an effort, Nathan dragged his mind back to the present. "I'm almost done." Pushing down his previously troublesome thoughts, he briefly glanced at the doorway before giving her a reassuring look. "There's no one waiting on us. Your teller buddy is just keeping an eye on you. Bay Island must be like any other small town where everyone knows everyone—and their business." It pleased him when Judi managed a tiny smile of agreement, lightening the tension. "So, what's a bank teller inclined to do if a regular customer comes into the bank with a perfect stranger and this customer wants to get into her safety deposit box for the first time in two years? The teller is suspicious—as well she should be."

Judi seemed to think this over. "You're probably right."

"Actually," Nathan said with a small smile of his own, "I think the entire employee pool has waltzed by that door in the past half hour to make sure I haven't absconded with all your jewels and worldly possessions."

"If only they knew," came her reply with a quiet but impish laugh. Her coloring was beginning to improve dramatically.

"But all the same," Nathan continued, smoothing down his tie, "I'll finish copying this last letter so we can get out of here."

Diligently he printed the last few lines and sat back in the uncomfortable chair to appraise his work. The words needed to be exact if he was to make any sense of these letters and the possible motive behind them. Carefully, he twisted the tip of the pen until the point retreated inside and then leisurely secured it into the pocket of his shirt.

He glanced at Judi, who sat solemnly across from him, and wondered if he dared risk the fragile truce they'd developed. "Judi, I know you said that you wanted all of these letters to remain in the safety deposit box, but I'd like to keep one of them."

"But why?" Alarm spread across her face.

Nathan hesitated, rubbing his thumb across the sharp edge of his jaw. "I came here believing you had deserted me for one selfish reason or another—all of which I couldn't understand." He rested a hand on the metal box. "You believed me to be the author of these notes." Leaning forward, he caught the gaze of her guarded look, her eyes unabashedly veiled in wariness. "Can I assume we've come to some point of agreement where you might consider another explanation as a plausible alternative? We need to take a closer look at this whole thing, including the wording and handwriting. To do that, an actual sample of the letter will be necessary."

Judi surveyed him with large emerald eyes, uncertainty still lingering in their depths. "I don't know."

"It's up to you," he assured her, spreading his hands nonchalantly before her. "I do think it will help us sort out the who, what, and why of this problem. You can choose which note comes and which ones stay."

There was a measured but deep intake of air as Judi mulled over his words. "All right. One note can't make that much difference—if it should disappear." She regarded him with a narrow gaze. "For the record, though, you need to know that I'm not convinced of your innocence."

"Fair enough!" He shrugged. "I have my own reservations when it comes to your part in this death-disappearance ploy. So we're even."

Judi's brows arched a fraction.

He launched his own quizzical look her way. "But I'm willing to concede other possibilities might exist. Are you?"

"I suppose."

"That's a starting point." Instinctively, he dropped his voice a tone or two and inclined his head toward the box. "Why don't you go ahead and choose a letter. We'll work from there."

"Fine!" Determination, sprinkled with a light dusting of edginess, crept into her voice; yet when she began to reach forward to select a note, Nathan saw her hastily pull back. Her eyes darkened in dismay as she looked up at him. "On second thought, why don't you choose one; maybe the note you were just working on."

"If you're sure?"

She nodded. "Yes, I'm sure—if you think it will help."

"I do!" Nathan cast her a troubled glance as he folded the letter and tucked it alongside the pen in his shirt pocket. Getting her to discuss the letters might be more of a challenge than he thought if she couldn't even touch them.

"Would you mind putting away the box?" she asked quietly.

Without delay, he closed the box lid, scooped it up, and slid it back into the dark, narrow cavity. The small metal door closed easily. "Are you ready?"

Judi nodded and gathered her purse while Nathan rang the bell. The ever-vigilant bank teller wasted no time in coming.

"Find everything all right?" the teller asked with a smile.

"Yes, thank you," Judi replied as the teller relocked the vault and returned Judi's key.

As they walked through the doorway and into the lobby, several heads turned their way.

Nathan leaned close. "I think we've stirred some interest," he whispered, his hand naturally resting at the small of her back to speed her along. He felt her back grow rigid and quickly let his hand drop.

Judi looked at her watch as soon as they stepped outside into the warm rush of island air. "It's almost two o'clock," she remarked with a groan. "I need to get back to the church. I'm already an hour late."

"But you haven't eaten," Nathan pointed out with logic as they walked to the golf cart. "We also have a lot of work to do. Why don't we grab a bite to eat and then discuss what we're going to do?"

"I don't think I could eat a single bite right now."

"But I could," he quickly protested.

"Well, I can't just not show up for work," she reasoned. "My job's flexible, but not *that* flexible."

"If it's bothering you, call the church and see about taking the afternoon off. They already know you have an out-of-town visitor. I'm sure they'll understand."

"I really shouldn't." There was a sigh. "It might generate gossip and I do have work to finish for the camp."

"Your policeman friend again?" Nathan moved to unsnap a small cell phone from the holder on his belt. "Then call your friend and explain that you're tied up this afternoon. See if the work can wait until tomorrow."

There was an awkward silence. "But I've never called off before."

"All the more reason why they shouldn't mind."

Judi hesitated.

"Call him and see." Nathan flipped open the phone and turned it on. A tart musical rumba danced across the silence as the network booted up. He handed her the open phone. "I'm sure the church and camp can spare you for a few hours."

Judi placed her purse on the driver's seat of the cart and grudgingly took the phone. "Let me see if Pastor Taylor's in first."

Nathan glanced down at her as she poised a slender finger to dial. Unbidden, his memory shot back to happier times when Judi would tenderly trace the outline of his lips with those soft, silky fingertips, nearly driving him out of his mind with longing. He closed his eyes over the burning recollection.

Suddenly, the phone came to life with a loud, annoying ring and he jerked his eyes open.

For a breathless moment, Judi stared at the offending noise before pushing it toward him. "I think it's for you."

Frowning, Nathan took the phone. When he saw the caller's name on the screen, he quickly snapped the cover down. Lindsey! That was another fine complication he would have to deal with.

"Aren't you going to answer?" Judi asked.

Nathan rested his gaze on her. "They can leave a message. I'm busy right now." There was curiosity in her eyes, but she seemed to accept his words and he went on. "So, where were we? Calling the church, I believe." He extended the phone to her again. "Let's try it once more."

Their fingers touched lightly as she reached for the phone, and he hesitated a moment before relinquishing his hold. She lifted her gaze questioningly. Again, an electronic noise interrupted, and she slowly pulled back, her hand dropping to her side.

"Sounds like the person left a message," Judi reasoned, nodding toward the phone. "Maybe you should listen to it before I call the church."

Shaking his head, he adamantly refused. "Go ahead and make your call—and do it fast before we're interrupted again."

But Judi was already looking beyond him. "Too late!"

Nathan turned to follow the direction of Judi's gaze. Instantly, he recognized the large-boned woman named Tilly he'd met that morning striding quickly across the parking lot toward them.

"Fancy meetin' the two of you here," Tilly greeted as she drew closer, her full-mouth smile embracing both of them.

"We're in trouble." He heard Judi breathe in a soft whisper.

Nathan remained silent.

"I'm glad to catch up with you, though," Tilly continued when she stopped in front of them, her purse handles swinging wildly from her arms. "The two of you are officially invited to my house tomorrow for a good old-fashioned pot roast meal." Nathan caught her piercing gaze, his own wavering slightly in surprise when she winked at him. "It would be a mighty shame for you to visit the island without me extendin' you one of my home-cooked dinners."

"That's kind of you," Nathan attempted to cut in. "But—"

"Won't take no for an answer," Tilly went on as pretty as she pleased, glancing between the two. "Just picked up the roast at the butcher shop a few minutes ago for this very occasion and it's a real beauty." She inclined her head toward Nathan with a twinkle of determination in her eyes. "I reckon you like banana cream pie?"

"Well—" Nathan must have hesitated one nanosecond too long, because Tilly instantly picked up talking where she had left off.

"I'll bet you've never had authentic stollen bread, either." Her mouth curved into a wide grin, and she turned her attention to Judi. "It's one of Judi's favorites. Tell him what a treat he's in for. Nothin' like a fresh, hot, steaming loaf of bread to tickle the palate."

"No one can beat your cooking or baking," agreed Judi. "But—"

"Does six o'clock sound about right for tomorrow?" Tilly asked with obviously no intention of waiting for an answer. "Judi knows the way well enough." Then a number of wide wrinkles creased her forehead as she smiled again. "Come a bit earlier and show Nathan the flower garden." Her sharp eyes swiveled back to Nathan. "It's the peak bloomin' season and somethin' not to be missed."

Judi gave Nathan a helpless look and opened her mouth to speak when Tilly interrupted for the third time.

"No need to thank me!" Tilly waved a casual hand at Judi. "Any family of yours is a friend of mine." Before anyone could protest further, she reached into her purse and brought out her checkbook. "I'd better stop jawin' and skedaddle to get my bankin' done." She turned to go and waved a happy finger. "Don't forget, now. Tomorrow at six. I'll be waitin'."

Tilly strode away with purpose and vanished into the bank, leaving the pair alone. Then silence fell.

"What just happened?" Nathan asked after a moment, shoving a hand into his pocket as he stared at the clear glass bank doors and then at Judi.

"We've just been shanghaied, counselor," Judi said, her lovely eyes widening in resignation. "That's what happened."

*Tilly must be slicker than oil to get through my fingers like that,* Nathan mused. That didn't happen too often. He didn't have time for a home-cooked meal with a woman who obviously knew how to navigate the waters to her advantage as well as, if not better than, he. This posed a new question.

He drew his hand out of his pocket and rested it firmly on his hip. "What's behind this invitation?"

"My guess is she knows something's up and believes she can help." She shrugged her delicate shoulders. "It will be useless to try to extricate ourselves from the invitation—she won't give you the chance, as you can see."

"I noticed," he muttered flatly. "She's something else. I could have used her on the House Floor last week. She would have made chopped liver out of every senator and representative there."

Judi nodded in agreement, looking up at Nathan.

"Better take advantage of the lull in the action," he advised, pushing the phone toward her. "Maybe you can make the call before any other interruptions and distractions come our way."

Again Judi nodded, and he wondered what was going through her mind as she dialed the numbers and what he was going to do with all of his pent-up frustration.

Judi held one hand over the wild strands of hair happily taking flight as the wind sliced through the golf cart, and she continued to tightly grip the seat back with the other. The wind died down as Nathan pulled into the Dairy Barn parking lot.

"I knew the church wouldn't mind your taking some time off," Nathan remarked as he parked the cart and climbed out.

"The pastor and the people at church are wonderful," she commented, sliding out of her seat. "I don't want to take advantage of their generosity."

He only nodded and she fell into step beside him as they went into the restaurant. When they had ordered and brought their food outside to the red painted picnic table, Nathan pulled out a crisp white handkerchief to dust off the seat. Judi laughed.

"What?" Nathan bluntly asked, giving her a quick flash of annoyance as he refolded the handkerchief. "This is one my finest pairs of slacks."

"Some things never change," she replied, finding it hard to keep the silly grin off her face. She pressed her skirt close to her legs and plunked herself down on the other side of the table. "The first thing you need to learn about island life is to lose the dapper duds. We're a laid-back lot and like to go casual."

"I feel more comfortable dressed up," he defended, slipping the paper wrapper off the straw and stabbing it into the perforated lid of his cup. "People respect the starched and pressed look."

"I didn't mean to offend you," she apologized, biting her lip to keep from grinning again. Somehow she felt considerably lighter and more relaxed. "Around here, folks respect you for who you are, not what you wear."

"You like it here, don't you?" he asked, as if the idea surprised him.

She sobered, knowing how she clung to Bay Island like a climbing tea rose to a trellis. It was her home. "I absolutely love this place."

Nathan peered into the food bag, pulled out a foil-wrapped hot dog, and handed it to her. "You seem to have made a lot of friends."

Judi pushed her own striped straw into her cup, pumping it wistfully up and down. "I know this may sound strange, but starting a new life on Bay Island gave me an opportunity to change who I was—and I like the new person I've become." She swallowed the sudden lump in her throat. "And yes, I've made quite a few new friends who I'll always cherish. It will never take the place of my own family, though." A sigh escaped. "I still miss them terribly."

Nathan seemed to regard her carefully. "Really?"

She nodded pensively. "Have you kept in contact with my father?"

"Some," he answered, lifting the bun of his hamburger to inspect the contents. He moved the pickles in a symmetrical pattern and replaced the top. His gray eyes regarded her closely. "Your father never cared much for me and in some small way has blamed me for your death, so our contact has been limited." He shrugged. "But as far as I know, he's still living in the same place and doing as well as expected." One eyebrow lifted. "He took your death rather hard."

Judi felt her previous lightness slip away and guilt move in. "And your family?"

"Mother and Father are still in good health and active as ever," he answered. "My sister, Laurie, has been promoted to senior editor and brother Jeff is seriously in love for the tenth time. Nothing new." He gave a wry smile and took a bite of hamburger.

"That's the part I hated the most, causing pain to the people I loved. It was a choice I didn't want to make." She cast a pleading look asking for understanding. "There was no other way."

"Did you think to ask God if your plan was the only way?" Nathan demanded to know, wiping his lips with the thin paper napkin.

"God?"

"You know," he went on, pointing to the sky, "the God of heaven and earth."

"I know *who* you mean," she assured him. "I just—"

"You're simply not used to me talking about Him," he finished for her. He gave her a searching look. "You'll appreciate the irony of this. After your so-called death, I turned my life over to Christ. . .mind, body, and soul. Your faith seemed so strong and just what I needed to grab on to during those agonizing days." His expression hardened. "But you probably never thought about how I might be affected by your death, did you? Not when you thought I was the devil incarnate."

"Nathan—"

"Did you ever stop to think that I might not have been the person threatening you and that I really had loved you?"

There was that past tense version of his love declaration again. Judi tensed. "I did what I had to do, Nathan."

"Without regard for what I might have to go through, the devastation of losing a wife?" he asked, taking a sip of his drink. He paused, studying her in a way she found disturbing. "I can't begin to describe to you what that felt like. Do you know what my nights have been—" He stopped midsentence, the last coming out rushed, as if he suddenly realized how transparent he was being. "Finding you alive brings more questions than answers, Judi. It also makes me wonder if my relationship with God isn't as much of a forgery as yours."

"Don't say that, Nathan," she pleaded, a fresh sense of urgency coming over her. This wasn't how it was supposed to be at all. "I've learned so much more about God since coming to the island. My faith looked strong before, but it wasn't. My view of God and my relationship with Him wasn't right. There was so much I didn't understand then." She laid an insistent hand on his arm. "It's different now! My relationship with Christ has grown to a much deeper level."

"But you're living a lie!" he pronounced, his mouth grimly tight. His scrutiny of her face was calculating, as if he were sizing her up. "You can't say you have God and blatantly ignore His laws."

She protested. "It's not that black and white."

"What's not so black or white about it? Either you obey His laws or you don't. How do you justify it?"

"I don't," she answered. "But what could I do? Once I finally understood what it meant to have a real live relationship with God, I was in too deep to back out." Her grip tightened on his arm. "Can you understand that? What would going back to Pennsylvania do, anyway? It would have put me right back into the hands of the person writing those letters, ruined your career, and crushed our families all over again. There was no turning back once my new life began—not without serious repercussions."

"You already have serious repercussions."

"I know!"

"No." His glance swept over her. "I don't think you do."

"What do you mean?"

Nathan leaned forward, thoughtfully propping his chin on the ball of his thumb. "I mean. . .I'm engaged to be married!"

# Chapter 6

"Engaged!"

Judi felt her heart stop as she waited for him to say something—anything. Since Nathan's arrival earlier in the day she had endured one shock after another, but his most recent bombshell moved her world like the shuddering shift of the San Andreas Fault.

"I guess this is another complication you didn't foresee," Nathan exclaimed, his words as sharp and clean as a two-edged sword.

Judi sat perfectly still, barely breathing. "Oh, Nathan."

She heard how thin her voice sounded, but how could she stand it? Engaged to another woman! Had the thought of him seeing other women ever occurred to her? Yes; once or twice, early on. Yet, when Mrs. Judi Whithorne died and Miss Judi Rydell's identity firmly took hold, the menacing Nathan faded off into non-existence. She had hardened her heart against the love she knew with her husband. Not once did she seek information on him or her family in fear that someone might take notice and blow her cover. There were no harsh realities to think about if her former life was erased from the books. Now, however, she was face-to-face with this previously hidden world and the lives of those affected by her *death*.

"Certainly you understand the difficult position I've been thrust into." His gaze was indecipherable; his face set as if in stone. "What would have happened if I had already married this woman? It's inconceivable enough to think that I, a married man, am engaged to another woman. Could this be in any way fair to her? Fair to me?" He rapped an unyielding finger on the table. "Although innocent in heart, I'd be a bigamist in God's eyes. Does any of this begin to cut at your heart as deeply as it does mine?"

"I'm not a horrible, unfeeling person, Nathan," she muttered, feeling wounded. "I'm hurting inside, too. Can't you see that?" To know he believed her capable of such self-seeking, deliberate treachery and deceit was too much to endure. Yet hadn't she thought as much of him? "I'll admit, when I formed this plan, your comfort and well-being were not highly considered. After all, you were the reason for the plan." Taking a steadying breath, she rose from her seat and faced him. "You claim to know nothing of the threats, but how do I know?" She felt a rush of heat come into her cheeks. "I'm not sure what scares me more—the possibility that you're innocent or the prospect of your guilt."

Nathan gave her a long, searching look. "Finding me guilty would make it so much easier for you, wouldn't it? Then you could write me off as getting what I deserved." Judi felt her pulse quicken as his eyes darkened. "But if I'm innocent—then what? Then I've become a victim, maybe even more so than you, and at the hand of my very own wife, the one who vowed to love and cherish me until death."

Judi sank back onto the hard, unforgiving bench seat, her stomach already sinking even lower. Like a lightning-fast whiplash to the back, his words stung appallingly close to home, leaving her flesh exposed. He was right! It would be much easier if he were guilty of the crimes she'd laid at his feet. If she was wrong... an unbearable weight of sin lay at her door. Which scenario was right? Her whole body moaned in fear of what the answer might be. Could she have mistaken the circumstantial evidence and foolishly blundered into a wrong conclusion? She was so sure at the time. Would she never get things right...not during adolescence... not now...not ever?

"And what about you?" Nathan continued with force. "Did you plan to stay alone and single for the rest of your life? Or have you already violated our marriage as part of your new life and identity?" She saw a muscle tighten in his cheek. "Maybe that's not black and white enough for you when you account to God."

Judi felt the heat and color drain from her face. "I've always honored our marriage and not once, not ever, have I broken my vows of faithfulness to you, not even after what you"—she broke off for a second—"or what I thought you had done."

His accusation burned like acid against her core. She was a woman running for her life and the lives of her family, not a promiscuous floozy on the make. What did he take her for? She knew going into this plan that she would never know another man's companionship. That was part of the sacrifice that had to be made.

They stared at one another, reluctantly squaring off into opposite corners of throbbing hurt. She knew this would be a match with no winners—only losers.

"Ah, Judi!" he suddenly exclaimed, breaking the silence in what she recognized as exasperation. He leaned forward to grasp both of her hands and held them tightly. By the intensity of his gaze, she knew he was fighting powerful emotions. "I'm trying to deal with this as best I can. I know I'm angry. I can't help feeling angry with you, with the person who wrote you those notes—even with God." His voice turned husky. "Somehow, I have to get past this anger if we're going to solve this problem." He gazed down at her hands, still tightly held by his. "We'll have to settle our trust issues to make this work."

Judi slanted a wary look at Nathan. "Exactly what did you have in mind?"

He looked up. "Prayer!"

"Prayer?"

"I don't know if my commitment to God is a counterfeit or not, but I have to give Him a try. I have to put Him to the test." His handsome face assumed a pained but determined expression. "So, from this point on, we're going to approach this problem God's way. No more deceptions, no more lies, and no more hate."

His last word sprang instantly to the forefront. Hate? Nathan hated her? If he was innocent of the accusations, she knew he had every right to detest her. Yet it didn't make it any easier to stomach. She blinked back the stinging pain at the thought.

"Agreed?" Nathan was still talking.

Judi wondered how she could stay so calm. Nathan hated her! It wasn't love motivating his concern for her. Then what—his Christian duty? Would his hate turn into revulsion once he discovered the secrets held by the letters? That she could sit across from him while he held her hands and not totally break down from the upheaval within was something she couldn't comprehend. Casually, she looked back at him. "Agreed!"

He seemed satisfied with her answer. "Then we start by asking God what we should do."

When Nathan closed his eyes and dropped his head to pray, Judi could only watch him, feeling the penetrating warmth of his hands. What she wouldn't have given for Nathan to have shared her faith during their first year of marriage. Now he was acting like the man of God she'd always wanted. Yet this man no longer loved her, and their bonds of devoted loyalty had been broken long ago.

"We need Your help," Nathan prayed as she observed with interest. "Judi didn't ask for advice before becoming this new person, and I didn't ask for Your guidance in coming to Bay Island. Then I came here in anger and for that I need to ask Your forgiveness." He paused, and she noticed his eyelids tightened, his thick, dark lashes compressed firmly. "We don't know who to trust other than You—we can't even trust each other. Give us wisdom about how to proceed, and show us whom we can consult with in confidence. This time we want to do things Your way and not ours. That might be a sticking point for both of us, but we'll do our best." Judi could hear him take a deep cleansing breath. "Help me to know if I'm doing this Christianity thing right. If I'm not, show me what I need to do. In Your Son's name, amen."

When he looked up, Judi didn't bother to hide the fact she'd been gawking at him. With a prayer like that, how could Nathan even question his commitment to God? His humble prayer was so much more than her stuffy prayer list of complaints and wants, and tenfold better than the most eloquent churchy prayers. For the first time, a seed of hope began to sprout. Although there seemed to be no good ending to their dilemma and ominous consequences would still have to be faced regardless, knowing that God was going to run the program gave her hope.

Nathan slowly released her hands and gave her a wry grin. "Better eat your food before it gets cold."

"Too late, I'm afraid," she returned with a small laugh. Surprisingly, she did feel a twinge of hunger where a cumbersome ball of worry had previously occupied. She carefully unwrapped the foil and sniffed at the cool but delicious aroma of the frankfurter buried within the butter-grilled bun.

"Here's some mustard." Nathan handed her a yellow packet. "You were never one to eat a naked hot dog."

"Thanks!" She tore off a corner and spread a strip of velvety mustard down the length of the hot dog.

Nathan was watching her over his hamburger as he prepared to take a bite. *"Bon appétit."*

She threw him a tiny smile and, swinging her hot dog up to him, touched his hamburger in a toast. "Bon appétit."

"I know this is difficult for you, but we need to go over what is written in each of the letters," Nathan said, spreading his sheets of notes on the coffee table in Judi's living room. "If we're going to get to the bottom of this God's way, it will require knowing the whole truth."

Judi stared plainly at him from across the table, curled up in a wingback chair with her bare feet tucked under her, a cup of tea in one hand. There was a slight trembling of her hand that belied the calm look on her face, and the cup clattered faintly when she placed it on the table. "I'm ready."

"It makes sense to start with the first letter and try to track them chronologically." He looked through the small sheets of notepaper until he found his first handwritten copy. Once again, he held it at arm's length, wishing he'd remembered his reading glasses. "You mentioned that this one was sent to you around the time when the sugar was poured into the gas tank of your car. I'm assuming the good Amish girl the person speaks about is you. What does the writer mean about you having your hand in the till and a mug shot?"

Judi's gaze faltered for a moment, and he watched her gnaw slowly at her bottom lip. "Yes," she finally answered with disdain in her voice, her gaze switching to the plush carpet. "I'm the good Amish girl with the 'hair full of curls.' You already know that I wasn't born into an Amish family, but like you, we lived among the Amish in the community. I was often referred to by my schoolmates as the Amish girl because of an old-fashioned bonnet my father bought me for Christmas one year while in elementary school."

"Go on."

"The mug shot refers to a time during my youth when I tried to shoplift an especially expensive piece of jewelry from Langerton's department store." She paused long enough to look at him, and Nathan willed his features to stay neutral.

"To make a long story short, I was caught and because the item was rather costly, I was sent to the juvenile center and then to court."

Nathan leaned back. "Then what happened?"

"There were the mandatory private and group classes for a year with a county juvenile corrections counselor." She pursed her lips. "I attended like I should and kept my nose clean. In return, the county cleared my juvenile record."

"Tell me about the mug shot." He made every effort to keep his voice sounding professional, much like he would when talking with a client. He knew he was a skilled interviewer who could maintain a poker face, even though the information might bounce around like an emotionally charged firecracker inside his brain—like it was right now. This professional demeanor, however, would be hard to sustain. She was his wife, not a client.

"The mug shot?" she repeated, shaking her head slowly. "It wasn't a mug shot in the real sense. It was a picture the juvenile center took for their files, that's all. They used the photos for identification to make sure the right teen, not a paid substitute, showed up for the classes."

"You're sure this is the mug shot the writer is referring to?"

"Quite sure!" she said with certainty. "A copy of the photo accompanied the note." When he tossed her a questioning glance, she quickly added, "I tore up the photo in anger. But I assure you it was the same picture."

"How do you suppose the person acquired it?" he asked. "If your record was purged, the photo should have gone with it years ago."

Judi spread her hands halfheartedly in front of her. "I honestly don't know."

"Did anyone else have a copy of the picture?"

She shook her head. "No one!" Straightening slowly, she cocked her head. "I did have an identification badge with the same picture, but I don't remember what became of it. I'm assuming it had to be turned in."

Nathan penned the information inside a black spiral-bound notebook and looked up. "The note mentions you having a hand in the till. What do you make of that?"

"I'm afraid that refers to another unflattering time when I was seventeen." She took a sip of tea and lowered the cup a little, the slight tremor becoming more pronounced. "I was working at the Old Village Inn at the time."

Nathan fingered through his sheets. "The same Old Village Inn noted in the ugly rat letter?"

"Yes." This seemed especially hard for her. She finally put the cup down on the table, let her legs drop to the floor, and sat nervously on the edge of the chair. "I worked as a cashier at the restaurant and. . ." Clearly agitated, she popped up from the chair and wrapped her arms protectively around her waist. "I'm not proud of what I did, Nathan. You have to believe me about that."

"It's all right, Judi," he soothed, his attorney persona taking over. "Just tell me what happened."

"Here's the whole ugly truth." Her small voice quivered on an uncertain note. "For weeks I would make change for some of the customers without entering in the ticket at the time of sale. Then I would later change the server's slip to reflect lower charges by either deleting a meal, a dessert, or sometimes the entire order, and pocket the difference."

Nathan rubbed the nape of his neck in thought. How could he have been so ignorant of Judi's past? More importantly, how did this past line up with the woman he married—the woman she was today? He didn't like being deceived and made to look like a fool. Others had tried to tell him the match between them wasn't right. Could they have seen what he so blindly missed?

With effort he kept his tone even and asked, "You were caught?"

"The manager suspected me and gave me the option of quitting or being fired. So I quit."

"No formal charges or investigation?"

She shook her head. "I was lucky that time."

"Who else knew about this?"

"There might have been one or two classmates who also worked at the restaurant," she answered slowly, her mind evidently searching back in time. "I'm sure my father suspected and my brother Tony probably knew."

"Anyone else?"

"No one I can think of."

"Why did you steal the money, Judi?" He was working to keep his reaction and resentment in check, remembering his pledge to God. Still, he had to know what had motivated her to live under such an umbrella of indiscretion.

By the look on her face, it was evident Judi was looking for just the right words. "That's a hard question."

There were so many other questions he wanted to ask, each exploding through his brain like popcorn. Had Judi kept her past a secret out of shame or self-interest? What more did she have to reveal? Why hadn't she warned him before they married, especially knowing his political aspirations? A bombshell like this had the power to derail him permanently if he were unaware and not prepared for it with damage control.

"I know what you're thinking," she said perceptively. "You're not only wondering why I felt the need to steal, but why I felt the need to keep my past hidden from you." When Nathan shifted slightly, she sadly smiled her acknowledgment. "I stole because I wanted what I could never have living on a poor father's salary. Designer jeans and the latest shirts made it easier to fit into a world where I didn't belong." She gave an indifferent shrug. "I never shared my sordid past with you because I realized early in this game of life that a straight arrow like you wouldn't have given me the time of day if you had known. Besides, I had no idea someone would dig up the information that should have been expunged decades ago and use it against me."

"You thought I wouldn't understand, much less marry you," he remarked with studied civility.

"I know you wouldn't have." She frowned grimly. "Especially if you had known that I never graduated with a degree from Penn State."

Nathan narrowed his eyes. "What do you mean?"

Judi wandered over to the sliding glass door, and Nathan twisted around and followed her with his eyes. Her fingers touched the vertical blinds as she looked out at the lake, her back toward him.

"Why not make a clean sweep of my prior misdeeds?" she exclaimed, turning to face him. "This is the last thing those letters held over me." The blinds swayed lightly behind her as she let go. "I went to a nine-month secretarial school and took a mail-order class on being a legal assistant." She flung her arms in the air. "When I went to apply for the job at your law firm, I lied on the application to get the job. There was no Happy Valley and there was no four-year degree as a paralegal."

"But your skills were impeccable!"

"Impeccable, yes," she agreed. "Honest, no. There was no way I could afford to go to a real college, and a scholarship was out of the question." She gave a bitter laugh. "I wasn't the most interested or best student in high school, and no college would give a scholarship to a student with my grade point average. Instead, I studied on my own and learned everything there was to learn about being a paralegal. I had the skills and know-how, just not the degree. And I knew your firm wouldn't hire me without that little piece of paper proving my educational worth."

"Anything else?" he dared to ask, with trepidation firmly entrenched in his mind of what she might say.

"No," she answered. "I think you'll find that these three big sins are the ones recalled in one letter or another." Her voice softened as she moved slightly toward him. "I do want you to know that when I met you and then God that year, I turned my life around. I went straight after that." She clasped her hands together nervously. "I had left that past behind when we married and erased it from my memory—until the first letter arrived."

"That put you into a bind, didn't it?"

She nodded. "I couldn't come to you for help, not without revealing my past and losing everything. Your family hated me and mine was distant. If I went to the police, my secret past would be made public. There was nowhere to turn." A deep sigh escaped. "I almost decided to risk telling you after the scary bird nest letter came."

"The one mentioning how birds didn't like breathing carbon monoxide?" Nathan asked, turning slightly to sort through the letters once more.

"That's the one." Her face turned grim. "Remember when my father's chimney flue became clogged with the makings of a bird's nest and the house filled up with carbon monoxide?" When he nodded with a frown, she continued. "The clog was no accident. Someone had stuffed it under the chimney cap and blocked the shaft." She nodded toward the paper in his hand. "The letter had come two days before the incident, but I didn't understand the significance. The other letters had come *after* the deeds." She paused. "I almost came to you when I realized my father could have died and the person who wrote the notes was responsible."

"Why didn't you?"

"When I went into your office at home, you were gone. I don't know. Maybe you received a call from your campaign manager and had to leave—that happened a lot." Pressing her fingers over one temple, she lightly shook her head. "But you had been in the middle of paying the bills and left the checks lying on the desk. It was then I realized how much the writing looked like yours. When I compared the letter to your writing and it matched, things started to add up."

"That's when you started planning a way to escape?"

"What else could I do?" she pleaded. "By then, I'd realized that you had somehow found out about my past and wanted me out of the picture. But you wanted me to be the one to leave, not you. I thought it was all about your aspirations to become a U.S. senator."

"I wish you would have come to me."

"How could I?"

"You should have had a little faith in me."

"My faith in everything was gone by that time." Her eyes grew somber. "You would have wanted an explanation of the letters. Then what? Would you still have loved me after learning about my past? Would your family have let you love me?"

It took a moment for Nathan to sort out exactly what his reaction might have been. "I don't know what I would have done," he finally answered. "But I know that I wouldn't have abandoned you."

She acknowledged his answer, but her eyes told him she didn't quite believe that scenario would have played out as he said.

He tried again. "My coming here should tell you one thing."

She lifted one brow. "What is that?"

"It should convince you that I'm not the author of these letters." He thrust a hand out in front of him. "Think about it. If I had written these letters and you disappeared from the scene so nice and tidy, there would be no reason for me to come searching for you. Am I right?"

"Maybe." She seemed to think it over. "That is a logical conclusion."

"And you weren't easy to find."

This perked up her attention. "I was very meticulous in securing my new identity."

"I know!"

"Yet you found me."

"True!"

"How?"

"It's a long story."

She sat back in the chair. "That's all right. If you have the story, I have the time."

# Chapter 7

Judi settled back in the chair across from Nathan. Finally, the worst of the interrogation was over. She'd spilled her guts and lived to talk about it—for now. What Nathan thought of her past was anyone's guess. His expression never changed from one of concentration and study. But he was good in that way. There were times when clients would give the most horrendous accounts of their dealings and Nathan held the same you're-in-capable-hands air people found comforting.

She found it disconcerting!

Did Nathan loathe her more than ever before? Was he repulsed and disgusted, wishing he had listened to his family? Maybe he was already envisioning the inevitable I-told-you-so party his mother would throw. If so, then she, as his wife, had done him a terrible disservice. Could Nathan be telling the truth? As he had mentioned before, if he had been the author of the threats there would be no feasible reason for him to come to Bay Island.

If it wasn't Nathan, then who did write the letters? Two possibilities sprang to mind: his campaign manager and his mother. Both disliked her! Yet neither would have access to her cleared juvenile records. She glanced at Nathan, his head still bent over the papers, organizing them for the second time into some type of order. Again, she sensed he was having trouble seeing clearly and wondered if he had been struck with the dreaded forty-and-over farsightedness that turned ordinary people into trombone players. What the man needed was a pair of glasses.

Nathan looked up, seemingly unperturbed by her stare.

"I'll tell you what," he told her, fitting the papers neatly into a folder. "I'll fill you in on how I came to find you, if you'll do two things."

She cocked an eyebrow at him. "Just two?"

He stood and stretched his back; she heard it crack, cringing at the sound. He only smiled at her reaction. "Sorry! You never did like the snap, crackle, pop unless it was in your cereal, did you? But sometimes a guy just has to loosen the spine." He looked at his watch. "We've been at this thing for several hours, which brings me to my first request. Would you be kind enough to scavenge through your refrigerator and make me a sandwich of some sort?"

"That's an easy one," she lightly answered back, still intently watching him. He was tired, she could tell, reminding her of those long days he used to put in while campaigning. "What's your second request?"

"I'll tell you all about my journey to locate a lost wife if you'll fill me in on a few details of your plan-of-escape that also seem to be missing."

"Sounds like a bargain." She moved toward the refrigerator. "Although it's just a matter of curiosity on my part, I am interested to know what bases I failed to cover."

He followed her to the kitchen counter where his glass of water was sitting, the ice now melted, and lifted it to take a drink. A droplet of condensation fell haphazardly on his tie. He brushed it away and looked back at her. "It should be more than just a matter of curiosity."

The warning tone in his voice told her he was hinting at something serious. "If you were able to locate me, then the person who wrote those notes could find me, too. Is that it?" She pulled a bag of deli ham from the fridge and two plates from the cupboard. "Not a comforting thought."

"True," he agreed solemnly, a measure of concern etching his face. "But it's something we should consider."

He did have a point. She had been so upset at his unexpected appearance, she hadn't considered that angle before. Closing the freezer door, she automatically dropped a handful of ice cubes into his water glass. "Does anyone else know why you're here?"

"Just my assistant, Thomas," he answered, his eyes following her as she opened the bread bag. "You don't need to worry about him. He's extremely good at what he does and is even better at keeping things under wraps. Then there's the fact that he came on staff after you were gone and didn't even know you."

"Then I'm sure he's safe." She took four slices of bread out and twirled the yellow bread bag shut until it formed an airtight wrap and grabbed the twist tie. She held the plastic-covered wire tie toward him. "Still losing twisty ties and eating stale bread?"

"Of course," he answered with a reluctant but slow, mischievous smile.

She laughed. How an intelligent, grown man could misplace every twist tie he'd ever had the misfortune to handle was a mystery. How many times the vacuum cleaner had eaten those twist ties couldn't be counted.

Judi put the finishing touches on the sandwiches and handed him a plate. "Heavy on the cheese and light on the mayo."

He murmured his thanks as he accepted the plate and grabbed his drink. Sliding her own plate off the counter and into her hand, she trailed him into the living room. Again they sat in their same places, opposite each other, only the coffee table serving as a buffer between them.

Sitting in the chair, Judi rested her plate on the makeshift lap of her legs, both feet slipped securely beneath. "Your story has to start at the very beginning," she informed him, watching him take a bite of the sandwich, "starting with the reason for your search. I'm certain there was nothing left behind to cause doubt or raise any suspicions that my death was anything but an accidental drowning. Everything went off without a hitch."

He waited to finish chewing and chased it down with a swallow of water. "Everyone was convinced; the police, your family, my family—even me."

"Then something must have happened to change your mind," she guessed, trying to read his face. "What was it? What did I leave behind?"

"It's not what you left behind," he answered, his long mouth twisting ruefully. "It's what you didn't leave behind."

Judi racked her brain. She hadn't taken anything! Her purse, keys, clothes, jewelry, makeup—they were all left behind. Not even a toothbrush was taken. "That's impossible," she finally concluded.

"You probably thought I wouldn't notice," he consoled. "Of course, I was having a difficult time dealing with your death and admit I was grabbing at straws, but you were acting very distant and peculiar before the so-called accident. So, when I noticed the ruby brooch missing, I began to have my first suspicions about the drowning."

Puzzled, Judi shook her head. "You're not talking about my grandmother's ruby pin?"

"That's the one."

"The ruby brooch is gone?"

"By the surprise in your voice am I to presume you didn't take it with you?" It was his turn to look mystified.

The brooch was missing! Judi wanted to jump from the chair and had to snatch the sandwich plate before it went flying to the edge of the cushion. "I didn't take the brooch with me. It can't be gone!"

"I assure you the pin wasn't in your jewelry box." He seemed troubled by her outburst, a wary line creasing his forehead.

"Nathan, I'm telling you; the brooch was left in the jewelry box. I never took it with me." She dropped the plate on the coffee table rather hard but didn't care and slumped back in the chair. "How can it be missing?"

He shrugged. "When the ruby wasn't there, I assumed you had taken it with you. I knew how important it was to you, being your grandmother's heirloom."

"But I didn't take it with me," she protested, her hands clutching angrily at the arm of the chair. There were only two worldly possessions she owned that meant anything—the heirloom pin and her vintage 1972 yellow Volkswagen Beetle. Both had to be left behind, but if she had known the ruby pin would be taken, she would have risked bringing it with her. She thought it would be safe with Nathan. At the very least, the brooch should have been given to her father. "This is terrible news!"

Nathan seemed at a loss. "Could you have placed it somewhere other than the jewelry box? Maybe you put it somewhere for safekeeping and forgot."

"It was in the box!" She wasn't crazy. The pin was left where it had always been. It was more than just the loss of an expensive gem. It was all that was left of her grandmother and a mother she barely knew. To be motherless was difficult enough, but the less than respectable reason for her mother's departure had marked her with embarrassment and then anger throughout her childhood. *She's run off with another man*, her father explained to her one hot summer day so many years ago. She never asked again why she had no mother. It was easier to make believe her mother left unwillingly than to cope with the reality that her mother didn't care enough to take her only daughter with her.

"I don't know what to tell you," Nathan finally said, breaking the silence. He cocked his head sympathetically. "Maybe God let it happen so I would come looking for you."

Judi pulled a face at him. "God didn't come down and take it."

"I wasn't suggesting God physically came into the room and took it," he softly returned. "I only know the ruby pin was not in your jewelry box when I went through your things. It seems an odd thing to go missing. I'm only suggesting that God may have orchestrated its disappearance—*how* I don't know—to cause me to begin a search."

Nathan was right! If the pin was missing, it was missing. There was nothing she could do about it now. How ironic! She had left the ruby behind to make a clean, total break from her former life and to prevent any suspicion. Yet the ruby had started a search ending in her discovery.

"Listen," Nathan said soothingly. "We'll add the missing ruby to our list of things to resolve. We'll find it!"

She lightly waved her hand in resignation. "You're right! It's not that important in light of my current situation." What good did it do to hold on to a pipe dream? The jewelry brought her no closer to the mother who abandoned her at the age of four. It did nothing to keep her father from drinking away his sorrows. No power was held in the red sparkle other than what she chose to believe. Taking a deep breath, she tried to calm herself. "Tell me what happened after you found the ruby missing."

Nathan seemed to hesitate as if waiting to see if she really wanted to move on.

"It's all right," she assured, taking the plate up again in her lap to prove it. "I'm ready to hear the rest of the story."

"If you're sure, but I have to warn you that my methods of tracking might put you to shame—I'm almost as clever as you," he remarked with an impish smile.

"Really?"

"Really! I did a thorough search of everything and came up with nothing. But then I took a long shot and it paid off." He wagged a finger at her. "I knew one day your addiction to that awful angelic hash fudge would be your downfall."

"You can't be serious," she sputtered in disbelief. "There is no way you could have traced me from that."

He only gave her a knowing glance and took another bite of the ham sandwich.

"You're telling me that you were able to get a list of customers buying this particular fudge and with that list you found me?" He was bluffing. There had to be hundreds, if not thousands, of people who ordered that exact fudge flavor.

He held up a waiting finger as he finished his bite. "The job was daunting. Did you know that there are over seven hundred people who regularly mail order the angelic hash? Five hundred eighteen of them are women, and 362 of those women have been customers for more than three years. That left me with 156 women who were customers for less than three years to check on."

"You are kidding, right?"

"Quite serious." He smiled, evidently amused by her befuddlement. "If you were alive, I knew you would somehow obtain this fudge. You wouldn't risk buying it in person from the shop, though. No, you would mail order it. So that's where I started."

"Even at that," she protested, "I used the name Amanda Rydell, not Judith."

"I know. The birth certificate you acquired was for Amanda Judith Rydell." He leaned back. "It was the process of elimination that narrowed it down."

She folded her arms across her chest. "Tell me."

"Back to the 156 women," he directed. "Of those, 61 were over the age of 55 and 10 were under 25. That left 85."

"You obtained their ages?" Fascinated now, she watched him intently.

"That's where my assistant, Thomas, comes in." He gave her a knowing look. "He first was able to secure the list with a little persuasion, and he did a basic, systematic check on every female customer who ordered that particular fudge, including their ages. Then he did an in-depth search of the remaining eighty-five and eliminated several more by profession, race, and marital status over the past two years. He arrived at nine names and you were one of them. Once he perused the driver's license photos of the nine, you seemed like a good bet. Then he came to Bay Island."

"Your assistant was here?"

"He even came into the church office one day to ask directions," Nathan went on. "You gave him directions to Levitte's Landing."

"I remember him," she exclaimed, thinking back just a week ago. "Clean-cut, tall fellow with black hair."

"That was Thomas."

Judi mockingly tapped at her forehead. "I should have been suspicious. He would have passed Levitte's Landing on his way to the church from the ferry dock. He shouldn't have needed directions." She gave a mental shake of her head. "You'd be surprised, though, at how many tourists get lost on an island no more than three miles long."

"Thomas followed you around for two days." He raised his eyebrows her way. "Did you know that?"

Slowly she shook her head. "No idea!"

"He even took pictures of you outside the pastry shop."

"This is sounding more and more like an espionage flick."

Nathan smiled. "I'm quite impressed with Thomas's abilities in this area. He might be more clever than either of us." Then he sobered. "But you can imagine my shock when he showed me the pictures. I almost couldn't believe it was you, but I knew it was. What I didn't know was why."

"Which now you know."

"Yes! It's still mind-boggling."

"I know!"

He nodded meaningfully, and then as if switching gears, placed his plate on the table and slapped his hands lightly together. "Now it's your turn. I've explained the breakthrough that brought me here. I have a few questions for you."

"All right."

"I figure you traveled to Allegheny County two times using your legal knowledge and a computer-forged court document to gain access to birth and death certificates. I'm guessing this happened in February of that last year when you were supposed to be visiting an old college roommate." He sat up straighter. "You searched for several days until you found a birth and death certificate that matched; an infant with the name of Amanda Judith Rydell. How am I doing so far?"

"Keep going."

"You obtained an official copy of this birth certificate and began to build your new identity—a false apartment address, driver's license, and even a credit card that you had the postal service forward from an apartment you never lived in to a post office box. What I haven't figured out is how you were able to gain a Social Security number." He gave her a fixed look. "It's not every day a thirty-two-year-old woman comes in for a number."

Judi nodded. "It took me a long time to figure out that logistical problem, but obtaining a legitimate Social Security number was crucial if this new identity was to work," she explained. "I had to get a job. To provide a false number would only gain me a year, maybe two at most, before the jig would be up and I'd be on the run again."

"But you came up with a plan," he remarked assuredly, regarding her with new awareness in his eyes.

"Do you remember my work with the Hampton House?"

"Of course," he acknowledged. "You volunteered once or twice a week with the developmentally delayed handicapped children and adults."

She smiled, remembering those she had come to care a great deal about. "I came up with a plan to take one of the adult patients with me. Tracy Stecky! I took the birth certificate I'd obtained in Allegheny County and told the Social Security clerk that Tracy was Amanda and that she would need to apply for benefits soon. Since she was never able to work due to the severity of her disability, they never questioned why she didn't have a number previously." She shrugged. "Actually, it was easy."

"And unbelievably ingenious," he remarked as Judi sensed a note of wonder and then disappointment in his voice. "Ingenious, but quite illegal."

Sadly, she had to agree. "Disappearing completely required more than the law would allow."

"You've broken a number of laws—some very seriously." He drew a deep breath and exhaled slowly. "Even the federal government will be on your case with the fraudulent Social Security number."

"After the city, county, and state have a go at me," she added grimly. "I know the law well enough to easily envision the mile-long list of charges that will flow from one prosecutor to another. It should be enough to keep several of them busy for quite a long time."

"Along with the life insurance company asking for their money back," he speculated. "That might be a problem."

Judi's head jerked up and she felt a pang of hurt. "You've spent it?"

"Not exactly," he answered, taking a deep breath. "Twenty-five thousand dollars of it I gave to the Hampton House in your name. The rest is sitting in a bank account."

Judi's heart swelled with hope and fear at the same time. "You did that for me?"

"I knew you would have wanted it," he responded awkwardly. Sadness overtook his face. "I couldn't have spent a penny of the money on myself."

She sagged back into the seat. "This is getting complicated."

"I agree!" Nathan bent forward and pressed the palms of his hands against his eyes. "It might have been better if I'd never searched for you and even better if I'd never found you. It's been like opening Pandora's box."

"What you really mean," Judi clarified, "is *I'm* like Pandora's box." When he let his hands drop and looked at her with a degree of uncertainty, she could see extreme exhaustion in his eyes. "Oh, I already know it. Everything I touch and everyone I know is somehow affected by me that way. Even my own mother left, and eventually my brother took off for Florida and never returned."

"You really believe you're the cause of these events?"

"Yes," she told him quietly. "Just look at your family. Did I ever do anything to your parents? Yet they treated me like the plague." Reluctantly, she met his gaze. "And you let them." Saying the words ripped through her chest like fiery knives. It was true! Nathan always tried to soothe the tensions between them and his parents, but not once had she ever heard him defend her honor. Because he knew what everyone else knew—she wasn't good enough.

"I had no idea you felt that way."

Judi heaved a sigh. "Why is it that other people just live their lives, but I have to scratch and claw for everything?" Their eyes locked. "When I came to the island as Judi Rydell, they accepted me for who I was. I was finally free to live life as others do." A fresh wave of despondency came over her. It was a freedom that would soon end. The prospect of losing what she valued so highly hurt terribly. The very people who taught her how to truly love God and trusted her implicitly would soon find out her secret and realize how undeserving she was of that trust. It would devastate those in the church. "I'm tired of fighting life by outwitting others with tricks up my sleeve."

There was a moment of silence until he said very gently, "Then it's time you stop trying to bend life around you and begin bending yourself. Maybe you need to start trusting a little more in yourself and giving others the benefit of the doubt." When she began to protest, he stopped her. "We promised to face this thing God's way and that will require both of us to bend. I never realized you blamed yourself for your family's troubles, and I suppose I have to share part of that responsibility for not seeing this before. Besides, you're right, as a husband, my place was to protect you—even from my own family."

"Nathan—"

"Wait until I finish," he interrupted softly. "I'm convinced that with God's help, we can get through this thing." He rubbed his hands together thoughtfully. "I'm equally convinced we need to keep clear minds to continue sorting through the details of what everything means." He swiped his hand across the back of his neck. "I don't know about you, but I've just about hit my saturation level for one day."

Judi let her gaze roam over his face. She was again struck by the lines of fatigue on his handsome features, the dark five o'clock shadow accentuating his deep chin cleft, and the vulnerability of his candid gaze. Her throat constricted at the sight and more at the fierce emotions accompanying her thoughts. Love! It was love stretching out from behind the locked door of her heart. Right now, at this very moment, she loved Nathan more than she'd ever loved anyone.

"I'm going to head back to my cabin," he told her, obviously unaware of her churning emotions. He stood up. "We both need our sleep. Tomorrow morning I'll start working on a way to help you. I'd like you to go about your day as usual at the church." He looked at her questioningly. "Can you do that? Then I'll stop by and pick you up for lunch."

Quickly, she drew herself out of the chair. "Are you sure you're okay? You look beat." Thankfully they had retrieved his car earlier so he could leave right from her place, but the truth was—she didn't want him to go. Then the words were out of her mouth before she could stop them. "There's an extra room here."

Something passed across his features she couldn't read. He shook his head. "That's not a good idea."

Disappointed, she only nodded. "It was just a suggestion. But please be careful."

He moved toward her and gave a weak smile. "I will."

When he paused long enough, she waited in hope that the look on his face was more than just concern over the situation, but concern for her. Slowly, he bent and gave her a quick peck on the forehead. "Everything will be all right."

With that he wordlessly turned around and walked to the door, closing it silently behind him, leaving Judi looking at the white decorative wood. It was as if the warmth had suddenly been sucked out of the room and left a cold, damp chill in its place. Already she missed the man whom she had previously hoped to never see again. It was craziness! She knew beyond a shadow of a doubt she still loved him, and right now it was coming at her full force. But why? Because he believed her story? Because she finally believed in him? Because he was finally stepping forward as her protector? If possible, the love she felt was deeper and more encompassing than the day they married.

And it scared her!

She was about to lose everything, even if Nathan assured her he'd find a way to fix the problem. What if he couldn't? What if she went to prison? What if God chose not to intercede? Could she bear to lose Nathan all over again?

# Chapter 8

Nathan opened his laptop computer on the kitchen table and flipped it on, turning the screen away from the morning sun. It was already past eight o'clock. He should have rolled himself out of bed at his usual time three hours ago, but he gave in to the fatigue claiming his body and burrowed in for a few extra hours. A hot shower welcomed him into the day, along with a strong cup of black coffee. Still he was drained. It made him question whether Judi had awakened yet. She would be due at work in less than an hour.

He had almost called her earlier to make sure but stopped short. Last night he was having trouble keeping his eyes focused, much less his thoughts. Seeing Judi for the first time in two years brought the enormity of his anger to the forefront until it slowly gave way to a painful bout of incomprehension, protectiveness, and then—what? If he wasn't careful, he'd fall for her all over again. He could feel the old familiar draw and knew this would be a dangerous path to follow.

She'd lied to him in the past, craftily enough to whiz right under his usual radar of perception without detection. Then her death had wrung him dry. He wasn't sure he could withstand another blow. Nevertheless, she was still his wife and whatever had passed between them couldn't change that fact. He would do whatever he could to shield her from the maniac who wrote the notes—and the law, if it came to that. The price would be steep! There was no naïveté toward the outcome. He stood to lose a great deal.

The computer came alive, and Nathan pulled his glasses out from the case, resting them squarely across his nose. Much better! Yesterday would have been so much easier if he'd remembered to take them. He let his finger roll across the pad, tapping where needed until his e-mail program opened. Quickly, he scanned the mounting mail as it downloaded. One caught his attention. Thomas had written only one word late last night: Urgent!

Without waiting he flipped open his cell phone, scrolled through the numbers, and connected. When Thomas answered, he pulled his glasses off and propped them on the top of his head.

"What's up?" he asked, not bothering to identify himself.

"You got my message, sir. Good!" Thomas cleared his throat and lowered his voice. "You need to get back here right away."

Nathan heard voices in the background. "Where are you and can you talk?"

"Hold on, sir." A minute passed as the noise gradually faded until there was silence. "All right, I'm back. The Speaker of the House only gave you a one-day reprieve on the eminent domain bill. If you don't get back here by Friday, we might have to wait until the September session starts again to get this bill passed."

"I thought we had another week or two before the session was out for the summer," Nathan replied, trying to remember his calendar. His life at the statehouse already seemed like weeks ago.

"We did have two weeks," explained Thomas, "but they passed the budget yesterday, much sooner than expected."

"I missed the budget!" Nathan couldn't believe it. How many times had they haggled for weeks over one line item after another, inevitably holding up the vote until the deadline of July 1?

"We were all surprised, sir," Thomas commiserated. "But now that the budget is passed, they want to recess early. A sort of bonus, I guess, for all their hard work."

Nathan had to think. "The speaker is willing to put my bill on the floor Friday? That's two days from now."

"Yes, sir. I already told him you had a family emergency, and he's willing to keep the session open until you can get back since you are the prime sponsor of the bill—but the sooner the better. If you wait until next week, they might pressure him to postpone it until the fall or at the very least, your fellow representatives might vote against it for spite." He gave a snort. "You don't mess with their time off."

"Don't I know it!" Nathan drummed his fingers on the table. This would shove his timetable downhill like a runaway locomotive. He had no other option. "All right! I'll be back by Thursday night. Have the committee ready and in place."

"I will, sir!" Thomas assured and then paused. "How's everything on your end going?"

"Very problematical! Has anyone been asking questions?"

"Just Lindsey."

Nathan blew out a mouthful of air. "What did you tell her?"

"I told her you were out of town attending to business, sir. She seemed very anxious to talk with you."

"I'll call her!"

"Anything else, sir?"

"Thomas. . ." Nathan paused a moment to gather the right words. "Things might get ugly very soon. It's imperative that you keep this matter about Bay Island out of sight until this bill is passed. The people are counting on me to protect their property rights, and the opposition's too strong to wait for others in the committee to try to gather support again in the fall. I might not be there to rally a comeback."

"What are you saying, sir? You're going to step down from office?"

"I don't think I'm going to have a choice." The words nearly stuck in his throat. All of his life he'd wanted to make a difference and finally he'd achieved the position to do it on a grand scale. If God saw fit to let him keep his post, Nathan would be most grateful, but realistically, he didn't expect it.

"Then I wish you best of luck on the island, sir."

"I need more than luck," he said. "I need God's intervention."

"Yes, sir."

"I'll call you as soon as I get back." Nathan closed the phone thoughtfully and laid it on the table.

He would have to call Lindsey. She might call his parents and have them worried enough to cause trouble. He already had his fill of trouble. Reluctantly, he opened his phone and scrolled through the numbers again until her name appeared. It rang only twice before she picked up.

"Where have you been?" Lindsey scolded, her restless voice shooting through the airwaves. "I've been worried sick. You weren't at the house, and Thomas wouldn't tell me where you were."

"Everything is all right," he soothed, instantly regretting the lie. He'd promised to do things God's way and that included the avoidance of perjury, no matter how innocent. "I can't explain right now, but I need to talk with you when I get back."

"But where are you?" she asked, her voice rising with anxiety.

"I'll explain that, too, when I get home." He pulled the glasses off the top of his head and placed them on the table. "I need you to be patient."

"Why do I get the feeling that something is terribly wrong?"

"Probably because I've never been evasive with you before," he answered honestly. "Can you trust me on this?"

"I suppose," she answered somewhat hesitantly.

"I'll be home soon."

"Soon enough for our dinner engagement with my parents tonight?" There was a hint of hurt in her voice as if she already knew the answer.

"Lindsey, I completely forgot!" Nathan could have kicked himself for not placing the date in his planner. Thomas could have headed this off. It was just the beginning of the damage he was going to cause her, and he hated it. "I'm so sorry," he apologized with genuine grief. "Please send my regrets to your parents."

"I wish I knew what was going on, Nathan," she said pleadingly. "Maybe I could help."

"I know you would help if you could, but there's nothing you can do." Nathan pinched his nose between his thumb and finger. "I promise you'll understand fully when I get back and explain everything." She would understand the situation better, but he also knew she wouldn't like it.

"Can you tell me when you'll be coming home?"

"I'll be back in time for us to get together either late Friday or Saturday," he answered vaguely.

"Then I'll wait for your call," she returned with conviction. "I have total faith in you."

Nathan winced, feeling as though he'd been slammed in the chest. "I know."

"You will call when you get home?" she asked, her insecurity resurfacing.

"Promise!"

"Please be careful," she went on, "and I love you."

Another kick to the gut. "I know." He wouldn't give her the chance to question why he didn't reciprocate the words and hurriedly ended the call. "Be good. I'll call you soon."

He couldn't snap the phone closed fast enough. He felt like a total, absolute heel. Lindsey was an innocent bystander who would be crushed under when the steamroller started moving at Judi's official comeback.

It wasn't fair to her. He and Lindsey had a comfortable relationship. For his part he had no illusions of profound love for her—all of which she accepted. But he did care for the woman. Sure, he could say the obligatory I-love-you when the situation seemed right, but it wasn't a love like he'd had with Judi. There would never be another love like that in a lifetime.

Lindsey had been the right woman at the right time. She was beautiful, smart, and exciting. Marrying her seemed the reasonable thing to do; he was lonely, his family loved her, she was good for his political career and made him feel wanted.

Only one thing had stood in his way, causing him to hesitate about setting a wedding date—she didn't believe in God. It was quite simple to her—life was life, and then it was over. Finished! One day you exist, the next day you were gone.

Nathan, conversely, couldn't reconcile the two of them living in unity with their faith, or lack thereof, at opposite poles. It probably would have never worked out in the end, but he certainly didn't want to conclude their relationship like this. He thanked God that his hesitation saved Lindsey and himself from an even more unbearable and intolerable situation. Not that the current news wouldn't be any less demoralizing to her.

His head was beginning to ache from the complexity of the moment. He'd assured Judi that with God's help he would find a way out of this problem. It was a tall order he wasn't sure could be delivered.

He took a tired breath and stood up. It would be so easy to walk away and let each of them live their lives as they had done for the past two years. He could keep his job in the Pennsylvania House, and she could continue the new life she loved. Everyone would be happy—except for God. Okay. . .he wouldn't be happy either. How could he be happy to marry the love of his life, lose her, find her again, and then leave her under such circumstances?

Slowly he walked to the bedroom and brought out his Bible. He needed a reminder of what he was doing and quick. Turning to Matthew 6:33, he read aloud. " 'But seek ye first the kingdom of God, and his righteousness; and all these things shall be added unto you.' "

"God, I'm seeking You," Nathan prayed aloud. "I think there's a strategy to help Judi, but I want to clear it through You first. You say in the third chapter of Proverbs to trust and acknowledge You and You will direct my path. I'm trying my best to trust. If at any time the path I'm taking isn't the right one, stop me. I'll accept Your decisions as they become apparent to me." He paused to look at the ceiling and ludicrously wondered if God heard prayers better when you looked up. "I'll call my brother this morning and get the ball rolling. Look over Judi—and Lindsey. Protect them both. In Jesus' name, amen."

Why did he feel like such a fish out of water? There were so many things in life he could manage with confidence, but trusting God to handle this wasn't one of them. How long would God allow him and Judi to stand in the fire before leading them out of the flames? What if God was trying to tell him something and he didn't recognize it in time to be of help? This faith business scared him—bad. It was all well and good when life skated along on smooth ice, but a significant bump or crack in the surface could bring a person down fast.

Nathan fell into a thoughtful silence. God would help! Why did he worry so much when he knew God would hold up His end even if Nathan faltered with his own? Hadn't God delivered on other life projects with or without his help?

Besides, he did have the makings of a plan, a plan his weary mind began yesterday.

The clock chimed the half hour and he looked up. His brother would be in his office by now, probably nursing his third cappuccino. It was time to put this plan in action. Again, he took up the phone and began dialing.

"Jeff," he greeted when his brother answered. "It's Nathan."

"Man, it's good to hear your voice!" he exclaimed, and Nathan could almost hear a smile cracking across his face. "I haven't heard from you in a couple of weeks. To what do I owe this unexpected call?"

It did his heart good to hear the lightheartedness in his brother's voice. "I need your help."

"Sounds foreboding," teased Jeff. "I'm the one usually calling you for help. What can I do you for?"

Nathan envisioned his blond-haired brother sitting at his desk, feet propped on an outstretched drawer, the computer blinking before him. "I need to know if you have any computer software that can do handwriting analysis? It needs to be as professional as possible."

"Can I ask what you need it for?"

"No!" Blunt and to the point, Nathan softened his answer with a slight chuckle.

His brother gave a low whistle. "No? You sure have been acting weird and grouchy lately—almost back to normal." He laughed at his own joke. "What is this. . .a romantic handwriting analysis for you and Lindsey to see if you're compatible? I could save you the time and money. All that palm reading and personality testing is a bunch of hooey!"

"I don't need the program for a personality profile," Nathan answered, trying to hold back a smile. "This is much more serious than that."

"Then what? More statehouse stuff, amateur sleuthing to save the commonwealth of Pennsylvania?"

"In a sense," Nathan answered, knowing if he waited long enough, Jeff's curiosity would be drowned out once he started talking computer programming. "I need a software application that can read, decipher, and compare handwriting." He thought for a second. "It would have to be able to tell the difference between handwriting samples that were meant to look alike."

"That's a big order," he remarked without sounding the least bit perturbed. "So you want professional software like the police department uses to identify forgeries, but available to the public?"

"Right! Do you have it or know where I could get it?"

"It's possible," he answered somewhat distractedly, and Nathan could hear the computer keys tapping in quick succession in the background. "The question to be asked is whether a graphology program could interpret the data like a professional. Software of this caliber is usually operated in conjunction with someone skilled in the area."

"I was afraid of that."

"Don't give up so easily," his brother encouraged, the sound of keyboard movement still evident. "Do you know anyone on the Harrisburg or Lancaster police force who would be willing to help?"

"No." Nathan sighed. He had plenty of contacts, but no one he could involve without jeopardizing the situation. The words "accessory after the fact" came to mind. How would the district attorney or public feel about him not immediately reporting the fraud once he'd discovered Judi's new life? Would they consider him an accessory to this charade? "Do you know of anyone?"

"I might," he returned, his tone suggesting his mind was preoccupied with the computer. "Our sister, Laurie, might be the one to help you." The keyboard sounded furiously again. "Remember that detective story she did in Pittsburgh about a murder suspect they convicted by using handwriting analysis? If I could just find it. . ." His voice dropped off. "There it is!" he almost shouted.

Nathan tried to recall the story and couldn't. "Did this detective do handwriting analysis?"

"That's what I'm trying to find out." There was a pause. "First I have to sign up for a free trial subscription to the online archives of the newspaper. Just give me a minute." Another pause. "Let me read the story. . .yada yada yada—here it is. Yes, I think you're in luck."

"You found it?"

"Yep," he answered. "I can talk with Laurie about it if you want. I have to call her anyway."

"Please!" Nathan exclaimed, excited that God had opened at least one avenue. "If she thinks this detective will do her a favor, I'd really be grateful. All I need is to match a short letter with the handwriting on a check."

"Can do!"

"Have her call me on my cell phone and I can fill her in."

Something in Nathan's urgent tone must have triggered Jeff's next question. "Are you all right?"

"I'm not sure," he answered honestly. "I'll be better if Laurie can help me out."

"All right, big brother," he responded affectionately. "I'll see what we can do."

When Nathan closed the phone, he again thanked God. He wanted to prove beyond a shadow of a doubt to Judi that he was not the author of these notes and possibly, possibly. . . find the identity of the person responsible. He would need to scan the letter and obtain an electronic copy of a few old checks he'd written. Buoyed by the possibility of help from Laurie, he placed the glasses back on his nose and turned back to the laptop. Quickly, he accessed his banking records and flipped through several secured Web pages until he reached the copies of his old checks. It would be best to go back to the time when the notes were written to make all things equal.

There were the checks! Gas bill, credit card payment, mortgage—he supposed it didn't matter. Then he saw a check written to Judi's father for five hundred dollars. He frowned. What he'd meant as a gift to help his father-in-law pay medical bills was met with scorn—but it didn't prevent the old man from cashing the check, Nathan thought wryly. Mr. Porter told him in no uncertain terms he didn't need any handouts. Thankfully, Judi never knew of the fiasco. Nathan had let it go and never mentioned it.

Why he'd kept it secret he couldn't remember. His goodwill gesture flopped, but he hadn't shirked his duty. Maybe it was time Judi realized he wasn't as unfeeling as she believed. This check was as good as any to print and use for analysis. Nathan saved a copy of the check and two others in the computer. These he would send as one file.

Now, for the threatening note. With a few cable connections to the computer, he set up the portable scanner-printer and within minutes printed out the perfect copy of the note he planned to have compared. This he also saved into a file.

That was the first step. When he met with Judi for lunch, they would plan step two and try to figure a way to keep Tilly Storm from scavenging information at dinner that evening. It wouldn't be easy, but imperative. The world would rain fire down on their heads if the situation wasn't handled just right. Their lives depended on it!

# Chapter 9

Judi sluggishly dropped her purse into the desk drawer and locked it. She felt depleted and knew her appearance let it show. Without purpose she sank down into the chair and plucked her hairbrush from the top drawer, running it through the out-of-control curls that looked more like a twirl of pink cotton candy on a paper stick than her usual soft, smooth waves. She'd taken a shower soon after Nathan left the night before, but was too tired for the usual blow-dry and curling iron routine. Then after a night of fitful turning in her sleep, the damp hair had turned into the Bride-of-Frankenstein beehive by morning. Wetting it down with copious amounts of gel and trying to finalize the disaster with hairspray hadn't improved matters.

She gave a sour grimace at her reflection in the small mirror on her desk, sticking out a rebellious tongue at the less than flattering result. "Who cares what you think!" she demanded of the object.

Just as she figured, the mirror didn't seem to care.

Suddenly, she heard the church office door pop open and caught a glimpse of Larry Newkirk strolling in with a smile. Quickly, she dropped the brush back into the drawer and shoved it closed.

"Good morning," he cheerfully greeted as she turned toward the counter. He was dressed in his customary crisp police uniform, evidently pulling another double shift from evenings to days. The poor guy worked all the time.

"Morning," she mumbled back with as much enthusiasm as she could muster. She noticed a momentary break in his concentration when he took in her appearance, but thankfully he said nothing of it.

"Did you have a nice afternoon yesterday?" he asked politely, checking the small wooden mailbox slots in the outer office.

Judi managed a slow smile. "Yes, thank you."

"I saw your cousin coming back to the Stantons' cabin last night," Larry went on, sounding nonchalant while he opened an envelope retrieved from the mail slot. "That is where he's staying, isn't it?"

Larry was on a fishing expedition and she knew it. "No," she finally said. "I believe he's staying at the rental next to the Stantons'. The old McGreevy place."

He moved toward the counter and set the letter down. "You're sure everything's all right? You seemed a little uncomfortable yesterday."

"Just a little surprised, that's all." That was an understatement.

He gave a grim nod. "You know if you ever need help, Becky and I are only a phone call away."

"I know," she said, her smile widening. "I appreciate knowing there are good friends to rely on when needed."

The office door immediately pushed open again and Becky burst in, her face bright with excitement.

"Did you hear the latest?" Becky asked, her long black hair swishing lightly from side to side as she looked between Judi and Larry. When they shook their heads, Becky clapped her hands together in delight. "Jason and Lauren Levitte are expecting twins. Isn't that marvelous?"

"Twins!" Judi repeated in pleased astonishment. Now here was a couple God had managed to bring back together in what seemed like an impossible situation. After five years of separation, Lauren came back to the island to set right the accusations Jason had made that caused her to leave the island in the first place. Although Judi wasn't around to witness the breakup several years ago, she was there in time to see the reunion. The entire island talked about it for weeks. Finally, they married and were now expecting twins. If God could heal their botched love and hurts, maybe there was hope for Nathan and her after all.

"It's true!" Becky bobbed her head, continuing with vigor. "Won't the residents be surprised in the spring? It will be like a population explosion. I'm not sure the island has ever had three babies at one time."

"Three?" Judi asked, immediately noticing the bright shade of red creeping up Larry's neck. Becky was looking aghast and subconsciously planted a hand over her abdomen. Then Judi knew. "You're expecting, too?"

"Oops!" Becky's hand instantly flew to her mouth in chagrin.

Larry gave a lopsided, almost shy grin. "We weren't going to tell anyone yet, at least not until we had talked with our parents."

"My lips are sealed." Judi laughed, mimicking the pull of a zipper across her mouth. "But please accept my early congratulations."

"Thank you!" both said in blissful unison.

There was another of God's miracles. Becky was a missionary forced out of the Congo due to political unrest that made it unsafe for Americans. While furloughed on Bay Island, she became involved with the building project of the Thunder Bay Christian Camp and its lead committee member—Larry. They fell in love. It was a wonderful romance, blemished only by Becky's rich father, who couldn't accept her life as a missionary or as a wife to a "lowly" police officer. Her parents never even bothered to come to the wedding. Judi had met the father once—and once was enough. He was a tough egg to crack. Yet Becky mentioned how much peace God gave her over the situation, and she believed one day her daddy would come to know Jesus. That was real faith.

Even the cantankerous church elder Van Edwards seemed to find love. Judi hadn't missed the ogle-eyed looks Mr. Edwards and Tilly Storm had been exchanging the past several months. Ever since Tilly's heart attack last year, Mr. Edwards thought he was Tilly's personal trainer. It was heartwarming to see, really. Both were alone and made the perfect couple. Yes, romance and now new life were in the air on Bay Island. She hoped there would be enough romance left for another unlikely couple.

Was it possible? Maybe it was too much to ask. She would have to win Nathan back and clear herself in the bargain. There was also another woman in the picture, one Nathan loved. She'd seen God work in the lives of so many, but none were tackling the love triangle and legal battle she now faced. Was He up to the challenge?

"I need to get back to rounds," Larry finally announced to the ladies. Giving the counter a light slap with the palm of his hand, he gave Judi a pointed look. "Call if you need us for *anything*!"

"Yes, sir!" Judi gave a mock salute.

Becky laughed and gave her husband, the new daddy-to-be, a kiss on the cheek. "Isn't he handsome when he's so commanding?" She smiled back at Judi. "I need to meet the plumbing contractor at the camp, so we both better get going. We'll see you later, Judi."

Like a whirlwind that blew in, the two blew right back out, leaving Judi relieved for a quiet moment. She immediately busied herself with the ever-growing stack of paperwork and phone calls. Totally immersing herself in her familiar world of secretarial duties and tasks helped bring back a stabilizing calm to the morning.

One last keystroke completed the Sunday bulletin, and Judi pushed back her chair, critically looking at the screen text for errors. So deep was her absorption, she didn't notice Nathan enter the office until she looked up to see him standing at the counter watching her. How long he'd been there she didn't know. Immediately, she felt color rushing into her face.

"Nathan!" Judi swiveled in the chair to fully face him, wishing she could control her blushing reaction. "Is it noon already?" She looked up at the clock in surprise.

"Almost," he answered. "Are you about ready for lunch?"

"Just give me a minute!" Slightly unsettled, Judi quickly set about saving the files on the computer and rearranging the piles of papers on the desk to be finished that afternoon. She retrieved her purse and knocked on Pastor Taylor's door.

"I'm off for lunch," she announced after cracking the door open wide enough to pop her head inside. He gave his blessing with a smile and went right back to work.

"Where would you like to go for lunch?" Nathan asked when they stepped out of the building.

"There's a great taco place at Levitte's Landing," she said after some thought, smiling inside again at the reminder of the news announcing Jason and Lauren Levitte's twins. Twins! Even Jason's shopping center masterpiece couldn't compare to this development.

"That will be fine," Nathan was saying as he directed her to the golf cart. "Do you mind if we take your *'coupé de* cart'? I'm beginning to get the hang of this island transportation business. I wasn't sure at first, but it kind of grows on you."

Judi gave a light laugh at his pun and handed him the keys. "Be my guest."

By the time they'd ordered lunch and sat on the pier overlooking the boat dock, Judi was ravenous. Nathan hadn't even blinked when she ordered three tacos and must have sensed her mounting hunger for he gave a quick prayer for grace.

Judi took a hasty bite, immediately splitting the hard taco shell in two. Half of the meat and cheese contents spilled into the wrapper. The lettuce and tomatoes soon followed. "Sorry," she apologized with a shrug. "These can be a little messy."

Nathan looked at the disintegrating taco then back at her, seeming to take in her appearance for the first time. His eyes widened slightly when his glance lighted on her frizzy hair.

"Bad hair day," she explained, taking another bite of her food. The open ride to the dockside shopping center hadn't helped.

A short but deep one-syllable hum was his only response. It seemed his mind wasn't on her hair for too long—or his food, for that matter. His burrito remained untouched.

Finally he spoke. "I talked with Laurie this morning, and I think we've found someone who can analyze at least one of those threatening notes you received. I sent her a copy of the one note and three checks that I wrote during that time period."

Judi stopped eating. "You told your sister about me?"

"No," he answered, his gray eyes on her. "Laurie doesn't know the how or why of the project. That's the marvel of trusting someone—they do what you ask without questioning, even though they don't understand why."

Judi felt a blush come to her cheeks again. She wasn't sure he'd meant to zing her, but his words held a bitter sting, and behind those deep, penetrating eyes lingered a hurt she knew she had placed there with her mistrust. He was being more aloof today, and she wondered at his changing mood. For the moment she would choose to ignore the barb, if that's what it was, and move on. "What do you hope to find by having the analysis done?"

"First, it will prove that I'm not the author of the notes," he stated plainly, and when she tried to protest that she had already figured out that fact, he stopped her. "I think you'll feel better if it is in writing. The other reason is to gain information about who *did* write the letters."

"Then what?"

"Then we have to get through dinner tonight without this Tilly woman discovering who I am."

Judi scooped the meat back into the fractured taco with a plastic fork. "That will be hard to do."

"It's imperative she not find out," he insisted. "I have a very important eminent domain bill coming before the House. If anyone, especially the media, finds out about you before the vote, that bill will be dead in the water."

"It sounds really important."

"It is!" His serious, handsome eyes turned to the lake waters, a passion taking over his voice. "People are losing their land to private developers who are abusing the eminent domain laws. This bill would put a stop to that. Unfortunately, the legislative session is closing earlier than usual, and I have to be there to present the bill for a vote on Friday."

"This Friday?" Judi nearly choked on the last bit of lettuce.

He gave a solemn but decisive nod. "It couldn't be helped. The vote was due earlier, and I've already stalled it once. They won't keep the session open just for this bill, and waiting until the fall will seriously jeopardize its passage."

"That means you'll have to leave tomorrow," Judi pronounced, pointing out the obvious. "What am I supposed to do?"

Nathan took a deep breath. "I haven't worked out all the details yet, but I was thinking it might be best if you stay on the island until I send for you—maybe on Saturday. We'll need to retain an attorney, and then I'd like to gather our families together to explain the situation before going to the police. It depends upon a lot of things falling into place at the right time."

"But if I leave on Saturday, when will I get a chance to talk with those close to me here on the island?" she asked, her pulse quickening. "I can't just leave and let them find out about me on the news. What about my job? This will leave the pastor and the church in a terrible spot come Monday morning."

"I'm still working on that part," he countered, turning his face to meet hers squarely. "What's important right now is that Tilly doesn't detonate the bomb before its time."

Distressed, Judi shook her head. "I'll do my best, but you've seen firsthand how tough she can be."

"I know."

She knew Nathan was doing his best to hold the situation together with so many delicate threads of circumstance hanging in the balance, any of which could snap between now and Friday.

A deep sigh erupted within. Nathan should never have come looking for her. It was disastrous for both of them. Yet another passion pulled just as hard at her heart, if not harder, telling her she was glad he did. But what could she do about that now? If only she could just disappear again. She wondered if he'd considered the possibility and decided to pose the question. "How do you know I'll be here when you send for me?"

A flicker of surprise registered in his eyes, but his voice remained even and calm. "You'll be here," he said confidently, "because I believe you've told me the truth and there's no reason for you to run from me now." Suddenly he frowned. "You're no longer frightened of me, are you?"

"No!"

He leaned forward. "Don't you have some level of trust in me?"

"Yes."

"Then why would I think you might not be here when I send for you?" His rhetorical question seemed suspended in the air, a feather sustained only by a slight updraft. Then he added, "And I trust you, Judi!"

The conviction of his words caused two things to happen: It kept Judi's hopes afloat that Nathan might still have some love left for her within his bruised heart, and the words caused her to rethink the risk Nathan was taking for her. He trusted her and this trust caused him to act gallantly on her behalf. Although it would break her heart to lose him again, it was extremely painful to know this allegiance might cost him everything.

"Nathan," she approached softly with her voice, daring to take his hand in hers, "you said that your assistant is the only one who knows that I'm alive and no one here knows about us. Have you considered going back to your own life in Pennsylvania and leaving me to my own here?" She looked down at his strong hands. "It might be easier that way."

"Is that what you want?"

She raised her eyes and saw that his face was very quiet and serious, his gray eyes unfathomable, as if her next words meant a great deal to him. "It's not what I want that matters anymore, Nathan. I can see how important the people of Pennsylvania are to you. They need you! Your family needs you. How can I ask you to chance all of that?" She shook her head despairingly. "Look at what it has already done with this important bill that needs to be passed on Friday. I don't want to be the one to mess this up for you or the people who are depending on you to obtain justice for them."

A slow smile crept across his face in what she could describe as relief. "We promised to do this God's way, right?" She nodded noiselessly and he continued. "Then that option doesn't exist for us."

"So what option does exist when it comes to us?" she asked, anticipating and dreading the answer at the same time. "If we're going to publicly come out with this, where do we stand as a husband and wife?"

He was silent for a long moment, and she feared he might not answer. Then he took a deep breath and met her stare.

"For now," he finally conceded with some hesitancy, "we stand together."

Judi should have known she was pushing too hard, too fast. She could feel it. Nathan was a man of action. Once the dust settled, he'd look at their marriage and determine whether it was worth salvaging or if the woman waiting in the wings was his destiny. She only hoped what was left of their love wouldn't be trampled when all was said and done.

Nathan looked over at Judi in the passenger seat, her wild hair flying in the wind as she pointed to the next road. She directed him up the pine needle-covered driveway to a quaint cabin shaded by a swarm of mature trees.

"This is it," Judi declared when he stopped the cart and turned off the ignition.

Nathan glanced at her again. She'd given him a scare that afternoon with her talk about disappearing. The thought hadn't occurred to him until the moment she spoke it aloud. He supposed the possibility existed, but it seemed, at least on the surface, her thoughts of escape had been born out of a concern for him.

Then again, maybe he was being suckered. Wouldn't that be a kick in the pants? Yet, when she reached for and held his hand within hers, her forceful green eyes looking vulnerable and alive, he had wanted to kiss her—badly. But he didn't! He wanted to drive away her pain. But he couldn't! Their problems had begun well before the threatening letters were ever sent. Certainly, his feelings and even passion for her were still strong. He wouldn't, however, leave his heart exposed and bleeding again until he was sure she was through conning herself and other people. She had to be serious about sticking around to save their marriage.

Suddenly, the sound of a screen door flying open and the twang of the metal spring broke his deliberations, and he saw Tilly racing out to meet them.

"Come on up," she said, beckoning with her hands as she quickly ambled toward them.

By the time he climbed out and was waiting for Judi, Tilly was upon them. First she gave Judi a mammoth hug, totally eclipsing the tall, slender figure. Then Tilly turned on him.

Nathan quickly held out a hand. "Thank you for inviting us for dinner."

Tilly gave a dismissing look at his hand and then barreled forward, wrapping her thick arms around him, pushing the air clear out of his lungs. "We don't stand on ceremony, honey. We're friendly people." A few swats to the back made him cough until she finally drew him back with a wide, toothy smile. He delicately tried to withdraw himself, feeling as if he'd been put through a wringing machine, but Tilly kept a tight grip on his arm. "I'm mighty glad you're here."

Nathan barely had time to catch his breath before she swept them up onto the porch landing and into the cabin.

"Sit yourselves right down and relax," she demanded, scurrying around the small living room. "Dinner is almost ready."

Tilly disappeared around the corner and into what he presumed was the kitchen. The living room opened into the dining room where a beautiful table was set for four.

Judi sat down on the small sofa and Nathan dropped down next to her, adjusting his long legs in an effort to get comfortable.

"Who else do you think is coming for dinner?" he whispered, his mouth within inches of her ear.

Judi turned toward him, but before she could utter a word, the answer appeared out of the kitchen. An older man with pure white hair and the most enormous blue eyes bulging from behind thick glasses came into the room. A frilly and quite unmanly apron was tied around his waist. A somewhat grumpy look was planted on his face.

Although Nathan was sure he'd not seen this person up close before—he would have remembered those eyes—the man did look familiar. Nathan racked his brain to place him.

"Hello, young man," the older man said gruffly, stepping forward. "I see you found the place all right." He nodded a greeting at Judi. "And you brought the missus."

Nathan stood silently to his feet, and he felt Judi scramble up beside him. An uneasy feeling settled over him, but he momentarily shook it off and held out a hand to the old man.

If possible, the elder one's eyes grew wider as he intently looked at Nathan's face and then his outstretched hand. He seemed to be taking inventory, and Nathan wondered if the old man would find him up to snuff.

When the man finally grasped his hand in a viselike grip, he blurted only two words. "Van Edwards!" Then he scrutinized Nathan's face again as if waiting to see if the name meant anything to him.

"Nice to meet you, Mr. Edwards," Nathan returned, wondering if he should recognize this man who didn't seem inclined to let go of his hand. Yet the name meant nothing. "I'm Nathan and I think you know Judi."

Mr. Edwards peered out from his thick glasses, aiming his sharp gaze at the two of them. "I know who you are, Representative Whithorne." He paused only briefly as he zeroed in on Judi. "And I know this is your wife!"

# Chapter 10

Nathan stared at the old man in stunned silence until he felt Judi sway lightly against his arm, the coolness of her skin shocking him back into reality. He turned to see her colorless face and hastily placed a steadying hand around her waist, guiding her back to the couch, where she sank down without an argument. Even Mr. Edwards's eyes grew pensive when he glanced at the pale figure. Nathan straightened and, like a shield, slowly moved into position between Judi and the white-haired man, keeping both within sight.

"Now look what you've gone and done," Tilly scolded as she came into the room and took in the scene. "I told you to wait until we had finished dinner." She brushed past both men, her ample hips swishing loudly against her polyester skirt as she did. Sitting down solidly beside Judi, she threw another reproachful look at the unsmiling elder before turning her attention back to Judi. "There, there," she soothed, firmly patting her hand.

"Well, it had to be said," the old man argued, his lips firmly set.

"And I told you there had to be a logical explanation if you'd just give 'em time." Tilly blew an upward, frustrated breath that lifted the few wisps of gray hair loose on her forehead. "Now look at the poor girl. You've shaken her bad."

Nathan returned his gaze to Judi, who seemed to be thunderstruck, but recovering, and then he turned to Tilly with barely concealed anger in his voice. "What's this all about?"

Tilly in turn looked at Mr. Edwards and then to Nathan. "Now let's everyone stay calm like. It doesn't do a body a bit of good to get all riled up. There's a plain and simple explanation for everything." Her head tipped toward the old man. "Van here saw you eatin' at the Dairy Barn yesterday and recognized you as the lawmaker from Pennsylvania. With a little searchin' on the library computer, we found a news piece about the drownin' of your wife whose picture was lookin' remarkably like our Judi here." She thumped Judi's hand a few more times. "Guess we kinda put two and two together."

Nathan remembered the man now. He was the one cleaning tables at the restaurant where Judi and he had eaten the day before. Knowing this made him even more confused. Why should an old man playing busboy in his retirement years recognize a state representative from another state when 80 percent of his own people in Pennsylvania didn't even know the name or face of their own representative, let alone someone not in their district? Yet this man from Ohio knew who he was.

"Are you denying that this woman is your wife?" Edwards challenged, ignoring the warning look Tilly gave him.

Nathan narrowed his eyes. "I'm not confirming or denying anything until I find out what your interest is in this matter. Tilly invited us to dinner tonight, and yet it seems more like an ambush party with accusations for the main course, apparently meant to cook our goose instead of the pot roast. I want to know why!"

"I invited you to dinner—that's what I planned and that's what you'll get," Tilly quickly interjected, shaking her head in frustration. "I love Judi like one of my own. It's just that being the observant body that I am, I noticed a slight tan mark where a weddin' ring used to be on Judi's finger when she first came to the island. I figured she'd be talkin' about it one day when the time was right." Her keen eyes gave Nathan a knowing look. "But when you came waltzin' in yesterday with her, I figured you must be the ex. Thought maybe I could help the two of you, that's all." Unperturbed, she casually took a balled-up facial tissue from her apron pocket and loudly blew her nose into it. "Findin' out about this other nonsense didn't happen until today."

"When Mr. Edwards supposedly recognized me, the two of you decided to do some investigating, is that it?" Nathan asked bitterly, not liking the story one bit.

"Tilly thinks there must be a mighty good reason why you've misled people to believe Judi's dead when she's been living right here on the island." Mr. Edwards seemed bent on being unpleasant. "Now I'm not so easy to fool."

"Please stop!" Judi stirred restlessly to the edge of the seat, seeming to rally at last. "Nathan had nothing to do with this, Mr. Edwards. This whole thing is my fault."

"Don't say any more, Judi," Nathan immediately warned, holding up a hand to silence her.

"Nathan," Tilly pleaded, hoisting herself up with effort from the couch. "Listen to what Van has to say. If you're in trouble he can help. I'm a pretty good judge of character, if I have to say so myself, and I've seen your record at the statehouse. You're a good man."

"That still doesn't tell why the two of you are so interested," Nathan reasoned, a sudden blaze in his eyes. He didn't care for Edwards's highhandedness any more than he liked Tilly's nosiness.

"First of all, young man," Mr. Edwards retorted, pointing a bent finger his way, "Judi is our church secretary. If she's not who she says she is, then I want to know the why and how of it. I don't take lightly to our church people being duped. As a church elder who has served more years on the board than you've been breathing, I have a right to know the extent of this pretense." The man squinted his eyes. "No funny stuff, either. I'm warning you to be careful with your words, and you'd better tell the truth the first time around. I won't waste any time getting Officer Newkirk over here. That boy's right smart. He'll sort this whole thing out lickety-split."

"Please, Mr. Edwards," Judi implored, scooting closer to the edge of her seat. "It's not Nathan you want, it's me."

Nathan shushed her, not so gently this time. "Let me handle this."

He needed time to think. He'd asked God to provide a path to follow and the wisdom to guide him to the right people. Then why did he suddenly feel like he was on a challenging downhill slalom course without the benefit of skis? It wasn't like there was a fork in the road where he had a choice of paths. There was only one steep and icy path, taking this trust thing with God to an entirely different level of technical difficulty—perhaps beyond his capabilities of faith. What could God have possibly been thinking to send him a grumpy old man who wore women's lacy aprons and an island busybody whose loyalties, and possibly brains, seemed scattered?

"Well," the old man groused, "what'll it be?"

Frustrated, Nathan frowned. What choice did he have? It irked him to be shoved into a cage like a cornered dog.

"It's all right, Nathan," Judi insisted with resignation. Grabbing his arm, she stood to her feet. "We have no other choice but to confide in them. If Larry comes, he might be understanding of the situation, but he would be bound by duty to take action." She lowered her voice to a hush and lifted her face close to his. "And I know Mr. Edwards. He won't back down for anything. We can only hope to pacify him long enough so you can leave tomorrow to complete what you need to do."

"You two can stop the whispering!" Edwards's blue eyes darted accusingly between the two.

"Simmer down, all of you!" Tilly shook her head vehemently. "I've about had my fill of this! Now, Van, you get off your high horse for a minute and let these young folks decide what they want to do." She turned to Nathan and Judi. "And the two of you can take a few minutes to talk over this thing while I get the food situated. I promised you a dinner and heads are gonna roll if this perfectly good roast goes to ruin."

Mr. Edwards harrumphed but backed off and strode irritably back into the kitchen, paying testament to the equality of stubbornness he and Tilly possessed.

"That's better." Tilly seemed appeased for the moment. "Nathan, you take our Judi here and get comfortable at the table. Don't let the old coot scare you off." Her tone suddenly turned soft. "He's just a big ol' teddy bear on the inside."

Nathan could hardly believe the audacity and outright perjury of her words. Was the woman blind? Her "teddy bear" rivaled the great black bears roaming the countryside of his home state, and these bears were anything but cuddly. He was tempted to enlighten her about this fact, but instead turned toward the table, doing as he was told, still smoldering inside over the turn of events. He didn't want to eat, and he was sure Judi's appetite was spoiled, as well. He was sure, however, that Tilly's threat about heads rolling wasn't an idle warning if the food went to waste.

"What do you think the old-timer is up to?" he asked Judi as soon as they were alone.

"Just what he said," Judi answered matter-of-factly. "He's no lightweight and a real fighter. You should see him during the church business meetings. Only a few brave ones dare to take him on." She paused in thought. "There's also something strange about him."

"Other than the fact he's wearing a lacy apron?" Nathan couldn't help asking.

This brought a small smile to her full lips. "Other than that," she answered. "I don't know how to make sense of it, but a con artist can usually spot another con artist. You know what I mean?"

"Possibly," Nathan answered hesitantly. "Are you saying this Edwards guy is a con man?"

"Rumor on the island says that he has to work at the Dairy Barn to make ends meet. I don't buy it!"

"In what way?"

"It's hard to put into words, but things seem to happen when Mr. Edwards becomes involved."

"Things happen? Like what?"

"Take the new camp for example," Judi began. "Old man Edwards fought hard against the development of this camp for the longest time. The church was even having second thoughts since the camp committee couldn't secure the land—at least not until Mr. Edwards finally agreed the Thunder Bay Landmark might not be such a bad site for a Christian camp after all." She flung her hands out. "Then all of a sudden, the land is donated and money starts pouring in—and I don't mean hundreds—I mean thousands."

"You think he's a rich entrepreneur who tries to pass himself off as a helpless old man?"

"Maybe," she conceded.

"What about Tilly?"

Judi visibly relaxed and gave a fond smile. "She's creative and devious, but genuine. No doubt she thought her dinner tonight was going to be a matchmaking experience. She must be extremely disappointed." She gave a light chuckle. "You wouldn't believe how good she is in the romance territory—it's almost eerie. With Tilly on your side, you can't go wrong."

"She seems nosy to me."

"You won't think that once you get to know her," Judi argued amicably. "There's not a person on this island who doesn't love her."

Nathan frowned, trying to make sense of the information. "I still don't like it!"

"Neither do I, but what choice do we have?"

Nathan signaled her to be silent with a squeeze of his hand on hers when he heard movement from behind. Tilly bustled into the room carrying a platter overflowing with carved roast beef, followed by Van Edwards juggling steaming bowls of mashed potatoes and green beans.

"Go ahead and get your drinks," Tilly directed to Nathan and Judi, pointing beyond the head of the table. "There's soda, iced tea, and a pitcher of ice water on the sideboard over there."

The older couple disappeared again into the kitchen. Judi looked tentatively at Nathan before rising from her seat.

"Iced tea for me," Judi said. "The caffeine might come in handy for what's ahead. What about you?"

Nathan puckered his brow. "Make it the same." It would take more than caffeine to make this evening bearable or palatable.

In a matter of minutes, everyone seated themselves around the table Tilly had completely loaded with food. Mr. Edwards gave a short, stiff prayer. When he finished, a tomblike silence engulfed the room. The quiet made Tilly scowl.

"Go on, now," she demanded. "Dig in before it gets cold. No sense in sulkin' when everything's gonna be all right."

Ever so slowly, the clinking of serving ware and dishes being passed filled the void, but tension remained high throughout the meal. The delicious down-home food seemed to be squandered on such a dour group, and Nathan knew this upset the matronly woman. Soon the meal drew to a close, and Mr. Edwards seemed ripe to start their previous discussion by suggesting the group retreat to the living room.

"Which one of you is going to tell me what's going on?" the old man asked when the four assembled, flopping himself down into the overstuffed chair, linking his fingers together across his slightly plump belly.

Nathan was about to speak when Judi put a restraining hand on his arm. "I'm responsible for this mess. Let me tell it." She looked sadly at the couple. "All I ask is for you to keep an open mind and to be reasonable at any requests Nathan might make of you."

"I'll keep an open mind," Mr. Edwards retorted, "but that's all I'm promising."

Judi fidgeted, bouncing one foot nervously. In a sense, she should be glad to let loose her haunting past. Maybe Mr. Edwards would be able to help—or not. She didn't have a handle on the man yet. He was too much of an enigma.

She began her story slowly, gaining speed and strength as she continued, relating the threatening notes and sparing nothing of her former life that gave the menacing letters their power. Nathan sat stiffly beside her on the couch, brooding and unhappy. Occasionally, they exchanged glances, and he would give a slight reassuring nod of his head, bestowing on her the much-desired encouragement she needed to continue.

"So, as you can see," Judi concluded, "Nathan didn't know anything about my faked death until he arrived on the island to see for himself that I was alive and well." She threw a penitent glance at Nathan. "I falsely believed he was the culprit. I was wrong! Because of this, he's spent the last two years going through the horrific pain of losing a spouse and ironically came to personally know Christ through the experience. Now we're just trying to find our way by doing what God would have us do." She drew her chin up as she looked at the old man. "I know the trouble I face is tremendous, but Nathan is innocent and shouldn't be made to bear the brunt of my problems."

A silence covered the room, and she heard Nathan take a tired breath.

"What do you say about that, young man?" Mr. Edwards's large blue eyes nailed Nathan like an arrow, his docile tone indecipherable.

Nathan shot back a look under frowning brows. "I say she's been quite patient, more so than I would have been, and bared her soul truthfully to the two of you." His gaze hardened. "Now I would like to know your intentions."

The old man's lips thinned. "I already know she's been truthful. I'm asking what your position is on what she said about your role as it relates to her problems."

"What are you getting at?" Nathan asked.

Judi drew a frustrated breath. Why couldn't Mr. Edwards understand? "I've already told you Nathan didn't know anything about the letters or my faked death. He's innocent!"

Nathan shook his head. "I don't think that's what he's talking about."

"You're right, young man," Mr. Edwards sternly agreed. "It's not my intentions but yours that concern me. You are still her husband. What do you plan to do about that?"

Judi could tell Nathan was growing weary and angry at this line of questioning. What was Mr. Edwards up to? From his tone, it was difficult to know if he was seeking to help or harm. Tilly seemed to be taking everything in, processing the information like a court reporter. All she needed was a stenotype machine.

"Let me tell you something," Nathan said, his voice dropping dangerously low, "Judi is still my wife, and I'm going to do everything in my power to help her—including walking all over you if need be. She's played fair with the two of you even though you've drawn her here possibly under false pretenses, bullied, threatened, and frightened her—much like the person who wrote those menacing notes." He leaned forward on the seat, taking a stance similar to those Judi recalled him using in the courtroom when he wanted to intimidate. "If you want to threaten her with the law, then you'll have to go through me first."

A brief and puzzling smile lit on the old man's lips. "Don't go spitting fire like a sea dragon," the old man strangely responded. "You'll wear yourself out. If you plan to fight this thing sensibly, you'll need to conserve your strength."

"What are you saying?" Nathan demanded.

Tilly finally came to life with a knowing grin. "He's saying you're gonna get some help."

Nathan looked unsure, but Judi knew Tilly was right. Help had arrived!

# Chapter 11

Nathan stared at the ceiling, drawing his arms up then under the satin-covered feather pillow. What a strange and bizarre day. It might take him weeks, if not months, to straighten out what had gone on at Tilly Storm's house. How Mr. Edwards went from a grumpy old codger to a multi-tasking thinking machine couldn't be explained. Before Nathan had known it, the man was writing down the names and numbers of people he wanted Nathan to contact—the last being an extremely well-known and definitely expensive criminal lawyer.

"Don't worry about the cost," the old man had told them. Don't worry about the cost? Nathan could only dream of making in a lifetime what this fellow lawyer probably grossed on just one client. How could he not think about the cost?

The whole thing was off the wall, and he knew Judi's observations had been right. Mr. Edwards was more than he made himself out to be—more than a busboy at the Dairy Barn and more than a church elder in a small, obscure church on Bay Island. He knew too many important people, including congressmen and federal agents. Why Mr. Edwards should be living incognito among the islanders was a question worthy of asking. Why play out his golden years wiping down tables and hauling leaky, soda-filled trash bags to the restaurant Dumpster? It just didn't make sense. Surely, if the man was a wealthy philanthropist or even some type of retired government agent, why reside in an everyone-knows-everybody's-business place like Bay Island?

The old man was full of advice, as well. Nathan was to return as planned to Pennsylvania in the morning and immediately contact the criminal attorney who would be awaiting his call. He was to say nothing of Judi or his trip to Bay Island to anyone else as he prepared to present his eminent domain bill to the house floor. Nathan would then make a return round-trip to the island the following Monday to collect Judi for an appointment with the attorney in Harrisburg. In the meantime, Mr. Edwards would take care of the writing analysis, which he insisted could not be performed correctly unless an FBI expert executed the examination. Nathan tried to explain he was already in contact with a detective who was a pioneer in the field. This news didn't even faze the man.

The white-haired man just went on looking again at the copy of the threatening letter Nathan carried with him, the note so close to the man's thick glasses Nathan wondered how he could read it. When Mr. Edwards asked rhetorically whether Nathan had left his fingerprints on the notes when he copied them, he and Judi merely blushed in reply.

Mr. Edwards seemed so sure about what to do. Nathan wasn't so convinced, his head still swimming with the possibilities and complications of the new plan.

Somehow, through all of the intricate scheduling, he would have to fend off questions from his family, friends—and Lindsey. That could prove to be difficult.

Judi, however, had quickly embraced the old man's plan and seemed encouraged with the news that he believed her case was a winnable one. Most of all, the couple hadn't openly judged her poor choices and insisted she was still a valuable and much-wanted resident of the island and the congregation at their little redbrick church.

The sanguine expression on Judi's face said it all. Knowing she was still loved and accepted by those on the island was more important to her than the legal outcome of her dilemma. Yet a thick cloud of sadness exuded from her features when their eyes met. He knew she was thinking about what was at stake—including their husband and wife relationship.

Was this relationship salvageable? Could their marriage withstand the strain? Could he really trust Judi knowing what he did about her propensity toward secrecy and mistrust? God could change people. He knew this firsthand. Yet a person had to be willing to hand their life over to Christ for this transformation to happen. Judi claimed to have totally given her life to God—and Nathan believed her. But what he really wanted to know was if she was absolutely committed to giving up her previous methods of problem solving to focus on God's plan—not her own.

Another consideration needled him. What if Judi's con game had also included her marriage to him? She'd admitted her former insatiable need to achieve a lifestyle where she wouldn't have to scratch and claw to be like everyone else. Did that include marrying a man who could financially acquire such a position on this ladder of success? Maybe love never entered the picture where she was concerned. If so, would she admit to such treachery and willingly release him from a loveless marriage? The thought made his chest tighten. The fact was, he didn't want to be released. He still loved her in spite of everything. The realization didn't give him any satisfaction; it made him feel weak and foolish. How could any self-respecting man settle for anything less than a spouse who could fully return his love?

At best, even if she truly loved him, several obstacles stood ready and willing to drown them. Neither of their families seemed the least bit flexible concerning their marriage—not three years ago, and he could safely assume the new turn of events would exacerbate the tension. Judi would wither in such an environment after experiencing the love and acceptance she knew on the island.

Would these factors doom them to become another in the long line of couples joining the dismal ranks of the divorced?

*I'm lying on this bed with a lot of questions and few answers. God, I'm in need of serious counsel where Judi is concerned. I'll live in a loveless marriage if that's what You want, but it's not what I want. Yet living without her seems just as unbearable. It's not how You planned it, I'm sure!*

*I know her honor should have been defended when my family often treated her with disrespect. I'll make that right! I'm pleading with You to bring back the love I thought Judi had for me. If this is not to be, then please take away the desire that's gnawing at me. I don't think I could stand the pain of losing her again. Give me the perseverance to see this thing through. Your honor is at stake, too, and I never want it to be said that I've dishonored You in any way. Help me to trust You. I can't do this alone.*

He turned to glance at the bedside clock. Time was quickly gaining on midnight and he knew sleep would not come easily. He checked the alarm setting one more time. A confirming red dot glowed back at him. He couldn't afford to miss the morning plane, not when so much depended on timing—and a stellar performance on the house floor.

As Judi stood in front of her bedroom mirror adjusting the collar of her blouse, she was only too conscious of the shadows and strained lines etched around her eyes. Even her mouth looked strained and tight. She smiled experimentally, but her reflection looked stiff and artificial. Tilly wouldn't be happy with her peaked appearance, either, when she came by the church office to take Judi to lunch. She was sure of that.

There was a reason for the droopy appearance. Despondency! Yes, that's what it was. Nathan's plane would be halfway to Harrisburg by now and already her heart felt empty without him. He had called earlier to say his transport had arrived on time and to see if she was holding up after their taxing evening at Tilly's. She was holding up well, actually, mostly because she had felt so protected by Nathan during Mr. Edwards's inquisition and because his actions almost made her believe there was some spark left of their love.

Over the phone, Nathan's voice resonated with husbandly concern, and when he paused for several seconds, she was so sure he had to be sensing the growing fire within her coming through the airwaves that he was on the verge of pouring out the words she desired to hear. She waited, willing for any expression of love to come.

The words never came.

Instead, he told her to take care while he was gone and that he would call her sometime the next day after finishing with the house session.

What had she really expected, anyway? A fairy-tale ending to a mixed-up Cinderella turned modern-day runaway bride story? Tilly and Mr. Edwards assured her the church would continue to love and welcome her. Those words meant more than their weight in gold. Yet she wanted Nathan's love and acceptance even more. She was afraid she might not gain either.

Deciding not to morbidly dwell on the unforeseeable, she quickly finished dressing. Breakfast consisted of nothing more than a few gulps of orange juice and one very burnt piece of toast on her way out the door.

The morning went quickly as she worked on the lengthy quarterly report. She was thankful when Tilly turned out to be the only visitor to the church office. Tilly, however, was wired, evidently happy to be put in action again, and immediately tried to usher Judi out the door.

"You're lookin' a mite peaked today," observed Tilly, situating her purse over her forearm as they walked into the parking lot. Judi gave her a mocking I-knew-you'd-say-that smile, which the woman chose to ignore. "The burden of this bad business can't be good on a body."

Judi couldn't have agreed more. "I'm just worried about Nathan, that's all."

"God'll take care of him. Ain't no use to carry on when you can't do anything but pray about it." Tilly flopped herself into the driver's seat of her beat-up two-seater cart. "Thought we might ride over to Bell's Market for a bite to eat. They're havin' a mighty good Thursday special on their fried bologna sandwiches in the deli today."

"Who can resist fried bologna?" Judi remarked with a laugh, not daring to mention the island delicacy was not on Tilly's heart-smart diet. She felt her spirits lift a little. Tilly must have known how difficult the day would be for Judi and offered—no, demanded—they have lunch.

When they'd arrived at the market and ordered the special, Tilly hustled them outside to the backless, sun-drenched blue bench positioned against the storefront window.

"We can situate ourselves right here on the liar's bench," Tilly chuckled, letting her purse drop onto the sidewalk and giving it a swift kick under the wooden seat with her bone-colored orthotic shoes. "Hoggin' up the bench should keep the community gossipin' down for a spell. Too much lollygagging and jawin' going on here, anyway."

Judi smiled as she sat down, knowing that Tilly had spent more than her fair share of time *jawin'* on this very same bench with her own lady friends. The store was a popular hangout for the older crowd in the warm months. Taking a deep breath of the island air, Judi let her glance skip along the tree-lined street. How she loved this island with its small, oddball shops and family-owned businesses. The colorful characters inhabiting the island, nosy as they might be, could be counted on in a pinch. They really cared about people—took care of their own. She would hate to lose this priceless companionship and solidarity that had become so ingrained in her life.

Yet she knew her life was about to drastically change. The possibility of prison even loomed on the horizon. Nathan would leave her for sure if that happened. Then she would be totally, irrevocably alone.

Tilly gave Judi's hand a maternal pat, evidently sensing her poignant mood. "Everything's gonna be all right, you hear? Van will help get matters under way right quick. He's given Nathan a heap of sound advice to get the two of you young'uns through this briar patch."

Judi remained silent for a moment and then turned to face the matronly woman. "Just who is Van Edwards?"

Tilly looked momentarily flustered. "Whatever do you mean? You know who he is!"

"I know who he *appears* to be," Judi answered. "But there's more to him than meets the eye, isn't there?"

The question seemed to befuddle the woman further. "That's just a bunch of foolishness now. I really don't know why such a notion should enter your head."

"Really?"

"Really!"

"He does seem sweet on you," Judi went on, deciding to try another tactic, and was pleasantly surprised to see the shocked expression lighting up Tilly's face. Judi laughed. "You're not the only observant body on the island."

Tilly smoothed her tightly pulled-back hair with a busy hand. "That's gibberish!"

"Oh, come on," Judi said with a laugh. "The man's not left your side since last summer when you had the heart attack. You're like Frick and Frack together, bread and butter, Lucy and Desi—"

"Now stop all this foolishness," demanded Tilly, playfully swatting at Judi. "Seems to me this here liar's bench is havin' a terrible effect on you. And I'd be much obliged if you'd stop speculatin' on such matters."

Judi was finding great enjoyment in turning the tables on Tilly but decided to have mercy on the woman. "I'll quit for now. It just seems proper for the one who's always playing Cupid to occasionally be the recipient."

"That's for the young folk," Tilly asserted with a firm nod.

The thought caused Judi to linger over the words for a moment. "Sometimes it doesn't work for the young folks, either."

Tilly must have heard the slight catch in Judi's voice. Her face softened. "Nathan will do right by you."

*But I haven't done right by him*, Judi's soul accused right back. It was true! How could she argue with this self-judgment? Nathan always chose the high road, the straight and narrow—the path to help the greatest amount of people.

He had the right character to take on the world. Even now, she could recall a time when he would have done anything for her.

"Do you know what caught my attention the first time I met Nathan?" Judi asked contemplatively, her mind actively going back in time.

"What was that, girl?" Tilly was at full attention, her eyes bright with curiosity.

"I had come to interview for a job as a legal aide in the law firm where he worked, an interview he'd obviously been relegated to perform for the first time." A wry smile came across her lips. "He was so handsome—and nervous. He wouldn't crack a smile for anything throughout the entire meeting, cross-examining me like a witness on the stand instead of a potential employee. Then he kept fidgeting with his papers and constantly writing things down on a clipboard. I could hardly take my eyes off of him with that cute cleft in his chin. I'm sure it made him tenser, but I didn't care. Not when I knew right then and there that he was someone I had to know everything about, someone I'd been waiting for."

Judi shifted on the bench and laughed as she continued. "Finally, when we'd finished, he asked if I would fax over my references. I decided it was time for the poor man to loosen up a little. You should have seen the expression on his face when I told him I'd gladly fax over the original if he would send it right back since it was my only copy."

Drawing her eyebrows together in bewilderment, it only took a moment for understanding to light Tilly's eyes. "Did you finally get the smile you'd been waiting for?"

Judi nodded, feeling the prick of tears dangerously close to the surface at the endearing memory. "He looked at me with this stunned expression at first and then, like a closed flower opening for the first time, he just let out this huge, uninhibited laugh. He didn't stop for the longest time, as if his happiness had been trapped inside for too long. It was hard not be caught up in the contagiousness of the moment. I was laughing right along with him." Staring at her hands, she clasped them tightly together. "It was then he told me he'd do anything for me—since I seemed to be the only one who could not only make him laugh, but also knew so much about operating office equipment. He hired me on the spot—without the references."

"That's a sweet story, Judi."

"And now he's still doing everything he can for me."

"That's what love does for you."

"Love?" Judi could feel her heart shrink at the word. "He's doing what's right because he's respectable. I had hoped, but I think the love is gone." She let a sigh build and slowly let it loose. "Our love has been steadily siphoned away by my distrust and deceit. I think it's too late."

"That's a bunch of hogwash, girl," Tilly replied, her voice firm.

"No," Judi argued, shaking her head despondently. "You weren't there. You didn't see the look in his eyes when I accused him of sending those vile letters and then told him about my past. The whole thing disgusted him."

"He said that?" Tilly demanded.

"He didn't have to."

"Seems to me you're buying a peck of trouble without even knowin' what's in the basket." Tilly wagged a finger at her. "Don't go assumin' anything. You listen to ol' Tilly. I know what I'm sayin'." Her intent eyes snapped forcefully. "I'm tellin' you that boy loves you—but he's scared. You're gonna have to fight, to let him know how much you still cherish and trust him. No man likes to be made a fool of. He just wants to be loved and respected."

"I do love and respect him!"

"Then you gotta show him!"

"I don't know how," Judi lamented. "There's so little time."

"Then it's a good thing you got ol' Tilly around to give you some pointers," the older woman said with a wide, toothy smile. "Anything worth anything in this ol' world is worth fightin' for."

Judi wanted to believe. Could she fight and win his love back? Another thought caused her to halt briefly. If she won the prize of his love, would she lose her precious Bay Island in the exchange? Only God knew. One thing she did know: As much as she loved her newfound life on the island, her heart could never be complete without Nathan.

She had to fight—and win.

The small aircraft bumped leisurely to a stop along the short island airstrip, and Nathan closed his eyes, still thanking God for allowing him the chance to complete the house session and see his dream bill passed by a wide margin. Pieces were falling nicely into place, including his call to the attorney. Mr. Edwards had certainly pulled enough strings to set him wondering again about the old man's true identity.

He was sure Judi would be relieved to know such a competent attorney was working on her behalf. They would fly back tomorrow, Tuesday, to Harrisburg and meet the attorney face-to-face. Nathan hoped Mr. Edwards had been able to secure the handwriting analysis he'd promised in time for the meeting.

The weekend had been difficult. He had managed to dodge his family—but not Lindsey. They'd had a terrible quarrel, with Lindsey accusing him of seeing another woman. Little did she know! Nathan's evasiveness only made it worse, yet he knew there was too much at stake to risk telling her the truth. It hurt to know what he was doing to her. He had no other choice.

Thomas, his legislative aide, had proved himself invaluable, seeing to every little detail at the statehouse. He'd offered his help, gone about his business, and kept Nathan's matters to himself. What more could Nathan ask for?

Nathan unclipped his lap belt and followed the pilot as he opened the door. Standing in the arch, he saw Judi waiting patiently by the small airport tower in her golf cart. She waved her arm in greeting. He waved back and stepped off the plane.

They had talked twice on the phone while he was away. She seemed different somehow, more confident perhaps, or just calmer knowing the statehouse session had gone well and the attorney was already working on her case. He, on the other hand, had become more restless. He shouldn't have given in to the urge to go through Judi's belongings at their house, or worse yet, spent hours intently going through their picture albums.

The deep emotions and pain he felt were inexplicable. It was like plodding through their courtship and marriage, again leading up to the big climax where she died—where the pictures suddenly stopped. The emotions tore through him once more, like watching a movie over and over, knowing the ending, yet the suspense leading to the conclusion still gripping terribly at the heart every time.

The occasion gave him time to reflect on their past as a couple. Yes, Judi had deceived him and maligned his integrity. At the same time, he'd dismissed her concerns and legitimate needs over his desire to achieve a lifelong goal of serving the people of Pennsylvania. Noble as his gesture might have been, he'd failed as a husband. He could see that now. How he had been so blind while taking the journey was still a mystery. A man of detail should never have missed the obvious signs of his own shortcomings.

"How was your flight?" Judi greeted when he finally reached the end of the tarmac. Her strawberry-red hair flipped lightly in the afternoon breeze and her rosy cheeks seemed kissed by sun. She looked relaxed behind the wheel.

He gave her a grin. "It was a beautiful day for flying," he answered, suddenly glad to be back on the island. "Have you been doing okay?"

"Much better now that you're back," she answered with a welcoming smile, her green eyes meeting his. "I'm glad you're here!"

He frowned, tossing his bag into the back of the cart. "Why? Is something wrong?"

"No," she said with a delicate shrug. "I just missed you, that's all."

Something in her eyes sent a spark along his chest and triggered his pulse to racing. The look reminded him so much of the photos he'd just seen when they'd first married, reviving yet another forgotten ember.

"Is that so hard to believe?" she went on as he slid into the passenger seat.

He turned easily toward her, resting his elbow on the seat between them. His gaze fell on her face and then her lips. Her slight smile was openly disarming.

"You're sure everything is all right?" he asked again, marveling at her composure. This was not the same woman he had left on the island.

Slowly, she leaned close. "I'll prove it," came her whispery-light response. One soft hand cupped the side of his face as she gently pressed her lips to his.

Her kiss momentarily stunned him, but when she began to withdraw, her green eyes openly questioning his reaction to her gesture, his arms quickly pulled her forward again, claiming her mouth with his. The feel of her mouth and breath caused an explosion of familiar longing within him, taking him back to the happier times they had enjoyed early in their marriage. Feeling her eager response filled him with joy—and fear—that she was once again, at that moment, completely his.

Slowly, he drew her back and they stared at each other. He searched her face for recognition or acknowledgment of what they had just shared. What he saw was a mirror of his own uncertainty mixed with a strong longing and desire to be one again.

Judi traced his chin with her finger and he turned to see if anyone was watching. It was ludicrous to be sitting in a golf cart in the middle of an airport kissing like passionate lovers. The islanders would think they were kissing cousins. Thankfully, there were only two lonely bystanders wandering around the small airport tower. He didn't know where his pilot had gone.

Judi dropped her hand. "Are you angry?" she asked, her voice husky and low.

He drew his gaze back to her. "No."

"You're embarrassed, then?" It was her turn to peruse the tower and airfield.

"Frankly," Nathan said, scratching at the back of his neck, his eyes roaming back with a will of their own to her lips again, "I'm not sure what I am." The intensity of his emotions scared him more than anything he'd encountered in the past week.

"Then I have to tell you something."

Nathan's heart sank. A bomb was going to land, he was sure of it. "What do you need to tell me?" he asked, bracing for the worst.

"I love you, Nathan Whithorne!"

# Chapter 12

Judi refused to turn her gaze away as she tried to capture the various emotions stirring across Nathan's face. She had just bared her soul, open and unprotected, laying everything she had on the line with three little words. It was a risky business. He had just returned from home, and although it pained her to think about it, Nathan had most certainly spent some time with the woman he'd previously pledged to marry—another who claimed to love him. Which way would Nathan eventually turn? Was his heart torn between the two women? Right now, she was his wife and decidedly had the edge, but eventually one would be the winner and the other the loser. Surely the love they had shared in the past counted for something and the way he'd just kissed her revealed he wasn't totally devoid of feelings for her.

"Well," she finally asked in frustration, watching him rub the back of his neck in contemplation, "aren't you going to say something?"

His hand dropped and he lifted one eyebrow. "Wow!"

"Wow?" Judi frowned. Was that all the man could say? Kissing Nathan had produced more than a *wow* for her—much more. It had awakened every fiber of her consciousness to the love she knew was ready to let loose. It had been suppressed and held dormant for so long, it could no longer be held against its will. If Nathan rejected her—if God chose this to be—she would resign herself to live with this one-sided love, a strong bond she would never fully realize.

But she hadn't lost the battle yet. The fight had just begun, and she didn't plan to give up easily. With determination, Judi started the ignition.

Nathan immediately grasped her hand, his features impossible to interpret. "Now you're angry."

"No," she answered, turning back toward him, feeling the warmth of his hand. "There's no anger. Matter of fact, I can't tell you how good it is to have you back on the island." She returned his stare, captivated by the intensity of his exquisite gray eyes. "But we do have to get back to the business at hand. Mr. Edwards received the handwriting analysis this morning and wanted me to bring you to Tilly's as soon as you arrived."

His eyes immediately narrowed in interest. "Did he say anything about the results?"

"No," she said with a shake of her head. "He just seemed anxious for me to get you there."

"Then I suppose we should do as he asked." Nathan dropped his grip on her hand and settled back into the seat, his eyes momentarily closed.

Judi turned the cart around and started down the long drive next to the runway. She gave him a quick sideways glance. "I turned in my resignation today."

His eyes snapped open, and he seemed to study her a moment before speaking. "Are you sure that was wise?"

"What else could I do?" she asked, stopping at the end of the road and then turning right. "We'll be leaving in the morning to see the attorney, and I can't leave the church in a bind if I'm not able to come back." She slowed down to make another turn. "I've already secured a temporary replacement for the next two weeks. After that—I guess they'll have to hire someone."

Nathan didn't comment but quietly kept his gaze on the road ahead while looking deep in thought. Judi didn't want to make too much of his comment about her resignation, but she had to wonder at the surprise, or perhaps it was disappointment, in his voice. Surely he knew for her to remain on the island two things would have to happen—exoneration from all criminal charges and the church's willingness to let her continue in their employ. Did Nathan believe she was going to come out on top of this legal tangle? Was he already planning for her possible return to the island—alone? She didn't hold much hope of him leaving his beloved Pennsylvania. A terrible thought struck. Maybe he had already made his choice. That might explain his mixed reaction to her kiss and verbal declaration of love.

Judi stopped the cart to let a laughing group of tourists cross at the next intersection, instinctively waving back at their friendly gestures. She smiled. Like her, the strangers seemed to be under the island's spell, and she felt a responsive bond with the affable visitors. The island was her sanctuary, a calming hideaway from the rest of the world.

"Is the island always this busy during the weekdays?" Nathan asked as they moved forward again.

Judi turned and gave him a brief look. "From Memorial Day until Labor Day. The weekends stay full until the end of October."

Nathan nodded and fell silent again until they reached Tilly's cabin. When Judi cut the ignition and slipped off her seat belt, he gripped her arm lightly, and she looked at him expectantly.

"Mr. Edwards has secured one of the best lawyers money can buy," Nathan remarked, looking quite serious. "But I think we should still be careful around the man until we know more about his real interest. He could be a humanitarian who goes about helping people in need, or he could be something more. As a public representative, I need to be careful."

"You think he might be a political saboteur?" she asked, trying to picture the opinionated old man working for one of Nathan's opponents. The vision was too ridiculous for words. Although their approaches were vastly different, Mr. Edwards and Nathan held a likeness when it came to being a straight arrow. No, the two of them were working on the same side. "I don't believe you have anything to worry about, Nathan; but I'll be careful all the same."

Nathan nodded and led them onto the porch deck where he rapped on the door. Tilly came to greet them looking unusually solemn, and Judi immediately felt on the alert. Nathan's taut expression let her know he'd sensed the change, too.

"Come on in, you two," Tilly said, ushering them inside.

Mr. Edwards stood stiffly behind the living room chair. "Have a seat," he directed when the two entered the room.

"Think I'll stand, if you don't mind," Nathan returned, and Judi tensed when he passed on the niceties. "You have the results of the analysis?"

The old man nodded grimly. "It found a credible match."

The room turned stone cold and silent. Judi felt her heart slam against her ribs, pounding like a hammer. It couldn't be true!

"That's impossible," Judi blurted, breaking the unnerving silence. She shook her head. "I don't care what the test says; it must be wrong. Nathan did not write those letters."

"I didn't say it matched with him," the old man asserted, staring at Judi with his magnified blue eyes. "The test cleared Representative Whithorne."

Nathan looked as stunned and confused as she felt. "I don't understand."

Mr. Edwards and Tilly didn't speak right away, but both continued to look at Judi with a mixture of pity, uneasiness, and regret.

"What?" Judi demanded. Slowly it all registered in her tired brain. "You think I wrote the notes?" Disbelief sent shock waves through her numb body. "That's crazy!"

Immediately Nathan sent her a cautionary glance and slowly turned to the old man. "Exactly what did the test reveal? You weren't given a sample of Judi's handwriting."

"Will the two of you stop conjecturing and just sit down so I can tell you what the test did say?" Mr. Edwards barked, firmly sitting down in the chair, obviously expecting everyone else to follow suit.

Tilly quickly swished over and lowered herself into the chair beside Mr. Edwards. Judi heard Nathan sigh and felt his hand on her back as he led her to the couch where he indicated for her to sit. He dropped down beside her without a sound.

"Please continue." There was palpable constraint in Nathan's voice.

"That's better," the old man responded. "Let's get something straight. The writing didn't match Nathan, and as he just mentioned, we didn't have a sample for Judi. It was neither of you."

"Then who?" Judi murmured, totally mystified.

"It was the person who endorsed one of the checks Mr. Whithorne gave me to analyze," answered the white-haired man, his piercing eyes zeroing in on Judi. "It was a man by the name of Stanley Porter!"

"There's no way!" Judi felt unwell. A sick feeling at the pit of her stomach burned like fire, and her stricken lungs needed air. "My father?"

"It just doesn't make sense," Judi said, wiping her nose again. In her shock she hadn't cried at Tilly's place last night, but she'd let loose once she'd arrived at the condo. Now she was on a commuter flight with Nathan, and the tears were on the verge of coming again.

Nathan squeezed her hand. "I can't explain it, either."

"Your campaign manager would have made a better suspect than my father," she contended with a sniffle. "I didn't even know you'd given him money. He had never said a word about it."

Nathan shrugged. "He seemed low on funds after his last hospitalization. I was only trying to help, but he wasn't very receptive."

"Why has it been so hard for our families to accept us?" Judi balled up the tissue in one hand. "Why couldn't they just be happy for us?"

"Maybe we should have given them more time to warm up to the idea and had a proper church wedding," speculated Nathan. "Eloping solved our problems but not theirs."

"How could something so trivial cause a father to hate his child enough to threaten her life? Some of those letters were so vile." She looked at Nathan, unshed tears blurring her vision. "I suppose he did have opportunity. He knew all about my past and could have taken my juvenile rehab identification badge." She shook her head in disbelief. "To think I went to such great lengths to make my plan work to protect him. I thought he was in danger."

"You need to listen to me, Judi," Nathan insisted, gently tipping her face toward him with his hand. "I don't know why your father sent those terrible letters, but you need to let go of it for the next few hours and save your energy for the attorney's visit this afternoon. We need to concentrate on getting you through the legal difficulties first." His thumb traced the line of her jaw. "I promise we'll get to the bottom of this."

Judi nodded and yielded to his touch when he soothingly brought her forward to lean on his chest. The comforting, even beat of his heart resounded against her ear, and she could feel the softness of his shirt, smell the scent of his familiar aftershave. Experiencing his protective arms around her shoulders calmed the wild beating of her own heart. With Nathan on her side she could almost believe the nightmare would work out into a manageable dream.

*God. . .I didn't see this last development coming. My own father! Am I to lose my family, too? I don't think I can bear it. Now, more than ever, I need to keep the husband*

*You gave back to me. It feels so good to have his arms around me, to hear his steady breathing. I don't want to ever move from his hold. Please give Nathan the desire to keep our marriage together. What a joy it would be to serve You together. We'd make a great team! Change my heart to be what You desire, to make this thing work, even if it means forgiving those who have wronged us.*

Judi snuggled further into his embrace, letting her heavy eyelids close and carry her tired body to a place of rest.

"Come on and wake up, sleepyhead." Nathan gently shook Judi's shoulders and she stirred. He removed his anesthetized arm from behind her back, experimentally stretching his fingers to regain some circulation. "We've landed."

Judi's eyes fluttered open and she stared blankly at him for a moment. "We're here?" She let a yawn break free and immediately covered her mouth with her hand. "Sorry."

He gave a smile, glad to see her features more rested. Mr. Edwards's bolt from the blue the night before had taken a toll on both of them. They had to remain strong for what lay ahead. Quietly, he ushered Judi from the plane and to the airport parking lot.

"What a beautiful car," admired Judi when they reached the metallic blue sedan. She settled into the bucket seat, letting her hand slide over the expensive leather. "Isn't this the European car reputed to go from zero to sixty in fifteen seconds?"

"Actually it's seven seconds!" Nathan nodded appreciatively. "And it handles better than any car I've ever driven." He threw her a grin. "Although I must say, I'm growing quite fond of your golf cart. I might be hard put to choose between the two."

"I don't know," she said, cracking a small smile. "I'm willing to trade with you for a while."

"Perhaps I'll take you up on that offer." Nathan maneuvered into the heavy traffic and onto the freeway. Judi seemed lost in thought, looking out the window as if seeing civilization for the first time. The companionable silence let Nathan think through his plans for the next few days.

Thirty minutes later he pulled into a space in the law office parking lot and shut the engine off. "Ready?"

Nodding solemnly, Judi slipped out of the car and looked up at the tall building. Quietly they walked into the office and waited while the secretary looked at the scheduling sheet.

"Mr. Winslow is waiting for you," she announced, ushering them directly into the plush office.

As soon as the polished wood doors opened, Nathan caught sight of the huge plate glass window. But it was the enormous desk with a distinguished-looking man seated behind it that commanded the room's attention.

The man instantly looked up and smiled. "Ah, you've made it. Come on in and make yourselves comfortable." He stood to his feet, and Nathan could see that he was rather short and stocky. The middle-aged man firmly shook Nathan's hand and immediately turned his gaze to Judi. "And you must be Judi Whithorne. Nice to meet you."

Judi timidly took the offered hand. "Thank you for taking my case."

"A very interesting set of circumstances, I must say," Mr. Winslow noted warmly. "But I think you'll be happy with the news today."

Nathan liked the man; his warm, professional demeanor gave a welcoming feeling of interest and loyalty. "Then I take it you've had time to look over the information I gave you last week?" Nathan asked.

The attorney nodded and turned to Judi. "From what Representative Whithorne has told me, you had obtained the birth certificate of a child who had died and with this document you made a new identity, subsequently obtaining driver's licenses in Pennsylvania and Ohio as this new person. You then faked a drowning death and have been living on Bay Island, Ohio, since that time. Does that sound correct?"

"Yes!" Judi looked nervously reserved.

"Let's deal with the licensing issue first." Mr. Winslow slowly swiveled back and forth in his chair. "The most either state could do for falsification is charge you with a misdemeanor, slap you with a fine, and put you in jail for six months if they felt so inclined."

Judi tensed and Nathan placed his hand reassuringly on her arm. "But you have good news about that, right?"

The lawyer gave a reassuring smile. "The fact that you came forward of your own accord has worked in your favor across the board. To be honest, neither state has a desire to waste their time on a misdemeanor case where there's been no intent to perpetrate a major crime. They are struggling enough trying to track down illegal immigrants and check scammers. It would be hard to justify spending several thousand dollars to collect a one-thousand-dollar fine or to make an example of you. So we're going to destroy both driver's licenses and the birth certificate and pay the fines."

Judi leaned forward, gnawing at her bottom lip. "But I also have a Social Security card."

"Not a big deal," Winslow asserted with confidence, chuckling at Judi's look of disbelief. "Although it goes against the grain of the American justice system, the feds aren't terribly interested in you, either." He scratched at the side of his nose. "The Social Security number will be revoked, of course, but the worst that will happen is that all the monies you paid into the system using that number will be lost. If you had tried to withdraw money from the program, that would be another story, but without any theft, and because of the circumstances that caused you to falsify your identification, they don't care to prosecute."

"That is great news!" Nathan's confidence in the man was growing. Right now he was thankful Mr. Edwards had steered them in the right direction.

"I believe," Winslow continued, tilting his head in thought, "I can get you through this entire process without any criminal charges being filed."

"None?" Judi perked up. "How can that be?"

"It can be done, but it will be cost some money."

Nathan knew this was coming. "How much?"

"Your biggest outlay will be in restitution to the city and county," he said matter-of-factly.

"Restitution?" Judi asked.

"The city and county will want to be reimbursed for the rescue and recovery attempts they made. It won't be cheap!" Winslow began ticking off items on his fingers. "There will be the police department's man hours, canine units, dive teams, and the detective's investigation to recoup—to the tune of around fifty thousand dollars."

"Fifty thousand dollars!" There was awe in Judi's voice.

"And if we make restitution," Nathan asked, still sorting through the details, "then the city and county prosecutors won't press charges, is that right?"

"They'll probably kiss your ring for saving them the time and expense of attempting to prosecute such a case." He shrugged his bulky shoulders. "If you don't or can't pay back this money, or if they decided to formally charge Judi, there's a good chance I could still get a jury acquittal. Realize, however, there are some risks and there will still be court fees and possibly fines to pay. Another possibility if you were charged would be for you to agree to plead guilty to lesser charges and make restitution, which brings us back to where we started."

"Then we'll pay the city and county up front!" Nathan looked determinedly at Judi and then at the attorney. "There's no sense in taking a chance."

"I have absolutely no money, Nathan," protested Judi. "Where would we be able to scrape up that kind of money?"

"Let's not worry about that now!" Nathan would find the money, even if it meant selling their house. He turned back to Winslow. "What else?"

"There's the matter of the life insurance policy." Winslow tilted his head toward Nathan. "From what you've said, twenty-five thousand was donated to a charity. Unfortunately, the insurance company could not care less where the money went—they'll just want it back immediately."

"That's over seventy-five thousand, so far," Judi needlessly pointed out.

"The last matter will take more time than money to fix." The lawyer leaned back in his chair as he looked at Judi. "A judge has declared you to be legally dead. We have to get that reversed and revive your real Social Security number. Until those steps are done, you won't be able to hold a job or apply for a driver's license—anything that requires identification or a background check."

"How much time do you think that will take?" Nathan asked.

He shrugged again. "It might take weeks, but I'll do my best to speed the process along."

"Anything else?" Nathan was roughly calculating what it would take to pay the debts.

"I think we've discussed all the major issues."

"Except for your fees," Nathan added.

A surprised look crossed Winslow's face. "My fees? They're already covered."

"Covered?"

"An anonymous donor is paying my fees," he answered. "I thought you knew that."

Nathan looked at Judi, who returned a suspicious nod. "Mr. Edwards?"

"I really can't say," he said with a knowing smile. "All I can tell you is that my services have already been taken care of, and I'll do the best job I can." His smile slowly faded. "I understand that you have recently discovered the identity of the author of the threatening notes. If you need my help in that matter, I'll represent you." He looked at Judi. "Do you have any plans to file charges?"

The stricken look on her face answered the question. "No matter what my father has done, I can't do that to him."

The attorney nodded with understanding. "Unfortunately, I can't solve or heal family problems like the one you're facing." He leaned forward, his elbows on the desk. "Are there any other questions I can answer for either of you?"

"No," Nathan answered. "You've been very helpful. I'll let you know when the money is secured to make restitution."

"Very well," concluded Winslow. "My secretary has some papers for you to sign and then you're free to go. Will you be staying here or going back to the island?"

Nathan felt Judi's gaze on him. "We have some family business to take care of before we make any career or relocation plans."

"Another set of decisions I can't help you with." There was empathy in the attorney's eyes.

"I know!" Nathan stated.

*Only God can!*

# Chapter 13

Judi stood alone in the master bedroom slowly turning in a circle to take in the surroundings. The memorable sights and smells belonging to her previous life were coming alive and rushing at her with thrusters on full burn, penetrating her soul with unbearable longing. It was as if she was returning to the pages of a suspenseful but unfinished novel she laid aside years ago. With a heavy sigh, she sank onto the king-size bed and absently smoothed out a crease along the wedding ring quilt.

Like a fog lifting, she could feel her heart respond to the surroundings. She had purposely closed away these pictures of her past and now they were being dusted off and put back into service.

She wished Nathan was with her at this moment; but in the silence of their house, she was quite alone.

Instead, Nathan was with Lindsey, explaining what he couldn't convey in a phone conversation. He hadn't volunteered any insight into what he was going to say to the woman, and Judi had been too afraid to ask. With a sense of foreboding, she watched him back out of the driveway and speed off toward the west end of town. It was hard not to worry about the outcome of his visit with this woman who also claimed to love him, but Judi had to preserve her physical and emotional energy to focus on what was scheduled next—her father. It was a visit she dreaded but desperately needed in order to understand why her father would have done such a thing.

How was she going to get through this meeting with her father when she'd been a total basket case just listening to Nathan's phone conversation with him? There had evidently been some hesitancy at her father's end of the line when Nathan explained his urgent need to see him, but Nathan had been firm and the older man eventually agreed to meet.

If that weren't enough, Nathan's entire family would be gathering at the house in less than four hours. Although she understood the necessity for the announcement of her return to be quick and efficiently executed, the sheer weight of the project besieged her. Nathan had warned that the media would be onto them within twenty-four hours and they needed to reach their family members before it had a chance to blow up. He had already been in contact with the statehouse, though she didn't know the particulars. Nathan wouldn't discuss it—not yet.

Judi took a deep breath and blew it out between pursed lips. Her gaze landed on the jewelry box sitting cockeyed on the dresser—her jewelry box. Getting up, she made her way across the room and carefully lifted the lid. Several glittering gems sparkled in the light. Piece by piece she examined the necklaces and rings, tilting her favorite opal ring to see the brilliant fire of color. Slowly she placed the ring back in the holder and continued her search. Her grandmother's ruby brooch was glaringly absent.

It was then she saw another ring—a gold band.

Nathan's wedding ring.

Carefully she lifted the ring and held it between her fingers. The beaded edge was slightly worn and Judi smiled sadly. The jeweler had explained that over the years the edging of their matching rings would eventually wear down into a radiant, shiny gold—a tribute to a long and happy marriage, the man had said.

Judi wondered how long Nathan had worn the ring before taking it off for the final time and placing it in the dormant jewelry box. What went through his mind when the decision came? Lost in thought, she stared at the gold band.

There was a slight sound from behind and suddenly she knew she was no longer alone. Slowly she turned to see Nathan leaning against the doorjamb watching her, his face solemn. For a long moment neither spoke.

"I thought you might be in here," he finally said, breaking the spell of the silence. His tired eyes pivoted to the ring she held then back to her. He gently pushed off from the door frame and came near. "My wedding band."

Judi nodded, instantly feeling intrusive. "I'll put it back."

His hand shot out and captured hers. "I don't want it back in the box."

Confused, but hopeful, she looked up to meet his captivating gaze. The expression on his face made mincemeat of her insides. He was fighting against the same stresses threatening to take her under and yet there was vivid fire in his eyes. With awareness he took the ring from her hand and slid it over his finger.

"This past week has thrown my entire world into a vortex of chaos." Nathan's voice was low and expressive. "So many choices and possible directions to go." He gave a slight shake of his head. "I had no idea what I was going to say to handle Lindsey today, and I asked God to show me how to make an impossible situation a possible thing for Him."

"And what did He show you?" Her breath felt suspended as her chest ached for the answer.

"That I have already committed to love and cherish the woman I married." Nathan gently took her face between his hands. "We said it would be for better or for worse. We're experiencing the 'worse' part now, and I'm willing to hold out for the 'better' portion to come." He sighed. "I've not always been the best husband. I know that!"

"It's not true," Judi cried, clasping her hands over his. "I'm the one to blame. It was immature of me to be jealous of your political work. I should have trusted you enough to know your long hours of work weren't a reflection that you loved your job more than me—or that you weren't trying to get rid of me. If only I had come to you. I'm so sorry!"

Nathan leaned closer. "We've both made mistakes in the past, but we have to look to the future. We have something very solid to bond us together that was missing before."

"God!"

"Are you willing to see if God can bring us together as one again?"

"Willing?" she cried, drawing one hand endearingly down his chin. "I've been desperately praying for it."

Nathan imprisoned her hand and pulled her close, his lips beginning an exploration of her face, kissing her cheeks, chin, and eyes, moving into the hollow of her neck. "I've missed you so much. When you disappeared—"

The obvious pain in his voice tore at her heart, and she gently put her fingers to his lips and hushed him. "I'm here now and I promise to stay this time." Judi felt a great surge of happiness when he kissed her again.

Slowly he pulled her back. "I wish we didn't have to deal with our families this afternoon."

Judi sagged against his chest feeling the tightening of his grasp. "I can do anything as long as you're beside me, Nathan."

"I love you, Judith!"

Closing her eyes, she reveled in the depth of his tone, the beauty of his words. For several minutes they stayed in the close embrace, Judi never wanting to leave the warmth of his touch.

Suddenly, she heard a gasp from the doorway and both jerked toward the sound. Nathan's sister stood in the doorway, her mouth gaping in utter surprise.

"Judi?"

"Are you sure Laurie's going to be all right by herself?" Judi asked when they pulled out of the driveway. "She looked absolutely floored."

Nathan sent her a sideways glance. "She'll be okay! I never thought she might make it into town this early and use the spare key. That was my fault." He looked in the side-view mirror before changing lanes. "I'm sure my cryptic message insisting that she meet at the house tonight with the rest of the family sent her into a panic."

"She won't tell the rest of your family before tonight, will she?" Judi looked at him doubtfully.

"She promised not to, but one can never tell."

Remembering the shocked expression on Laurie's face sent shivers through

Judi. If Laurie had reacted with such alarm, Judi could only imagine how her own father was going to respond. Her hands were beginning to sweat as they drew closer, finally turning into her father's driveway.

Nathan turned to her. "Stay in the car until I give you the signal. We don't want to give him a heart attack. Let me talk with him first."

Mutely, she nodded and once again sent up a prayer for guidance. Nathan got out of the car and walked onto the porch stoop and rapped on the door. She saw the front door open and a second later Nathan disappeared inside. Nervously, she clenched her hands together, feeling the tremors of apprehension coursing through them. Her emotions were seesawing with joy from Nathan's affirmation of love and God's mercy to exonerate her from criminal litigation, to despair over her father's behavior—and over seventy-five thousand dollars in debts she had no idea how to pay.

Suddenly Nathan appeared at the front door, beckoning her to come. As she opened the car door, she caught a glimpse of her father trying to see around Nathan. When she reached the front steps and then the door, she heard his surprised intake of breath.

"It can't be true," her father sputtered as he hurriedly skirted around Nathan and embraced her with a fierce hug that threatened to break her ribs. He pulled her back to look into her face. "It's you. It's really you!" Once again, he held her close, and she felt him shudder, a sob reverberating against her shoulder.

"I've missed you, Daddy," she exclaimed, tears forming in her eyes as she looked questioningly at Nathan. The old man seemed genuinely overcome with elation at her return. How could he be the one who'd sent her such hateful letters? "Can we talk, Daddy?"

Reluctantly, her father released his hold and stepped back, wiping his face against the sleeve of his worn shirt. His thinning gray hair looked unkempt and wild, a scraggly three-day beard prickled over his jowls.

"Let me straighten up a little so we'll have a place to sit," her father said, immediately setting about to clear strewn newspapers from the couch. He dumped the papers behind a chair and turned to the couple, thrusting out an anxious hand indicating for them to sit. "When Nathan told me you were alive, I just couldn't believe it. I'm not sure I can believe it now even though I see you." He dropped into a chair and shook his head as if to clear his mind. "What happened to you? Where have you been all this time?"

Judi sat on the edge of the sagging couch within easy reach of her father. "I've been living on an island off Lake Erie for the past two years. The drowning accident never happened. It was all a fake."

Stanley Porter cradled his forehead with one hand. "A fake? But why?" Then he turned to Nathan. "You knew about this?"

"Listen to me, Daddy," Judi intervened, touching her father's knee. "Nathan didn't know anything about it until last week." She waited until her father looked at her again. "I left because someone was sending me threatening notes. I feared for my safety and yours." Contritely she gave Nathan a look. "I mistakenly thought Nathan had sent them. I was wrong!"

"You faked your own death because of those letters?" The old man's face paled. "That can't be!"

Judi pressed on, her heart thumping wildly. "Did you write those letters?"

"Me!" A haunted look pierced his eyes.

"I need to know the truth."

The old man seemed winded, his eyes darting riotously. "It wasn't supposed to turn out like this."

"Like what?"

"You were supposed to come back home to me," he blurted breathlessly, "not kill yourself."

Judi looked at Nathan, who shrugged his shoulders and nodded for her to keep talking. "I don't understand. Why was I supposed to come home?"

There was agony on the man's face. "Don't you see? Nathan didn't love you, and his family was killing your spirit day by day with their uppity snobbery. I could see how unhappy you were."

"But the letters were so. . .hurtful." Judi had to pause a moment to gain control of her voice. "How were those awful notes going to help me be happy?"

"By coming home where you belong!" her father answered, one shaky hand resting on his knee. "I wanted you to come to me for help, but when you didn't come, I figured you might have gone to Nathan about the notes. That just wouldn't do. He didn't care about you. He only cared about making money and being a famous politician." He looked accusingly at Nathan. "You know it's true!"

Judi closed her eyes for a second. "Oh, Daddy!"

"Don't you see? I had to change tactics. That's when I stuffed the chimney flue with a bird's nest after sending you the letter about the carbon monoxide. I thought for sure if you believed Nathan was trying to harm me, you'd have to come to me then." His voice cracked. "But you died instead! I assumed you'd been so distraught that you committed suicide."

"Is that why you've treated Nathan so badly?" Judi asked. "You thought he was ultimately responsible for making those threatening letters necessary? That was wrong, Daddy, no matter what your reasons were."

The old man nodded. "He's no good for you, Judi."

"Daddy, he's the man I love." Her voice was gaining strength. "You shouldn't have tried to come between Nathan and me. We would have worked it out."

Nathan rested a comforting hand on Judi's back and began to speak. "Sir, I do take partial responsibility. You were right about the fact that I should have been a better husband and not let my family treat her with disrespect. I plan to change all that." He stared back at her father's wide-eyed expression. "We can't alter what's already happened. We can only move forward. In light of that, Judi and I have agreed that it would be of no use for anyone else to know that you wrote those notes. We would like to clear the slate."

"He's right, Daddy," Judi chimed in. "We want you to be part of our lives." She grew serious. "But you have to promise not to interfere with our marriage again. That's between Nathan and me."

"But what are you going to do now?" her father asked, consternation on his face.

"I don't know!" Judi answered truthfully.

Stanley looked at Nathan. "You don't have any plans?"

"We have a lot of details to work out with our attorney, families, and my career," Nathan told him. "My first priority, however, is to protect Judi, and I'll do what it takes to accomplish that. In the meantime, we're going to go wherever God leads us."

"God?" The word sounded foreign on her father's lips.

For the next few minutes, Judi expressed how God had miraculously changed their lives. "God can help you as much as He's helped us. You need Him."

The old man shook his head. "I don't have time for no religion."

"I'm not talking about religion, Daddy," she said with a rueful smile. "I'm talking about a personal relationship with Christ."

Her father took a deep breath. "Another time, Judi."

Nathan cautioned her with a nod. "I think he's been through enough for one day. He's still in shock by your appearance." He looked at his watch. "And we need to get back to the house before my family comes."

"You'll be coming back, right?" There was alarm in her father's voice.

Judi stood and gave him a big hug. "I'm not going anywhere. I already promised Nathan I'd never run off again."

It was a promise she planned to keep!

Nathan rounded the street corner and spotted three cars in the driveway. That could only mean Laurie had spilled the beans and the family was already gathered. Great! Just great! The day had been extremely draining, and he wondered if he would be able to keep pace on the last leg of the relay.

The visit with Lindsey had taken a toll on him. She had gone from being devastated and angry one minute to cajoling and pleading the very next. Just when she seemed accepting of the inevitable, she would beg him to reconsider what he was doing. Nathan was torn by her grief, but no amount of pain could keep him from making the decision he knew God wanted—the one he himself desired. Judi's response to him confirmed he had made the right choice.

"Nathan, your family is already here," Judi said with dismay.

"I know." Nathan parked the car behind his parents' luxury sedan and shut off the engine. He saw the living room curtains move and felt several pairs of eyes on them. "Laurie never could keep a secret."

"I was hoping to have time to talk with you before meeting them," Judi remarked jadedly, clutching her purse.

"I know! There's so much we have to discuss."

"Before we go in, I want to show you something." Judi rummaged around inside her purse and brought out a velvet bag. Tipping it up, a glimmering diamond ring and band spilled into her hands.

Nathan looked at the jewelry. "Your wedding rings."

"I brought them with me, hoping. . ." The color heightened in her cheeks. "I thought maybe, if you didn't mind, I'd like to wear them again."

Taking the rings from her trembling hand, he placed them on her finger. "I was hoping you still had them." He gently kissed her, feeling the warmth of her lips. She tasted so sweet.

The sound of the front door opening caused him to sit back with a sigh of exhaustion and look over at his parents standing impatiently in the doorway. He unsnapped his seat belt.

"Be brave," he instructed, squeezing Judi's hands.

Utter chaos reigned for the first five minutes when they entered the house. Questions began flying back and forth until Nathan's head ached.

"Quiet!" The loud reverberation of his voice instantly had an effect and a hush settled over the room. "I can't answer twenty questions at one time. I've already explained that Judi's drowning did not happen, and I've told you about the threatening letters that caused this whole chain of events."

"Have you seen these notes?" his normally soft-spoken father asked, throwing a suspicious glance Judi's way. "You say she knows who wrote the letters, but you won't tell us. How do you know these letters even existed?"

Nathan gave his father a stern look, a rush of anger coming over him at his father's tone. "Yes, I have seen the notes, and yes, I know who wrote them. It will serve no purpose for you to know the identity of this person."

"But—" His mother began to interrupt, holding up her delicate hand.

"Let's get something straight." Nathan's voice grew harsh as he looked from face to face. "Judi has been treated shamefully by this family, and I will not let it happen again. It's time I stood up and acted like the man of this house. Maybe we were wrong to go off and get married without anyone knowing, but that doesn't give anyone in this room the right to bully or slight her. She is my wife, and we come as a package deal. You'll treat her as you treat me."

Nathan's mother drew a delicate handkerchief to her mouth. "But we've always treated her well."

"Please don't deny what I already know." Nathan's features refused to soften as they usually did when addressing his mother. "Everyone in this room has been disrespectful to Judi in one way or another. Again, I want you to know I love Judi and we are still a married couple."

"But what about Lindsey?" asked Laurie, a worried expression intensifying across her brow.

"I've already explained the state of affairs to Lindsey and although it's been an unfortunate situation for her, she will come through this."

Once again questions began. Nathan fielded each subject as best he could, explaining the complexities of the circumstances.

"What about your elected seat in the statehouse?" his father asked, still giving sour looks to Judi. "You can't just give it up."

"I already have!" Nathan heard Judi's quick intake of breath, and he ruefully turned to her. "I'm sorry. I had hoped to discuss this with you before the family arrived." Judi's quick smile of understanding gave him courage to continue. "Although it is possible for me to retain the seat, it would mean a media circus that would inevitably hurt all of us and work against my fellow lawmakers."

"You're throwing away all your hard work," his father charged, the color deepening across his already ruddy face. "All you have to do is tell them Judi suffered from amnesia and recently got her memory back. It might even gain you points."

"Maybe it would," Nathan responded. "But spinning the story won't gain points with God. There will be no lies or deception. The people I serve have supported me because I gave them what they wanted—honesty and a genuine interest to see our state grow. Lies have no gain."

"Honesty has its place, son," his father continued. "But you're going to lose everything, and I don't think you're going to like living on the other side of the money belt."

Nathan smiled. "I'm not trying to build an empire. It's more important to lay my treasure with God where it belongs. The book of Matthew tells us to seek God's kingdom first." He looked at those gathered in the room. "No, I can't say that I want to live in poverty, but if I don't like it here, I'm certainly not going to like living like a pauper when I reach heaven because I have nothing to show for my life."

Jeff stood and shook Nathan's hand. "I'll support you, brother, in whatever you do. And if you need help searching online for a job, I'm your man."

Nathan smiled and gripped his brother's shoulder. "I appreciate that." He turned to Judi. "But I already have a job, if Judi is agreeable." There was uncertainty written across her face, and he gave her a reassuring grin. "I've been offered a partnership in a law firm in Cleveland with a new branch office on Bay Island."

"Nathan, when did this happen?" Judi asked, excitement in her voice.

Nathan reached for her hand. "The offer came last weekend, and I've decided to take it. I'll be handling the accounts for Kelly Enterprises—the company that donated the land for the church camp on the island. From what I understand, this company is a full-time job in and of itself. I'll also take on extra work like wills and probate for those on the island. It's the perfect job!"

"Van Edwards!" she whispered almost reverently, her eyes meeting his.

Nathan had to only smile his response. Whatever or whoever Mr. Edwards was, "rescuer" could easily be added to his résumé. In time, Nathan hoped to discover the real person behind this unusual and secretive old man. Mr. Edwards also indicated that the mayor's position might be opening soon if Nathan still wanted to remain active in politics. Nathan thought this might be a conflict of interest, but Van said on an island that small, everything was a conflict of interest. He was probably right!

Laurie broke in. "You'll be moving?"

Nathan nodded, his eyes never wavering from Judi. "If Judi is willing to go back to Bay Island, I'd like to sell this house and my car. With our savings and equity, we will have enough to clear our debts and start over."

"Are you sure you want to do this?" Hope was written on every feature of Judi's face. "You love this house and living in Pennsylvania."

"Yes, but I'm rather fond of the island and your golf cart, too," he answered with a laugh. "And your little VW Beetle should fit right in once we get it back in working order." Judi jumped up and hugged him with abandonment, and he leaned close to her ear. "By the way, the church turned down your resignation. Once your original Social Security number is back in order, your job will be waiting."

Obviously speechless, Judi snuggled against his shoulder. He closed his arms around her, feeling the fragility of her body.

"Besides, when we get settled," Nathan continued in low tones, "you're going to get that college education you always wanted—the honest way."

Judi looked up. "You promise?"

"I promise!"

Jeff stepped forward and placed his hand on Judi's shoulder. "I'm sorry that we treated you poorly. I can see Nathan has made an excellent choice. Right, sis?"

Laurie grudgingly agreed and walked over to join in a group hug. Nathan could tell Judi was happily reserved, but weary and near collapse. He needed to end this inquisition.

"Anyone else have anything to say to Judi or to me?"

His mother cleared her throat. "When Laurie called us this afternoon"—Nathan shot his sister a disapproving look, and she innocently shrugged—"I thought it might be good," continued his mother, unwrapping her white lacy handkerchief, "for me to give this back to Judi." A red ruby stone brooch lay in stark contrast against the white cloth.

Judi let go of Nathan and leaned forward, pale and uncertain, looking questioningly back at his mother. "It's my grandmother's brooch."

"You took it?" Nathan accused, unable to keep the disbelief from his voice.

His mother frowned. "Judi had shown it to me one time, and I knew it was something important to her. I saw it the day I helped you clean out her clothes and, well—I wanted something to remind me of her."

Like having the air sucked out of his lungs, Nathan felt sucker punched and at a loss for words. He knew the excuse was an outright lie and another example of his family's impertinence toward his wife. It was time to stand his ground.

Suddenly, Judi placed her hand on his arm and stepped forward.

"That was awfully sweet of you," Judi told his mother, taking the offered ruby. "Thank you for taking such good care of it."

His mother smiled contritely. "I should have told Nathan, but you know—"

"It's okay," Judi assured, smiling at the older woman.

Nathan was pleased to see his mother had the decency to blush. Served her right—she should be ashamed. His father remained silent throughout the exchange, but Judi didn't seem to notice.

"You're all invited," Nathan announced, breaking the intense moment as he pulled Judi to his side, "to Bay Island for a visit, especially for the ceremony to recommit our vows as we begin our lives together again. I believe our good friends, Tilly Storm and Van Edwards, have something cooked up that should prove to be a very classy celebration. You won't want to miss it."

Nathan smiled down at Judi and kissed her full on the lips. "Are you game?"

"I wouldn't miss it for the world, Mr. Whithorne!"

# *Epilogue*

Judi walked proudly down the aisle, her father's arm hooked inside hers, feeling like a redeemed Cinderella. Her simple, sea-foam chiffon dress felt light and airy, ready to sing like her heart. At the altar, Nathan looked undeniably handsome in his dashing gray suit. He sent her a quirky smile that sent waves of joy through her.

Nathan's entire family was present, attempting in their own way to mend fences. Funny how much easier it was to forgive when so much had been forgiven of her. Even her father looked attractive and clean-cut, and healthier than he'd been in years. She never thought happiness would be hers to embrace again, but here she was, sailing like a bird above crystal blue waters.

Nathan and she were stronger and better than before. Tilly and Van were insistent about planning and paying for the ceremony. Someone had to throw a party, Tilly had said.

The service was simple, but an absolute ball. Family and friends gathered at the church reception hall bubbling over with food and laughter. Judi tapped her foot to the lively brass quartet, watching Jason and Lauren sway to the music. Larry and Becky were having a great time, too, and Judi reveled in the happiness of the expecting couples. As she looked over the gathering, she realized new life was everywhere on the island.

Judi caught a glimpse of Tilly slipping through the crowd and into the kitchen. With a smile, she detached herself from the festivities to follow.

"Hey, where you going?" Nathan laughingly stole up beside her, taking her hand in his.

"To the kitchen!" Judi gave him a full smile. "I want to thank Tilly for all her hard work, including putting this together. I'm having the time of my life."

"We'll go together," he whispered in her ear.

They made their way toward the partially closed kitchen door and skidded to a stop. Judi put her hand over her mouth to keep from bursting out.

Nathan gave her a mischievous grin and immediately pulled her away into the deserted hallway. "You always said Mr. Edwards and Tilly were sweet on each other."

"But kissing in the church kitchen?" Judi laughed.

"How about in the church hallway?" Nathan asked, gently pulling her to him, his lips meeting hers. "Are you happy, Mrs. Whithorne?"

"Indubitably!"
"That's a pretty fancy word."
"I have a pretty fancy husband."
He kissed her again. "And a pretty awesome God!"

# A Letter to Our Readers

Dear Readers:

In order that we might better contribute to your reading enjoyment, we would appreciate your taking a few minutes to respond to the following questions. When completed, please return to the following: Fiction Editor, Barbour Publishing, Inc., P.O. Box 719, Uhrichsville, OH 44683.

1. Did you enjoy reading *Ohio Weddings* by Beth Loughner?
   ❑ Very much—I would like to see more books like this.
   ❑ Moderately—I would have enjoyed it more if ______________
   ________________________________________
   ________________________________________

2. What influenced your decision to purchase this book?
   (Check those that apply.)
   ❑ Cover ❑ Back cover copy ❑ Title ❑ Price
   ❑ Friends ❑ Publicity ❑ Other

3. Which story was your favorite?
   ❑ *Bay Island* ❑ *Bay Hideaway*
   ❑ *Thunder Bay*

4. Please check your age range:
   ❑ Under 18 ❑ 18–24 ❑ 25–34
   ❑ 35–45 ❑ 46–55 ❑ Over 55

5. How many hours per week do you read? ______________

Name ________________________________

Occupation ____________________________

Address ______________________________

City ________________ State __________ Zip __________

E-mail ______________________________